MARY LARKIN is Belfast's leading saga writer. She grew up just off the Falls Road and spent forty happy years living in the city before moving to the north-east of England. She is the author of a string of bestselling titles, including *Full Circle*, *Suspicious Minds* and *Ties of Love and Hate*.

MARY LARKIN

The Wasted Years

·THE·
BLACK
·STAFF·
PRESS

Author's Note

The Falls Road and St Paul's Parish portrayed in *The Wasted Years* actually exist, and historic events referred to in the story are, to the best of my knowledge, authentic. However, I would like to make it clear that the story is fictional, and all characters are purely a figment of my imagination and not based on anyone alive or dead, and any similarity is purely coincidental.

First published in 1992 by Judy Piatkus (Publishers) Ltd

This edition published in 2016 by Blackstaff Press
4D Weavers Court
Linfield Road
Belfast BT12 5GH

With the assistance of
The Arts Council of Northern Ireland

Supported by
The National Lottery®
through the Arts Council of Northern Ireland

Mary Larkin has asserted her right under the Copyright, Designs and Patents Act 1988 to be identified as the author of this work.

Typeset by KT Designs, Newton-le Willows, England

Printed and bound by CPI Group UK (Ltd), Croydon CR0 4YY

A CIP catalogue for this book is available from the British Library

ISBN 978 0 85640 959 2

www.blackstaffpress.com
www.marylarkin.co.uk

Acknowledgements

The author gratefully acknowledges the people who helped in the research, compilation and writing of this book. They include my late father and mother whose brains I constantly picked for any snippets of gossip from the past. For my sister Sue who first suggested that I could and should write a book, especially with a Belfast theme. To my oldest son Con for his help and encouragement, particularly with computer expertise. To all the staff at Blackstaff Press for their dedication to detail and especially Helen Wright who was always at the other end of the telephone with help and advice. And finally to my husband Con who is always there when I need him. My grateful thanks to them all.

Chapter 1

Belfast, 1938

The power went off, and as the looms ground to a halt the weavers changed their old, comfortable shoes for more serviceable ones, donned their coats and headed for the door. In spite of the glass roof lights being whitewashed against the glare of the sun, stifling heat still built up inside the factory and they were relieved to escape out into the fresh air. One of the many mills that provided work for the people of the Falls and the Shankill Roads, the Falls Flax Factory was situated in Cupar Street; right in the centre, at the 'T' junction where it curved sharply to the right and continued on up to the Shankill Road to the Protestant districts, while the left-hand turn became the Kashmir Road and ran on to the Springfield Road and the Catholic districts.

Arm in arm with Rosaleen Magee, May Brady felt the tension ripple through her friend as they walked out of the gates on to Cupar Street. She knew what was causing Rosaleen such concern, or rather who, and sure enough, there he stood, about six feet tall, jet-black hair and eyes as blue as a summer sky. This was the third night he had been waiting outside the factory. But for whom was he waiting? Mr Blair's secretary? Yes, it must be Miss Maynard he was waiting for. She was the only one May could picture him with, although May had seen and been dismayed by the look that had passed between Rosaleen and the handsome stranger on Monday night, the first he had been there. She was also aware that Rosaleen had her old work-coat lying open, disclosing the fact that she had taken the time to remove the overall she wore to protect her clothes when working, and May could see that she was wearing one of her better skirts and a cream-coloured blouse that was just a few weeks old; a blouse that enhanced the fairness of her skin and lightened the green of her eyes. This was unusual, very unusual, because dust from the weft in the weaving shop got embedded into everything, causing a fusty smell, and it was customary to wear old clothes to work.

Why on earth is Rosaleen wearing her new blouse? May mused. Surely she did not fancy the handsome stranger? A small frown puckered her brow as she pondered. All the same, she must. Why else risk ruining the new blouse? Oh, don't be ridiculous! she admonished herself, but was unconvinced. Isn't she engaged to be married?

Rosaleen's thoughts were running along similar lines to May's. Why was she so aware of this man? In four months' time she would be married to Joe Smith. Big, kind, handsome Joe. She loved Joe. So how come a single glance from a pair of blue eyes could floor her? She kept her own eyes demurely downcast, but she was very much aware that the man's eyes never left her face, bringing a bright blush to her cheeks, and that when they passed him, he turned to look after them.

'I wonder who the big hunk's waiting for?' May muttered, with a sidelong glance, covertly watching Rosaleen's reaction to her words. 'Probably Miss Maynard,' she continued, and jerked her head back towards the factory. 'She's the only one in there I can picture him with. I can't see *him* with a weaver or a winder.'

'Who are you talking about?' Rosaleen asked, trying to appear uninterested and failing miserably.

'Oh, that big, tall, handsome stranger that you never noticed,' May answered crossly. She was annoyed with Rosaleen and showed it. Why couldn't she be honest and admit that she found him attractive? Unless ... surely she couldn't find him *that* attractive?

2

Oh dear God no, that would never do. 'All the men around here wear Crombie overcoats and patent leather shoes that you could see yourself in,' she continued scornfully. 'So of course you wouldn't notice him.'

Hot colour brightly burned in Rosaleen's cheeks. She could not understand why, but she did not want to discuss the man with May. Perhaps because he affected her so deeply. On Monday night she had been laughing when he had caught her eye and an electric current seemed to run like a live wire between them. Time hung suspended as they gazed in awe at each other. Just a few seconds, but it had filled her with rapture, and she had recaptured the feeling often in the past few days and hugged it to her.

Joe did not have this effect on her and she felt guilty and uneasy at her reaction to this stranger. Last night and tonight she had avoided looking directly at him, scared of the effect he had on her, but she had been very much aware of his scrutiny.

Now she muttered, 'No, you're wrong. Miss Maynard stops work at half-five so she'll be long gone. It's not her he's waiting for.'

May shot her a sharp glance and saw the heightened colour. So, she had been giving him some thought and wondering who he was waiting for.

'Who do you think he's waiting for?' she asked, slyly.

But Rosaleen was no fool. She knew May's curiosity was aroused and did not want to continue the conversation, afraid of betraying the emotions the stranger had aroused. She wanted to put all thoughts of him from her mind; his obvious interest in her made her feel uncomfortable.

Shrugging her shoulders, she cried gaily, 'Oh, who cares?' And to change the subject, she asked, 'Are you going out tonight?'

She and May had been friends since their first day at primary school and only the arrival of Joe on the scene had come between them. They still had one night a week out together, a Friday night, and this they spent at the Club Orchid Ballroom. Joe did not like dancing but Rosaleen loved to dance and this way everybody was happy.

May was not hoodwinked. She knew Rosaleen was deliberately changing the subject, but decided to let her get away with it.

She gave a deep sigh. 'No, I'm washing my hair tonight and I've some clothes to launder.'

Being the eldest child of a family of six, she preferred to launder her own clothes than have them done with the family wash. Her mother was inclined to boil everything together in an old tin bucket and many a jumper and cardigan had been ruined, hence her desire to do her own laundry. She envied Rosaleen, who had only one sister and who was lifted and laid by her mother.

'Well, see you tomorrow.' She squeezed Rosaleen's arm before letting it go. 'Don't do anything I wouldn't do.'

'That gives me plenty of scope,' Rosaleen retorted, with a toss of her head that sent the blonde hair swinging about her face, making May wish, not for the first time, that she was blonde and beautiful, instead of plain and mousy.

With a deep chuckle, she turned down Clonard Gardens which joined Clonard Street and ran down on to the Falls Road where she lived, while Rosaleen continued on up the Kashmir Road.

As Rosaleen hurried along, her thoughts returned to the dark stranger. Why did he affect her so much? Chemistry, that's what it was! If they were to meet and talk they would probably bore each other to tears. With this observation she relaxed and turned her thoughts to Joe. Kind, handsome Joe. Nothing must interfere with her plans to marry him.

Her first and only serious boyfriend, he was a wonderful person who idolised her. He had put down a deposit on a house in Iris Drive, off Springfield Avenue, and was in the process of decorating it, for them to return to after their honeymoon in Bray. No greasing someone's palm with a tenner for the key to a rented house; no, not for them! Not every girl was lucky enough to marry a man with his own business. Just a small business, dealing in wrought-iron gates and railings, but there was room for expansion, and Joe was full of plans for the future. No, she would be foolish to let anything interfere with their plans. Why, it was wrong even to think of another man.

Nevertheless, in spite of her good intentions, the minute the alarm clock shattered the silence on Thursday morning, her thoughts returned to the stranger and she jumped out of bed. Dampening her hair, she rolled the long blonde strands in curlers and left it to set while she quickly washed herself down in the draughty scullery and then ate the breakfast her father prepared for her every morning. Her father was a good man; there were not many like him. Every morning he was downstairs first, and after lighting the fire he prepared breakfast. Then, without fail, he carried a cup of tea and a round of toast upstairs to her mother, before departing for Greeves Mill where he worked in the flax store.

Once ready for work, with her hair swept up at the sides and hanging to her shoulders in the current page-boy style, she gave in to the temptation to use a little make-up. Just a little. A light touch of Pan-stick and a hint of rouge. She did not want May to notice and comment on it.

But alas, she may as well not have bothered. There was no sign of the tall, handsome stranger outside the factory gates that night and she did not know whether to be glad or disappointed.

On Friday morning she was pushing away at her looms, lost in thought, when Betty Devlin came and stood beside her. She did not know Betty very well; a non-smoker, she did not therefore gather in the toilets where one met all the newcomers and was kept up to date on all the gossip. Knocking off the handle of the loom, Rosaleen gripped the comb and helped the loom to stop more quickly. Then, with a smooth, fluid movement, she exchanged the empty shuttle for a full one and set the loom in motion again, before turning to Betty, an eyebrow raised inquiringly. At the same time she removed the empty bobbin from the shuttle and put a new one in from the cage of weft that sat above the loom. Looms had to be kept constantly on the move or they left marks in the cloth, bringing the wrath of the examiners down on the culprit's head. So keeping an eye on the three looms, she gave half of her attention to Betty. She guessed the girl was probably collecting for something; someone getting married or maybe someone retiring.

While Rosaleen changed the shuttles, Betty eyed her closely. She had known right away who her brother was talking about when he had described her. There were not many girls as lovely as Rosaleen and she could understand why her brother was attracted to her.

Leaning close to make herself heard above the clatter of the looms, she cried, 'Did you notice a tall guy standing outside the factory a couple of nights this week?'

To her amusement, colour flooded Rosaleen's face and neck. Even her ears went a bright pink, causing Betty to laugh out loud.

'Obviously you did! You and half the factory! Well, he was waiting for me. He's my brother Sean and he wants a word in with you.'

Rosaleen found herself smiling in return. It was a long time since she had heard that expression: 'Wants a word in with you'. Not since she was about fifteen. Still, Betty was barely sixteen, so that would account for her using the term. Then the girl's words sank in and she went redder still. He wanted a date with her!

She shook her head and said, 'I can't. I'm engaged to be married.'

Betty eyed her bare left hand in disbelief and Rosaleen quickly explained, 'I don't wear my ring in here, the stone's too big.'

That sounded like boasting, but it was the truth. Joe had invested a lot of money in her engagement ring, a huge solitaire. She had demurred but he had said, 'May as well, while I can afford it. It's an investment, so it is. A ring like that can only grow in value and … God forbid … if we're ever stuck for money … well, it'll be there.'

However, she was nervous when wearing the ring, it was an awful responsibility, and she would not dream of wearing it in the factory.

Betty shrugged and gave a rueful smile. 'Oh, well.' She forced an exaggerated sigh from deep in her chest. 'Our Sean will be disappointed, but still I did my best.'

Deep blue eyes, just like his, laughed into Rosaleen's. Then, giving Rosaleen a wink and a nod, Betty turned and made her way down the shop floor, weaving in and out of the fast-moving machinery with graceful steps and a seductive sway to her small, neat bottom. Very much aware that her progress was watched avidly by two fitters who were maintaining a loom. Rosaleen watched her for some seconds, amusement in her eyes, then turned her attention back to her work, but her actions were automatic, her mind full of thoughts of 'Sean'. Imagine him wanting a word in with her. He had a cheek all the same. Sending word in like that, instead of asking her himself. This thought sent dismay flooding through her.

What if he was outside tonight and spoke to her? The very idea of it made her tremble and she chastised herself: Stop acting like a fool! He means nothing to you.

One of the looms dwindled to a halt and when Rosaleen saw the flaw that had been caused by a broken thread, she muttered to herself as she let out the web and started to rip out the flaw. That's what you get for daydreaming. Get your mind back on your work, you silly girl!

That night, keeping her head down, she gripped May's arm and hustled her quickly through the gate and past the corner where he usually stood. Not even trying to catch a glimpse of his well-polished brogues, should he be there.

May allowed herself to be propelled along Kashmir Road in silence, a resigned look on her face, but when they reached Clonard Gardens she said, with a gentle shake of her head, 'He wasn't there.'

'What?' Trying to look indifferent, Rosaleen tossed her head and added, 'I don't know what you mean.'

'Ah, Rosaleen, be honest!'

Shame-faced, Rosaleen muttered, 'He's Betty Devlin's brother. He wants a word in with me.'

May gaped at her and Rosaleen laughed softly before repeating with a smile and a nod: 'He wants a word in with me.' She chuckled aloud at the idea. 'Imagine! I felt about fifteen when Betty said that to me.'

'He actually wants a date with you?'

Rosaleen's smile deepened at May's amazement and once more her head dipped and her lips pressed tightly together to contain her mirth.

'And what did you say to that?' May asked, tentatively.

'Now what could I say? Eh?' Rosaleen's brows rose in surprise at the question. 'Me engaged to Joe?' A wistful look passed over her face and she added, with a deep sigh, 'Perhaps if he had come along sooner I might have been tempted. Oh, my, but he's a handsome brute, so he is.'

Alarmed at these revelations, May gripped her by the shoulders and shook her fiercely.

'Don't be daft! You'll never get anyone as good as Joe Smith,' she warned.

As far as she was concerned, the sun rose and shone on Joe Smith. If only he had fallen for her, life would have been marvellous.

'I know! I know when I'm well off. I won't do anything silly,' Rosaleen promised, and hit May playfully on the shoulder. 'Never fear. I've no intention of spoiling things.'

Relieved, May relaxed and laughed. 'Now, why couldn't he have picked me?' she jested. 'Eh? Twenty-one and fancy free.' But she knew why – the same reason that Joe had picked Rosaleen. Rosaleen was beautiful. She was mediocre.

Glad that he had not put in an appearance, Rosaleen heaved a sigh of relief and hurried home to prepare for her night out with May. This was the highlight of her week, Friday night at the Club Orchid. Not for the world would she admit it, but she felt as if she was already a staid married woman. Joe was wonderful but a bit dull, and their relationship lacked sparkle. They were both staunch Catholics and lived up to the rules of the Church. No long kissing or close embracing; no walking in dark lonely places that were an occasion of sin.

Still, sometimes she found it hard to bear when Joe put her firmly away from him, telling her that they must wait. He was able to control his emotions so much easier than she, and she felt frustrated and wicked because she longed to be held close and cuddled. Nothing serious, just a few kisses.

It will be different once we're married, she assured herself, not for the first time, and tried to picture Joe sweeping her off to bed on a wave of passion, but the man in her imagination had dark hair and deep blue eyes, and she blushed with shame as her thoughts ran on.

The Club Orchid was situated above a pub, on the corner where Castle Street met King Street, down near the town centre. As usual, Rosaleen met May at the bottom of Clonard Street and in high spirits they caught the tram down the Falls Road.

They felt very daring going to the dance at the present time, because since De Valera, the Prime Minister of Southern Ireland, had drawn up a constitution laying claim to the six counties, there had been trouble. The Protestants did not want a united Ireland, and Lord Craigavon had challenged De Valera by calling a general election a few months earlier. The campaign was low key in most places but in Belfast it was bitterly fought and the Troubles which had been dormant for a time were rekindled. The country had gone to the polls on February 9th and it was a day of bitter violence. Cars were wrecked and burned, and windows broken. Republican and Nationalist women had fought each other in the street and the hated B-Specials were on full alert, their guns prominently displayed.

To the delight of the Protestants, Craigavon won the election and the riots eased off a bit, but resentment still simmered, with the Catholics very much aware that the majority of those out of work were of their faith, and that any jobs going would be given to Protestants. However, Rosaleen and May thought it was worth the risk of going to the dance, in spite of recriminations from their families and Joe, because they knew the crowd, and Catholics and Protestants mixed quite amicably together in the Club Orchid.

The ballroom was packed, as was usual on a Friday night, and as usual Bill Murray (Joe's young cousin) lifted Rosaleen in the first dance. She often wondered if Bill kept an eye on her and reported back to Joe, but she did not misbehave so she had nothing to worry about.

It was a slow foxtrot and Bill was a good dancer so she gave herself up to the sheer joy of dancing. Then, suddenly, an awareness came over her and as surely as if he had hailed her, she knew *he* was there. She could feel his presence, and eagerly her eyes roamed around the dancers until they locked with his and a thrill coursed through her body, making her tremble.

'Are you cold, Rosaleen?' Bill drew back and gazed down at her in concern.

'No, no, somebody must've walked over my grave,' she assured him, and over Bill's shoulder she looked at his partner. It was Betty, who raised a hand in greeting, and chiding herself for feeling relieved, Rosaleen nodded in their direction before giving all her attention to Bill. When the dance ended she went to the side of the dance floor where all the girls gathered, and joined May, tugging anxiously at her sleeve.

'May! He's here. What am I gonna do?' she whispered urgently.

'Eh?' May's glance was blank. Her attention on the lad with whom she had just danced, and who was waiting for the next. 'Who's here?'

'Oh! Ye know! Him!' moaned Rosaleen, in anguish. 'Oh, here he comes.'

'Can I have this dance please?'

Worried by the effect he was having on her, she was determined to refuse him, but one look up into his intensely blue eyes and she was lost.

With a slight nod of her head, she silently entered his arms and was drawn close. Their steps matched perfectly, and lost in a bubble of joy, Rosaleen let his remarks on the music go over her head.

The dance was half over before he spoke again. Drawing back, he mouthed the words down at her. 'I'm sorry, please forgive me, I didn't realise you are dumb. How stupid of me.'

Her head reared back and she gaped up at him, her mouth opening in protest. Then she saw the twinkle in his eye and laughed ruefully.

'I suppose you can be forgiven for thinking so,' she agreed, and quirking an eyebrow at him asked, 'What would you like to talk about?'

'Well, let's start from scratch, shall we? Do you come here often?'

His face was alive with suppressed laughter and she dimpled back up at him. 'Every Friday night.' Both brows arched high, inquiringly. 'And you?'

'First time here. You see I'm in the Merchant Navy and I'm away from home a lot.'

'Oh.' Rosaleen wondered why she was so disappointed. Why she felt such a sense of loss. After all, he meant nothing to her.

'I have another week's leave,' he said, and drew her closer. 'Come out with me. Please!' His deep voice was low, pleading.

She shook her head. 'I can't, I'm engaged.'

He glanced at her left hand, at the large diamond sparkling there, and pretended to shade his eyes from the dazzle.

'Ooops, that's a whopper. Where's he tonight?'

'He's plastering the walls of the house we've just bought.' She gave a little laugh and added proudly, 'This is my night out alone.'

He pulled her closer still and his eyes scanned her face intently, marvelling at the purity of her skin and the beauty of her eyes.

'He's a fool! If you were mine I wouldn't let you out of me sight.'

She drew away from him, pleased but embarrassed, and with a toss of her head replied tartly, 'Well then, thank God I'm not yours. I need some time to myself or I would feel smothered.'

'When are you getting married?'

'The beginning of August, all being well. That's if the Troubles don't get too out of hand.'

'So soon?' he cried, dismayed. He had so little time to make her change her mind. 'Look, surely you can come out with me on one date?'

Seeing she was about to refuse again, he rushed on. 'Just once! One date.'

'No … I'm sorry, but I can't.'

She did not realise how regretful she sounded, but he did and asked softly, 'Are you afraid?'

Once more her head reared back, her small chin jutted forward, her eyes flashed green fire, and he fell more in love with her.

'Of course I'm not afraid! Why should I be?' she exclaimed.

'Why not come out with me then? Eh? Just once. We'll probably hate each other and I'll be able to go away with an easy mind. Come on, put me out of my misery.'

She looked up at him, a slight frown ruffling her smooth, wide brow as she digested his words.

Why not? Why not indeed? One date would not hurt her, and Joe need never know.

He could see that she was weakening and again pleaded: 'Please, Rosaleen, just one date.'

'All right.' Guilt and shame made her add urgently. 'But don't dance with me too often. Joe's cousin is here.'

He nodded in understanding.

'When?'

'Tuesday night. Does that suit you?'

Every Tuesday night Joe went to the confraternity in Clonard Monastery. He usually called to see her afterwards but she would make up some excuse to put him off.

Aware that the next three days would drag, Sean, grateful for small mercies, nodded in agreement. 'Where shall I meet you?'

'Outside the London Mantle Warehouse.'

'At the corner of Chapel Lane?'

'Yes, that's right. And please ... don't tell Betty we're meeting.'

Her eyes pleaded with him and he guessed, rightly, that she was having second thoughts.

'I won't tell anyone,' he promised, and after another dance he left the ballroom. He did not want Joe's cousin reporting anything amiss in case she did not show up on Tuesday night. Having accomplished what he had set out to do, he was contented. She was meeting him; it was up to him now.

Having told Joe not to call to see her on Tuesday night as she would be going out with May to visit a sick aunt, Rosaleen prepared carefully for her date with Sean.

Watched by her young sister Annie, she brushed her thick hair until it glowed like dull, pale gold, and highlighted her cheekbones with blusher. Her eyes needed no help to enhance them. Thick dark lashes framed clear green irises edged with a dark ring, and well-shaped dark brows arched above them as if in approval.

'Are you sure you're going out to visit May's sick aunt?' Annie queried, from where she lay sprawled on the bed eyeing Rosaleen. 'Are you telling wee porky pies, eh, Rosaleen?'

Her sister threw her a look of rebuff and did not deign to answer. Inspecting her clothes in the wardrobe, she chose to wear a white suit, knowing it would show off the translucency of her skin and that the green of the blouse she wore under the jacket would darken the green of her eyes.

Examining herself in the mirror she was aware that she looked lovely, all aglow! How come she did not look like this when she went out with Joe? It must be the secrecy; the idea of doing something naughty. That must be what added the sparkle.

Annie showed that she was aware of the difference also.

'Hey, our Rosaleen. Have you a date with someone else?' she asked, her face agog with excitement. Even as she said the words, her mind rejected them. Rosaleen would never do anything underhand. Dismayed at the question, Rosaleen gaped at her, but as she groped about in her mind for a suitable answer, she saw the doubt die in Annie's eyes.

It was with relief that she hugged Annie, who whispered wistfully, 'You look lovely.'

'Thank you, love. See you later.'

And bracing herself to pass her mother's scrutiny, she descended the stairs.

Her mother looked at her askance. 'Where are you goin'?'

'I'm going with May to visit her aunt, she's not very well,' she lied, and knew by the way her mother's face creased in disbelief that she was not fooled.

Rosaleen was consumed with guilt and shame. Why was she doing this? Usually honest, she found it hard to lie, but tonight she felt a person apart. Tonight she wanted to be different. Just this one time. One date with an exciting stranger, before she got married.

'See you later, Mam.'

'What about Joe? What will I say to him when he comes in with your da after the confraternity?' Thelma Magee was worried and it was apparent in her attitude. 'He always calls. Ye know he does.'

'He won't be calling tonight, I've told him I'm going out.'

And before any more embarrassing questions could be asked, Rosaleen closed the door firmly and hurried down the street. Just one date, she promised herself, but she was determined to enjoy every minute of it.

Sean Devlin was growing worried when at last he saw Rosaleen step off the tram at the bottom of Castle Street. He had begun to think that she had changed her mind. As she walked towards him, blonde hair bobbing on her shoulders, he noticed how many heads turned to watch her and wondered how this Joe fellow could bear to let her out of his sight. The suit she wore was close-fitting, the skirt below the box jacket hugging her slim hips and swinging gently to below the calves of her legs, and his breath caught in his throat at the beauty of her.

'Hello.' Her voice was shy, uncertain, and her even white teeth nipped at her bottom lip.

'Hello.' He smiled warmly down at her. 'Would you like to go anywhere in particular?'

She shook her head, her cheeks bright pink at the admiration in his eyes.

'Shall we go to the Imperial then? I hear the film's good.'

This time she nodded her head, feeling tongue-tied. She was annoyed at her shyness. He would think her a fool.

With one accord they turned and walked down Castle Street towards the town centre and when he reached for her hand and pulled her arm through his, hugging it close to his side, she did not demur. Tonight was her last night out alone with a man, before she wed. A kind of hen night. She did not worry that someone might see them and tell Joe. No! She felt that they were invisible, alone on a cloud, and as they queued up outside the Imperial Picture House in Cornmarket, she was enclosed in a bubble of contentment and happiness.

During the film he held her hand, and every now and again he lifted it and brushed his lips across her palm. The emotions this aroused frightened her and she had to keep reminding herself that it was only a date. The film was a sad love story, and she was unable to stop the tears from falling. Surreptitiously, she wiped at her cheeks with her free hand. She did not want him to think her a fool. Joe often chided her for being soft-hearted, but to her surprise Sean squeezed her hand in sympathy and presented her with a handkerchief. As the film drew to a close, she was sad that their night out was nearly over and when he asked her if she would like a coffee, she nodded eagerly, glad of the chance to spend more time with him.

They sat either side of the table in a dimly lit cafe and when he had ordered the coffee, he reached across the table and gripped her hands in his.

'It can't end like this.'

'It must! You promised! One date you said,' she cried in dismay.

His eyes held hers and his head swayed slowly from side to side as he denied this.

'No. I said we would probably hate each other if we were to go out together. Remember?'

'You did promise. You said one date,' she whispered, greatly agitated, and dragged her eyes away from the magic in his.

The warmth of his look embraced her. 'Ah, Rosaleen, I didn't promise. But even if I had promised, I would gladly break it … because I know now that I love you. We were meant for each other. Can't you feel it?'

His hands tightened on hers. 'Look at me, Rosaleen.'

The thick dark lashes that fanned her cheeks slowly lifted and their eyes met, and there it was again, that lovely, warm feeling of belonging.

'There now, you feel it too,' he chided her. 'Don't deny it.'

The arrival of the waitress with the coffee caused him to let go of her hands, and grateful to be free of his overpowering touch, she leant back in her seat out of his reach. There could be no more dates; it was too dangerous. She must make him understand that nothing had changed, that she was marrying Joe.

They argued the whole way home, but she was adamant and at the corner of Colinward Street, where she lived, offered him her hand.

Ignoring the outstretched hand he took her by the shoulders and drew her into the shadows where he kissed her; his lips persuasive, compelling. She stood for some moments, cold and passive, but then her body betrayed her and her lips moved hungrily under his and her arms crept up around his neck. They strained together for many moments and then he drew back and looked at her, a puzzled frown on his brow.

'Does this Joe fellow not satisfy you?'

Pulling angrily away from him, she cried, 'Don't talk like that! That was a sin! I shouldn't have let you kiss me like that.' There was a break in her voice as she lamented, 'Joe and I are saving ourselves for our wedding night.'

'Listen, love.' His voice was gentle, soothing. 'I'm not talking about heavy petting, but surely he shows his love like this ...' he pulled her close again and to her shame she let him, wanting to recapture the joy of the first kiss '... and this.'

His hands caressed the back of her neck and trailed down her back, before gently gripping her buttocks and fitting her body to suit his. Sending thrill upon thrill coursing through her, awakening emotions that she had not known existed; making her feel weak at the knees. Butterfly kisses covered her face, her eyes, then her nose, then gently, so gently, her mouth. She stood in a trance, unable to break the spell he was weaving around her, until his hand cupped her breast. Then sanity returned and she reacted in anger, pushing him roughly away, hissing: 'Don't! That's a sin! Oh, I never want to see you again. Never again!'

Her voice broke on a sob. Turning, she ran down the street, her cheeks hot with shame. Joe had been courting her for eighteen months and not once had he been disrespectful. Not once had he touched her breast. He respected her too much. And tonight she had let a stranger, an exciting, wonderful stranger, but a stranger nonetheless, touch her ... and, worse still, had wanted more. Much more, she realised, and shame engulfed her. She must never meet him again. It was too dangerous.

The rest of the week passed in a daze and she clung to Joe like a drowning person, feeling safe only in his company.

Sean was outside the factory on Wednesday and Thursday nights, but she refused to talk to him. In despair, he called May aside.

'Look, I go away tomorrow and I won't be back until the end of July. Talk to her. Please, talk to her,' he begged in a ragged voice. 'She doesn't love this Joe fellow. I just know she doesn't. She'll be unhappy married to him.'

Watching Rosaleen scurry ahead like a scared rabbit, May cried. 'I suppose you think she loves you?'

She was angry with him. Rosaleen had been unhappy and jumpy since her date with him and May placed the blame squarely at his door. However, Sean was sadly shaking his head. He had thought he would be able to make Rosaleen talk to him, listen to his pleas, convince her that they were meant for each other, but he had failed miserably. She was strong-willed, much stronger than he, and he had to admit defeat. If only he was not due back on his ship. If only he had more time to wear her down.

'No, she doesn't love me,' he said sadly. 'Or at least she won't admit she loves me, but she doesn't love Joe.'

He was so earnest that in spite of herself May was impressed and asked, 'What do you mean, she doesn't love Joe? Who are you to say?'

'So help me, I don't know. I only fear she will be unhappy with him.'

'You're wrong. Joe's a good man, and they're hard to come by. He has his own wee business, so he does. He'll provide well for her. She'll never want for anything.'

He looked astounded. 'An' you think that's all that matters? A meal ticket?'

'Yes, I do!' May was adamant. 'I wish I was marrying a man like Joe. I'd look to neither left nor right, I can tell you.'

He swung away from her in anger and then swung back again to bawl, 'In the name of God, are you all thick? Do you think money's everything?'

Stung, May put her hands on her hips, threw her head high and bawled back at him. 'No, but it helps to get everything.'

The look he bestowed on her was full of pity. 'You poor fool. You poor, poor fool.'

Without another word he turned on his heel and strode down the street, leaving her standing gaping after him.

The weeks flew past and Rosaleen, caught up in preparations for her wedding, managed to push all thoughts of Sean to the back of her mind. She would not fancy marrying a Merchant Navy man, she convinced herself. Her Aunt Margaret was married to a sailor and half her life was spent waiting for him to come home on leave. No, that was not for her. She wanted a man who was always there, someone to hold her close in the night. If, when Joe kept her at arm's length, she longed for the rapture she had experienced with Sean's kisses, she assured herself that it was worth waiting for. Just a matter of a few months, and then they would be married and Joe could show his love for her. Meantime, there was plenty to keep her occupied. What with decorating the house and attending fittings for her wedding dress and all the other things attached to preparing for a wedding.

A week before the wedding, her last day at work until after her honeymoon, she came through the factory gates laughing and happy. She was covered in confetti and in her arms carried a large box, her present from the girls in work. The laughter died on her lips and her step faltered when she saw him standing there, magnificent in his Merchant Navy uniform; the target of many admiring eyes. Then she was past him, almost running in her haste, her stupid heart thumping against her ribs, panic gripping her. Dear God, why was this happening to her? She did not want to feel like this. Why couldn't he have stayed away another week and then she would be safely married to Joe?

His long strides quickly caught up with her and, gripping her by the elbow, he forced her to slow down, at the same time throwing May a look which she rightly interpreted as, 'Get lost.'

Seeing May scurry out of sight, Rosaleen turned and faced him.

'You shouldn't have come. I have nothing to say to you.'

'Why didn't you answer my letters?'

'I've already told you why – I have nothing to say to you, Sean Devlin. Don't you understand? I'm marrying Joe next week and that's that!'

'Is that box heavy? Here, let me carry it.'

'No!' She resisted his efforts to take the box from her. 'No … I can manage it myself, thank you.'

'Are you going to the Club Orchid tonight?'

'Listen you!' she cried in exasperation. 'I'm going to the dance with the girls out of work tonight and I don't want you coming and spoiling it for me. Do you hear me? Leave me alone!'

With these words she stormed ahead and he let her go. She would be at the dance tonight and whether she liked it or not, so would he. Grimly, he nodded his head. Oh, yes, he would be at the Club Orchid tonight. Just let anyone try to keep him away!'

That night, he was the first person she saw when she entered the ballroom. He was dancing with a tall, attractive girl, whom, to her shame, she found herself avidly examining.

The evening was nearly over and although he had danced with May, Sean did not ask Rosaleen to dance with him. Annoyed for feeling peeved, Rosaleen reminded herself that she had warned him not to annoy her, had told him to leave her alone. And even if he had asked her to dance, she would have refused him. Wouldn't she? Still, she felt slighted and covertly watched him, annoyed with herself for noticing that he did not dance with any one girl in particular.

It was the last dance and she was moving sadly on to the dance floor with a partner when Sean appeared. Taking her firmly by the arm, he said, 'Sorry, but she promised me the last dance.'

Before she could object, he swept her into his arms and on to the dance floor.

Her heart was racing and she held herself stiff in his arms.

'You had no right to do that!' she stormed up at him, annoyed yet excited at the effect he was having on her.

'Would you have danced with me if I had asked you to?'

'No!'

Her shake of the head was definite and he said, 'That's why I did what I did.' He gave her a little shake. 'Relax, for heaven's sake. I'm not going to bite you.'

He was a terrific dancer, long smooth strides covering the floor expertly, and in spite of herself, she relaxed against him and they twirled around the floor as one. They danced in silence, each aware of the magic bond that held them, and as the music came to an end, he steered her over to the cloakroom door.

'I'm seeing you home, so tell your friends to go on.' She opened her mouth to protest and he growled, 'Do you want me to make a scene?'

When she hesitated, he insisted, 'I will, you know. I intend talking to you, whether you listen or not.'

'It won't make any difference,' she muttered. 'You're wasting your time. My mind's made up.'

'Then you have nothing to worry about,' he assured her, and abruptly turned away, saying over his shoulder, 'I'll see you outside.'

When she told May that Sean was walking her home, her friend eyed her with concern.

'Do you want me to tag along?' she asked anxiously.

'No, no … it's all right. I can look after myself. You go home with the rest of the girls and I'll see you sometime tomorrow.'

It was a beautiful, moonlit night and they dandered up Castle Street in silence. At Victor's Ice Cream Parlour in Divis Street, famous for its Italian ice cream, he stopped and bought two ice-cream cones.

She had to smile when he handed her a cone with a flourish, as if he was giving her the crown jewels.

He's very handsome, she admitted to herself, as she observed his straight nose and strong jaw. But then, so is Joe, she reminded herself. Once Joe and she were married and her frustration was at an end, she would not be attracted to another man. She would be fulfilled and need no other.

It came as a surprise to her when they arrived at Colinward Street. They had so much in common, so many shared interests to talk about, that the time had flown. It was with regret that she offered him her hand, but instead of shaking it, he pulled it through his arm and drew her on up the Springfield Road.

When she tried to break away from him, he begged, 'Please, Rosaleen. I may never see you again, please walk with me for a while.'

Against her better judgement she did as he asked. When they arrived at the Dam, that dark lonely place frequented by lovers, he steered her off the road and down a grassy bank.

She felt uneasy. She never liked being near the Dam, even in daylight. Too many people had drowned in it. Some accidentally, some by choice. Nevertheless, it was a favourite spot for courting couples, full of shadows and corners. Of course Joe would never dream of taking here here, he respected her too much, yet here she was with a stranger. But she did not really feel that Sean was a stranger. She felt as if she had known him all her life. It was not him she was afraid of, it was her own emotions. Feeling panic rise, she realised that this was an occasion of sin. Did the priests not warn them to stay away from lonely places when out with boys?

'I must go home,' she cried, and twisting out of Sean's hold, she started back up the grassy bank, but he grabbed hold of her arm and pulled her down again, into his arms. Her heart was racing and he was aware of her agitation.

'Don't be afraid, Rosaleen,' he whispered softly. 'I won't harm you.'

His hands caressed her back, sending sensual tremors shivering along the edge of her nerves, and in spite of her misgivings she sank against him, excitement a tight knot in her groin. In the moonlight her eyes were pale and glittered like diamonds, and her hair was like silvered silk. The moon's light was ghostly and as she cast apprehensive glances around in the eerie light, she shivered. Sean opened his jacket and drew her against the warmth of his body.

'Are you cold?' he asked, wrapping his jacket around her. She shook her head, her hair swaying like a silver bell. He put his lips against its perfumed softness and his pulse quickened. Excitement sent the blood pounding through his veins. He groaned, feeling real pain at the very thought that she was to wed another. He had to stop her. Aware of his anguish she drew back, looking up at him askance.

'You can't marry Joe,' he cried. 'I won't let you. Do you hear me? I won't let you.'

'Tut! Of course I'm marrying Joe. Don't you realise my parents have spent all their savings on this wedding? Haven't I told you Joe has bought and decorated a house?' she cried, annoyed at his persistence.

His grip on her tightened. 'You wouldn't be the first girl to realise she had made a mistake.'

This really riled her. 'Oh, but I haven't made a mistake! I love Joe,' she cried in exasperation. 'And next Saturday I'm marrying him.'

'Then why are you here with me?' he asked quickly. 'Eh? Tell me why.'

'Because I felt sorry for you, that's why,' she hissed, and once more turned to leave him.

He pulled her roughly back against him. 'Sorry for me? Sorry for

21

me?' His voice was hoarse. 'Well now, let's see a little more of your pity.' His grip on her tightened and his lips savaged hers.

She stood rigid, fear a tight knot in her stomach, as his lips angrily bruised hers, crushing them against her teeth; making her wince.

Coming to his senses, he turned aside, apologising.

'I'm sorry ... I'm sorry ... forgive me. I had no right to do that.'

He sounded so upset, compassion overcame her fear. Pulling him around towards her, her hands tenderly brushed his face.

'Hush ... hush. It's all right ... it's all right,' she soothed him.

Gently now, he pressed her close and his lips touched her face. She lapped it up, enjoying the sensual tremors that were rippling through her body; the mounting excitement. Why couldn't Joe kiss her like this, instead of constantly pushing her away and telling her they must wait? Surely kisses like this were not a sin?

Unconsciously, her face moved restlessly until his lips found hers, and as his kisses became more insistent, her arms crept up around his neck, and she returned kiss for kiss, caress for caress; pressing urgently against the hard lines of his body. When his hands gently explored her, seeking out the forbidden places, she knew why Joe did not take chances. This was wrong, one part of her mind insisted. Very wrong! She knew she should push him away, stop him, but her body would not obey her mind as his hands brought her to the edge of ecstasy, and over, and soon it was too late. There in the shadows they came together as naturally as night follows day. It was the easiest thing in the world. Not awful, as she had been led to believe, and she lost all track of time as he made her his own. Lost in a well of passion that carried them above all reason, senses alive to nothing but each other, they were as one.

They clung together for a long time, at peace with the world, but at last he pushed her gently away, until he could see into her eyes.

'Now do you know why you can't marry Joe? You're mine! All mine! We were meant for each other. I knew it the minute I saw you.'

His voice was gentle and confident, and smug.

It was the smugness that came across to Rosaleen as sanity returned and she realised just what she had done. She stood aghast, panic setting in. Was she mad? A week before her wedding and she had given herself to another man. She was a whore. A tart. A sinner. Dear God ... how could she have been so stupid? How could she have done this terrible thing?

Appalled, she hurriedly adjusted her clothing and groped about on the grass for her handbag. Without looking at him, she started to clamber up the grassy bank. Sean took her arm to assist her, aware that all was far from well, but not knowing why. Surely she understood? Hadn't he proved to her that they were meant for each other? Angrily, Rosaleen shook him off, hitting out at him with her handbag, deep sobs choking her.

Once up the slope she almost ran down the Springfield Road, the tears blinding her, and when he followed close behind, she rounded on him and hissed, 'Leave me alone! Leave me alone! Go away. I never want to see you again.'

'You're being a fool, Rosaleen. You can't possibly marry Joe after what happened back there.' His voice became pleading. 'Ah, Rosaleen, I love you. I love you so much. Surely you know that? Don't you feel the same?'

Stopping in her tracks she rounded on him. 'Love? You call what happened back there love? That was lust! We were like two animals. Now I know why Joe insists that we don't pet. That's what happens when you pet. You lose control and act like animals.' Her voice broke and she swallowed deeply before continuing. 'Let me tell you something, Sean Devlin. Joe wouldn't have lost control. In fact, he respects me too much to take me to a place like that. That's the difference between you and him. He respects me.'

Stunned at her words, he grabbed her and pushed her roughly against the wall.

'I love you! That's why that happened. Believe me, if I hadn't loved you, it wouldn't have. I'm no fool, I know the difference between lust and love... and you wanted it too, so don't act innocent with me,' he growled.

She stood, head averted, lips tightly pressed together, and he cried, 'Ah, Rosaleen, you wanted it too. Come on now, love, don't deny it. Don't put all the blame on me,' he begged, wanting to reach her, but he pleaded in vain.

'If you're quite finished, I'd like to go home.'

Her voice was cold, lifeless, and he knew he had lost her. He had not meant to take her. Not like that! No, he had wanted to woo her with flowers and gifts, but time was against him and he had let himself get carried away. He bitterly regretted his actions, but it was too late. At the contempt in her eyes, his arms fell limply to his sides and without another glance, she left him.

He watched until she turned the corner of Colinward Street and then he went to the corner and watched until she entered her own doorway. It was late and he wanted to be sure she got home safely. Then, with steps that dragged, he continued down the Springfield Road, his heart a heavy lump in his breast.

Inside the small hall, Rosaleen wiped her face and tried to compose herself. She knew her mother would still be downstairs; she never retired until Rosaleen and Annie were indoors. Sure enough, the light was on in the kitchen. Opening the door, she stayed in its shadow and said, 'Goodnight, Mam.' But she was not going to be let off the hook.

'Come in here a minnit!' her mother ordered, and slowly Rosaleen entered the room.

'You're late t'night! Were you with Joe?'

Her mother sounded suspicious and seeing her nose twitch, Rosaleen's heart missed a beat, feeling sure she could smell the sex on her; she felt she stank of it.

She lied abruptly. 'Yes, I was. I'm tired, Mam, I'm going to bed.'

And before her mother could ask any more questions, she withdrew into the hall. Climbing the stairs, she entered the room she shared with her young sister Annie, wishing they had a bathroom. She felt so dirty; wicked and dirty.

It was easy running away from her mother, but not so easy to escape her conscience. If only she had come home with May. Would Joe guess that she was not a virgin when they spent their first night together? Only one more week and she would have experienced that wonderful pleasure with Joe. Oh, why hadn't she come straight home? How could she have been so stupid?

Oh, dear God, please forgive me. Please don't let Joe guess and help me make him a good wife, she prayed earnestly on her knees, before crawling into bed beside Annie.

As she tossed and turned, causing Annie to twitch irritably at the bedclothes, she realised that at least now she would not be afraid on her wedding night. Some girls said that it was awful the first time, and a lot said that it didn't get much better but once the kids came they compensated for everything. Well, she shouldn't have listened to gossip. She had thought it wonderful. The most natural thing in the world. It had just been the wrong man. One thing she was sure of, she was going to enjoy married life.

May was surprised when, leaving the factory on Monday night, she saw Sean waiting at the corner of Cupar Street. He approached her. She was horrified at his appearance. He looked as if he had not slept for a week. When he humbly asked her if he could have a word with her she silently nodded her agreement. He walked the full length of Clonard Street with her. Right down to the Falls Road and over to the corner of Spinner Street where she lived, speaking all the while of how much he loved Rosaleen.

He was in such a state that she took pity on him and promised to try to persuade her friend to meet him once more. And, that night, calling to see Rosaleen, she did try. Pleading his case until she was blue in the face, but to no avail.

Rosaleen was adamant. Eyeing May reproachfully, she chided, 'You've changed your tune. I thought you didn't want me to have anything to do with him?'

'I know, Rosaleen, but to tell the truth, I feel sorry for him. He looks awful. Will you not see him just once, and put him out of his misery?'

'No, May. You don't understand. I like him, I like him a lot, too much … but I'm marrying Joe.'

May nodded. She did understand. Once more she lamented the fact that Sean had fallen for Rosaleen. Why could he not have picked her? Rosaleen was lucky to have two handsome men in love with her, but she had made the right choice. Joe would make a better husband and father than a sailor would. There was no doubt whatsoever in May's mind that Rosaleen had made the right choice.

Saturday dawned with clear blue skies and Rosaleen made a beautiful bride. Her dress was made of soft, ivory-coloured satin which swirled around her ankles above matching satin shoes, and she carried a bouquet of lilies and freesia. Annie had been horrified at her choice of flowers, saying lilies were for funerals and were considered unlucky. However, Rosaleen loved the waxed, pure beauty of lilies and she was not in the least superstitious. She had two bridesmaids; Annie was in pink, and May in blue, and each carried a small posy of mixed flowers. Oh, yes, her mother had been determined to splash out and Rosaleen felt indebted to her. Her parents too looked splendid in new outfits. The pale blue of her mother's matching coat and dress made her look younger, and her father was very handsome in his new grey lounge suit. It had all cost a fortune, and there was no way she could have changed her mind. No way! Her parents had scrimped and saved to make her day perfect and she could not have backed out. Not that she had wanted to, she reminded heself. She would soon forget Sean Devlin, now that she was married. All week she had been plagued by doubts, overcome every now and again by memories of the rapture she had felt in his arms, but when she saw the tears of pride in her mother's eyes, she knew she had done the right thing. Joe was the man for her. Everybody thought so ... and surely everybody could not be wrong? She was sorry she had hurt Sean but a handsome man like him would soon find someone else.

Then she saw him. He was standing on the far side of the Falls Road, facing the church, against the wall that used to house the old asylum. She gave a gasp of dismay when she saw how haggard and ill he looked. Immediately Joe was all concern. 'Are you all right, love?'

'Yes!' her answer was so abrupt, he drew back to get a better look at her face, and she hastened to assure him, 'Yes, I'm fine, fine. Just nervous.'

She moved closer to him and gripped his arm tightly. Would

Sean approach them? Would he say anything that would betray her? While the photographer took the wedding photos, she kept her eyes averted, and when she next dared to look, Sean was gone and she breathed a sigh of relief. She only hoped that she had not ruined the wedding photographs by her own stupidity.

Chapter 2

With a mumbled excuse, Rosaleen pushed her chair away from the table and hurried from the room. A slight frown gathered on Joe's brow as he gazed thoughtfully after her. This was the third morning she had rushed from the table, out to the bathroom that he had built on to the back of the house. It was almost as if she was ... but then, she couldn't be ... could she? His mind boggled at the idea. Could she possibly be pregnant?

In the bathroom, on her knees at the toilet bowl, Rosaleen retched and retched, her whole body contracting in an effort to bring up food from an empty, exhausted stomach. At last, flushing the toilet, she pushed herself wearily to her feet and turned to the wash-hand basin, despair in her heart. Whilst she washed her hands and splashed her face with cold water she examined her reflection in the mirror. She looked awful! There wasn't a vestige of colour in her face and her eyes were like saucers; saucers with great dark rims round them. A sigh left her lips, a great, deep sigh from the heart. She would have to tell Joe. There was no alternative. A shiver coursed through her body at the idea. In the short time that they were married, she had discovered that Joe was very strict where morals were concerned. Black was black and white was white.

There was no grey as far as he was concerned. You were either good or you were bad, mistakes ought not to happen. What would he do when he discovered that she was pregnant? Would he put her out? Where would she go? Back to her parents' home? Would they let her return.

In a state of terror, she pictured the horror on her parents' faces when she told them that she was pregnant and that Joe wasn't the father. The recriminations, the questions. Fearfully, she looked around her. What was that noise? To her dismay, she realised the strangled sounds were coming from her own mouth. A sob rose in her throat and burst from her lips, and she pressed the towel to her mouth to stifle the sounds as she fought for control.

This was all Sean Devlin's fault! What if she had not been getting married? She was in a state as it was, but what if she was single?

Her mind baulked at the very idea, filling her with panic. Imagine her pregnant and him away in the middle of the ocean. Not that it would be much better once she admitted to Joe that she was pregnant, but at least she had a wedding ring on her finger, Mrs in front of her name, and she could hope that Joe would not broadcast her shame to all and sundry.

Oh, dear God, help me, she begged. But how could she expect God to help her? Hadn't she been wicked? Even if God in all His mercy had forgiven her, how could she expect Him to make Joe understand?

With steps that dragged, she returned to the kitchen; she may as well get it over with.

Joe watched her sit down, watched her clasp the mug of tea with both hands, as if seeking warmth, and asked gently, 'Are you not feeling well, Rosaleen?'

Lost in thought, trying to find words to confess her guilt, she jerked upright, sending tea dripping down her fingers on to the table.

Immediately Joe was on his feet and around the table, bending over her full of concern. Taking the mug from her shaking hands, he gently dried them on a tea towel.

'Is it something you ate, do you think?' he asked, solicitously rubbing warmth into her cold hands; his eyes taking note of her lack of colour.

Closing her eyes, Rosaleen forced the words into her mouth and out. 'I'm pregnant.'

She sat still, waiting for words of condemnation, perhaps a blow. God knows she deserved it. At last, unable to bear the silence any longer, she glanced up and her mouth dropped open in amazement. Instead of the look of horror she expected to see on Joe's face, there was a look of bemused wonder.

Even as she gaped at him, he reached for her, drawing her up into his arms, muttering, 'Ah, Rosaleen, Rosaleen my love, you have just made me the happiest man in the world.'

He sank his face into her hair, and she felt his tears soak through and wet her scalp. 'I thought I wasn't able ... you know what I mean ...' His voice trailed off, then filled with awe. 'And to discover that I am ... why, it's an answer to my prayers.'

Bewildered, Rosaleen clung to him, trying to sort out her jumbled thoughts. Surely Joe did not believe that his few futile attempts at making love had resulted in a pregnancy? He could not be so naive. Could he? Another stealthy glance at him showed her that he did indeed believe.

It seemed *her* prayers were being answered too.

Leading her into the living room, he made her sit down on the settee. 'Put your feet up, love. There'll be no work for you today. In fact, perhaps it would be better if you left work.' He brushed the hair back from her brow and planted a tender kiss there. 'What do you think?'

Still in a daze, she answered him mechanically. 'I would like to work on for a while. We could do with the money.'

When she was settled with a rug over her legs and a cup of warm milk in her hand, he returned to the kitchen. Shouting in excitedly to her, making plans, as he washed the dishes. At last, after much fussing over her, he left for work.

Glad to see him go, Rosaleen relaxed and set her mind to work on her problem. Should she tell Joe the truth? She must! Surely she must? She owed it to him. To let him rear another man's child as his own would be a sin. One thing was sure: if she let him believe he was the father, her lips must be sealed forever.

What if she was found out? But then, she couldn't be found out. Only she, and she alone, knew the truth. No one would be able to blow the whistle on her; not even Sean. And, really, she would be doing Joe a good turn, wouldn't she? Because it looked as if he would never father a child. But had she the right to make such a decision?

Her thoughts whirled, making her head ache, and at last she could bear it no longer. Pushing the rug irritably away, she rose to her feet. For some moments she stood undecided; then she entered the bathroom and set the taps running in the bath, a determined look on her face. Her mind was made up. From now on, as far as she was concerned, this child she was carrying was Joe's. As soon as she had bathed she would go up and break the news to her mother and then make an appointment to see the doctor. Thoughts of a laughing face with dark blue eyes flitted across her mind, but she pushed them resolutely away. These thoughts she was beginning to dwell on so often lately must stop.

All of a sudden, against her will, she was blinded by tears as the memory of the night up at the Dam returned to haunt her. She could feel his arms around her, hear his declaration of love, and self-pity filled her. Lying in the bath, she wept long and hard for what might have been. Her only consolation was that she need never see Sean again. Need never know who he married or where he lived, and for this she was grateful.

Thelma Magee eyed her daughter closely when, after a light tap on the kitchen door, she entered the room. The signs of weeping were well camouflaged but she saw them and her heart sank. It dismayed her to feel Rosaleen's unrest, but what could she do? It would be wrong to interfere between husband and wife. Rosaleen had made her bed, now she must lie on it. Who would have thought that Joe would be found wanting? A big man like Joe? It was hard to believe.

'This is a surprise,' she cried. 'Why are you not at work?'

'I've some news for you, Mam. What do you think? I'm pregnant!'

Relief flooded through Thelma at her words. Everything must be all right; things must have sorted themselves out.

Rosaleen felt the relief that radiated from her mother and smiled wryly. Her mother would be sure to think that pregnancy solved all her problems. How wrong she was. It only added to them.

'Oh, that's wonderful, Rosaleen. Just wonderful. Wait 'til your da hears, it'll be another excuse for a drink. As if he needs one.'

'Ah, Mam, don't. Me dad's not that bad. Why, he only drinks at set times. In fact, I can't remember seeing him really drunk, just happy.'

'Humph!' Thelma turned away, a cynical look on her face.

Rosaleen couldn't understand her mother's attitude towards her father. Heaven knows he was always bending over backwards to please her, he lifted and laid her, but she never gave him credit for anything. He was such a quiet, inoffensive man, and was devoted to her mother, but still she was forever finding fault with him.

Rosaleen eyed her mother covertly. Why, she was absolutely beaming. She was certainly pleased about the baby. She remembered the day she had plucked up the courage to ask her mother's advice about her matrimonial problems. To her surprise, her mother had been more embarrassed than she. Bright red, she had refused to meet Rosaleen's eye and had pleated her apron, pulled it apart and pleated it again, and again, making Rosaleen want to scream, and sorry that she had broached the subject at all. At last her mother had muttered, 'That's between you and him. It's something you must work out between you. Because ... well... ye see, I ... really ... I ... I'll make a cup of tea.' And had sought refuge in the scullery. The conversation was never resumed.

'When's the baby due?'

'I'm not sure. I've to see the doctor yet, but I imagine ...' Rosaleen paused, remembering in time that her mother knew that she and Joe were having trouble.

'I think about June,' she finished, adding on an extra month. Was this the beginning of a life of deceit?

'Oh, that's a lovely time. You'll have the whole summer to get out and about. A summer baby gets a better start in life than a winter child, so it does. Ye know what I mean. It gets out in the sun an' all.

Our Annie'll be glad. She dotes on kids, so she does.'

'How's her romance going?'

'Oh, it's still on. I've warned her, mind. He'll never cross over this doorstep, I told her, but she's stubborn, so she is. You'd think she could find herself a good Catholic boy. The Falls Road's full of them. Somebody like Joe. That's one thing about you, Rosaleen, you never gave me any sleepless nights. You never ran around with Protestants.'

'George seems a nice lad, Mam.'

'You've met him?'

Her mother sounded so scandalised, Rosaleen laughed aloud.

'Yes! And he didn't bite me, and he didn't have horns.'

'Really, Rosaleen, I'm surprised at you, condonin' her behaviour. You're as bad as your da.'

'Oh? Does me da not object?'

'Hah! He keeps throwing every convert he knows in my face. A fat lot he knows. You're better with your own sort, I told him. But then, of course, he would be prejudiced.'

'Why? Why would he be prejudiced?' Rosaleen asked, her look intent.

Her mother grew flustered. 'Well, ye know what I mean. He's worked with Protestants all his life. He can see no harm in them.'

'Mam …'

It was on the tip of Rosaleen's tongue to ask her mother why she had married her father, but when Thelma quirked a brow inquiringly at her, the words died.

'Oh, nothing, just … about our Annie – don't push her. If you leave her alone, I bet you she'll stop dating George, but as sure as you nag her, George will seem more wonderful. We all go through these phases.'

'You didn't!'

'I know … I know … but times change. The young ones are more independent nowadays. Annie's no fool. She'll be all right!'

The door was pushed open. Annie's eyebrows raised at seeing Rosaleen. 'Who's taking my name in vain?' she cried.

'Nobody! What are you doin' home?'

With a discreet wink at Rosaleen, Annie solemnly answered her mother, 'I'm meeting George. We're going down to pick out an engagement ring.'

'In the name of God, are you mad?' Thelma rose from her chair in panic. 'You'll get out of this house, mind. Ye can pack your bags if you get engaged to that Prod.'

'Mam! She's only joking.'

Rosaleen gave Annie a disapproving look. Fond as she was of her young sister, there were times when she wished that she would date Catholic boys. Her mother was right; there were plenty of young men on the Falls Road, but so far Annie had dated only Protestants.

Now Annie grinned wickedly, and continued, 'Did you hear that, Rosaleen? She'd put me out and I'd have to go and live on the Shankill Road – in sin.'

Seeing her mother's face blanch, Rosaleen sought to change the conversation.

'Stop acting the fool, Annie. I've some good news. What do you think? I'm pregnant.'

Annie's mouth gaped slightly open and she gazed in wonder at Rosaleen. Then, nodding her head, she said: 'I'm glad for you. Surprised, but glad.'

Rosaleen gaped in amazement and cried, 'What do you mean, surprised?'

'Well, perhaps I shouldn't say this ... but I didn't think Joe had it in him. I always thought he was a bit of a wimp.'

Open-mouthed, Rosaleen sat in stunned silence, surprised at how perceptive this young sister of hers was. Just past seventeen and she was more worldly than Rosaleen would ever be.

'Oh, listen to knowall. From the mouths of babes comes rubbish,' Thelma cried in dismay. Annie was too forthright for her own good. What if Rosaleen took offence? 'Why are you home?' she asked again, to change the subject.

'We're on strike! We all walked out because Jean Morgan was given the sack for bad time-keeping.'

'An' you think they'll take her back? You think ye can blackmail the firm?' Thelma's face fell in disbelief. 'Sure, they could fill the factory ten times over, there's so many stitchers out of work. You'd never get another job. You're even dafter than I thought ye were, girl.'

'Mam, you can't let them get away with everything. Next time it might be me.'

Hands on hips, Thelma challenged, 'Why you? Eh? Tell me, why you? You're not a bad time-keeper. You're never off work. Why would they sack you?'

'They would find some excuse. My face doesn't fit.'

'That's because you can't keep your big mouth shut!' Thelma bawled. 'Ye fight everybody's battles, so ye do. You should mind your own business.'

'Tut!' Annie turned aside in disgust. It was no use telling her mother that Mr Benson didn't like Catholics. 'Anyhow, we're going back in tomorrow. I think Benson will give her another chance. He's too many orders in to do otherwise, but meanwhile we'll have made our point. He'll know that he can't push us around.'

Thelma opened her mouth to argue, but with a slight shake of her head, Rosaleen stopped her. In this mood Annie would only humour her mother so long, then there would be a blazing row.

'Will Jean go back?' she asked, seeking to ease the tension.

'Oh, yes, I think so. Mind you, she's been warned to pull up her socks, 'cause next time we won't back her. She'll be out for good.'

With an apologetic smile, she placed a hand on Rosaleen's shoulder and squeezed it. 'I'm sorry about what I said just now about Joe. You know me. Speak first... think later. He's a fine guy and I'm very fond of him. You know that, don't you?'

Rosaleen patted her hand and smiled, graciously receiving the olive branch.

Later, when Rosaleen had departed, Thelma rounded on Annie.

'Are you daft. Eh? That was a terrible thing to say. Joe's a fine figure of a man, so he is. Imagine saying to someone's face that their husband's a wimp ...' For some seconds words failed her. Then: 'Rosaleen could've easily taken offence, girl.'

'I know, I know.' Annie made placatory gestures with her hands. She sorely regretted her remarks. Would she ever learn to control her tongue? And now her mother was on her hobby horse

... keeping her in line. 'It was stupid of me, I admit! But luckily enough Rosaleen didn't take umbrage, so there's no harm done.'

'Your big mouth will get ye into trouble one of these days, so it will. Even in work ye can't keep it shut.' Thelma glared at her. 'What if you get the sack? Eh? If Benson gives you the push, don't come t'me for sympathy. Do ye hear me? An' if he doesn't give you the push ... keep yer big mouth shut in future!'

With a grimace, Annie turned away and headed for the scullery; afraid to retaliate; afraid of starting a full-scale row. Her father would be home soon, and although a kindly man, he always sided with her mother. She hadn't realized how much Rosaleen had shielded her from her mother's sharp tongue until her sister had married and her comforting presence was withdrawn.

Her mother's voice followed her. 'As for that Prod yer dating, don't you ever dare bring him near this door ...'

To escape further recriminations, Annie carried on through the scullery and out into the yard, closing the door with a sharp decisive click. Drawing deep breaths of air into her lungs, she fought for control. If only her mother would try to understand her. She couldn't help that she was different from Rosaleen, and the way her mother kept comparing them made her blood boil. All right, so she wasn't as good-living as her sister. Could not get interested in a Catholic boy. It wasn't from choice. Catholic boys just didn't ask her out, whereas Protestants did. One thing she was sure of: she certainly didn't want anyone like Joe for a husband! To her, he appeared a cold fish. Oh, he was kind, generous to a fault ... Rosaleen wanted for nothing. Still, he never showed her any affection in public; no wee spontaneous kisses or hugs. No warm 'I'm glad you're mine' looks. But perhaps he was different in private.

Or perhaps, as her mother was always pointing out, she read too many romantic novels. The man Annie dreamed of meeting would be loving and passionate; sweep her off her feet. Kiss her and hug her whenever the notion took him. She sighed as her thoughts ran on. Even the thought of how things could be made her feel all mellow. Her mother was right all the same ... she would have to learn to control her tongue or, awful thought, she might even scare Mr Right away. With these thoughts she entered the house, prepared to eat humble pie to keep the peace.

That night, as she sat on the opposite side of the hearth from Joe, Rosaleen found herself examining him but could not agree with Annie. As far as appearance went, Joe was all man: tall, broad-shouldered and handsome. Were his good looks a bit too pretty, though? No, not really. With his fair hair and thick-lashed pale grey eyes, he wasn't as rugged as Sean, but neither was he soppy-looking. Annie, not being aware of his problem, was doing him an injustice.

As the weeks passed and Rosaleen started to get bigger, Joe, released from the pressure of having to perform his duty now that she was pregnant, suggested moving into the spare room.

'You need a bed to yourself, love,' he explained with a tender smile. 'I don't want to crush you now you're getting bigger.' And he gave her stomach a patronising pat.

Annoyed, the look Rosaleen gave him was so long and appraising that he blushed bright red. He became so flustered she felt pity replace the annoyance, and thanked him bleakly for his thoughtfulness. She had not married him to sleep alone, but, she reminded herself, it would be better on her own than having to put up with Joe starting something he could not finish. Perhaps she would not feel so frustrated. Sometimes she was angry with Sean for making her aware just what she was missing out on. She had not expected to enjoy that side of married life and she would not have known any better, but then, she reminded herself, she would probably have ended up childless; this way she would at least become a mother.

Rosaleen worked up until six weeks before the baby was due, to help pay for the bathroom. Joe didn't want her to, because with the threat of war all the big engineering firms were making parts for planes and ships and his small business was doing well on smaller home jobs, but she preferred to be active and the money would come in handy. She knew how lucky she was; not many young married couples were able to afford their own house. And she got on very well with her mother-in-law, which was another blessing; none of the married girls in work could abide their mothers-in-law.

Joe's father had died when he was very young and he had left money in trust for Joe and that was how he had been able to start up on his own. He was an only child, so Rosaleen had been afraid his mother might be over possessive. But no, if anything, she clung more to Rosaleen than she did to Joe, and since she lived just around the corner in Cavendish Street, this was a blessing.

Annie's romance with George had died a natural death once her mother stopped talking about him and a delighted Thelma confided in Rosaleen that Annie had a new boyfriend, a Catholic!

Every Tuesday night, when Joe went to the confraternity in Clonard Monastery, Rosaleen accompanied him as far as Dunmore Street. There they parted company, Joe going down Dunmore Street towards the monastery and Rosaleen going on up the Springfield Road to visit her mother; to be collected later by Joe.

A smile curved her lips as she walked up the Springfield Road this particular night. Tonight she was meeting Annie's boyfriend. A paragon of virtues as far as her mother was concerned (although he had been on the scene just a few short weeks).

When she opened the kitchen door and saw Sean sitting at the fireside, she almost fainted. Why had she not asked the name of Annie's boyfriend? Clinging to the door for support, she drew long gasping breaths into her lungs, fighting the dark cloud that threatened to engulf her.

Sean was on his feet instantly, and putting an arm around her. He half carried her to the settee and made her sit down. He was dismayed; he had not meant to take her unawares. How come she did not know about him? Annie was a chatter-box, so how could Rosaleen be unaware that he was dating her sister?

'What's wrong, Rosaleen? Have you started? Do you think the baby's comin'?' Her mother's voice was shrill with panic. 'Will I send for the nurse? Eh? Will I? Some first babies come early.'

Pushing his arm away from her, Rosaleen turned thankfully to her distracted mother.

'I'm all right, Mam. Just a bit faint. Could I have some water, please?' She was playing for time, trying to still her racing heart.

Sipping the water, she smiled weakly at her mother. 'I think I had better go straight home again, Mam. Just in case.'

She wanted to get away from Sean's disturbing presence, but to her dismay he immediately said, 'I'll see her home.'

'Oh, would you, Sean? And will you stay with her 'til Joe comes home from the confraternity? I'll chase him home the minnit he comes.'

'Of course I will.'

'No! No ... what about Annie?' Rosaleen wailed. She could not bear to be alone with him.

'Sure she'll not be ready for another half hour. Ye know what she's like. She can go down with Joe when he comes. Sean won't mind. Sure you won't, Sean?'

'No, no, I'll be glad to see her home.'

'By the way, Rosaleen ...' Her mother bestowed a fond smile on Sean. 'I suppose you've already guessed that this is Annie's new boyfriend?'

Rosaleen nodded mutely and rose to her feet. She needed to get home, to be alone to sort out how Sean dating Annie would affect her life.

At last they were out on the street, away from her mother's fussing. Sean examined her from the corner of his eye. He saw the bloom of her skin, the thick lashes that he knew concealed the vivid green of her eyes. Here she was, full of another man's child, and still he wanted her; craved for her touch.

Rosaleen plodded along beside him, feeling fat and ungainly. Wishing that she had worn her green swagger coat. What on earth was she saving it for? She was aware that her ankles and hands were swollen and that her hair needed washing. Why hadn't she paid more attention to her appearance before she came out?

Dear God, what was she thinking of? What did it matter how she looked? She was another man's wife! Aghast at her thoughts, she quickened her step and Sean lengthened his stride to suit hers.

'Take your time, I'm not going to bite you.'

'Seems to me I heard those assurances from you once before. To my cost,' she cried bitterly.

His lips tightened, but he bit back the angry retort that sprang to them. He had thought that if he saw her again, especially as Annie had mentioned that her sister was expecting a baby, he would be able to lay her ghost. But, no, every pore of his body still ached for her.

At the door of her home, Rosaleen turned to him with a relieved sigh. 'Thank you for seeing me home. I'll be all right now.'

She made no attempt to open the door. She did not want to see him in her home; he would fill it with ghosts.

But Sean had other ideas. 'If you won't invite me in, I'll wait here until your … your husband comes.' He found his tongue stumbled over the word 'husband', and this made him more angry still. He glared down at her and growled, 'I promised to stay with you until your … until he comes, and I intend to do just that.'

Resigned, she silently opened the door and he followed her inside. 'Would you like a cup of tea?' she asked sullenly.

He was no bigger than Joe but seemed to fill the room. She felt an insane longing to fall into his arms and weep, which terrified her.

'No, thank you. Here … gimme your coat.' He gently helped her off with it. 'Now sit down and rest.'

She obeyed him and watched him hang her coat at the foot of the stairs, her eyes wide with fear.

Seeing the expression, he cried in exasperation: 'For heaven's sake, stop looking at me like that. I'm not going to tell anyone we went out together.'

'May knows.'

Alarm flared in his eyes, and his jaw dropped slightly. He did not want to cause her any trouble.

'She doesn't know about…' His hands made motions in the air and hot, vivid colour rushed to her face when she realised what he meant.

'Oh, no! No!'

He smiled slightly at her indignation. 'Well, then, you can warn her off, can't you? Isn't she trustworthy?'

Dear God … it sounded as if he intended being around for a long time.

'Are you serious about our Annie?' she asked, her look beseeching him to deny it.

'Why not?' he asked reasonably.

'You're doing this for badness, aren't you? You're getting your own back on me.'

'Don't flatter yourself.' His nostrils widened in disdain. 'I admit I first danced with Annie because she was your sister, but don't underestimate her. She's a lovely girl, warm and kind, and I find her charming.' His shoulders rose slightly. 'One thing led to another and … why shouldn't we date? We're both free.'

He refrained from telling her that she was often the topic of conversation; that he milked Annie dry obtaining information about her. He was surprised that Annie had not twigged on, but she was very fond of Rosaleen and enjoyed talking about her.

'She's too young for you, so she is!' Rosaleen cried indignantly. 'She's only seventeen.'

He smiled wryly. 'Well now, she says she's almost eighteen.'

'Oh, she's only a child, so she is!'

He watched her through narrowed eyes. 'Do you know something? Annie is more worldly than you. She has no strong beliefs about kissing and hugging.'

He saw her go pale and sinking to his haunches beside her, gripped her hands. 'Don't look like that,' he begged. 'Please … I was having you on. I assure you I've never taken advantage of Annie. As you say, she's very young. I'll never harm her.'

She looked at him, and although her eyes swam with tears, he could see the pain there.

'I wish you'd repected me, like that.'

Her voice was sad and he gripped her hands tighter still.

'Ah, Rosaleen … I did respect you,' he cried in dismay. Her lips pressed tightly together and she shook her head in disbelief.

Cupping her face in his hands, he pleaded, 'Believe me, Rosaleen, please. I did respect you … but I loved you, too, and one got in the way of the other.'

'Well then, please don't do this,' she begged. 'Leave our Annie alone.'

'Ah now, Rosaleen. That's not fair,' he countered. 'I'm a young man, and I intend to marry and have children, and I really am very fond of Annie.'

The child in her womb chose that moment to turn over and she thought wildly, It knows. It knows he's its father.

And soon everybody would know of her shame if she produced a dark-haired boy the picture of him. How would she be able to hide the truth if he was there for all to compare them?

The closeness of her, the soft trembling lips were his downfall. Unable to help himself, he kissed her. A kiss full of hunger and need. How she got the strength to pull her mouth away from his she would never know, because her whole body cried out for want of him, but with a vicious shove she sent him flying. Crouched on his haunches as he was, her push took him unawares and he found himself sprawled on the carpet.

'Don't you dare touch me again, do you hear me? Don't ever touch me again,' she cried, her voice rising hysterically. 'You're evil, and I hate you. I hate you. I hate you.'

The sound of Joe's key in the lock halted her tirade. Gulping deep in her throat for control, she cried, 'Get up, you fool. Get up. It's Joe and Annie.'

When Joe entered the room, she was lying back on the settee and Sean was coming from the kitchen with a glass of water in his hand.

'How are you, love?' Joe asked, hovering anxiously over her.

'I'm fine, Joe, fine.'

Sipping from the glass of water, dismay filled her when, over Joe's shoulder, she saw the anxious faces of her parents as well as Annie. They mustn't stay. They must go and take Sean with them.

Since she had left work, she had become very close to her father; him being on the sick this past four months and at home all day, and her mother doing home help to a neighbour, meant she saw more of him than she did of her mother. Now her eyes pleaded with him and he did not let her down.

'I think she should go to bed,' he said.

Then, as if in answer to her plea, he added, 'It's rest ye need, love, being so near yer time. Away t'bed. I'll come down tomorrow and see how ye are.'

'Thanks, Da.'

'Maybe I should stay off work tomorrow, eh, Rosaleen? Just in case,' her mother asked anxiously.

'No, Mam, that won't be necessary. Old Mrs Grant needs you. I'll be all right. If I need you, me da'll go for you. OK?'

'All right, love, we'll go now and let you get t'bed.'

To her relief, Annie and Sean left with them, Annie promising to bring Sean back when Rosaleen was feeling better. This caused Joe to insist that they come back on Saturday night, all being well, and Rosaleen thought she would die when Sean quickly took him up on the offer. How was she going to bear seeing Sean and Annie together, watching Annie fawn all over him?

Joe was working late the following night and Rosaleen decided to meet May coming out of work, to ask for her silence about the fact that Sean had once fancied her. She had worried all day about the coming Saturday night visit and felt the walk out in the air would do her good. It was some time since she had seen May and had come to the conclusion that she must be courting.

From where she stood waiting on the corner where the Kashmir Road met Cupar Street, Rosaleen saw May come through the gates of the factory deep in conversation with Billy Mercer, foreman over the fitters who maintained the looms. To her surprise, she saw Billy bend and kiss May before they parted, he heading for the Shankill Road and May walking towards Rosaleen. Her jaw dropped slightly and bright colour stained her cheeks when she saw Rosaleen, but her arms reached out and she greeted her warmly.

'Rosaleen! Oh, you're a sight for sore eyes. What brings you here?'

Returning her hug, Rosaleen jerked her head after Billy's retreating figure.

'What's all that about?'

'Oh, I've been out with him a few times.'

May's voice was airy and Rosaleen eyed her closely.

'Well, what brings you here?' May repeated.

'I want to talk to you about something. Can you come up to the house for a while after you get your tea and we'll have a natter? It's been ages since I saw you.'

'Ah, Rosaleen, I'm sorry, but I'm going out with Billy.'

All Rosaleen's problems receded when she thought of the implications of May going out with Billy.

'May!' she gasped. 'He's a divorced man. Your da will kill you if he finds out.'

John Brady was a violent man, a real bully, and May had many a time arrived at work with a black eye when she had been unfortunate enough to incur his wrath.

She shivered now and retorted, 'Do you think I don't know that? I've nightmares about him finding out.'

Bewildered, Rosaleen cried, 'Then why take chances?'

With a resigned sigh, May stopped in the middle of the pavement and faced her. 'Look, Rosaleen, it's all right for you to talk. With your looks you could pick and choose and you got the most eligible bachelor around here. You don't know what it's like to be an onlooker. You've never sat a dance out in your life, but me ...' Her finger poked her own chest to demonstrate her point. 'I'm twenty-two and I've never had a guy serious about me. Until now.'

Her gaze wavered and fell before Rosaleen's steady look.

'Billy wants to marry me,' she finished flatly, with a defiant tilt of the head.

'But you can't marry him! He's old ... and he's divorced. The Church won't let you marry him.'

The horror Rosaleen felt at the very idea of her friend wanting to marry Billy came across in her words, and May clasped her hand to her head and laughed. Then, with a deep sigh, she once more looked at Rosaleen. 'You're so innocent. He doesn't want to marry me in church, and he isn't all that old – only ten years older than me.'

Aghast, Rosaleen thought, this can't be happening. Why, May was too good-living to contemplate marrying anywhere but in church.

They had reached the corner of Dunmore Street. This would take Rosaleen out on to the Springfield Road near Iris Street and thus to Iris Drive.

As she paused, she sensed relief in May's voice when she said, 'Look, Rosaleen, I'll have to run now. I'm meeting Billy at seven and I've loads to do. I'll come up next Tuesday night when Joe's at Clonard and tell you all about it. OK?'

'OK. Don't forget now, I'll be waiting for you.'

'No, I promise. See ya.'

Rosaleen turned away, but May caught her attention again with a shout. 'Hey! What did you want to see me about?'

'Good Lord, I forgot about that.'

Rosaleen moved closer again and May said with a wry twist of her lips, 'It can't be very important.'

'Well, it seemed important until I heard about your romance,' Rosaleen cried indignantly. 'You knocked the wind out me, so you did.' She rolled her eyes at May. 'It's just – well, our Annie is going out with Sean Devlin. You remember Sean, don't you?'

May laughed. 'Tall, dark and handsome? How could I forget?'

'Well, I just want to make sure you don't let the cat out of the bag if you happen to meet them. Remember, I was engaged to Joe when I went out with Sean and it could cause all kinds of complications.'

May gaped at her. 'Ah, Rosaleen … do you think I'm daft? I would've known better than to say anything.'

'I just wanted to be sure, May. Didn't want you taken unawares. See you next Tuesday night, all being well.'

The week seemed to drag, but suddenly it was Saturday. Annie and Sean were coming at eight o'clock and Rosaleen had prepared a light supper for later on. As she dressed, she was angry at herself for wishing she was slim and attractive again. She felt huge and ungainly even though her new maternity dress had flattering panels that hid most of the bulk of her, and she suited the pale primrose colour. Joe had remarked at her use of make-up and she had been quite abrupt with him. If he had his way she would never use make-up. She had not worn any for a long time, but she vowed that in future she would take care of her appearance. She was not going to let herself go.

Even though she was prepared for the sight of him, she still felt winded when Sean entered the room. What on earth was going to happen to her if he married Annie? She could not exist in a state of panic like this.

The conversation was stilted, as was usual when a stranger entered a family group for the first time, but then Joe suggested having a game of cards and everyone relaxed.

As the evening wore on, Annie said, 'I'd better warn you, we won't be staying late. So if that spread you've out in the kitchen is for us, you'd better serve it now, Rosaleen, I don't think I mentioned it, but Sean's in the Merchant Navy and he's due back tomorrow.'

Rosaleen expelled a soft sigh of relief and rose from the table. He would be gone tomorrow.

'I'll make the tea.'

Annie followed her into the kitchen and said, 'Isn't it funny? In our street this is the scullery, and down here it's the kitchen.'

'It is a bit bigger, you have to admit,' Rosaleen retorted, pride in her home apparent.

'Well, I suppose so.' Annie's nose wrinkled in disdain and then she leant closer and whispered, 'What do you think of him?'

'Mmmm ... who?'

'Huh!' Annie eyed her in amazement. 'Sean, of course! Who else?'

'Oh, he seems very nice, so he does.'

'Oh, he is ... he is. And so different from the boys I've known.' Annie hugged herself. 'They all seem so childish compared to him. And he's so kind and respectful. I honestly don't know what he sees in me, why he singled me out, but I love him, Rosaleen,' she confided. 'I love him very much.'

'He singled you out because you're lovely! There'll be plenty of boys interested in you before you meet Mr Right,' Rosaleen retorted. 'He's a bit old for you, don't you think? Remember, not so long ago you thought anyone over twenty-one was an old man?' Seeing Annie's lips twitch with mirth at the memory, she added, 'So just watch you don't get hurt, won't you, Annie?'

'I know I used to think like that,' she agreed with a grin. 'But I've grown up. And I'm well aware that he's older than me, but I don't care. As for getting hurt... well, ye know what they say. Better to have loved and lost, than never to have loved at all. I love him and

I can only hope he doesn't tire of me. You're lucky, Rosaleen. You've always been admired. You're everybody's favourite. But me ... I've always been second best.'

'What on earth do you mean?'

'Oh, you know what I mean. You're the only one I've ever felt close to. Me mam thinks I'm too flighty, and me da ... well he thinks the sun rises and sets on you.'

'You're wrong, Annie. Me da has always treated us equally. As for me mam ... well, she worries about you.'

'I know, I know. But still, you're a hard act to follow. You never bothered with Protestants. You fell in love with the right man and gave no cause for concern. Anyhow, I hope Sean falls in love with me because I love him.'

Dreading the answer to her next question, Rosaleen asked it anyhow. 'Does he not commit himself?'

'Not so far,' Annie answered sadly. Then straightening to attention she vowed, 'But he will, he will, I'll make him love me. I'll make him want to marry me. Just you wait and see.'

And knowing that Annie usually accomplished anything she set out to do, Rosaleen believed her and her spirits sank.

It was with relief that she closed the door on them that night. She had been jittery with nerves all evening. She had noticed Joe watching her, a concerned look in his eyes, and fear had gripped her heart in case he guessed how she felt about Sean. She was glad when she heard that he would be away for six months. Surely by the time he returned, she would be able to control the emotions that he aroused in her? It was just because she was pregnant that he affected her so. Didn't they say pregnant women were unstable emotionally?

'Sean's a nice bloke, isn't he? Annie could do a lot worse than marry him.'

Joe's words brought her back to earth with a bang.

'He's a bit old for her, don't you think?'

'That makes him more responsible, and it's plain to see that he dotes on her. He'll be able to keep her in line. She's a bit of a rebel, is Annie. Likes to get her own way.'

Was it obvious that Sean doted on Annie? 'Well, six months is a long time. It will probably peter out.'

Joe drew her down on to the settee and sat with his arm around her. She squirmed uneasily. He was in one of his sloppy moods. He would be easily pleased; a bit of a cuddle, a few kisses and a lot of excuses for not disturbing her, but these episodes left Rosaleen frustrated and unhappy. Tonight she could not bear it! Unhappiness was already a deep pain in her chest.

Rising abruptly to her feet she said, 'I'm tired, Joe. I'm going on up to bed. Goodnight.'

She stole a glance at his face and saw chagrin there. Serves him right! she thought. He wouldn't be so ready for a cuddle once the child was born. No, he would be afraid to start what he couldn't finish.

The next morning she was up early, preparing for the midwife's weekly visit. Now that she was so near her time, Nurse Morgan came once a week. Rosaleen answered the door with a smile on her face which quickly slipped when she saw Sean standing on the pavement. She closed her eyes. She must be seeing things, the result of lying awake half the night thinking of him. But no, he was still there when she opened them again.

'I lost a glove last night and I wondered if perhaps it's here?'

Silently, she turned back into the house and he followed her.

'I never noticed any glove when I was clearing up,' she assured him. Well, she couldn't very well call him a liar, could she?

Going to the settee, he looked down between it and the wall, and then reached down and produced a black leather glove.

'You left that there,' she accused him, wide-eyed. When he nodded gravely in reply, she cried. 'Why? What did you hope to gain? I don't understand.'

'I just wanted to see you for a few minutes alone, Rosaleen. I'll be away for six months this time.'

'Ah, Sean ... Sean ... what am I going to do about you. Can't you see? If you keep this up you'll ruin all our lives. I'm married to Joe and ...'

Quickly, he interrupted her. 'But you regret it, don't you? Tell the truth, Rosaleen. You regret it. I could see last night that you don't love him.'

'No, you're wrong.' She shook her head. 'I don't regret marrying Joe.' Her gaze held his steadily. She must convince him that she was happy with Joe or he would never leave her alone.

'You're wasting your time. And Sean ... ?' Her look was beseeching. 'Annie and I are very close, please don't hurt her.'

He stepped nearer to her, a sceptical look on his face, but what he would have said she was never to know, because Nurse Morgan arrived. Tight-lipped, Sean wished Rosaleen goodbye and left the house.

Her daughter was born two weeks later, and Rosaleen sighed in relief when she saw that she was so blonde she appeared bald. Her eyes were blue but the nurse assured her they would probably change colour; that all babies were born with blue eyes. She was right. They did change colour – to green like Rosaleen's own. There was nothing about her in the least like Sean, and Rosaleen thanked God for letting her off the hook.

Her mother was in her glory helping to look after the baby. She came every day to see her, and one day, when the baby was two weeks old, arrived bursting with excitement.

'Who do you think called up to see me today?'

Not waiting for an answer, she rushed on: 'Kate Brady. What do ye think of that?'

Rosaleen's heart sank. She sensed that she was about to hear bad news. May had not paid the promised Tuesday night visit and when she had also neglected to come to see the baby, Rosaleen had guessed something was amiss.

She sat silent and her mother gaped at her. 'Don't tell me you knew all about it?'

'All about what, Mam? I don't know what you're talking about. I haven't set eyes on May for weeks.'

'She's gone! Took off a month ago. My, but they kept that quiet. I suppose they hoped she would get disillusioned and come back, before she was missed. But, no, she got married in the register office. I felt heartsore for Kate. She's worried stiff. It seems the big fellow waited ouside the Falls Flax yesterday and nearly killed the guy May married. It's as well May doesn't work there any more. He'd have swung for her.'

'Oh, poor May … poor May.'

'Poor May my foot! She should know better. It'll cause trouble ye know! Once the boyos hear about it, big John's life won't be worth living. I suppose that's why he beat the guy up. He was proclaiming his disapproval of May's actions.'

'Ah, Ma! She probably fell in love,' Rosaleen cried. 'Why can't we do as we please. As for the boyos … who are these faceless guys that everyone's afraid of?'

'Hush … don't talk like that.' Thelma glanced over her shoulder as if they might be overheard even though they were in Rosaleen's living room. This action brought home to her just how awful it must have been during the Troubles in the twenties, when you were afraid to speak your mind. 'As for May … well, she should've known better. She should've fell in love with a Catholic, so she should,' Thelma continued, then sighed and added gruffly, 'I suppose you're right. Ye can't help who you love. Ah, no, love makes fools of us all.'

Thelma's face reddened when she caught Rosaleen's appraising look, and she quickly changed the subject.

'Your da says there's goin' to be a war.'

Rosaleen just nodded, she knew her mother was changing the subject; the fact that her father was talking about the war was nothing new. He was always talking about the war. He ranted on about the government not making enough preparations to protect the people of Belfast. He kept explaining to anyone who would listen that Belfast was now a prime target, since it was turning out planes and ammunition for England, but no one listened to him. What did he know, working in Greeves Mill all his life? Hadn't the powers that be over in England assured the Stormont government that Hitler would not travel across England to bomb Ireland? Nevertheless, her father continued to point out that Belfast stuck out like a sore thumb, situated as it was on the edge of the lough, and that, mark his words, the Germans would come.

But there had been rumours of war for a long time now. Indeed, a new aircraft factory, Short and Harland, had been opened two years ago, bringing work to thousands. It had just completed its first Bengal Bombay last month and was working all out building more. Surely if the English government thought Belfast would be bombed, it would protect its assets? Rosaleen remembered the flurry of activity last summer when war had seemed imminent. Trenches had been dug around the harbour and in the parks, and sandbags had been distributed to all important buildings, shops and offices to protect against blast damage. But then all activity came to a halt as fear of war had apparently receded. The rumours had lingered too long now to cause Rosaleen immediate concern and it was May her thoughts dwelled on. Would Billy be good to her? Oh, she hoped so, she hoped so. May deserved a bit of kindness.

It was a month later that she received a letter from May, asking to meet her in the Dunville Park. Wrapping the child up warmly, she put her in her pram and near the stated time made her way down to the park.

May was already sitting on a bench near the fountain when Rosaleen arrived. She rose swiftly to her feet and embraced her friend fiercely.

'Oh, it's so good to see you.'

They clung together for some moments and then May turned her attention to the child in the pram.

'It's obviously a girl,' she stated laughingly, noting that everything was pink. Pulling back the blankets, she peered in at the sleeping child. 'She's lovely, Rosaleen. Just lovely. What did you call her?'

'Laura. Laura Marie. How are you, May?'

'I'm great, Rosaleen, never better. Billy lifts and lays me.' She winked, her tongue poking cheekily from between her teeth, causing Rosaleen to laugh outright.

'You certainly look great. Why, you're absolutely blooming.'

'Don't sound so surprised.' May gave her a playful push. 'Here, let's sit down and have a natter.'

Rosaleen's eyes ran over May's attire. She was dressed in a quality wool coat, dark green in colour, on her feet a pair of soft brown kid shoes, and she carried a matching kid handbag.

'Looks like you fell on your feet,' she exclaimed.

Somehow she had expected May to be sad and cowed. After all, she had acted foolishly, but instead she looked defiant. That was the only word Rosaleen could think of to explain how May looked.

'Well, Billy isn't short of a bob or two, and he's an only child. His parents dote on him.'

'How do they feel about you?'

'They love me.'

Seeing Rosaleen's look of disbelief, she nodded her head vigorously.

'They do! Honestly!' Her head bobbed up and down to lay stress on her words. 'Now if Billy had married me in the Catholic Church that would have been another matter. They would have disowned him, only child or not. They didn't like his first wife, so I consider myself lucky that they've taken to me.'

'Had he any children, May?'

'No. No children. And it was her fault the marriage broke up. She ran off with someone else.'

'Well, her poor taste was your good fortune, but your ma's breaking her heart, May.'

May's retort was quick.

'Not because of me, she's not. She's breaking her heart because I've left the Church. She doesn't care whether I'm happy or not.' She tossed her head defiantly. 'I suppose you heard how me da beat Billy up?' When Rosaleen nodded, May cried, 'I bet you didn't hear that he had two of his pals with him?' At Rosaleen's look of surprise, she cried, 'I thought not. If he had been alone Billy would have been able for him. But big and all as me da is, he needed help. The big bully! You should have seen the state Billy was in.' She gulped deep in her throat before continuing. 'His face was like a bit of liver. His mates wanted to retaliate, but he wouldn't hear tell of it. He said he felt he deserved the hiding for running off with me, and I was worth every last blow.'

Although tears were running down her face, she smiled wryly at Rosaleen. 'I never thought I'd hear a man say that about me. And, Rosaleen, he does love me.'

Rosaleen gripped her hand tightly.

'You underestimate yourself, May. You're worthy of any man's love.'

In her heart she could not help but wish that May had waited for a Catholic. Surely she must feel uneasy living on the Shankill Road? She found herself voicing her thoughts.

'Are you not scared living on the Shankill?'

May paused in wiping her face and giggled.

'Not a bit of it,' she declared. 'They're just like us. Honest to goodness, Rosaleen. Listening to them is just like listening to the ones on the Falls Road.'

Rosaleen found this hard to believe. She remembered the few times she had gone shopping on the Shankill Road. She had imagined everyone knew she was a Catholic. Hadn't she been led to believe that they could smell Catholics? Certainly she had been glad to hurry back down Conway Street to the Falls Road. Now she could not hide her disbelief.

'Honestly, Rosaleen,' May assured her again. 'Do you know something? Billy and his parents go to church every Sunday. They're a lovely couple, and the neigbours are friendly. Everyone talks to me.'

'You don't go to church?'

Rosaleen was scandalised at the idea of May attending a service in a Protestant church.

'No, I don't. But why shouldn't I? We all pray to the same God. *He* doesn't ask if you're a Catholic or Protestant.'

She couldn't bring herself to admit that she had gone to church one Sunday with Billy but had found the church cold and bare. Not in the least like Clonard Monastry, with its shrines and altars.

'Listen, Rosaleen, besides wanting to see you and your new baby, I asked you to meet me because I want to ask a favour of you.'

Wide-eyed, Rosaleen remained silent.

'I'm worried about me ma. With me da and our Colin not working, I know she depended on my money every week.'

She delved into her handbag and produced an envelope.

'Will you give this to her for me? Tell her I'll get money to you once a month for her.' Her look was entreating. 'That's if you don't mind ... Please?'

Aware that Joe would object to her being a go-between, Rosaleen hesitated.

'It's all right. I'm sorry I asked. I had no right to put you on the spot.' May opened her handbag to return the envelope, but with an abrupt movement Rosaleen stopped her.

'Here, give it to me. At least this way you will have to stay in touch.'

'Thanks, Rosaleen. You're a true friend. And I have another bit of news … I'm pregnant!'

Rosaleen forced herself to smile; to act pleased. However, inside she was worried. The child would be brought up a Protestant. How will May be able to live with that? she wondered. And another thing, what would big John do when he heard about it?

To her amazement, May eyed her keenly and asked, 'Are you happy, Rosaleen?'

'Of course I am. What made you ask that?'

'Oh, I don't know.' May gave a little laugh. 'You'd have a cheek not to be happy. Married to Joe … a beautiful home … and now a lovely baby.'

May's reply was appeasing; Rosaleen's answer had been too quick, too emphatic, and May wasn't fooled. Remembering Sean had come back on the scene, she inquired after him.

'Is Sean Devlin still going out with Annie?'

She was dismayed to see hot colour stain Rosaleen's cheeks.

Aware that she was blushing, Rosaleen answered abruptly. 'He's at sea at the moment, but yes, he is dating Annie.'

'Oh… I see.'

'What do you mean, you see? What do you see?' Rosaleen asked sharply.

'I … I … ah, now, Rosaleen, I just asked.'

Rosaleen managed to get control of her voice before she replied. May was no doser, she must never guess that Sean was still interested in her. 'I'm sorry, May. I'm just worried in case Annie finds out about me going out with him.'

'Rosaleen, it was just a couple of dates … Oh, I see. You're afraid of Joe's reaction, is that it?'

Rosaleen nodded, relieved that May was being diverted.

'Well, he'll never hear from my lips, so he won't. Not that I'm likely to be talking to him.'

She sighed. 'I miss you, Rosaleen. I have to admit, I'm a bit lonely.'

Rosaleen squeezed her hand. 'Why not come and visit me every Tuesday night when Joe's at the confraternity?' she asked.

'Oh no, I don't think that would be a good idea.' May turned the thought over in her mind and repeated sadly, 'No, me da might find out. I'm not just anxious about myself. I just don't want you involved. I'll have to be satisfied seeing you once a month.' She reached for a parcel that was lying on the bench beside her, and thrust it at Rosaleen. 'Here! Just a wee present for Laura.' She peered once more into the pram at the sleeping child. 'She's lovely, so she is. I wish she had wakened ... but perhaps next time.'

'Thanks, May, thanks a lot. She sleeps most of the day and night at the moment, but I've been warned that that state of affairs won't last long. Next time she'll winge and gurn and you'll be glad to get away from her.' For a moment they both gazed in wonder at the sleeping child, then Rosaleen said, 'I'll be here waiting, this day four weeks. If it's raining, I'll be in the summer-house. OK?'

May rose to go. 'That'll be great, Rosaleen. I'll look forward to seeing you.' She reached for her friend's hand and clasped it warmly. 'So long for now, and thanks for coming.'

Rosaleen watched her walk across the park towards the side gate that led out on to the Grosvenor Road. At the gate she paused and waved, before heading for the tram stop. Rosaleen waved back.

Lost in thought, she sat on until a hungry cry from Laura brought her back to reality. A glance at the face of the clock on the wall of the hospital opposite brought her hurriedly to her feet. If she didn't get a move on Joe would be home before her and that would lead to a lot of questions. She had no intention of mentioning her arrangement with May, so haste lent wings to her heels as she pushed the pram up Cavendish Street.

Chapter 3

Kept busy with the baby and the running of the house, Rosaleen looked forward to her monthly meeting with May in the Dunville Park. The park was a sanctuary where young mothers, after leaving their older children at St Vincent's girls' school in Dunlewey Street or St Finian's boys' school on the Falls Road, pushed their prams and, when weather permitted, spread rugs on the grass to sunbathe whilst their babies slept in the warm air protected from insects by pram-nets. When the weather was fine, Rosaleen often walked down and sat in the park to give Laura the benefit of fresh air, but the days she met May were special. On those days she wore her best clothes and carefully made-up her face, knowing a new, splendid May would arrive in the latest maternity wear. She was happy that things were working out for May, although she could not understand how she could be happy living among 'Them' on the Shankill Road.

As she sat waiting, Laura blissfully asleep in her pram, the sun warm on her plump, bare limbs, Rosaleen examined the park and took delight in its layout. She was sitting on a bench with her back to the hospital, so she had a view that seemed like countryside. This was deceptive as the park was completely surrounded by a built-up area. The Royal Victoria Hospital loomed high on the far side of the Grosvenor Road behind her, and to her left the busy Falls Road was hidden from view by high hedges and bushes, the other two sides flanked by rows of terraced houses. However, the houses were blocked from view by thick bushes and it was easy to forget that they were there.

The park had been given to the people of the Falls at the end of the nineteenth century by William Dunville, owner of the whiskey distillery which, at that time, had premises off the Grosvenor Road. A family man, he had felt sorry for the people uprooting themselves from the countryside to come and work in the mills, their young children playing barefoot on the then cobbled streets. He had arranged for the building of the park, complete with washrooms, and had set up a trust to maintain it, for the enjoyment of the public and as a lasting memorial of his sister Sarah. His gift was appreciated by all and Rosaleen liked to believe that it was kindness that prompted his actions. Her grandmother had thought otherwise because of the comment 'Perhaps now the people of the Falls will manage to keep themselves clean', allegedly made by Mrs Dunville, and spoken in the hearing of the newspaper reporters. It caused an uproar when blazoned across the newspapers the next day and had made the older generation very bitter in their attitude towards the gift. But whatever the reason for the building of the park, it was a favourite spot for the younger generation.

The middle of the park was dominated by a huge fountain, once brilliant white, now weathered to a pale grey and at the moment out of order. Around the top were carved gargoyle heads and Rosaleen remembered the fear with which she had once regarded them. Were they not there to guard the fountain? To prevent naughty children from defacing it? Oh, yes, she remembered well the day Marie Brannigan, the school hero who feared nothing and no one, had carved her initials into the stone work with a nail. For days the rest of the girls in the gang had waited with bated breath for something terrible to befall her, but they waited in vain. If anything, Marie thrived.

No more did water tumble down from the mouths of the gargoyles, to be recycled in a continuous circle. She could well remember how breathtaking it was, remember paddling in the shallow water at its base, and in the winter, the naughty excitement of sliding about on the frozen ice. This was forbidden, for although not deep, many pairs of boots were destroyed when it cracked and feet occasionally went through. She sighed for times past, and continued her perusal of the park. To her left, in the far corner, the old weigh house still stood. Here, in the not too distant past, at the beginning of the century, the farmers had stopped to have their livestock weighed on their way down to the market – but that had been before her time, in the days of the horse-drawn trams, the days of mucky roads. Now the house was occupied by the caretaker and his family, the trams were electric and the roads concreted. Nearer the centre, to the left of the fountain, stood one of a pair of summer-houses, the other hidden from view by the fountain. These were where the older men of the parish played chess and dominoes or read their newspapers while having a quiet smoke or even forty winks.

Flowerbeds dotted the park as if thrown by a careless hand. Great big mounds of turned earth, a riot of colour at the moment, with sweet williams, stock, dahlias and pinks permeating the warm air with their heavy perfume. Four lawns of dark, lush green grass flanked the fountain, sloping gently down from a raised height, and in the centre of each lawn was yet another large flower bed; each one a different shape. Some distance to her right, at the very bottom of the park, was the play area, where there was an assortment of amusements to entertain the older children. Some slides, swings, swinging boats, a witch's hat, and in the centre, in pride of place, the maypole! Rosaleen recalled how, when she was younger, looping a rope around the handle of the maypole she had sat and swung for many a long hour. Oh, yes, the park was indeed appreciated by the people of the Falls, no matter what their age.

The thud of someone sitting on the bench brought Rosaleen back to reality with a start. She turned, and her mouth gaped in surprise when she saw it was Kate Brady.

'Sorry to startle you ... I just want to see May,' Kate explained apologetically. 'See for meself that she's all right, ye know? She'll not mind, will she?'

Wondering how Kate had known just when she and May met,

and not knowing how May would react to seeing her mother, Rosaleen confined her answer to an abrupt shake of the head. She hoped that there would be no unpleasantness, and made inane conversation as time passed with no sign of May.

She was aware that her friend took the tram to the stop at the bottom of the park to avoid meeting any neighbours at the busy junction where all the roads met. This was where the post office, home bakery and other shops were situated, and was always busy with shoppers. Rosaleen wondered if May had seen her mother as she passed by in the tram, and declined to meet her. However, the thought had just entered her mind when she saw her friend hurrying up the park, dressed to kill. From the corner of her eye, Rosaleen watched Kate's reaction to the new, stylish May. She saw her face twist with amazement and her mouth agape.

And no wonder! May was a sight for sore eyes. Dressed in a long pleated maternity skirt with a matching loose hip-length jacket, she looked every inch the grand lady. Made of slub rayon material, and blue in colour, the suit brightened the colour of May's eyes and Rosaleen noted that she had lightened her mousy fair hair to a pale ash blonde.

When she saw her mother, her arms stretched wide. 'Ma! Ah, Ma! It's good to see you.'

Rising slowly to her feet, Kate tentatively embraced her, all the while examining this stranger.

'Ye look well,' she muttered. Then, noticing the slight bump, she wailed, 'Are you expectin'?'

Some of the joy faded from May's face as she nodded confirmation to her mother's question.

Her face crumbling in distress, Kate wailed, 'Oh, my God. Wait 'til your da hears.'

'It's none of his business,' May retorted, tight-lipped. 'He won't be asked to rear it.'

'I should bloody well think I won't be asked to rear the bastard!'

The blast of these words brought Rosaleen to her feet to join the others, and all three turned to face big John Brady where he stood in the shadow of a tree. He must have entered the park by the gate near the weigh house and crept down to hide behind the tree.

Rosaleen's lips curled and she bestowed a look of scorn on him at the very idea.

Kate moved until she was between husband and daughter, but blind with rage, he pushed her roughly to one side. Rosaleen could see spittle foam at the corners of his mouth as he fought to find words low enough to degrade May. She pushed the pram with her precious child in it to one side, out of harm's way.

'You dirty wee bitch!' he hissed, as he advanced towards them. 'You dirty … friggin' … wee friggin' bitch!' His words were sliding into each other and he gulped for control. 'T' think of a daughter of mine, lyin' in the arms of a bloody Orangeman … It gnaws at me guts, so it does. Turns me stomach.' His mouth gaped and words failed him at the very thought of it. He hovered over May with clenched fists. 'An' an ugly bugger he is too. Surely even a plain Jane like you could have done better,' he sneered.

May flinched at these words. She was aware that Billy was no oil painting, and that neither was she, but it hurt to have it thrown in her face. After all, not everybody could be beautiful. Bravely she stood her ground, head high, lips pressed tightly together. Aware of people gathering to watch, colour burned in her cheeks and tears glistened in her eyes, but still she stood her ground.

Father and daughter glared at each other and then, seeing that May would not be cowed, with an angry oath, John's hand (as big as a shovel) rose in the air. May saw it coming and stepped back as it swung her way, but she did not move quickly enough and it caught her on the side of the head. The weight of the blow sent her staggering and she ended up sprawled on the gravel path, a look of outrage on her face.

As she lay stunned, Rosaleen hovered anxiously over her, glaring fiercely up at big John, daring him to strike again; protecting May from another blow.

This defiance caused him to turn his wrath on her.

'Why don't you mind your own bloody business, eh? Stay out of it! There'll be no more go-betweens. She's made her friggin' bed, now let her lie on it. We don't want any Prod's charity!' His glare swung back to May. 'Do ye hear me? We want no charity from a friggin' Prod. Our bloody windows have been put in … twice.' At

May's wail of dismay, he repeated, 'Yes, twice! Ye didn't know that now, did ye? An' it's all your bloody fault!'

With these words, and another glare of wrath, he gripped his wife's arm and pulled her roughly towards the gate at the far side of the park, leading out on to Dunville Street, at the same time shooing the embarrassed crowds away with threats of what he would do if they didn't shift.

Stumbling along beside him, Kate tried to shake off his hand but he was adamant. Throwing Rosaleen an apologetic look, she mouthed the words: 'Will you look after her?'

Rosaleen gave her a reassuring nod and, bending, assisted a bewildered, weeping May to her feet. When May saw that the rough path had scored through the elbow of her new jacket she started to howl. Great harsh sobs, from deep down in her chest, not caring who saw or heard her.

'The bastard! Oh, how I hate him, Rosaleen. How I hate the friggin' bastard! Hate him! Hate him! Hate him! The unfeeling brute!' Then her eyes fell on the few stragglers still hovering about, all eyes and ears, and leaning forward she bawled, 'Well? What are ye waiting for?' And flapping her hand at them: 'Go on ... go on now. The show's over.'

'Hush, now. Never mind them,' Rosaleen said consolingly. 'Do you feel all right?' She nodded down at May's stomach, and her friend's eyes stretched wide with alarm as she patted her bump.

'I ... think so. I haven't any pain,' she assured Rosaleen, anxiety dampening the flames of her wrath.

Pushing her gently down on the bench, Rosaleen said, 'Just take it easy for a while, 'til we see how you are.'

May buried her face in her hands, muttering, 'I'm sorry, Rosaleen. It's awful that you had to be involved in all this.'

'Don't be silly. It wasn't your fault.'

May's head jerked up and down as she disagreed with Rosaleen.

'It was. Oh, yes, it was. If I hadn't asked you to be go-between, all this would never have happened.'

'But you weren't to know that your mam would come round and that your da would follow her, so don't be so silly.' Rosaleen sighed and added, 'With hindsight, I suppose it was stupid us meeting here, so close to Spinner Street. It was obvious some of your good neighbours would see us and tell your da.'

'Did you know our windows had been put in?' May's brow was furrowed with worry.

At Rosaleen's shake of the head, she continued, 'It mightn't have had anything to do with me, ye know. Maybe me da or one of the boys have done something wrong. I'd hate to bring trouble to them … me mam has enough to put up with. Do you think it was because of me?'

Rosaleen thought it was more than likely that May was the reason for the broken windows. Really, she should stay away from the Falls Road. Coming in all her grandeur like she did was like thumbing her nose and saying, 'Look, see how well I'm doing on the Shankill?' Rosaleen realised that she should not have encouraged her back by agreeing to meet her, but they were best friends and she had wanted to keep in touch.

Not wanting to distress her more than she was already, she muttered, 'I don't know, May. I really don't.'

'I feel so guilty, Rosaleen. I wanted to send money, but it was guilt money. I was salvin' me conscience, giving money every month. I felt awful deserting me ma. With him not working she needs my money, and I didn't even get giving her any today. Him and his bloody pride! It's me ma that'll suffer most. An' our poor wee Jenny … I bet she's suffering an' all. With me not there for him to vent his temper on, me da will turn it on our Jenny.' Tears flowed afresh. 'Poor wee mite, she's terrified of him.'

Not knowing what to say, Rosaleen remained silent. She had guessed that big John was a bully, but it dismayed her to hear it put into words. Obviously, May had suffered more than the odd blow.

Picturing May's brother Colin, twenty years old and not very tall, but no scrawny wee thing either, and the next one down, thin, lanky Daniel, eighteen years of age, she ventured to say, 'Surely Colin and Dan will be able to stand up to your da, and look after Jenny?'

'They'll be getting picked on an' all. Because of me.' May smiled wryly. 'You don't understand, Rosaleen. You live a very sheltered life. He never touches the boys, not since they left school. Even our wee Kevin's left school now. Oh, he picks on them, but he knows better than to lift his hand to them. They'd all gang up on him.' She sighed and nodded. 'Yes, they'd hit back. It'll be Jenny he'll pick on most. Her being the youngest. An' he's a crafty aul bugger, he'll pick on her when nobody else is about.'

She turned to watch Rosaleen's expression when she asked the next question. 'Does your da ever beat your ma?'

When Rosaleen's face showed surprise, she laughed bitterly. 'No! I can see he doesn't. You don't know how lucky you are. Everything handed to you on a plate. You've always had it easy.' She gave a long heartfelt sigh. 'Ah, it's different in our house. My da can't get a job ... and to be honest, he does try ... but he just can't get a job, so he tortures me ma for the wee bit of money she has coming in.' She shot Rosaleen a derisive glance. 'Do you know something? When me ma pays all the bills – or I should say all the bills she can afford to pay, she has to decide every week whose turn it is to be paid – the little she has left to see her through the week she has to hide. She's running out of places to hide it. You should see me da hunting for it. He wrecks the house ... It would be laughable if it wasn't so bloody serious.'

She fell silent, then taking a compact from her handbag, tried to repair her make-up. Watching her, Rosaleen noticed that a bruise was already appearing on her cheek.

'How will you explain that?' she asked, dismay in her voice. 'What will Billy say?' She could understand letting big John away with his attack on him, but May was a different matter. He obviously loved her, so there could me more trouble.

May examined her cheek in the small mirror of the compact. 'I'll put some Pan-stick on it ... that should hide it.'

'It's very close to the eye. What if you've a black eye in the morning?'

A smile twisted May's lips. 'I'll accidentally fall and hit my face when I'm in the bathroom tonight.' Seeing Rosaleen's start of surprise, she added proudly, 'Oh, yes, I've a bathroom.' Then, squeezing Rosaleen's arm, she added, 'Don't look so worried. Remember I'm used to explaining bruises away. Do you remember at school? Miss Watson thought that I was accident prone. If she had only known ... I hardly ever fell.'

Rosaleen sat aghast at these revelations. She remembered how, apparently, May was always falling down the stairs or getting hit on the face with a swing in the park, but she had been so bright and cheerful when she explained her wounds that no one had ever doubted her.

Unable to think of any words of comfort, Rosaleen sat silent and was relieved when Laura chose that moment to let out a wail. Lifting her from the pram, she hushed her, rocking her gently over her shoulder.

'Can I hold her, Rosaleen?'

With a smile, she handed over the sweet-smelling bundle, and May stretched the child out on her knee, playing with the tiny hands and little bare feet, all the while exclaiming at her loveliness.

'God knows when I'll see her again,' she said sadly.

'Now listen, May. We're not going to let this stop us from meeting. We'll meet somewhere else.'

'Where, Rosaleen? Tell me where?'

'Would you not consider coming to my house, May?'

'And have me da put a brick through your window?'

At these words, Rosaleen drew back in disbelief. 'Surely he wouldn't dare?'

'Oh, he'd dare all right. You don't know him. Not that you'd ever be able to prove he did it. He's a cute aul bugger.' May watched Rosaleen from the corner of her eye when she asked the next question. 'I don't suppose you'd come to visit me?'

She saw the look of horror spread over Rosaleen's face and cried bitterly, 'For goodness' sake, Rosaleen, don't look like that! Nobody'll bite you. They're not a lot of savages, ye know.'

Shamefaced, Rosaleen smiled wryly as she replied, 'I know, I know. I believe you.'

May had never felt less like laughing in her life, but when she saw Rosaleen square her shoulders before declaring, 'All right!' as if preparing for battle, she laughed aloud.

'Good for you!' she cried, her eyes teasing, 'I'll write and tell you the easiest way to get to our street. I'll draw a wee map, and send it to you, so I will. Then next month, you can visit me.'

They smiled at each other and the time flew as they exchanged ideas and advised each other.

It was Laura starting to whinge and nuzzle about, looking for something to eat, that brought Rosaleen to her feet in alarm. A glance at her watch told her it was a quarter to five and she gasped in dismay.

'If I don't hurry Joe'll be in on my heels and there'll be no dinner ready for him,' she cried, settling Laura in her pram, and turning to May for a last farewell.

She was surprised to find her friend gaping at her. 'Surely Joe won't mind?'

'No, not really,' she lied, because Joe did mind, he minded very much. He expected his dinner to be on the table when he came home from work. 'It's just that, with me not working, I like to have a meal ready for him when he comes home.'

'Well, just let him wait today. Don't you kill yourself pushing the pram up that hill in a hurry … especially in this heat,' May admonished her.

'I won't. But, look, I'll run on now. Don't forget to write.' And with a final hug and wave Rosaleen set off at a trot, leaving a bemused May staring after her.

When Sean came home on leave, he always, weather permitting, caught an open-deck tram up the Falls Road to Beechmount, the estate where he lived. Today was no exception and as he sprawled on the seat looking about him, Rosaleen was not very far from his thoughts. As the tram trundled across the junction where the Falls divided the Springfield and the Grosvenor Roads, he sat up in delight, because there she was, waiting to cross the road, a brand-new pram in front of her, and looking young and sweet in a spotted cotton dress; the sun catching her hair and turning it to silver. On his feet instantly, he rang the bell for the tram to stop at the next stop and descended the stairs two at a time.

A short distance up the Springfield Road, he caught up with her and put a restraining hand on the handle of the pram.

'Why the big rush?'

Alarm brought her to a halt when his hand descended on the pram but when she saw who it was, taken unawares, joy lit up her face as she stared up at him in amazement.

'I thought you weren't due home for another couple of months!' she gasped.

His eyes twinkled down at her as he tried to steady the thumping of his heart. She would probably deny it but she was pleased to see him. It was in her eyes and the warmth of her greeting.

'Oh, have you been counting the weeks? Eh, Rosaleen?' he teased.

'Oh, don't be silly.' Her hand flapped at him, but a smile tugged at her lips and crinkled her eyes. 'I'm fed up listening to our Annie counting the days.' Her brows lifted slightly. 'Does she know you're home?'

'Not yet.' He shook his head, and peering into the pram, at the little red, screwed-up face, declared, 'My, but she has a fine pair of lungs.'

'She's hungry,' Rosaleen cried defensively. 'She's usually very good.'

'Here!' He thrust his holdall at her, and before she could demur, lifted Laura from the pram. The little rascal stopped crying immediately.

'She's spoilt rotten, so she is,' Rosaleen admitted, with a wry smile.

'Put the bag on the pram and I'll carry her home for you,' he ordered. And without waiting for her agreement, he started walking up the Springfield Road, leaving her to follow.

Noting the way he supported Laura's back and head, Rosaleen asked. 'How come you know so much about babies?'

'I'm an uncle four times over. Three nephews and one niece.' He tickled Laura under the chin and when she rewarded him with a big, toothless smile, he added, 'I must confess I've a weakness for girls. She's lovely, Rosaleen.' His eyes scanned her face and his voice caressed her. 'Just like you.'

Colour stained her cheeks at the compliment and she was glad it was one of her days for meeting May and that she was looking her best, in her new cotton dress with the squared neckline and puffed elbow-length sleeves. Seeing her blush, he had a great urge to hug her and kiss her. If only he was coming home to her and this was his daughter. Why, it would be like heaven on earth.

With the past events still fresh in her mind, Rosaleen found herself telling him about May and her father. He let her ramble on, just giving her an encouraging nod now and again. When her voice trailed off, he glanced at her, and seeing her nip in her lips and an apprehensive look pass over her face, knew at once what was wrong.

'It's all right, Rosaleen. I won't say a word.'

She flashed him a grateful smile and wrinkled her nose at him. 'I did go on a bit, didn't I? It's not like me. Usually I can keep a secret ... not that it was a secret, mind. I wasn't sworn to secrecy.' She hastened to explain. 'But, well, really I shouldn't have mentioned it.' She held his eye. 'You won't say anything to our Annie, sure you won't?'

'I won't say anything to anyone,' he assured her gravely, lost in the green wells that said far more than she realised.

'Thanks ... I got carried away. You're so easy to talk to, so you are and ... I trust you,' she added shyly.

Often he had recalled their last meeting but one, when she had called him evil, treated him with scorn. Her words had stung him, hurt him to the very core, and he had lost sleep over them. Now he took these words and tucked them away in his heart. She trusted him.

A frown puckered the smoothness of her brow. 'I'd better hurry. Joe will be home soon.'

With these words she walked faster and as he lengthened his stride to suit hers, it was his turn to frown.

When they arrived at the corner of Iris Drive, she turned to him.

'Put her back in the pram now, Sean. I'll take over from here, and you can go on home.'

She nodded along Oakman Street that ran down on to Beechmount Avenue.

'No, I'll carry her in for you. And I'll tell you what. Since you're behind time, I'll give her a bottle while you make Joe's tea. How's

67

that?'

To his delight, colour again stained her cheeks, deeper this time as she confessed, with lowered eyes, 'I breastfeed her.'

His eyes teased her again, bringing an answering sparkle to her face. 'I'm glad to hear that. If she was my daughter, I'd want her to be breastfed.'

She was glad that they had arrived at the small forecourt at the front of the house. Glad that she could bend down to open the gate, and that her hair swung forward to hide the dark blush that suffused her face and neck as guilt assailed her.

To think that he was holding his own daughter in his arms and didn't know it.

If he should ever find out … why, it didn't bear thinking about. Once more she tried to send him off, but he was adamant.

'While you feed the baby, I'll start Joe's dinner.'

'I can't ask you to stay, mind,' she lamented. 'I've only one chop.'

'I've already eaten,' he lied, and she knew he lied and was grateful to him. He was so kind, so understanding.

'But what about you? Are you not eating?' he asked, his glance keen. Surely she could afford to eat properly?

'I'm on a diet. I've another few pounds to get rid of. I'll have salad later.'

Having witnessed his sisters starving themselves to lose weight after the birth of each child, this reassured him and he relaxed.

Heading for the kitchen, she said, 'Since you insist …' and pulled open the door of a cupboard. 'The pots and pans are in there, the chop, a couple of sausages and cooking fat are on the top shelf in the larder, and the potatoes are under the sink. Now I had better get this wee girl upstairs before she turns blue.'

As she fed Laura, she thought how wonderful it would be if he was coming home to her. If only she had listened to him! With a sad smile on her face, she pictured how things would go. She would finish feeding Laura and then make him his tea, and they would talk for a while … She found herself laughing softly at the very idea. Who did she think she was kidding? The way he was looking at her, if she was his wife they would be at it hammer and tongs right away and she would not object. Oh no, she would not object … not one wee bit. Sadness settled like a mantle on her shoulders. If only she had met him sooner …

After she had changed Laura's nappy, she combed her hair and powdered her nose. Descending the stairs, she entered the kitchen.

He was turning the chop in the pan and the potatoes were bubbling away on the back ring. He had removed his jacket and donned one of her aprons but still managed to look all man.

'What about veg?'

Dismay filled her, and her face crumpled. 'Oh! I completely forgot about vegetables.' She ran her fingers through her hair, undoing all the careful combing and leaving it standing on end. At last she muttered, 'Tut! Joe hates tinned peas, but it's too late to do anything else.'

'If he's hungry, he'll eat anything.'

He was eyeing her intently and she grimaced, but did not reply. 'I'll take over now, Sean. Thanks very much.'

He was about to demur, but one glance at her face and he knew she did not want Joe to see him in the kitchen, so he whisked off the apron, gently took Laura from her arms, and with a wink at her, went and sat in the living room.

Joe must be a right sod. It was obvious that she had to be home before him, to have his meal ready. His heart ached for her. With hindsight, he realised that he should have phoned in sick last year and made her listen to him. But would she have done? He doubted it. Anyhow, now it was too late. Not that Joe was mean. No, far from it. As his eyes examined the room in which he sat, Sean was aware that money had been spent, and spent to advantage. The settee on which he sat was new, no second-hand things here, and made of a moquette velvet in deep rich autumn colours. Matching armchairs graced each side of the grey and black kitchenette grate, and curtains that toned exactly hung at the window, separated by fine nets. And setting all these off to a treat, a square carpet, thick-piled and dark rust in colour, covered most of the floor. Rosaleen was obviously being denied nothing, so why did sadness lurk in her eyes? Because it did; when her face was in repose, sadness was

apparent. But then, perhaps he had caught her on a bad day ...
perhaps Joe and she had had words this morning?

When Joe arrived, he paused just inside the door, his eyebrows
rising in surprise when he saw Sean.

'I met Rosaleen on the Falls Road and walked home with her,' he
explained, and thrust his hand at Joe in greeting.

Clasping his hand, Joe said, 'I thought you weren't due home for
another month or two.' His eyes were very intent as he examined
Sean's face. Somehow he looked too at home, too comfortable,
sitting here in his living room, young Laura on his knee.

'Well, it seems we're likely to be at war soon, so we're getting our
leave early.'

'Oh?' Joe reached down and tickled Laura on the tummy. 'So
we're going to war at last?'

'It looks like it.'

'I thought something was going to happen when they sandbagged
the City Hall last week and ordered a complete blackout, but when
everything slackened off, I imagined it was another false alarm.'

Sean shook his head, and his voice was grave. 'No, I think that
this time we'll be going to war.'

Rosaleen's voice came from the kitchen. 'Your dinner's ready, Joe.
Come eat it.'

Excusing himself, he entered the kitchen and when he saw the
table was set for one, enquired in surprise, 'Did you not make Sean
some?'

'He has eaten already, and his mother will be expecting him
home soon,' she explained, and raising her voice called, 'Sean, will
you have time for a cup of tea?'

'For tea, I'll make time,' he called back, glad of the opportunity
to stay in her company for a while longer.

As he drank the tea, she watched him, watched his hands as he
played with Laura, bringing squeals of delight from her small,
rosebud mouth. In spite of the tight rein she had on her feelings,
Rosaleen was remembering the excitement his hands had brought
to her, and she wriggled uncomfortably in her chair. If only she had
met him sooner!

Feeling his eyes on her face, she refused to meet them, afraid of what he might see. She was relieved when, tea finished, he rose to leave.

Placing Laura on her knee, he went to the door of the kitchen. 'I'm away now, Joe.'

Joe rose from the table, but with a motion of his hand, Sean stayed him. 'Finish your dinner, I'll see you before I go away again.'

'Come round on Saturday night with Annie, Sean. We'll be glad to see you.'

'Ah, well …' His eyes sought and caught Rosaleen's at last, and teased her once again. 'I'll have to see about that. Annie might not want to share me with anyone else.'

She grinned back at him. 'Oh, listen to the conceit of that! I'm sure she'll be glad of a break away from your brand of humour,' she retorted, but in her heart she thought that Annie would be daft if she didn't keep him to herself, and really it would be better for her if she didn't see him again. Still, she found herself hoping that they would come. At the door she mouthed the words, 'Thanks for everything.'

His eyes held hers, deep and soul-searching, and she stood entranced. At last he whispered, 'The pleasure was all mine.' And leaning closer he assured her with a nod of his head. 'And it was a pleasure, Rosaleen.'

As he strode along Beechmount Avenue, his thoughts were busy. He had seen the scepticism in Joe's eyes. He was no fool, and Sean was aware that if he wasn't careful, he could place Rosaleen in a compromising position. Joe must never guess that he was interested in his wife, or Rosaleen was the one who would suffer. Yes, he would have to be very careful. Joe must never guess. The best thing would be for him to break with Annie. He had used her to see Rosaleen, to find out how she still affected him, how, after months at sea, he would react to her presence. Now he knew the answer to that. He loved Rosaleen with a deep abiding love, but he would have to get out of her life before he ruined it. There was no way, no way at all, that she would be lured into an affair with him. She was too good-living and her conscience wouldn't let her. Even if by some chance he managed to play on her feelings for him, because he knew that physically she was very attracted to him, and they started an affair,

71

what would happen? Why, the guilt and worry of it would kill her. Besides, he didn't want an affair; he wanted a wife and children. No, he must get out of her life. Joe was providing a comfortable lifestyle for her and it was up to him to leave her in peace.

That evening when he called at Colinward Street to visit Annie, all Sean's good intentions were forgotten. Annie's delight at seeing him, her warm, eager embrace, touched his heart. She was lovely and they got on well together, so why not court her? Because she was Rosaleen's sister ... that was why not! If only she wasn't. But then, he would never have met her otherwise. He would never have danced with her, asked her out. Oh no! He would have considered her too young.

Annie rushed upstairs to get ready to go out with him, wrapped in a bubble of happiness. When her mother had answered his knock on the door and ushered him into the kitchen, she had been unable to believe her eyes. Even when she was in the scullery making him a cup of tea, she had found herself going to glance into the kitchen to make sure that he was really there.

Since meeting him, her thoughts had been full of him; he even managed to invade her dreams at night, where she was forever chasing him, only to see him fade away as she approached. However, his letters to her had been friendly ... no more ... the kind of letters that he would write to his young sister. Even she, in her bemused state, had been unable to read anything serious into them. Now, as if in answer to her fervent prayers, here he was! He had just arrived home today. Surely this would not have been his first port of call, unless he cared for her.

To make things even more perfect, her mother doted on him and she could see that her father respected him. It would be lovely to do something that had her parents' blessing for a change. If only ... Oh, if only he would fall in love with her, she would spend the rest of her life making him happy. But, according to Sean, her father had been right in his prophecy of war. If it happened, Sean would be plunged straight into it. What if he was killed? This thought dampened her happiness and brought her to her knees beside the bed. Please ... please God, don't let anything happen to him, and bring him safely home to me. He's the best thing that ever happened to me, and if you do, I promise ...'

Her muttered prayer trailed off and aghast she chastised herself. What was she thinking of? You didn't try to blackmail God. God was good! You trusted him. His will be done! And with a muttered excuse, she rose to her feet and finished her preparations.

Annie called in on her way home from work the next night to inform them that, bar word from the Navy, she and Sean would be down on Saturday night, and when Rosaleen saw the happiness that spilled from her, she envied her. A man should be able to excite you and make you happy like that. Not dampen your spirits by making everything seem sinful.

As she prepared for their visit on Saturday night, there was a quiet happiness in her heart but she was aware that she had better be careful. Neither Annie nor Joe was a fool, and she did not want them to become suspicious.

These thoughts startled her, brought her to a standstill, to examine her thoughts with dismay. Suspicious of what?

She was acting as if she and Sean were lovers. If only they were! Oh, if only they were! Shame made her cheeks burn at the longing in her, and she wept as she begged God's forgiveness for her sinful thoughts. What on earth was she coming to?

On Saturday night, she remained in the kitchen when Joe went to answer the knock on the door. She was so worked up that she was afraid to greet Sean under Joe's watchful gaze. Afraid of blushing and stammering like a schoolgirl. That was what she felt like – a teenager in love.

Annie joined her in the kitchen and Rosaleen was pleased when she exclaimed at the assorted dishes that had been prepared.

'You're becoming a proper wee housewife, aren't you?' she teased.

'It helps pass the time. I find the days long, even with Laura to look after. She's such a good baby.'

'Dad would mind her for a few hours a day, Joe's mother even would take her,' Annie exclaimed. 'Either of them would be glad to earn a wee bit of money. Why don't you go back to work, part-time? It would give you a bit of independence, so it would.'

'Joe would never hear tell of me leaving Laura. Oh, no. Not that I would anyhow. She's far too young to leave,' Rosaleen cried, surprised at Annie for suggesting such a thing.

Aware of many friends who had no choice but to leave their children, and had to work to keep the wolf from the door, Annie grimaced at Rosaleen's indignation and holding a hand up in protest, retorted, 'It was just a thought. No offence meant.'

'Sorry, Annie,' Rosaleen apologised. 'I'm awful edgy lately. I must be run down.'

'Perhaps you're pregnant again?'

'No, no ...' Rosaleen could not help smiling faintly at this idea. Chance would be a fine thing. Joe had yet to offer to share her bed again, and she had vowed that she would not invite him. The first move must come from him.

'What's so funny?' Annie asked huffily. She hated to be treated like a child, and she thought Rosaleen was being patronising.

'Ah, Annie, I didn't mean to offend you. Let's not squabble. Let's enjoy ourselves, eh?'

With a smile, Annie acknowledged the logic of what Rosaleen said and in good spirits they entered the living room.

At first, Rosaleen thought she was imagining that Sean was slighting her. Not that 'slighting' was the right word, but considering all that they had been through together, he was treating her like a casual acquaintance. As the evening wore on, she became more and more depressed. What had she done wrong? Did he think it was all right to tease and flirt with her, as long as Annie wasn't present? Was he serious about her? Could she bear to have him as a brother-in-law? Her thoughts swung this way and that, and dismay filled her when she realised that he was in the right and she was wrong. She was a married woman, and he was making it plain to her that he was interested in Annie, and only Annie.

Well ... she didn't want him to be interested in her. Had she implied that she did? Had she been too forward? Red blazed in her cheeks at the very idea, and she found herself sitting closer to Joe, hurt and bewildered.

Since he could read her like a book, Sean knew that she was

confused and hurt. He wanted to get her alone, to explain why he was acting so strangely, but the opportunity did not arise. Anyhow, he knew that to explain would only undo all his careful work. He knew without a doubt that Joe was suspicious, had seen it in his eyes as he watched them together. Sean's lips tightened when he saw Joe put his arm around Rosaleen and draw her close in a possessive manner, and he in turn placed his arm around Annie's shoulders. With a pleased smile she moved closer. Too late, Sean realised that he had made a mistake. He was acting like a callow youth instead of a mature man. Joe had every right to put his arm around Rosaleen, after all, she was the man's wife, and the sooner he accepted that fact the better. With war about to be announced, he should be thinking of getting married. He was the only son in a family of five, and it was up to him to keep the family name going.

The evening dragged a bit, and it was with relief that he agreed with Annie when she suggested that it was time they were getting a move on. At the door he took Rosaleen's hand in his, a cold limp hand that did not return the pressure of his fingers. And when he bent to kiss her cheek she drew away from him, and the hurt, reproachful look she gave him cut him to the heart. It also made all his efforts appear to be in vain because he saw Joe's eyes narrow at Rosaleen's action, and guessed that Joe probably thought that he and Rosaleen had disagreed in some way or other. And now he would be wondering how and when they'd had the opportunity to disagree.

He was making a mess of everything. With a curt farewell, he left the house, a happy Annie hanging on his arm.

As she brushed her hair before retiring for the night, Rosaleen went over the entire evening, word for word. No, she had not been mistaken. Sean had kept her at arm's length. How dare he! HOW DARE HE! To come into her home and treat her like that. Remembering the wonderful rapport of Tuesday afternoon, her heart sank. Had she made a fool of herself? Did he think that she was trying to charm him? Was this his way of warning her off? Her lips tightened angrily at the thought. Well, he would never get the chance to humiliate her again. From now on, as far as she was concerned, he just did not exist. She would show him! With this thought, in despair, she threw herself on top of the bedclothes. This would never do. She was a married woman. In future she must act like one.

Joe's hand on her shoulder startled her.

'Are you all right, Rosaleen?'

Glad that she had not given in to the desire to weep, she assured him. 'Yes. Why shouldn't I be all right? What would be wrong?'

She was surprised to see him in her bedroom; he usually avoided the intimacy of that setting. Now he sat down on the edge of the bed and his eyes roamed over her face, then down the soft curves of her body. She was lovely ... desirable and sweet. He did not blame Sean for fancying her, but she should know better than to encourage him.

'Have you and Sean had a disagreement?' he asked casually.

She gaped at him in amazement, 'Of course not. Whatever gave you that idea? Why, I haven't seen Sean since he left here on Tuesday afternoon, so I haven't.'

Her surprise was obviously genuine, and he began to doubt the evidence of his own eyes. Was it jealousy that had made him think that there was something going on between her and Sean? His eyes searched her face, but she held his gaze steadily and his eyes were the first to fall away.

'Was that what brought you into the lion's den, eh?' she hissed. 'Did you come in to make accusations? Are you not afraid to be alone with me?'

To her surprise, he rose and slowly drawing her into his arms, sank his face into the softness of her hair. She stood stiff as he hugged her close, feeling the desire mount in him. She did not want this ... could not bear, tonight of all nights, to be left frustrated. Unhappiness was sharp within her breast.

'Rosaleen ... please be kind. Please?' He gulped deep in his throat, 'I can't help myself. Do you think I like being the way I am? Do you think I don't want... to ... to ... oh, you know what I mean.' His voice trailed off miserably and compassion smote her.

'You could see a doctor.' She drew back and gazed up at him

beseechingly. 'I'd go with you,' she offered.

'No.' His voice was stubborn. 'No, I won't see a doctor.' He swallowed deeply and continued haltingly. 'Rosaleen, I don't think ... that you understand.'

Wide-eyed, she returned his look. 'Don't understand what?'

'Well, you see, the physical act of love ...'

She interrupted him angrily. 'You mean intercourse?'

His eyes narrowed and his lips tightened. 'Don't be so crude.'

'Oh, but I'm not being crude,' she assured him, adding with a knowing nod of the head, 'That's the name for it.'

'Well, whether you believe it or not, the act is not all that important. It's for procreation, not for pleasure or lust.'

Again she interrupted him. 'What about love, eh? Aren't you forgetting about love? Do you love me, Joe?'

'Of course I love you!' he cried in amazement. 'How can you doubt it?'

'Huh! With little difficulty.' Her voice became coaxing, 'Joe, if you love me ... go to the doctor. Find out what's wrong with you.'

His look remained mutinous and he drew her close again. 'Perhaps if we try again ... Eh, love?' he pleaded, and as his hands began their exploration of her body, she cringed inside. Now she knew why he always made her feel so dirty. He believed he was committing a sin, and unconsciously the message came across to her. Closing her eyes, she prayed that this time it would be different; that this time he would succeed, but she was not really hopeful ...

Sean was also angry with himself. All he had succeeded in doing was hurting Rosaleen and making Joe more suspicious than ever. And another thing ... Annie was getting more serious about him. It was not fair leading her on, just because he wanted to be in Rosaleen's company. Since he did not intend to marry her, he must break it off and leave her free to meet someone else. Yes, he would break it off, but not until the end of his leave. He wanted to see Rosaleen one more time ... just one more time.

He sighed. He was kidding himself. There would always be one more time, and he was using Annie while she was falling in love with him. Would it be so wrong to marry her? He was very fond of her, and he knew that he could make her happy, and he had enough money saved for a deposit on a house. They could buy one far away. Up the Glen Road, or even on the other side of town – Glengormley, for instance. It was a nice village, and he would still see Rosaleen now and again.

His thoughts were in a turmoil when they arrived at Annie's front door, and to his surprise she did not invite him in for coffee as she usually did. Instead, she stopped in the hall and when he followed her in, closed the hall door. In the intimacy of the enclosed space, she leant against the wall and eyed him expectantly. In a dilemma, he returned her gaze; dark blue eyes locked on green, so like Rosaleen's. Contrary to what Rosaleen might think, he had never touched Annie. Just a chaste kiss on the cheek or brow, in spite of much encouragement. Now he was tempted ... he would be going back to sea soon and, who knew, he might not return.

He knew Annie well enough to ask her to marry him and on his next leave, if God spared him, they could get married. It would be nice to know that he had a wife waiting for him and perhaps, in time, a child. If war was declared, and there didn't seem any doubt about it now, it would be no picnic, and Annie was lovely and sweet and in love with him. Slowly, he reached for her and when her arms crept up around his neck, and the soft curves of her body pressed close to his, he felt passion rise. His lips sought hers and he kissed her long and hard, but try though he did to dispel it, Rosaleen's face, swimming behind his closed eyelids, kept him from going any further. With a sigh of regret, he put Annie firmly away from him. Her mouth opened to protest, but he was saved by her mother's voice, coming from the kitchen, inquiring suspiciously what was keeping Annie.

With a grimace, she gave him a reproachful look and asked, 'Well, will I be seeing you again?'

As though she had said it, he realised that she was going out on a limb; that she was giving him an ultimatum.

After some thought, he found himself nodding. 'Tomorrow night? Shall I pick you up at seven?'

With a relieved sigh, she nodded, planted a quick kiss on his lips, and bade him goodnight. She was happy; without speaking, she had managed to inquire whether or not his intentions were honourable. He, much to her delight, had indicated that they were, and now all was well with her world.

Rosaleen stayed away from her mother's house while Sean was on leave, afraid of meeting him. Afraid of betraying how he affected her. Although she longed to see him in case war was declared.

If it was, she might never see him again. She saw Annie, and in a happy confiding mood her sister told her that Sean had committed himself, that his intentions were serious. The future stretched before Rosaleen, long and painful, as she pictured him as her brother-in-law.

The declaration of war came as a surprise to the people of the Falls Road. First the general election and then the riots had hogged the headlines of the newspapers, and although everybody was aware that Hitler was taking all in front of him, they had their own troubles and strife, and had not expected England to declare war on Germany.

Rosaleen heard the announcement as she stood at the kitchen sink peeling potatoes.

'Today, England has declared war on Germany.' The rest of Mr Chamberlain's words coming over the radio were lost on Rosaleen as she stood aghast. With sinking heart, she wished she had not been so proud and foolish. Sean would be called back at once, and what if he did not return? What if he was killed? She might never see him again. Panic gripped her. She just had to see him again. She must see him somehow! Joe visited his mother every Sunday night, so tonight when he was round in Cavendish Street she would nip up and see her parents. Annie had remarked that her mam was inquiring if anything was wrong, it was so long since she had visited them, so tonight she would keep Laura up late, and go up to Colinward Street and, with a bit of luck, see Sean.

Fate was against her, however. Sean had taken Annie out for a meal, to celebrate their engagement. As soon as he had heard the announcement of war, he had proposed to her with a ring ready – a ring that had belonged to his grandmother. For an hour and a half Rosaleen listened to her mother rave about the virtues of Sean. Describing how big the stone in Annie's ring was. 'Every bit as big as yours Rosaleen,' she gushed. Just when Rosaleen thought she could bear it no longer, Joe arrived from his mother's. After a quick cup of tea, a relieved Rosaleen wrapped Laura's blanket around her, settled her in her pram and prepared to go home.

As they said their farewells at the door, her father casually let drop that Sean had been called back to his ship, and that he was leaving first thing in the morning. Tears stung Rosaleen's eyes at this news. To think he was leaving without saying goodbye to her and Joe and Laura. She would never forgive him, she vowed. Never.

On the way home, she only half listened to Joe moaning on about taking Laura out in the cold night air.

'Your mother looked all right to me,' he fumed. 'What was wrong with her?'

To cover the lie she had told him as an excuse to visit so late at night, Rosaleen assured him that her mother had been unwell but was recovering. Still, he lamented, she wasn't bad enough to justify taking Laura out at night; it could be the death of her. And on and on he went. As usual, when Joe kept lamenting about something, she began to worry in case the cold night air did affect Laura. What if she caught a cold and one thing led to another and she died? It would be her fault, and Joe would not let her forget it. She wished he would, now and again, be a comfort to her, instead of always making her feel in the wrong. Even when she was in the right and he was in the wrong, he was able to twist things about until she was the one who ended up feeling guilty and miserable.

He made her feel so inadequate, her life was becoming one big well of guilt and remorse. Arriving home she bade him an abrupt goodnight and carried Laura straight up the stairs, away from his recriminations, vowing to bathe her in the morning.

Each in their own room, they were about to retire for the night when a knock on the door brought a frown to Joe's brow.

Putting his head around the door of Rosaleen's room, he asked, 'Are you expecting Annie to call?'

'No … no, she never mentioned anything to me.'

His eyes flicked over her in her negligee set, and he warned, 'You stay here,' before descending the stairs.

Rosaleen examined herself in the full-length mirror. Joe would not agree with her but her negligee set was quite modest, hinting rather than revealing, and when she heard Sean's voice in the hall, she descended the stairs without hesitation.

Sean felt a lump rise in his throat as he gazed at the beauty of her. Face free of make-up and hair loose around her face, she looked about seventeen. Frowning fiercely, Joe turned to her. 'Sean has called to say goodbye,' he said unnecessarily.

'So you're off tomorrow, then, Sean?' she said softly.

He nodded, and when Annie proudly thrust her left hand forward, displaying the solitaire diamond ring, watched Rosaleen closely.

Glad that she had been forewarned, Rosaleen exclaimed in admiration and hugged Annie warmly, before offering Sean her hand in congratulation.

He sighed. He did not know whether to be glad or sorry; Rosaleen obviously did not care one way or the other whether or not he married Annie.

'Look … why are we all standing around?' Rosaleen cried. 'Sit down, sit down, and I'll make a cup of tea.'

At this suggestion, Joe interrupted her. 'I'll make the tea. You had better put on something warm or you'll catch cold,' he admonished her. And with another disapproving look at her night attire, headed for the kitchen.

'I'll have to use the bathroom. Excuse me, please. Too much wine … ye know what it's like.' With these words, Annie followed Joe, to go through the kitchen into the bathroom, and Sean and Rosaleen were left alone in the living room.

Aware of Joe in the kitchen, she whispered, 'I thought you were going to leave without saying goodbye.'

'Never, Rosaleen. I could never do that,' he whispered back.

Not another word was uttered, but his eyes spoke volumes. Rosaleen lapped it all up, and wept inwardly for the loss of him.

As they drank their tea, it was Joe who asked the question that

Rosaleen desperately wanted to know and did not dare to frame.

'When's the big day then?'

It was Annie who answered him.

'I'm going to set things in motion. You know … see about letters of freedom and the like, and get the banns read. With us both belonging to St Paul's Parish, it should be all right. Then the first chance Sean has of a pass, no matter how short, we're going to be married. Isn't that right, love?'

Sean answered her question with a nod, and avoided looking at Rosaleen. Knowing full well that without a word he had just been telling her how much he loved her. He felt ashamed; he had no right to exploit Annie like this. Why did life have to be so mixed up? he thought in anguish. Annie was lovely … why wasn't it her he desired?

At the door, when they were about to leave, Sean said to Rosaleen, 'Give Laura a big kiss for me.'

'Would you like to see her before you go?' she asked quickly, and when he nodded in delight, turned and led the way upstairs.

Glad that Annie did not accompany them, and good manners forbade Joe to leave her, Rosaleen entered her bedroom, followed by Sean. The big double bed and large cot took up most of the floor space, and there was not much room for manoeuvre. Laura was stretched out in the cot, the clothes kicked away from her body, her chubby arms and legs spreadeagled, her cheeks flushed with sleep.

'Ah, Rosaleen, she must be a delight to you and Joe.' Sean's voice was sad. If only Laura was his child.

Close beside him in the confined space, Rosaleen nodded, her eyes hungrily devouring his profile as he gazed down at the sleeping child. Etching it on to her memory.

'Are you not training her to sleep alone?' he asked in surprise, knowing that his sisters swore that the earlier you started, the easier it was to train babies.

To his amazement, Rosaleen blushed crimson and muttered, 'It's time enough. We haven't the back room ready for her yet.'

She doubted very much that Laura would ever have a room to herself; Joe's problem was no better, and he was adamant about not seeing a doctor, saying there could not be much wrong with him for: 'Haven't I given you a daughter?'

And what answer could she find to that?

Becoming aware that the other bedroom door was open and that he was bound to see the bed with the clothes turned down ready for occupation, she added quickly, 'We're going to space our family.'

Sean felt a great surge of resentment against Joe rise in his breast. Was the man a fool? Did he not know that Rosaleen needed to be loved? Such a well of sensuality going to waste. Did Joe not know that children could be spaced out without the withdrawal of warmth and comfort from the matrimonial bed?

Then he remembered how good-living Joe was. Still, how could the man stay away from the beauty of Rosaleen? If only he was her husband … there'd be no separate beds. What's more, he would take full responsibility for their actions. He would be the one to confess to birth control. Rosaleen would be free from worry.

Now he questioned her. 'Is that what you want, Rosaleen?'

'Of course. Especially now that we're going to war.'

He smiled slightly at this. 'I don't think Hitler will be too bothered about Ireland. It's too far from Germany. No,' he shook his head and smiled reassuringly at her, 'he'll be concentrating his wrath on England for daring to stand up to him. They didn't come near Ireland during the '14–'18 war, so I can't see the Germans bothering this time.'

'Me da disagrees with you. He says that this time we're building far more planes and ships for England, and that Hitler's no doser and is sure to try to bomb Short and Harland and the shipyard.'

Sean pursed his lips and a frown puckered his brow. 'He could be right … yes, he could be right at that,' he agreed.

The urge to hug her one last time became overpowering and he turned away. Her hand on his arm, long slender fingers tipped with pale pink nails, stopped him.

'You'll take care, won't you, Sean?' she whispered softly.

Placing his hand over hers, he fought the desire to raise it to his lips. 'I'll take care,' he promised.

When they had departed, she sadly climbed the stairs again, Joe on her heels.

'I hope you realise that you were an occasion of sin in that negligee,' he grunted, his lips a hard, tight line in his face.

On the small landing, mouth agape, Rosaleen turned to face him.

'I was no such thing!' she cried, but already her conscience was beginning to plague her. Had she deliberately set out to make Sean desire her?

'Of course you were. Look at it. It shows more than it hides.'

For a moment she was at a loss for words, then she lashed out at him in retaliation. 'Well, it doesn't turn you on. So how was I to know, eh? Tell me that. How was I to know?'

And with these words she entered her room and only the thought of the late hour and her sleeping neighbours prevented her from slamming the door.

Burying her face in the pillow, she wept long and sore for chances lost. To think that she had not wanted a seaman for a husband because she had wanted someone to hold her close in the night! Chance would be a fine thing. Well, she had made her bed and now she must lie in it. And – miserable thought – Sean was to be her brother-in-law.

Chapter 4

At first the war made no difference to Rosaleen. Life went on as before, and remembering that Sean had said Hitler would not be worried about Ireland, she was inclined to agree with him. Then she became aware that Joe was worried and waited anxiously, knowing that he would confide in her when he was ready and not before. And sure enough, one night after they had finished tea, he confessed to her that work was drying up.

'It's a bad business I'm in at the present time, Rosaleen. Wrought-iron railings and gates.' He grimaced. 'Trust me! I couldn't have been in a worse one. Iron's like gold dust at the moment. It's all being channelled into munitions factories.'

'Why not concentrate on the brick building side of the business?' she asked, thinking about the small sheds and garages he had been building lately.

He shook his head and a rueful smile twisted his lips. 'No one in their right mind is building anything at the moment ... they're afraid that Hitler will come and bomb it.'

'There's not much chance of him bombing here, is there?' she asked fearfully.

He shrugged. 'It's hardly likely. His troops are in the north of

France now, and I can't see them travelling a thousand miles across England and back again.' With lips pursed, he shook his head. 'No, I can't see Hitler sending bombers all that distance ... but who knows just what that madman will do? After all, we are supplying planes, ships and ammunition, and ... God forbid! ... if they take England, we're sitting ducks. Still, I can't see England falling to them. Churchill's a great man ... he knows what he's doing. Ah, well,' He sighed deeply. 'Who knows? Maybe everyone will have the same idea and business will pick up,' he finished on a more cheerful note, and Rosaleen breathed a sigh of relief.

The war did make a difference to her father. He was in his glory. On the sick for months with a bad chest, he had despaired of ever getting work. The doctors in the Royal Victoria Hospital had forbidden him to return to Greeves Mill, where he had worked for thirty odd years in the flax store, and where he had picked up the linen dust that was the cause of his congested lungs. They had issued him with a blue card, stating that he was only fit for light work, so that he was compelled to obey their orders. However, light work was hard to come by and Rosaleen had watched him grow quieter and more depressed. Her heart ached for him, a young man of forty-five, on the dust heap. Her mother, pushing the Irish News open at the vacancies column at him every morning, had not helped any. It was as if she thought he wasn't trying to get work, as if he was lazy.

This wasn't true. The vaguest possibility of a job that was suitable had him away, trying to get an interview. It had been no use telling her mother that he hadn't a snowball's chance in hell of most of the jobs advertised. Not with a blue card and the added stigma of being a Catholic.

Now, at last, he had obtained employment. He had been started as gatehouse man in the Blackstaff Linen Factory. This was another one of the mills that flanked the Falls Road, whose books were full with orders for heavy duck material for tents and rucksacks, and other less heavy material for uniforms for the forces. Not great money, but being just down the Springfield Road a bit, within walking distance from Colinward Street as it were, there were no tram fares to worry about. No wonder his step was lighter, his mouth more ready to smile. At last, he could feel independent. It was indeed true that it was an ill wind that didn't blow some good. If war had not been declared, resulting in a mad rush of young men to enlist, her father would never have got this job, and Rosaleen was happy for him.

Her visits to May had become fortnightly instead of monthly as May drew near the end of her pregnancy. The first time Rosaleen had visited May, her heart had been quite literally in her mouth, and her knees had knocked hell out of each other as she nervously pushed the pram up the street where her friend lived. But, to her surprise, she noticed that the rows of terraced houses looked like any street on the Falls Road, with the same mixture of houseproud and couldn't-care-less occupants. There was only one difference; some of the footpaths had the kerb edge painted red, white and blue. It looked ugly, took away from the quiet nature of the streets, and Rosaleen was glad that none of the street kerbs on the Falls Road were painted green, white and gold.

May's house was one of the houseproud: windows shining, net curtains snow white, and a well-scrubbed half circle around the spotless doorstep. It was with a mixture of pride and diffidence that she ushered Rosaleen in and, before settling down for a cup of tea and a gossip, took her on a tour of the house. It was a parlour house with three bedrooms, and in the smallest of these Billy had installed a bathroom suite, while the second bedroom was all decorated, ready for the arrival of the baby. Lovely nursery wallpaper and curtains made Rosaleen jealous as she pictured her own spare room crammed with Joe's belongings.

'It's lovely, May. You must be proud of it,' she said graciously, and smiled. May smiled in return.

'It is nice, isn't it, Rosaleen?' she agreed shyly. 'I never dreamed I would ever own a house like this. Billy's a lovely man.' She leant closer and her eyes begged Rosaleen to believe. 'Honestly, Rosaleen, he really is.' Her head nodded to emphasise her point. 'Ye know, you don't have to be a Catholic to be good.'

Mouth agape, Rosaleen cried aghast, 'Have I ever said otherwise?'

May smiled faintly as she shook her head. 'No, of course you haven't. Still…' her head tilted slightly and an eyebrow rose '… I get the feeling that you don't approve of him.'

'Ah, May, that's not fair,' Rosaleen cried in despair. 'I think he's a lovely man. It's just … well, ye see … I worry about your soul,' she finished lamely.

At that, May laughed aloud. 'Well now, how's about you letting me do the worrying, eh?'

'Willingly! Willingly! I'll say no more.' Rosaleen held up her hand, palm facing outwards, as if to ward off the reproach in May's voice, and then gave her friend a sly glance from under lowered lids. 'Does this mean that you want me to start being nice to Billy? You know, the odd wee embrace and the odd wee kiss? Just to show how much I like him.'

'No fear. You keep all that for Joe,' May warned her with a laugh, and Rosaleen turned away to hide her pain. Her joke had backfired. She had been caught on the raw. Joe did not want… all that.

May's son was born in February and all hell broke loose when Big John heard about it. Rosaleen was kept up to date on all the happenings by Annie, who, when the stitching factory closed down due to lack of material for ladies underwear, had found herself a job in Mackie's Foundry.

During the First World War Mackie's had played a prominent role, producing bullets and components for planes, so it was no surprise when they were roped in by the ministry to supply ammunition. Now they were working round the clock. Annie worked alongside Colin Brady (that was another thing about the war, it supplied employment for many on outdoor relief), and brought all the news home to Rosaleen.

It seemed that for a solid week Big John was drunk and eventually ended up in jail for being drunk and disorderly. When he was released, Kate and the lads would not let him back into the house and got a court order to stop him molesting her and the family. Of course Big John heaped all the blame on May's head, calling down vengeance on her. Vowing to get even with her for ruining his life. Not wanting to worry May, Rosaleen never repeated a word to her.

She could only hope that Big John's threats to get his own back were idle ones.

It was August of 1940 before work was started on the first air-raid shelter in the parish, but nobody worried about this. After all, during the First War, the Germans never came near Ireland and why should this time be any different? The shelter was built behind St Paul's Parochial House and was large and fitted out with padded seats. It was much more comfortable than the other air-raid shelters that followed it along Cavendish Road. It was said that this was because it would have to accommodate the policemen from the barracks on the Springfield Road.

August 24th was the day they started to build. Rosaleen was always to remember that date – it was the day Sean and Annie got married.

Rosaleen was Matron of Honour, and with Sean being an only son and all his close friends at sea, he asked Joe to be best man. For her wedding dress, Annie had chosen cream chiffon, shot with a tiny pink flower pattern. The dress was long and swirled around her slim ankles and clung to the curves of her slim body. To her mother's dismay, she shunned the conventional veil, saying that picture hats were in fashion, and wore one of these on her dark chestnut hair. She was breathtaking: her eyes glinting like emeralds, her skin clear and pure, and happiness radiating from her.

Seeing the adoration in her eyes as they followed Sean about, Rosaleen could understand his wanting to marry her, in spite of the complications that might arise. She only hoped that he would make her happy, but not for one minute did she doubt that he could satisfy her. Annie was a very lucky girl.

One thing was sure: as effectively as if he had used bricks and mortar, he had put up a wall between them, because by marrying Annie he had placed himself even further beyond her reach.

Although Rosaleen was not aware of it, she was every bit as beautiful as Annie. Her dress was pale blue chiffon, and her picture hat was caught under the chin with a swathe of white chiffon, throwing into relief the pure oval of her face and turning her eyes to silver. Since the birth of Laura she was heavier, but this just added a seductive curve to her bust and hips and did not detract from her beauty.

Much to Thelma's annoyance, the reception was held at home in Colinward Street, but with not knowing just when Sean would obtain leave, this was unavoidable. Also to her annoyance, there were not enough clothing coupons for both Tommy and she to get new outfits, and he had to make do with the lounge suit purchased for Rosaleen's wedding. Not that he was annoyed. Far from it! He hated breaking in new clothes and was happiest when wearing clothes that had matured. However, Thelma wanted Annie's big day to resemble Rosaleen's as closely as possible. They were both her daughters and she meant to do her best for them. To her delight, although rationing was beginning to be felt, she had managed to get caterers in at short notice, and the spread was lovely.

To Rosaleen's relief, Betty Devlin, having joined the WRENS, was not at the reception. She had been worrying about meeting Betty, but when she had inquired after her, Sean had smiled and told her to stop worrying, that everything was going to be all right. She did not agree with him, but then, how was he to know that things would never be all right with her again? Annie and Sean were having a few days in Dublin for their honeymoon and lying alone in the big double bed that night, Rosaleen tried to block the picture of them together from her mind, but fought a losing battle in which tears were shed. She awoke heavy-eyed the next morning and descended the stairs to find Joe still in the kitchen.

Normally he was away to work before she descended the stairs and she greeted him with surprise.

'Did you sleep in?'

'No, I want to talk to you. You were too tired last night. Too preoccupied …' His eyes scanned her pale face, noting her heavy eyes, and he frowned. 'Are you all right?'

'Huh? Oh, yes, I'm fine. What do you want to talk to me about?'

He grimaced before saying, 'I don't know how to say this … you'll think I'm daft … but, well, I've joined up.'

Bewildered, she asked blankly, 'Joined up what?'

'I've enlisted. You know … joined the army.'

'But why?' Rosaleen was dumbfounded. Everybody was thanking

God that there was no conscription here in Ireland; that there was no need for married men to worry about having to leave their wives and children, and here was Joe saying he had joined up. 'You're right. I do think you're daft. You don't have to go.'

'It's like this, Rosaleen. There is just not enough work for me and Owen.' Seeing that she was still bewildered, and guessing what she was thinking, he reached over and took her hand in his.

'I know what you're going to say. I'm the boss. Let Owen Black go. But, Rosaleen, he's in his forties, he's got four kids, and besides, he's too old and won't be able to get another job. Especially now the big foundries are all closing down for lack of material to carry out repairs. Rosaleen, things are in a bad way ... hundreds are being thrown out of work every week. I think it's a ruse to get more young men to join up, but whatever the reason, it's up to the young men to join. Leave what jobs there are for the older men.'

Realising that what he said was true and not wanting to whinge, she remained silent. He continued, 'With me away, Owen will keep the business going. Even if he only gets the odd wee building contract, it will keep it running until the war's over, and I can trust him to put something away every week, no matter how small. It'll be waiting for me coming home ... but it'll be in a joint account, so that if you should need any money, you have just to go to the bank. I doubt if he'll get any iron. In fact, they're talking about taking the railings off the parks. That's how bad it it. But he should get enough work to keep one man going.' He chucked her under the chin. 'At least one thing's sure – there should be plenty of work for me after the war.'

'You could concentrate on building garages or sheds,' she cried. 'Expand a bit.'

'I've already explained that to you, Rosaleen. People are just not building anything at the moment.'

'You could at least try to get a job,' she interrupted him indignantly. 'What about me and Laura?'

'Ah Rosaleen ... I couldn't work for anybody else, not after being me own boss all these years. Besides, you know there aren't any jobs. Why do you think so many are enlisting? And you and Laura will be all right. I've money put away. If anything happens to me, you'll be comfortably off.'

'I don't want to be comfortably off. I want you here with me and Laura.'

The idea of being in the house alone with her baby when the sirens went off did not appeal to Rosaleen. Joe might not share a room with her, but at least he was there. He often fetched his mother round to sit in the cubby-hole under the stairs with them. She couldn't picture herself and Laura sitting alone under the stairs when the sirens went off. So far they had all been false alarms, but what if the Germans did decide to come over? They heard daily on the radio how badly England was being blitzed. What if the Germans came over here? What if it was their turn next?

'That's another thing ... I want you to go with the rest of the women and children, out into the country. I want to go away with an easy mind.'

'Hah! Be evacuated?' Her face screwed up at the very idea. 'No way! If you go ... if you decide you must fight for Britain ... I'll do my bit. I'll get a job in Mackie's.'

'I'm not fighting for Britain.' The anger he felt came across in his voice. 'I'm fighting for a safe future for my wife and child. That's why I've joined up. And I want you away from Mackie's. It's like a big bomb sitting up there, in the midst of all the houses.'

She knew what he said was true.

'I'm sorry ... but you took the wind out of my sails,' she said appeasingly, then asked, 'When do you go?'

'In two weeks' time.'

'Oh my God!'

The strength left her legs and she groped for a chair. With an arm around her he led her to the settee and sat beside her, drawing her close. As she cuddled against him for comfort, she was beseiged by doubts. Was he going just to get away from her? She had started to repulse him; hating the way he always ended up crying in her arms. It had been driving her insane.

Now she regretted her actions. Joe crying in her arms would be better than being on her own.

'Joe ... are you going because of ... you know?' Her shoulders lifted in a despairing gesture and she swallowed deep before finishing the sentence. 'How things are between us?'

'No. No, Rosaleen, I'm not,' he consoled her. He smiled slightly and squeezed her closer still. He didn't blame her for her actions; the fault was all his. Now he tilted her face up so that he could look into her eyes. 'That's not the reason I'm going. I'm going because I think Hitler is a madman and must be stopped. I really don't think the war will last long. Maybe another year. And although I hate you being so near Mackie's, I don't really think that Hitler will come. He hasn't bothered with Ireland so far, has he?'

He held her gaze, and she shook her head as she agreed with him. 'No, he hasn't.'

'Are you feeling all right, now you're over the shock?'

When she nodded sadly, he said, 'I'm going round now to break the news to Mother. You'll keep an eye on her for me, won't you?'

'Of course I will.' Her eyes lit up and she nudged him excitedly. 'Now there's an idea! She can stay here with me while you're away. We'll be company for each other.'

His faced closed up and his nod was non-committal. Rosaleen turned away, annoyed. She could not understand Joe's attitude to his mother. She got on very well with Mrs Smith, but Joe did not encourage their friendship; he kept his mother at arm's length. Not that he wasn't good to her. He was. She wanted for nothing. But still, he did not encourage her to visit them. Did not make her at home in their house, saying that he did not want her popping in and out all the time, and he was not pleased if Rosaleen called in too often to visit her. Well, if he chose to go to war, she would be her own boss and would ask Mrs Smith to live with her in spite of his attitude. It would solve a lot of problems.

Two weeks later, Joe, handsome in his new uniform, left for England. Rosaleen, his mother, and the delight of his heart, Laura, accompanied him to the docks. They stood amidst the crowds and he crushed Rosaleen and Laura together in a fierce embrace.

'When I come back ... when the war's over ... I promise to go and see a doctor. All right, Rosaleen?'

Wet-eyed, she gazed up at him in amazement and nodded mutely. The kiss he gave her was full of promise.

Planting a more sedate farewell kiss on his mother's lips, he climbed the gangway and, with a final wave, disappeared from view. He had warned them not to hang about in the cold with Laura, and sadly they made their way through the crowd waiting to wave farewell to their loved ones. Leaving the quayside, they made their way to the tram stop.

Sure that Mrs Smith would be delighted to move in with her, Rosaleen put the suggestion to her, and was surprised when she regretfully declined the invitation.

'It's very kind of you, Rosaleen, but I don't think Joe would approve.'

'But why? You needn't give up your house. We can keep an eye on it. It's just 'til he comes back.'

Mrs Smith laughed softly. 'I'm not worried about the house. No, it's just… look, I can't explain. Someday I will, but not now. Besides, I don't want to be a nuisance. And Rosaleen? Do you think you could ever get used to calling me Amy?'

'Amy … that's a lovely name. But don't change the subject! What about when the sirens go off? What will you do? I'll be worried sick about you, so I will.'

'I'll be all right! I'll go in next door. Besides, it won't take them long building the shelters. But never mind me, what will you do?'

Determined that in time she would be able to make Amy change her mind, Rosaleen's answer was airy.

'Oh, I'll manage … I'll manage. Me da's an air-raid warden, he'll look after me. Don't you worry about me.'

In the following weeks, try though she did to persuade Amy to change her mind, she did not succeed, but they became close friends.

When Amy offered to look after Laura, now a mischievous eighteen months old, while Rosaleen took a part-time job, she at first demurred.

'She's too boisterous for you, so she is, Amy. You'd never be able to handle her.'

'Look, if you got started in the Blackstaff on the afternoon shift, she'd be asleep most of the time. You know rightly she sleeps for at least two hours every afternoon, and it would do you good to get away from her for a few hours every day. Go on, Rosaleen. I'm sure the money would come in handy.'

This argument helped to sway her. Joe had been gone six weeks, and so far no money had come from the ministry for her. Whenever he could afford to, Owen was depositing some money straight into an account for her but she knew that it would not be much and had vowed not to touch it unless she had to. But, with Joe's money being held up, she would soon have to dip into their savings. Therefore Amy's offer tempted her. She was aware that it sometimes took months for the army wages to get through, and Amy was right, the extra money would come in handy.

'Are you sure?' she asked diffidently.

Seeing that she was weakening, Amy hastened to assure her, 'Of course I'm sure. I wouldn't have offered otherwise.'

So Rosaleen sought and obtained employment in the Blackstaff, just five minutes' walk away from Iris Drive.

She was in charge of three looms, weaving heavy black duck and drill material which would be used for making tents, and life became so busy she did not feel so frustrated. Her only regret was that it put a stop to her visits to see May, as she did not want to leave Laura in the evenings and felt that she was too young to keep out in the evening air. Besides (to May's disgust), she did not fancy being caught on the Shankill Road if the sirens went off. She wanted to be amongst her own kind.

May wanted her to visit at the weekends, but Rosaleen had so much shopping and cleaning to do then that it was impossible to trek away across to the Shankill Road, and anyhow she did not want to intrude when Billy was at home with his wife and child.

She began to dread her mother's daily visits. Every time she came she lamented in her ear about Annie's behaviour. After the disappointment of not being pregnant, Annie had started going to dances with the girls out of work. Bringing home men from the forces to meet her parents. Going to the pictures with them and entertaining them generally. Seeing the furrow of worry on her mother's brow, Rosaleen sought to console her.

'Listen, Mam, she's not doing anything wrong. If she was she wouldn't be bringing them home, now would she?'

'How do we know what she's doing, eh? She's not like you. You know your place.'

Rosaleen felt hot colour blaze her face and turned aside to hide it, fussing over Laura; hoping her mother would not notice. Why did everybody assume that she was a good girl? She could not picture Annie having it off up at the Dam. Yet here *she* was, considered a goody-goody, and Annie who was forthright and open about her actions was considered fast. It was true what they said, quiet ones were the worst.

'She'll go too far, so she will. What will Sean do if he hears about her actions?' her mother continued, too preoccupied to notice Rosaleen's manoeuvres. 'That one doesn't know when she's well off, so she doesn't.'

'I don't think Sean will mind ... who knows? Perhaps some girl somewhere is being nice to him. I'm inclined to think that you're worrying unnecessarily. Annie won't do anything to jeopardise her marriage.'

'Will you have a word with her, Rosaleen? Eh? She'll listen to you, so she will. Go on, love ... have a wee word in her ear.'

Against her will, Rosaleen promised to have a word with Annie. It certainly wasn't her place to criticise anybody, especially Annie, but having promised, she waited her chance. It came sooner than she expected; the following evening her sister called down from work for a chat.

'This is a pleasant surprise,' Rosaleen greeted her, a happy smile on her face. 'My, but you don't half suit that boilersuit,' she added enviously, her eyes roaming over Annie's slim figure.

And the boilersuit did indeed become Annie. Not so long ago it had been considered a scandal for a woman to wear trousers, but the war had changed all that, and the long slim lines of Annie's body and legs were emphasised by the navy boilersuit which all Mackie's workers wore.

'You look lovely, Annie. Really nice.' Her look turned reproachful and she childed, 'Long time no see.'

'I know.' Annie lifted Laura up in her arms. 'How I've missed you, love,' she cried, hugging the child close and covering her face with kisses. 'You're a wee bundle of joy, so you are,' she added, as Laura squirmed and giggled in her arms.

'Well, what kept you away then? It must be two weeks since you've been down,' Rosaleen chastised her.

'Longer,' Annie agreed with her. 'Too long, but I've been very busy.'

'So I hear ...'

At that, Annie sat Laura down on the settee with a plop. 'You sit there a wee minute, pet, and be a good girl. I've something nice for you,' she promised, and turned to face Rosaleen.

'You've been talking to me mam,' she said resignedly as she removed the turban that bound her hair, and ran her fingers through her long, chestnut tresses. 'Gosh, but these turbans are warm. I wish we didn't have to wear them.' She moved to the mirror above the fireplace and fluffed her hair out, pouting at the attractive picture she made, before asking, 'And just what has Mam been saying about me?'

'She's worried about you. And from what I hear, I don't blame her.'

Anger flared in Annie's eyes and she turned on Rosaleen and growled, 'Just what did you hear, eh? What? That I'm carrying on with soldiers and sailors? Is that what you heard?'

At the look of guilt on Rosaleen's face, she grunted.

'Huh! I can see I'm right. Well, let me tell you something. I hope some girl, somewhere, is being nice to Sean. You can be nice and entertain a man without doing "that", ye know, and I'm not doing anything wrong. Would I bring them home if I was carrying on? Eh? Tell me ... would I? No. I'd bring them where some of the girls bring them. Up to the Dam, or over Daisy Hill. That's where I'd bring them, and no one need be the wiser.'

The anger left her and a wry smile crossed her face. 'Honestly, Rosaleen, most of them just want company. Someone to talk to about their wives and girlfriends. And I supply that company. So the neighbours can gossip all they want! That's all Mam's worried about... what the neighbours'll think.'

At the mention of the Dam, Rosaleen felt the colour leave her face. Did Annie know? Had Sean confessed to her? She made herself look Annie in the face but her sister's attention was back with Laura. Giving her a small bar of chocolate, Annie once more lifted the child up in her arms and hugged her close.

Close to tears, she muttered, 'I wish I was pregnant. If only I was pregnant... If Sean's killed, I have nothing ... nothing.' She broke off on a sob, burying her head in a silent, wide-eyed Laura's neck.

Going to her, Rosaleen gathered her close to her breast. 'Ah, Annie, don't talk like that. Sean will come back. I just know he will.'

Clinging to her, Annie sobbed for some seconds, at the same time trying to smile to please Laura who was wiping at her tears with a chubby fist, muttering. 'There now, Auntie Annie ... hush now ... it'll be better soon, so it will.' Repeating like an old woman the words that Rosaleen used to comfort her when she wept.

'I hope you're right, Rosaleen. I hope you're right. You're lucky. If anything happens to Joe, you've got Laura.'

They drew apart when Amy, after a tap on the door, entered the room.

'Oh, I'm so sorry... I didn't know you'd company. I'll come back later.'

Seeing Annie's tear-streaked face, her voice trailed off in embarrassment and she made to back out again but Laura wriggled from Annie's arms, slid down and ran to Amy, tugging her skirt for attention.

'You're all right, Amy,' Rosaleen assured her kindly. 'Come on in. I was just going to make Annie a wee cup of tea. Do you fancy one?'

Amy's eyes searched both their faces and when Annie said graciously, 'Sit down, Amy. I'm just feeling sorry for meself, it's nice to see you,' she accepted the offer of a cup of tea.

'Well, if you're sure. A cup of tea would be lovely, thank you.'

They talked and laughed for a couple of hours, and when Annie left, at the door she confided to Rosaleen.

'Sean might be home for a couple of days. His ship's in port in England, for repairs and he's going to try to get over for a while. Who knows? I might get pregnant yet. Here ...' she extracted a small packet from her pocket and thrust it into Rosaleen's hand '... a wee present for you.'

'What is it?' Rosaleen asked, feeling the parcel with inquisitive fingers.

'A couple of pairs of silk stockings. With seams!'

'Oh, really?'

'Really,' Annie said smugly. 'And they really are pure silk. Save them 'til Joe comes home and give him a treat.' Her head tilted back and her brows rose. 'What's this they say about an ill wind?' she jested. Then, observing the worried look on Rosaleen's face and guessing the reason for it, she bawled, 'Oh, for heaven's sake, Rosaleen ... I didn't do anything wrong to get them. You can take them with a clear conscience, so you can!'

Rosaleen grimaced, guiltily. 'I'm sorry, Annie. Thanks very much.'

Appeased, Annie grinned at her. 'You're welcome. And there's more where they came from, so keep your fingers crossed that I see that particular sailor again.' She backed away from the door. 'See you soon.'

'Don't wait so long next time,' Rosaleen warned her.

Grinning wickedly, Annie retorted, 'Now I'll not know whether you want to see me or are hoping for more stockings.'

'Oh, you! See you soon!' And with a flap of her hand, Rosaleen waved her on her way.

Sean did manage to get three days' leave but this time Rosaleen only saw him in passing; a hello and goodbye, as it were. When he returned to sea, Annie counted the days, jubilant when her period was late, inconsolable when it arrived.

Christmas came and went practically unnoticed except for the religious ceremonies, more profound and beautiful than ever because of the war. The priests said that was how it should be, and they were right of course. Still, it would have been nice to have been able to splash out a bit, but rationing and shortage of clothes and sweet coupons put paid to that.

Early in 1941 the sirens were going off more regularly; still false alarms as the planes continued to blitz England and returned to base without approaching Ireland at all, but nevertheless disrupting lives and causing worry.

When Billy, accompanied by May, visited her and urged her to seek refuge out in the country, Rosaleen was tempted. The bombings on the west coast of England were too close for peace of mind and she felt guilty leaving Laura with Amy and going off to work every afternoon. Felt that she should be taking Laura to apparent safety, especially now Joe's money was getting through.

So when Billy pleaded, 'Think of Laura, Rosaleen,' she was tempted, although she had to laugh at his reasoning.

Realising the trend of her thoughts, Billy reddened, and giving a shamed laugh, confessed: 'I suppose you're thinking I'm only worried about Laura because May won't go away without you? And in a way you're right. I *am* worried about May and Ian ... but I really do believe that you should take Laura away too.'

She smiled kindly at him. 'I know how you feel, Billy.' She turned to May. 'But suppose we're sent to different parts of the country?'

'That's what I said to him.' May sniffed and tossed her head defiantly. She had no intention of going anywhere without Rosaleen, danger or no danger. 'I said you can't pick and choose. I told him you've to go wherever they send you.'

'Tell you what, I'll have a word with me da. He might be able to fix something up for us. He'll certainly be glad of the chance. He's at me every week to take Laura away.' She looked at Billy. 'So will you leave it in my hands? I'll see what can be done and I'll get in touch with you.'

Happy to have set things in motion, Billy agreed to leave it in her hands, warning her not to delay too long.

Glad that Rosaleen was at last consenting to be evacuated, Tommy Magee did all in his power to find them accommodation together. It was during lent, three weeks before Easter, that he at last succeeded. When he called in to tell Rosaleen of his success, she was far from pleased.

'It's too near Easter, Da!' she exclaimed. 'Can we wait 'til after it?'

'No, ye can't wait. Look, I've knocked me arse out of joint getting you and May on the same farm, so you'd better not let me down.'

'A farm?' Rosaleen interrupted him, her face alarmed. 'A farm? We don't want a farm. I thought we'd be in some wee town or village.'

At these words Tommy blew his top.

'Now you look here, madam, you're goin', like it or not. You're goin'. You're not goin' to make a fool out of me. There's no bloody vacancies left in wee towns or villages. Do ye think that they were just waitin' for you to make up your mind to go? Eh? Do ye?'

His anger startled Rosaleen; in all her life she had only seen him give vent to it on a couple of occasions, and with just cause. Now she found herself meekly agreeing to get in touch with May.

After that, once Billy heard, there was no turning back and Saturday found them in Great Victoria Street Station, waiting for the train that was to take them to Dungannon, in County Tyrone.

Rosaleen hugged her father tightly, glad that her mother and Annie had consented to say their goodbyes at home; this was heartbreaking.

'You'll come for me if I hate it, won't you, Da?' she asked anxiously.

'Of course I will love ... ye know I will. But now give yourself a chance to get used to it, won't ye?'

She nodded and pushed him away. 'Go on ... go on home before I change me mind,' she cried, thinking that perhaps it was not such a good idea leaving Belfast.

With a brief glance inside the coach at the closely entwined figures of Billy and May, her father rolled his eyes and pursed his lips.

'I'll wait outside for Billy. Goodbye, love.'

One more hug and kiss for his beloved grandchild, who was taking everything in, wide-eyed, and he left the platform.

Rosaleen chatted and played with Laura and hovered in front of the door to the carriage, preventing other people from entering, giving May and Billy a few precious extra minutes alone. She tried to keep her eyes away from them but did not succeed, envying them their closeness. How wonderful, after two years of marriage still to desire each other with such intensity. May did not know how lucky she was.

When at last the train roared into life, and its great frame shuddered and puffed, Billy pushed May away from him, patted his young son on the head, and hugging Rosaleen, whispered, 'Look after her for me.' He rushed from the train, cheeks wet with tears.

Hanging from the carriage, May watched him out of sight and

then wiped the tears from her own cheeks before lifting Ian from the seat. Hugging the child tight, she sat down on the seat facing Rosaleen, at the window. Glad that they had a compartment to themselves and could talk freely, she said wryly, 'I'm sure you think I'm a fool, Rosaleen. You'd think I was going to war instead of safety.' She gave an embarrassed laugh. 'It's just not being able to finish what we started that frustrates me.' She wrinkled her nose. 'You know what I mean.'

Oh yes, Rosaleen knew exactly what she meant. She knew all about the frustration of starting what couldn't be finished. Now she just nodded her head in agreement. How she envied May; to be loved like that must be heaven.

Observing the sad droop of her mouth, May reached across and squeezed her hand sympathetically.

'It must be awful for you ... Joe away fighting. You must miss him something awful, and here's me, rambling on about Billy.'

Embarrassed, Rosaleen nodded her head again. She did miss Joe; read and re-read his letters, longed for the comfort of his presence about the house, but she did not miss him in the way that May meant.

At Dungannon they were met at the station by a tall, thin, young man in a small, open-backed lorry. Into the back of this, the surly owner loaded their cases, prams and gas masks. Then, barely glancing at them, he hoisted Rosaleen and Laura, followed by May and Ian, up into the cabin. The nearest he came to an apology for the tight squeeze was a muttered, 'It won't be for long. Just fifteen minutes,' as he swung up in beside Rosaleen.

The journey was conducted in silence, and after thirty minutes Rosaleen was just about to ask sarcastically if time stretched longer in the country when the lorry turned off the road and bounced and trundled up a rutted track and around the back of a low, sprawling, one-storeyed building. The big, sturdy, oak door was pulled open immediately and a small, plump woman bustled out. Reaching up with great difficulty, she wrenched open the door of the lorry and assisted May to the ground, at the same time introducing herself.

'Hello, hello ... I'm Mrs Magill, Maggie ... call me Maggie. An' you must be ...?' Her eyes noted the young child in May's arms and she finished, 'Mrs Mercer. I'm pleased to meet ye. You too, missus,' she shouted up at Rosaleen, and turning to the young man, exclaimed testily, 'Well, don't just stand there, Vince. Help her down.'

Reaching up, the man lifted Rosaleen bodily from the cabin and set her on her feet. When he lifted Laura down and placed her in her mother's arms, Rosaleen thanked him.

He shot her a swift glance. Only then did Vince Magill realise that Rosaleen was attractive, very attractive indeed.

Head back, he looked down the length of his long thin nose and examined her face. Noted the bright pale gold hair escaping from the headsquare that covered it, and interest kindled in his eyes, bringing a blush to her cheeks. Then he startled her by smiling, something she had not thought him capable of, and the smile changed his face completely. It exposed even white teeth against the dark, rugged tan of his skin, and made her aware of bright blue, mocking eyes. It was with relief that she turned at his mother's direction and followed her as she led the way into the house and through a big, spotlessly clean kitchen. Rosaleen was pleased to note this: the big wooden table was scrubbed white, and the long range that ran the length of one wall was well black-leaded, no mean feat, as Rosaleen well knew. It took her hours to keep her own small kitchenette grate in apple-pie order. A quick glance around also showed copperware gleaming on the wall above the range, a well-scrubbed redstone floor, a big brown jawbox in the corner, and brasses on the wide stone hearth, shining in the firelight.

After showing May into a room, Mrs Magill led the way to the front of the house, and stopping outside a door, explained, 'I've put you in the parlour, Mrs Smith. I only had one spare room but when we heard you an' your friend wanted t'be t'gether, I offered t'put a bed in the parlour. I think you'll find it comfortable.' With these words, she opened the door and ushered Rosaleen in. 'Vince, that's me son, will bring in the pram and yer gas masks, and then he'll fetch ye some hot water, so that ye can refresh yerself and the chile b'fore tea. I've made the tea early 'cause I'm sure you're hungry. The laverty's at the bottom of the yard, so it is.'

Rosaleen stood and took stock before she answered her. It was an attractive room, with a deep bay window that looked out over open countryside. The bed was double, with a bright, clean, patchwork quilt. She noted that there was no sign of a cot.

'Thank you very much, Mrs ...'

'Don't be formal ... please call me Maggie. An' I know that you're Mrs Smith.'

Rosaleen acknowledged the introduction with an inclination of her head.

'I think I shall be comfortable here, thank you.'

When the door closed on her, Rosaleen pulled back the bedclothes and felt the mattress. It was dry; no sign of dampness, and the bedclothes were freshly laundered. Perhaps it wouldn't be too bad staying here after all. Maybe it would be just like a holiday.

'I trust it meets with your approval?'

Rosaleen swung around, embarrassed colour staining her cheeks. She had not heard Vince enter the room.

'And I trust that in future you knock on the door before you enter my room,' she retorted angrily.

'I did knock ... but you were too preoccupied to hear me.'

He accompanied the words with a derisive smile, and wheeled the pram into the corner. Rosaleen longed to call him a liar, but bit on her tongue. She did not want to antagonise anyone, not when she was going to have to live here. He swung the gas masks in her direction and with a deft movement she caught them.

'Ye might be interested to know that we were worried about you too,' he informed her. 'We've been hearing all kind of reports about very dirty refugees. Ye know, lousy heads an' all.' His eyes took stock of the soft shining cloud of hair, now released from its headsquare, and her clean, tidy appearance. 'But you look clean enough.'

Before Rosaleen could think of a suitable reply to his accusations – which she knew to be true, from reports she had read in the *Irish News* – he added, 'I'll fetch ye some hot water now, but this is no hotel. In future you'll fetch your own. And tea will be ready in fifteen minutes.'

Another derisive glance was thrown her way, and then, lifting a big jug from a basin on the dresser, he left the room. While she waited for him to return with the water, Rosaleen decided to find the toilet. Laura was starting to squirm, any minute now she would be whimpering. 'Wee wee, Mammy,' and as she usually left it to the last moment to inform Rosaleen, it would be as well to find out just where it was.

Taking Laura by the hand, she made her way out to the back of the farm, bumping into May, in like mind.

'Well ... what's your room like?' she asked.

'Not bad. Not bad at all. Will you be all right in the parlour?'

'It seems comfortable, but there's no lock on the door.' Rosaleen eyed May anxiously. 'Perhaps it'll be all right here. Eh? What do you think?' she asked, seeking reassurance.

'I hope so.' May snorted. 'Huh ... I've often heard tell of the arsehole of nowhere, and now I know where it is.' She smiled wryly at Rosaleen's outraged expression. 'I'm sorry to be so crude, but you have to admit I'm right. How on earth will we pass the time?'

'At least the children will be safe,' Rosaleen said consolingly, but as they approached the toilet, her nose wrinkled in distaste. For one horrible moment, she thought it was a dry toilet. Her eyes met May's in distress.

'It's all right. That's the piggery you smell, so it is. On a farm like this one, they're bound to be civilised enough to have toilets that flush,' May assured her, and a relieved Rosaleen was glad to discover that she was right.

The toilet was clean, with whitewashed walls and a well-scrubbed wooden seat, and on the wall, hanging from a nail, were neatly cut squares of newspaper threaded on a piece of thick string. This brought a smile to her lips; not so long ago, that had been a fixture on her parents' toilet. Back when money was scarce, before she and Annie had started work and added to the family budget. This was something she could tolerate. The smile broadened as she imagined Laura's reaction when she had to use the newspaper squares; she was a fussy young madam.

Tea was an uncomfortable meal. Rosaleen was dismayed to find that what she had assumed was butter was instead margarine; she had lavished it on the scones and home-made bread before her discovery. She thought she would choke trying to force it down her throat. She sensed May's amusement at her predicament and smiled grimly at her. May smiled demurely back. Margarine was all right when you were used to it, and May never ate anything else. Halfway through the meal another big, surly man entered the room. Built like a bull, he had a thatch of bright red hair and bushy eyebrows that curled upwards, giving him a demonic look. Rosaleen was not surprised when Laura, without removing her eyes from the man, left her chair and stretched her arms up to her mother to be lifted, aware that if she had met him herself in the dark, she also would be frightened. When Mrs Magill introduced him as her husband, Rosaleen and May greeted him politely, but he just acknowledged them with a grunt and Rosaleen felt her temper rise. How were they going to manage to live with these surly people? You would think that they were taking in refugees out of the goodness of their hearts, instead of receiving a tidy sum from the ministry for their trouble. Well, she would see that she and Laura got their money's worth, Rosaleen vowed. Tomorrow she would ask for butter; she had never eaten magarine in her life before and she did not intend to start now. She was also very much aware that Vince watched her covertly and this dismayed her. Life would be bad enough here without any other complications and she determined to keep him at arms' length.

After tea they decided to go for a walk while there was still daylight. Both children had slept fitfully during the day and on the journey down, and were now wide awake. So deciding the country air would help them to sleep, they set off down the lane, pushing their prams in the direction of Dungannon. A lane that Mrs Magill assured them would cut their journey in half. They walked quickly, hoping to make it to town and back before dusk; they wanted to get their bearings and see what treats the future had in store for them. An hour later they arrived on the outskirts of Dungannon and pushed the prams with arms that ached up a long narrow street, arriving at last in the heart of the town. Bigger than they had anticipated, Dungannon was prosperous-looking and they stood in the great market square and looked around them with interest. It was now late afternoon and most of the shops were closing but Rosaleen noted that the Belfast Bank and Post Office were up in the right-hand corner, beside the Police Barracks. She pointed these out to May, knowing that they would be needing to draw money during their stay in Dungannon.

'Well, what do you think?' she asked.

'Looks all right… bigger than I thought it would be. Pity all the shops are closing, but we can come back in on Monday and browse around.'

Failing light and rising winds decided them to return to the farm but the size of the town had raised their spirits and they were in a happier frame of mind as they retraced their steps.

Mrs Magill met them in the hall. 'You're welcome to sit in the kitchen with me and Vince t'night, if ye feel like it. We listen to the radio.'

Before May could open her mouth, Rosaleen answered for them both.

'Thank you very much, but we've very tired … and Mrs Magill? Since there is no cot for Laura, I wonder if I could have a rubber sheet? She rarely wets the bed, but her routine has been upset today and I'd prefer to be safe than sorry.'

Immediately, Mrs Magill was all apologies. 'Oh, that was a mistake, so it was. Not on our part, mind ye. Vince has already put a cot up in the parlour, Mrs Smith. We just didn't realise that your child was so young. We were told a four-year-old would be comin'. Obviously there has been some mix up. An', remember, you're welcome in the kitchen any night. There's not much to do about here, once the light goes … except tomorrow night. Every Sunday night there's a dance in the town. I'm sure Vince would be glad to give you a lift in, he goes every week.'

This time May forestalled Rosaleen. 'That would be very nice, thank you, Mrs … Maggie.'

When Rosaleen had settled Laura for the night, she made her way down the hall to the back of the house, to where May's room was situated. To her surprise Ian was soundly asleep in his cot but of May there was no sight. Puzzled, she slowly entered the kitchen.

'Oh, so you've changed yer mind, have ye?' Mrs Magill greeted her. 'Come over here and sit down near the fire.' She reached across and poked the turf in the grate, sending a warm welcoming glow around the room. 'It's quite chilly t'night. Come on, come over to the fireside.'

Only when she saw May up to her elbows in suds at the big brown jawbox did Rosaleen realise that she would have nappies to wash out each night.

'Were you looking for me, Rosaleen?' May asked. 'I'm almost finished. Is there anything you want me to rinse out for you while I'm at it?'

'I'll do me own, thank you, May.' She turned to Mrs Magill and asked politely, 'Is that all right, Mrs Magill?'

'Of course! Of course! We've always plenty of hot water, and don't be so formal... call me Maggie.'

'Thank you, Maggie. I haven't much ... just a few wee things ... I'll fetch them.'

They did stay in the kitchen after all, bringing Mrs Magill up to date on things in Belfast and discovering that twice a week, Tuesdays and Saturdays, a bus passed close to the farm, should they want to go into Dungannon. At eleven o'clock, after a cup of hot cocoa, they retired for the night. A relieved Rosaleen was glad that Vince had not put in an appearance.

Awakening early next morning, she rose and thrust the curtains wide open, raising the blackout blinds. Back home in Belfast, she had often wondered what it would be like to awaken to a beautiful view, to see the sun rise and set. Now she would find out. To her dismay, everything was shrouded in mist. All she could see was the hedge that surrounded the house and barns. Everything else was grey and dreary. Disappointed, she closed the curtains again, remembering that she would be in full view as she washed herself down.

At breakfast, when she asked if she could have butter for her toast, Mrs Magill informed her that although they made butter, it was all for the market and if she wanted any she would have to pay extra for it. Annoyed, Rosaleen agreed to do so. She was more annoyed still when she discovered that if she wanted one of the big brown eggs that were abundant for Laura each morning, this would also have to be paid for.

As she spoon-fed a soft-boiled egg to Laura, she asked, 'How far is it to the Catholic church?'

'Ah… I was wonderin' about that. Did ye not notice it in town yesterday? But never worry, Vince goes t'church every Sunday. Not the Catholic church, mind, the Church of Ireland, but he'll give ye a lift in, so he will. You can leave the bairns with me, if ye like.'

'Why, that's very kind of you, Maggie,' May gushed, seeing a refusal hover on Rosaleen's lips. 'What time have we to be ready for?'

'Half-past ten.'

A glance at the clock made May cry, 'Oh … then we'd better get a move on, hadn't we? Come on, Rosaleen, come on.'

She gathered Ian up in her arms, leaving Rosaleen to shovel the last spoonful of egg into Laura's mouth and follow suit. Entering May's room, Rosaleen rounded on her.

'You're not going to leave Ian with her?'

'Why not?' May asked, reasonably.

'We didn't come here to palm the kids off on to someone else. That's why! We'll take them with us.'

'Look, Rosaleen, I'm going to Mass to please you … remember, I don't go to church any more. So if you want me to stay at home and look after the kids, that's all right with me.'

'Of course I want you to come to Mass, but…'

'But, nothing,' May interrupted her. 'The church will probably be tiny, and the kids won't like it, so they'll probably play up and cause everyone to look at us. We don't want that, do we?' When Rosaleen's head swung slowly from side to side, May added, 'We'll stick out like a sore thumb as it is, so let's be grateful to Maggie for offering to mind them. Not everyone would offer, you know.' And a disgruntled Rosaleen had to agree with her.

May was wrong: the church was big, old and beautiful, and after Mass they took a walk along the market square, window-shopping. The shops contained the usual regulation coats and dresses, but there were some other shops displaying the latest fashion and Rosaleen nudged May with delight. They beamed at each other, thinking of the hours of pleasure they would spend in these shops, a bit like browsing around Smithfield Market, only on a much smaller scale. On the lower corner of the square they saw a poster stating that tonight the local band would provide music for dancing. One look at the hall and Rosaleen sneered, 'You won't find me going to any dances there.'

Tight-lipped, May retorted, 'Well then, perhaps you'll look after Ian for me, 'cause if I get the chance I'll go.'

'You'd go to the dance?' Rosaleen turned a horrified look on her.

With an exaggerated sigh, May exlaimed: 'Honestly, Rosaleen, you astound me! You sound as if you were about fifty, instead of twenty-four. I didn't think you were such a stick-in-the-mud. I, for one, will be glad to get to the dance. Do you realise that there's nothing else to do in this Godforsaken hole?'

Hurt at May's attitude, Rosaleen replied huffily, 'We didn't come here to enjoy ourselves. We came to protect our children, so we did.' Her look was reproachful. 'I don't understand you, May. I thought you loved Billy.'

'What on earth has my love for Billy got to do with going to a dance? Eh? Come on ... tell me. I'm all ears.' And then the absurdity of their quarrel struck May, and slipping her arm through Rosaleen's, she apologised. 'Look, I'm sorry. You're right, of course. We should be respectable, staid, married women. We'll just sit in every night and talk to Maggie,' she said appeasingly. 'All right?'

Her apology only served to make Rosaleen feel guilty, just as May had known it would, and Rosaleen found herself compromising.

'Look ... if Maggie will keep an eye on the kids, let's try the dance tonight. It will probably be awful and we won't want to go back, all right?'

And a relieved May agreed with her, happy to have won her over.

Maggie good-naturedly did consent to keep an eye on the children, and it was with trepidation that, once Laura was settled, Rosaleen left her bedroom and entered the kitchen. Not realising that there might be a bit of a social life, she had just brought a selection of skirts and jumpers with her, and now she wore a pale green skirt and a cream twinset. She was dismayed to see that May had come prepared, and looked lovely in a dress of floral colours, with a full flowing skirt, a white cardigan draped around her shoulders.

'You both look lovely, so ye do. Now away ye go!' Maggie urged. 'Go on, Vince is waitin' outside for ye, an' ye better hurry up. He's very impatient, so he is.'

'Laura's asleep, but she's a bit restless … you will listen for her, won't you?' Rosaleen asked anxiously.

'Never ye worry. I've reared six of me own.' Maggie laughed at the surprised reaction these words provoked. 'Yes, six, and they're all married except Vince. So I know how to take care of babies.'

Once outside, Rosaleen motioned May up into the cabin of the lorry first, then climbed in beside her, receiving a mocking smile from Vince. May gave her a puzzled look but remained silent, and only when they were in the cloakroom of the dance hall did she query it.

'Have you anything against Vince, Rosaleen? He hasn't been too handy … ye know what I mean?'

At this, Rosaleen drew back and laughed aloud. 'No, of course he hasn't. Do you think I'd hold me tongue if he had?'

'Perhaps.' At Rosaleen's surprised look, May sighed and added, 'I keep forgetting you led a sheltered life. If you knew the things I've had to pretend never happened, just to keep the peace, you'd swoon away.'

'Ah, May …' There was a wealth of sadness in Rosaleen's voice and May laughed.

'Oh, it hasn't done any lasting damage, so it hasn't,' she declared. 'I mean, it wasn't anything serious … you know what I mean.' When Rosaleen still looked concerned, May became flustered and with a final look at her reflection, tossed her ash-blonde hair and said, 'Come on … let's go in and see what the local talent is like.'

In spite of herself, Rosaleen enjoyed the dance. The last time she had danced had been at her own wedding reception. The sound of the music set her feet tapping and soon she was twirling around the big wooden floor, to quick-steps and slow foxtrots, and even enjoyed the Gay Gordons, a dance she usually avoided.

It was after the Gay Gordons, as they stood flushed and breathless, that Vince approached them and offered to buy them a drink. As they waited for him to return, May confided in Rosaleen.

'I often wondered what it would be like to be lifted in every dance, and now I know. It's heaven.' She hugged herself, then gazed beseechingly at Rosaleen. 'You will come back next week, won't you, Rosaleen?'

'Of course. It will be the highlight of our week by the looks of it… and Joe and Billy won't mind if we enjoy ourselves, sure they won't?'

'No! Of course they won't mind. For heaven's sake, relax, Rosaleen. Anyone would think it was a sin to dance,' May admonished her, then leant forward confidentially. 'Did you notice the big horsey girl that Vince dances most with?' When Rosaleen nodded, May whispered, 'Well, that's his future wife.'

'Really?' Surprise made Rosaleen's voice shrill, and she covered her mouth with her hand to try to contain her astonishment. 'Really?'

'Yes, really.' They fell against each other and giggled at the idea. 'So you needn't worry about not having a lock on your door. He's "promised", and by the look of yon one, he'll be afraid to look sideways at anyone else.'

When Vince returned with two orange juices, he was accompanied by the big horsey girl whom he introduced to them as Mavis Cartwright. Avoiding each other's eyes, Rosaleen and May politely shook hands with her. Still afraid to look at each other, for fear a single glance would make them start to giggle, they made inane conversation and were relieved when the music started up again. Then, to Rosaleen's amazement, Vince turned to her.

'May I have this dance, please?'

Flustered, she looked at May for guidance but, relieving her of her glass, May gazed somewhere above her head, looking as if butter would not melt in her mouth.

A glance at Mavis showed tight-lipped disapproval, and Rosaleen was just about to refuse to dance with him when Vince put his arm around her waist and drew her on to the dance floor.

Once out of earshot, she looked up at him. 'Won't your friend be angry?'

'Who cares?' His shoulders lifted in a shrug of indifference and his narrowed eyes examined her face. 'Every time I tried to dance with you I was beaten to it, so I took the opportunity when it was offered.'

'Are you engaged to Mavis?'

He nodded and his face closed up and Rosaleen knew he was

warning her not to trespass.

Most of the farm helpers and country lads plodded around the floor, but Rosaleen had to admit that Vince had class. His steps were light and his long strides covered the floor expertly. She gave herself up to the joy of dancing with a good partner.

They danced in silence and when the music trailed off, Vince looked down at her flushed, happy face and whispered, 'I thoroughly enjoyed that.' And Rosaleen could only nod her head in agreement, knowing that he was aware that she had enjoyed it also.

'Will you save me the last dance?' he asked softly.

Uneasy again, Rosaleen countered, 'No ... I don't think that would be right. Won't Mavis object?'

'No. Mavis and I have an agreement. She won't object.'

Against her better judgement, Rosaleen nodded her consent. 'All right.'

Somehow or other, she thought that Vince meant that Mavis did not dare to object and she felt sorry for her.

After the last dance Rosaleen had to admit to herself that the priests really did know what they were talking about when they preached from the pulpit about close dancing. An uneasy bond had been formed between Vince and herself, a bond that would never have shown itself had they not danced, and Rosaleen was apprehensive and quiet on the drive home.

Not so May; she eyed Vince and asked demurely, 'Are you and Mavis engaged?'

He nodded, and to Rosaleen's surprise volunteered information.

'She's an only child and will inherit the farm adjoining ours. It should be a good match.'

And that explained everything. Obviously, Mavis wanted Vince and Vince wanted the farm, and there would probably be a lot of strings attached ... like him doing as he pleased when it suited him. Poor Mavis. It seemed like she would get the thin edge of the wedge.

When they arrived at the farm, Rosaleen was relieved when May whispered, 'Are you going down to the loo?'

She nodded, and bidding Vince goodnight, they made their way down the yard. She was glad of May's company, had been afraid of meeting Vince in the dark, feeling that somehow she had given him the wrong impression by enjoying her dances with him. And in spite of what May had said, she was more worried than ever that her door did not have a lock. Much more worried. She had seen the desire in his eyes.

Once back in her room, Rosaleen looked around for some means of securing her door. Something that would make a noise and awaken her should anyone try it during the night. The only chair in the room was too low and the back did not reach the door handle, so she abandoned that. At her wit's end, she at last tied a belt to the door handle and then secured it to the pram. Next she piled the pram high with objects and at last crept into bed.

Should Vince try to enter her room during the night, she should be forewarned, and consoled by this thought she drifted off to sleep.

The clatter that brought her from the bed in confusion and panic, to stand shivering on the cold oil cloth, resounded through the quiet household. The room was pitch black because the dark blinds and heavy curtains that prevented any light from showing outside also prevented natural light from entering the room. She heard a muffled oath outside the door, then voices.

'What on earth's wrong, Vince?'

She heard Mrs Magill approach her door and Vince answer her.

'I don't know, Ma. I heard this awful noise … I think it came from Mrs Smith's room.'

Quietly, Rosaleen removed the belt from the doorknob and opened the door slightly.

'I'm sorry,' she apologised. 'I'm afraid I had a nightmare and accidentally knocked over the pram.'

'Oh? The pram?'

Rosaleen sensed Mrs Magill's doubt and added appeasingly, 'I really am sorry to have disturbed you.'

'Rosaleen … are you all right?'

Glad to hear May's voice, Rosaleen opened the door wide and entered the hall, forgetting that she was in her nightdress until Vince's eyes scanned her body, making her feel naked. Crossing her arms over her chest, she sank her chin on to them and answered May.

'I had one of my nightmares, you know how it is? I forgot where I was, and in the dark knocked the pram over. I'm sorry to have awakened everybody.'

May frowned. She had not been aware that Rosaleen suffered from nightmares ... then she saw the chagrin on Vince's face and the penny dropped.

Why, the cheeky bugger! Giving him a look of venom, she backed Rosaleen up. 'Oh, you poor dear. Will I stay with you the rest of the night?' The look she bestowed on Vince was derisive. 'Just in case your nightmare returns?'

'No, no, I'll be all right now. You go back to Ian. Goodnight, everybody.'

With these words, Rosaleen entered her room and closed the door, glad that Laura had slept through all the noise. She did not think that Vince would risk trying her door again but to be on the safe side, she secured the door as before and fell into a sound sleep the minute her head hit the pillow.

The next morning it rained, and on Tuesday they awakened to more rain. Bored, they decided to brave the elements and catch the bus into town. And when Mrs Magill offered to mind the children, Rosaleen did not hesitate to take her up on her offer, having come to the conclusion that she was fond of children. She was also aware that farmer's wife though she may be, Mrs Magill had time on her hands. It was the woman and two young girls who came to 'do' every day who scrubbed and polished and black-leaded, while the men attended to all the outside work, leaving Mrs Magill free to attend to the cooking.

In Dungannon, they spent some hours browsing in the small shops full of old second-hand stuff, Rosaleen bought some ornaments, which she was convinced would grow in value, and May bought a shawl made with silk threads and shot with all the colours of the rainbow. Pleased with their purchases, they had tea and scones in a small cafe and returned to the farm in a more settled frame of mind.

On Wednesday they awoke to more rain and were glad to break the monotony by lending a helping hand in the dairy.

They churned butter and helped to make cheese and then assisted

Mrs Magill in baking bread. Then donning Wellingtons, amidst squeals of laughter, they collected the free range eggs, letting a delighted, giggling Laura help them. The week passed slowly, but at last Sunday dawned, bright and dry, and Rosaleen had her first experience of watching the sun rise. When she opened the curtains, she knelt on the window seat and gazed in awe at the scene before her. A huge red ball of flame slowly rose and swelled, its rays colouring everything it touched, setting the sky on fire and awakening birds and wildlife as it spread its glow. As she gazed in wonder, her breath caught in her throat at the beauty of it, and her belief in God was strengthened. It was an experience she knew she would never forget.

As before Vince, who had been gone before they entered the kitchen for breakfast each morning, and had been absent each night, gave them a lift into church. On the way home, he casually asked, 'Will ye be wantin' a lift into the dance t'night?'

May remained silent; it was up to Rosaleen, it was she Vince fancied. Rosaleen was in a dilemma. All week she had silently vowed that she would not dance with Vince again. It was too dangerous! However, she knew that May longed to go to the dance, and to be truthful, so did she. It would ease the boredom. So she found herself nodding her head.

'Yes, thank you.'

And May's happy smile was her reward.

As she prepared for the dance that evening, Rosaleen found herself taking care with her make-up and brushing her freshly washed hair until it seemed to have a life of its own and sprang from her head, full of electricity. Becoming aware of her actions, knowing in her heart that she was making herself attractive so that Vince would admire her, she was aghast.

With a damp flannel she wiped the make-up from her face, leaving it clean and shining, but there was nothing she could do about her hair, it framed her face in a soft silver cloud, and none of her efforts to make it lie down were successful.

She chose her most dowdy sweater and skirt, a dark grey that did nothing for her, and entered the kitchen feeling virtuous; she had done her best. May gaped at her, her eyes roaming over Rosaleen's old skirt and jumper in amazement. Then she twigged on. Rosaleen was playing down her good looks. She would be afraid of feeling that she was encouraging Vince, afraid of being an occasion of sin to him. May had yet to meet anyone as scrupulous as Rosaleen; she simply let her conscience torture her.

May sighed and smiled wryly at her. Little did she know that she could never look plain. The drab grey of her sweater only emphasised the silver of her hair, and her skin did not really need make-up to enhance it, while the dark grey deepened the green of her eyes, making them dark and mysterious-looking. She simply glowed, and May could see by the look in Vince's eyes that he agreed with her.

The minute they entered the hall they were rushed for dances and as the night wore on and Vince ignored her, Rosaleen heaved a sigh of relief. He had learned his lesson; he was going to leave her alone.

She was wrong. Toward the end of the evening, Vince approached her and asked for a dance. She assured him that she had promised the next dance, but when the music started, his arm circled her waist and without a word she allowed herself to be led on to the dance floor.

Hadn't she been waiting all evening for this? And didn't Vince know it? They danced in silence, their bodies twisting and turning to the steps of the tango. She had heard the tango called the dance of seduction and she could well believe it true, as their bodies moved as one to its suggestive steps. When the dance was over, he drew her to one side.

'I want to talk to you.'

Her eyes sought May. She did not want her to be left standing alone, but May was talking to a partner, and resignedly Rosaleen sat down on the chair away from the crowds that Vince ushered her to. He sat beside her, one arm along the back of the chair, and she squirmed uneasily.

'Ye made a right fool of me last Sunday night, didn't ye?'

'You shouldn't have tried to enter my room,' she retorted angrily.

'You led me on. I thought ye wanted me t'come,' he growled.

'I did not!' she cried in dismay. 'You're a good dancer and I enjoy dancing with you, but that's all.'

'Come off it!' His voice and eyes mocked her. 'Hey! Where do ye think you're goin'?'

She had risen swiftly from the chair and was making her way down the hall. He caught up with her in three strides, just as the band started to play. Expertly, he swung her into the quickstep.

'All right, you win. We just dance.'

'Promise?'

'I promise ... Unless you decide otherwise.'

Her head reared back and she gave him a startled look. 'Don't bank on it.'

Vince eyed her from under lowered lids. He couldn't understand her. She wanted him. He had not lived all his life on a farm without learning the signs of arousal, and he was sure that she wanted him. It was in her eyes, in her awareness of him. The way she coloured when he eyed her. And what harm would it do? She was a married woman and you never missed a slice of a cut loaf. No one need ever know. Well, time would tell; he would try to wear her down. In fact ... he was confident that he could wear her down. He danced the last two dances with her and then informed her that he had arranged a lift back to the farm for her and May, as he was seeing Mavis home.

That night, as she lay unable to sleep, Rosaleen kept seeing the look in Vince's eyes when he had promised – unless she decided otherwise – and she was more confused than ever. He had sounded as if it was just a matter of time, and this frightened her. Why was her body reacting to Vince even though she didn't like him? Was she a bad woman? One part of her mind assured her that it was because she did not have a proper marriage, and she latched on to this belief. That must be the reason ... it must ... otherwise, she would make a first-class whore.

Once more Monday dawned dull and wet. March had been a miserable month – at least this past week in Dungannon had been awful. Hail, rain, winds, everything but snow. Was it only dry on Sundays in Dungannon? Rosaleen wondered as she made her way down the mucky yard to the toilet, a whinging Laura by the hand. The child hated it here, whinged all the time to go home, and Rosaleen did not blame her. How long were they doomed to stay? Would the war last much longer? Joe's letters always came in bunches and she had received three that morning, forwarded by her father.

He tried to sound happy and assured her he was well, but she sensed his loneliness and her heart ached for him. He admitted that there was no sign of the war ending in the foreseeable future and no hope of leave.

The week dragged past, with Rosaleen and May putting on a happy face when in the presence of each other, but secretly longing for home.

Vince had not put in an appearance since Sunday night, so on Thursday night, when the need to use the toilet drove Rosaleen out into the dark yard, he was far from her thoughts.

There was a moon, but it was obscured by clouds. By the faint light, Rosaleen retraced her steps back up the yard. A hand on her arm brought a squeal of terror from her lips but this was quickly stifled as another hand covered her mouth. She was lifted bodily into the barn and the door closed. For one horrible moment, in the darkness, she thought it was Mr Magill and panic set her heart thumping within her breast. Then, as her eyes became accustomed to the dark, she saw that it was Vince and breathed a sigh of relief.

She could handle him. He had promised.

To her dismay, she saw that he stood with his back against the door, blocking her escape.

'Just what do you think you're doing?' she asked, trying to appear calm.

'I think we should have a wee talk, Rosaleen. Rosaleen ... now that's a lovely name. It rolls off the tongue. Ros ... a... leen.'

His voice was caressing and slurred. Dismayed, she realised that he had been drinking. He moved slowly towards her. She backed away until she could go no further, and when her back was to the wall, he placed a hand on either side of her head and gazed down at her. She could smell the sweat of him and instead of filling her with distaste, to her dismay it just emphasised the maleness of him.

'Now, my teasin' Rosaleen, how's about a kiss. Mmmmmm … come on now, ye know ye want me. Ye know ye do.' One hand left the wall and as she stood unable to move, it trailed down her face. Surprised that he was receiving no opposition, he cradled the nape of her neck, and tilted her face up to his. Even in the dim light, she could see the hot passion in his eyes, and as his breath quickened, panic gripped her.

Thick with passion, his voice muttered her name over and over. As his face slowly bent toward hers, she came to life and jerked her head aside. His lips landed on her ear. To her amazement, this appeared to excite him.

'Ah! What have we here? Do ye like it rough? Eh? Do ye like it rough, me lovely Rosaleen?'

His pleasure at the idea was unmistakable. Terrified, she tried to break from his hold, but his arms bound her fast against him.

As he thrust his body at hers, probing, seeking, to her horror and dismay she felt excitement shiver through her and fill her loins, and she relaxed against him, her body craving fulfilment.

At his soft laugh of triumph, sanity returned. Only once before had she known and given into desire, and look what it had cost her. At this thought, anger and bitterness swept through her, lending strength, and her sudden surge to life caught him unawares. Remembering stories from long ago of how to defend oneself, her knee rose in the air and viciously landed where it hurt most, desperation making her aim accurate. Gasping for air, he doubled in two, and she broke free and leapt for the door. But she was not going to get away so easily. In pain though he was, he managed to grip her ankle and she crashed to the floor, rattling every bone in her body.

Aware that he was moving towards her, she ignored the pain that throbbed through her and on all fours scrabbled towards the door. Obviously still in pain, he managed to throw himself on top of her and his fingers were vicious on the soft flesh of her arms. Realising that if he regained his full strength, nothing would save her, she sank her teeth into his hand and bit as hard as she could; pleased to taste that she had drawn blood. With a howl, he relaxed his hold on her and before he could regain control, with a mighty thrust, she got to her knees again, throwing him off her back and to one side. Rolling away from him, she managed to get to her knees again. Then she was up and at the door, sobbing as she pulled it open and staggered outside.

His voice, full of venom, followed her. 'I'll get ye for this, ye damned wee temptress. You mark my words, I'll get ye.'

And not for one minute did she doubt him. She would have to get away from this farm. Belfast with all its dangers beckoned like heaven and she resolved to return there as soon as possible. In her mad scramble back up the yard in the dark, she fell, scraping her knee and the palms of her hands as she tried to save herself. Thankful to escape to her room unnoticed, the tears ran down her face as she removed her soiled, mucky skirt and jumper. She looked as though she had been through the wars. Her hands and knee were bleeding and bruises were already appearing on her upper arms. Why did she have to get into these predicaments?

She should have entered a convent, so she should. At least there she would have been free from this kind of temptation, because in her heart she knew that Vince was right. Her body had wanted him, and only the fact that her heart hadn't agreed had saved her.

Next morning, as she and May worked side by side making butter, she tried to form words to explain why she must leave the farm. May, suddenly gripping her hand and exclaiming at the raw scratches on her palm, gave her an opening.

'How on earth did you do that?'

Haltingly, Rosaleen recounted the events of the night before, bringing cries of pity and concern from May's lips.

When she had finished, her friend gasped. 'You actually kneed him?' At Rosaleen's nod, May cried in approval, 'Good for you! Good for you! I hope he can't use it for a week.'

These words brought a reluctant smile to Rosaleen's lips and her reply was heartfelt. 'So do I! But, May ... I can't stay here. To tell you the truth, I'm scared of him.'

'Of course you can't stay. Look, tomorrow morning we'll catch that bus into town and order a taxi ...'

'Wait, May!' Frantically, Rosaleen interrupted her. 'There's no need for you to come. Billy'll go daft if you arrive home.'

May smiled smugly. 'No, he won't. I can tell by his letters that he's missing me something awful, and only Ian is preventing him from asking me to come home.' She smiled shyly, making Rosaleen aware of just how much Billy had changed her life. 'I want to go home, Rosaleen. I just didn't like to say ... after all the bother your da went to, to get us fixed up.'

'Ah, May. We've both been suffering in silence.'

May grinned, a great beam of happiness. 'Looks like it. Listen, we'll pack our things tonight, go to town in the morning, find out the time of the train, and order a taxi to collect us in time to catch it. How does that sound?'

'Heaven.' Rosaleen's smile reflected the joy in May's. 'You've forgotten just one thing.'

May frowned, and thought deeply, 'What's that?' she asked, at last.

'We'll have to send wires to Billy and me da, so that they can meet us at the station.'

'Imagine me forgetting that. But once we get to Belfast, there'll be no holding us. We can walk home if necessary. And another thing ... you come for me if you need to go to the loo tonight. OK?'

'OK,' Rosaleen agreed gratefully.

The price of the taxi to the station took their breath away. Luckily, they had enquired first, and by promising a tight-lipped, angry Maggie to forward the money owed for butter and eggs, they managed the fare between them. Rosaleen felt sorry for Maggie, whom she had grown to like. She was bewildered, poor soul, saying that she had thought they were settling in nicely. But how can you tell a woman that you are afraid of her son?

The train arrived in Great Victoria Street Station at eleven o'clock, and tired and weary they stood on the platform, surrounded by their belongings as the crowds thinned out, until they were alone in the station.

'What do you think happened, May?'

May bit her lip and shook her head, a puzzled frown on her brow.

'They can't have received our telegrams.'

They had deliberately caught the last train because they had been warned that the telegrams would not be delivered until about six o'clock. Now here they were, stranded. They could have managed the tram fares, but the last tram was away.

'Well, it looks like we'll have to walk, Rosaleen.' May sighed. Somehow it didn't sound so inspiring as it had done when they had planned their return. 'Here ... gimme the cases, they can go on top of my pram – it's bigger. You tie the gas masks to the handle of yours, and let's get a move on. I only hope the sirens don't go off.'

The long climb up the Grosvenor Road seemed endless, but at last they were at the Falls Road junction. They had long ago stopped trying to cheer each other up, and started across the Falls Road in silence, knowing that the road still ahead of them was as long as the one they had just climbed. Then, miraculously it seemed, Tommy Magee was in front of them. Peering at them in the darkness, crying, 'What on earth are you two doing out at this time of night?' Then, eyes getting accustomed to the gloom, 'Good God! It's our Rosaleen.'

Next thing they knew, they were inside the pub at the corner of the Springfield Road, sipping cups of tea, after assuring the pyjama-clad landlord that they did not want anything stronger.

'Why on earth didn't you order a taxi, Rosaleen?'

'We had no money, Da. We're broke,' Rosaleen reproached him. She had already explained their predicament to him.

'Good God, do ye think we'd have turned you away from the door?'

May and Rosaleen looked at each other and started to laugh. It had never occurred to them to get a taxi and someone would pay at the other end. Wiping tears of mirth and relief from their faces, they shared a happy smile. They were home, and that was all that mattered.

Chapter 5

The relief and joy of being at home was short-lived. On Monday, the start of Holy Week, Rosaleen was preparing for bed when, shortly before midnight, the siren sounded. Rosaleen actually smiled to herself as she got Laura ready. It was great to be home, even with broken nights. Unruffled, she took her time: dressing the child in warm clothes, cushioning the pram with pillows, and filling a bottle with juice, before setting off to enter one of the new air-raid shelters. There was no great urgency. The planes never reached this far. It would be a false alarm as usual. After breathing a prayer for the poor people in England who were being blitzed, she debated whether or not to bring the gas masks with her. They were a nuisance to carry about, and the rattlers that would signify they might be needed had yet to sound. As she stood undecided she remembered the meeting she had attended in the Broadway Picture House when they had been shown how to use the masks. They had also been shown a newsreel portraying the effects of the mustard gas on humans, and recalling the horrific sights, she decided not to take any chances and tied them to the handle of the pram, just in case! It would be silly to take chances.

To her amazement, when she reached the corner, chatting away to her next-door neighbour, her father descended on her. Gripping her pram with one hand and her neighbour's with the other hand, he urged them down Oakman Street, away from the air-raid shelters, begging them to hurry. Quickening their step, Rosaleen and her bewildered neighbour obeyed him, wondering why he was so agitated.

They're comin', love,' he gasped, in answer to their unspoken question. 'They're comin'. Now! There was no bloody early warnin'. Listen! They're right above us.'

Another tortured breath escaped from his poor, weak lungs before he could continue, 'Can't ye hear them? They'll be after Mackie's.'

Only then did Rosaleen become aware of the drone of the planes which was getting louder every second. Her legs turned to jelly, causing her to stumble. Dear God, the Germans were coming … it was their turn to be bombed. Her father hauled her roughly upright and pulled her along, past dalliers, shouting for them to get a move on.

'Lift your feet! Lift your feet! Can't ye hear the planes?' he scolded. And to Rosaleen, 'Come on, love … come on – if they hit Mackie's the district will go up an' we'll all be goners.'

Never had Oakman Street seemed so long, but at last they left it and hurried along Beechmount Avenue towards Daisy Hill and open fields.

Once they were safely away from buildings, without wasting breath on words Tommy turned on his heel and headed back the way they had come, just as the first bomb fell. It was some distance away, in the direction of the docks, but they heard the great 'BOOM!', saw in the distance the sky redden from its glow.

'Da! Da, don't go back. Stay here,' Rosaleen beseeched him.

But he didn't pause, just gasped over his shoulder, 'I must go back. I'll be needed … if there are fires … in the parish.'

It was a bright moonlit night, and the fields were crowded, everyone coping in their own way with the fear that gripped them. Some seemed too stunned to do anything, just sat gazing in front of them, cringing closer to the ground at every shot, every blast. Some actually sang between bombs falling, causing others to laugh and jest that if they sang loud enough the planes would certainly go away, to escape the awful din. Someone else started the rosary and as others joined in, Rosaleen added her voice to theirs and prayed. She prayed that somehow or other the Germans would not see Mackie's, in spite of the clear moonlight. If they did, she would have no home to go back to. As her father had stated, the district would go up if Mackie's was bombed. She prayed that her mother and Annie were safely away from the houses, away in the fields further up the Springfield Road, and prayed for the brave men, like her father, who were putting out the flares that the Germans dropped to help to identify their chosen targets.

Their prayers were answered. It was a long night, with bombs and incendiary devices falling constantly, causing fires and doing God knows what other damage. Dawn was breaking when at last the all-clear sounded but, as everyone started the weary journey home from the parks and countryside, Mackie's still stood!

Although as raids went it was deemed a small one, it caused a lot of damage. On Tuesday morning Rosaleen heard on the radio that the fuselage factory attached to Harland and Wolff, the shipbuilders, had been completely demolished, and that the docks had also suffered severe damage. Fear gripped her bowels, sending her running to the bathroom every time she thought of Mackie's Foundry, just a short distance away, surrounded by houses; a huge bomb in itself, so easily detonated. The raid brought home to her how vulnerable Belfast was, and she regretted bringing Laura back from Dungannon. Prayed that if her baby was killed she would be taken also, because she would never be able to forgive herself, never!

How come her father, a mill worker, had been aware of the danger they were in, while the brains of the country had not? Or had they? Had they known and thought Belfast not important enough to worry about?

Some of the fear abated when the morning newspapers stated that the planes were just a half dozen strays that had lost their way while on a raid over Liverpool and Manchester on the west coast of England, and would probably not return.

However, her father disagreed with the newspapers. 'They'll be back ... you mark my words. Now they know how few defences we have, they'll be back,' he predicted.

'Huh! How do you know what kind of defences we have, and you working in the mill, Da!' Rosaleen ridiculed him.

'I'm an air-raid warden, ampt I? And I hear a lot of criticism of the government,' he retaliated. 'You mark my words! I know what I'm talkin' about and we've very few defences.'

'What do you mean, Da, few defences?' she asked fearfully.

'I mean the government has neglected to provide us with enough planes and machine guns to retaliate. We've some Hurricanes at Aldergrove and some anti-aircraft guns, and that's about it.'

And hearing this, Rosaleen was inclined to agree with her father that if the Germans were now aware of their vulnerability, they would return. The final casualty figure for that night was thirteen dead and eighty-one injured, twenty-three of them seriously, but the Falls Road had escaped without a scratch and everyone went about their business as usual.

The rest of Holy Week passed uneasily. Each night Rosaleen prepared for a hurried departure from the house should the dreaded sirens sound, which they did frequently, but, thankfully, they were all false alarms. Although enemy planes were heard, and sometimes seen high in the sky, no bombs were dropped and each morning she thanked God for a night free from terror.

All the Holy Week ceremonies were well attended; the crowds spilling out into the church yards at each Mass and each Way of the Cross, and the queues for confession hit an all-time record.

At Mass on Easter Sunday, Rosaleen noted that she was not the only one to have splashed out on new clothes, as she had for herself and Laura. Indeed, no. Clonard Monastery was full of women and children in new dresses and hats, determined to use some of their precious savings while they had the chance, and not to be outdone the men were sporting new jackets and, once outside, new caps. Not that there was anything really fashionable in the shops. Annie and she had travelled the length and breadth of Belfast before managing to buy two dresses. One was green, the other blue, but in style they were much alike, the regulations being that as little material as was reasonable must be used in all clothes, and nothing was to be wasted in fancy work or pockets. Being slim, they both suited the square-shouldered, belted-waist design; not like the plump girls who it did nothing for. The only concession given to femininity was the slightly flared skirt with pleat back and front.

Easter Monday morning brought a knock on Rosaleen's door and when she answered it, who should be standing on the doorstep but Billy Mercer looking very dapper in a smart sports jacket and grey flannel trousers. His dark hair was slicked down with Brylcreem, and he carried a holdall slung over one shoulder.

'Billy! This is a surpise.' Her eyes darted beyond him. 'Where's May?'

'She's down in Spinner Street visiting her mother.'

Her hands reached out and she drew him into the living room.

'Come in ... come in. It's good to see you.'

'I'm ashamed, Rosaleen.' He hung his head, eyed her from under dark brows and looked embarrassed. I'm afraid I'm using you, as usual. You'll be saying the only time ye see me is when I need something. I've an hour to waste before I meet May at the corner of the Springfield Road and she said you'd gimme a cuppa, to pass the time.' He raised an eyebrow inquiringly at her, and when she smiled and nodded, swung the holdall to the floor and added, 'In fact, I've been ordered to persuade you and Laura to accompany me down. We're going to Bellevue, to the zoo.'

'Is it safe to go so far from home, Billy? I mean ... well... after that raid on Tuesday?'

'Ye wouldn't think there'd been a raid!' he exclaimed. 'Why, the trams are packed, and there's crowds going into the railway station. There's an offer on "To Bangor and back for a bob", and it looks like it'll be a sell out. And you should see the queues outside the picture houses! Honestly, Rosaleen, it's hard to believe that we were bombed on Tuesday.'

'Me da says they'll be back. Do you think they'll come back, Billy?'

'To be truthful, Rosaleen, I don't know. Maybe they were just strays, like the papers say, and Hitler isn't going to bother about Ireland. But anyhow ... I can't see them bombing during daylight.

So come on, get yourself ready and come to the zoo with me and May. She'll be disappointed if I land down on me own. You wouldn't want her to be scrowling at me all afternoon, would ye now?'

'No, Billy, that would never do,' she assured him with a chuckle, and glad of the opportunity to get away for the day, she quickly changed Laura's clothes. By the time Billy had finished his fresh Hughes bap and mug of tea, she was dressed and ready for the road.

'What about eats, Billy?'

He pointed at the holdall, a wry smile on his face. 'May's enough in the bag to feed an army, Rosaleen. No need for you to bring any,' he assured her, with a wink and a nod.

First, Rosaleen called into Amy's house and informed her where she was going. Her father called regularly to check that she was all right and he would worry if no one knew where she was. Then, excitement mounting, she accompanied Billy down to meet May.

Rosaleen and May had not seen each other since their arrival home from Dungannon and once on the upper deck of the tram they chatted and laughed, bringing each other up to date with gossip, all the way to Bellevue, watched by an amused Billy.

The Cave Hill, on the outskirts of Belfast, was the favourite spot at Easter for trundling eggs, and right on the side of the hill was Bellevue Zoo. It looked down over Belfast Lough and today, in spite of the fear of air-raids, it was packed. They joined the crowds that thronged the animal pens and caves, delighting in the joy and happiness of the two excited children. It was after their tour of the zoo, as they made their way along the Cave Hill to watch older children trundle their brightly painted eggs, as was the custom, and to eat the picnic lunch May had packed, that the mournful sound of the sirens filled the air.

The crowds scattered in all directions and Billy, who had often climbed the Cave Hill as a boy and remembered its terrain, quickly guided them some distance down the hill into a cave where they sheltered. To their amazement, although the planes were high they could clearly see them. They made no effort to hide; it was as if the pilots knew that there was no danger and were thumbing their noses at them. It was awesome to see them, as well as hear their drone and some people, in spite of the danger, actually stood out in the open, shading their eyes and gazing up at them in wonder. Luckily, no shots were fired, no bombs dropped, and soon the planes were but specks in the distance. When the all-clear sounded the crowds carried on in their pursuit of pleasure.

From their picnic spot on the top of the Cave Hill they discovered that looking across Belfast Lough, they could see where the bombs had demolished part of Harland and Wolff on Tuesday, and the desolation of it put a damper on their spirits and fear in their hearts. Had they just been stray planes that came over on Tuesday?

What about the planes that were spotted during the week? They had been spotted a few times. Why had those planes flown over today ... in broad daylight? What was their game? Were they lulling the people of Belfast into a false sense of security? Would they attack when they were least expected? Questions ... questions that no one could answer.

After a day that was quite enjoyable in spite of the ever constant fear of an attack, they parted in town in good spirits. May and Billy to catch a tram up North Street on to the Shankill Road and Rosaleen to make her way around to Castle Street and from there, take a tram up the Falls Road. They vowed to keep in touch, come what may, and Rosaleen arrived home in a happy frame of mind. However, this did not last long. Her neighbours were agog with talk of the lunchtime alarm, and of course gossip had it that the Germans were sizing up Mackie's and would return that night. Alone in the house with Laura, having refused to go and stay at her mother's, it struck terror to the very heart of Rosaleen and she was apprehensive as she prepared for bed.

The planes did return later that night. In the early hours of Easter Tuesday morning to be exact, and the sirens wailed warning of their approach at about ten-thirty. After all the false alarms during the week, Rosaleen was tempted to ignore them. Weary and sore after climbing the Cave Hill, she had retired early and longed to remain snug in bed. However, the thought of Mackie's, but a stone's throw away, made her swing her aching legs out of bed and prepare for another night in the fields.

They were lucky that the weather was mild, she consoled herself.

It would be awful if it was bitter cold or pouring down rain. One had to be grateful for small mercies. After all, it wasn't usually so mild in April. The planes passed over the city for over two hours, their drone deafening. Sitting on the grass in a corner of one of the fields beyond Daily Hill, trying to pacify a whinging child, Rosaleen's nerves were stretched to breaking point. She actually got to the stage where she wished that they would drop their bombs and get it over with, but to the surprise and relief of all, once again no shots were fired, no bombs dropped.

Next morning her father voiced his opinion to all who would listen. He said the Germans were probably surprised at just how little opposition they were encountering and had come back on Tuesday to see if any changes had been made.

Few had; after all, no one had expected German planes to come right across England. Not even those in higher places, so Belfast was unprepared, complacent, and few extra resources were forthcoming.

'They'll be back!' Her father prophesied. 'You mark my words. They'll be back. They'll make use of the full moon, and we're stuck out on the edge of the lough like a sore thumb.'

And once again he was right. On Tuesday night, when the moon was almost full, the planes came in force. They approached between the Divis and the Black Mountains and were very low. There seemed to be hundreds of them, and their drone was deafening. The sirens gave warning of their approach at about ten o'clock and five minutes later the streets were thronged. No one dallied now. They feared that the Germans were out to get Mackie's and terror lent speed to their feet.

Some, mostly the elderly, sought refuge in the shelters, but these were soon full. Of course this was something else to lament; something else that the government had neglected to do. They had not built enough shelters, so those able to run and those with young children headed for open country. Laura was teething and Rosaleen was glad that she had managed to get her to drink some water laced with whiskey and sugar, because tucked snugly in the pram, she slept like a log. At the corner of the street Rosaleen found Amy waiting for her.

'Can I come with you, Rosaleen? I could have gotten into our shelter but it stinks. Youngsters, an some aul lads too, use the shelters if they're caught short... and then we're expected to stay in them when the siren goes. It's a disgrace, so it is. I can't bear to be in them.'

'Of course you can come with me, Amy. Here, hang on to the pram.' And slackening her pace to suit Amy, Rosaleen assured her, 'I'm glad of your company, so I am.'

After a wet start to the day, the evening was mild with a light south-westerly wind and they picked their way across the fields by the light of the three-quarter moon, seeking a sheltered place to sit down. As they walked in the bright moonlight. Rosaleen was aware that the same moon would show the German planes just where Mackie's was and she kept heading as far away from this danger as she could.

However, she soon discovered that the Germans had no need for moonlight. The first planes over dropped huge flares. They fell from the sky like giant torchlights, hundreds of them, and as they hung over the town, suspended from parachutes, everyone stood in the fields and gaped at them. The sound of anti-aircraft guns thundered as they endeavoured to put out the flares, but more and more fell, and soon the sky became as bright and clear as daylight, making the moon look pale and insignificant. Belfast was shown in detail, as if under a huge spotlight. Huddled together on an old raincoat, Amy and Rosaleen prayed as the next lot of planes dropped a constant barrage of bombs, incendiaries, and parachute mines. Anti-aircraft guns woof-woofed in retaliation, and the ground beneath them shook, even though the bombs were falling in the city.

There was no singing now. Everyone was sure it was to be their last night on earth and each, in their own way, was begging God's forgiveness for past sins. The night dragged on; they saw flares fall in the vicinity of Mackie's and thought the bombs would surely not miss, but Mackie's fire-watchers were diligent in their labours, and as dawn broke and the all-clear sounded, Mackie's still stood.

St Paul's Parish had only one serious casualty, and that was a house at the corner of Springfield Drive (better known as Mackie's

Height), a row of posh houses, with three bedrooms and a bathroom, built just a few years earlier on an elevated sight facing Mackie's Foundry.

So close, so very close. Enough to make the blood run cold. The house had been hit by an incendiary device and was badly burnt, in spite of prompt action by the air-raid wardens, but it was empty at the time and there were no casualties.

The rest of the town was not so lucky, with the docks again suffering devastation, and at Shorts and Harland four Stirling aircraft that were almost finished were ignited by explosions and burnt to a cinder.

York Street spinning factory, said to be the largest of its kind in Europe, was hit, and brought down houses in Sussex Street and Vere Street in its wake, killing thirty people instantly. They also learnt that a bomb falling near a shelter in Percy Street had taken another sixty lives, and tram lines were wrecked and water and gas mains fractured.

In despair, firemen worked trying to keep the fires that raged all over the city from spreading. With the pipes having been cracked, the water pressure was low, and realizing that they were fighting a losing battle, help was sought from the south. And the south did not fail Ulster in its hour of need. Indeed, no. In spite of the obvious danger, in spite of being a neutral country, fire engines from Dublin, Dún Laoghaire, Drogheda and Dundalk rushed to their fellow countrymen's aid. With the Lord Mayor of Dublin himself riding up front in one of his city's engines, they fought the flames side by side with the Ulster brigades, until the fires were extinguished, leaving half of Belfast a smouldering mass.

Next day on the radio, Rosaleen learnt that five hundred were dead and this number was expected to rise steeply. Over a thousand were injured, thousands more homeless, and there was an exodus to the countryside as Belfast's inhabitants sought refuge with friends who lived outside the city.

Food kitchens were set up and the schools, closed for the Easter holidays, were reopened to house the homeless, who came mostly from Protestant areas. Everybody was urged to give all they could in the way of bedding, clothes and food to help the needy.

As Rosaleen piled blankets, clothes and tins of food ready to be collected, her mother arrived.

'Have you heard the latest?' she asked.

'Well, it all depends on what the latest is. I've heard so much today my mind boggles.'

Her mother smiled faintly as she asked, 'About the Pope leading the German planes in?'

Rosaleen's mouth dropped open. 'Ah' – she waved her hand in disbelief – 'you're having me on!'

'No. No, I'm not, the rumour's goin' around that the Pope must be leading the planes in. Ye see, a lot of Protestant churches were hit last night and not one single Catholic church was touched.'

'Tut! I never heard the like of it.'

'Aye, I agree with you.' Thelma had to smile at Rosaleen's outraged dignity. 'Are you goin' down to help out in one of the schools?'

'Yes, St Paul's. Are you?' When Thelma nodded in confirmation, Rosaleen added, 'I'm waiting for someone to collect these things.'

'We've a pile of stuff ready too. Your da has the key, he's calling to collect it.' Thelma's face puckered and there was a catch in her voice. 'It must be awful to lose your home … all your belongings.'

'And so many dead. We were lucky last night, but tonight we might not be. I'm not waiting for the sirens to go off. I'm going to take Laura up to the Falls Park the minute we get our dinner. As far away from Mackie's as I can. I learnt one thing last night: those fields beyond Daisy Hill aren't far enough away. If Mackie's got hit, there'd be pieces flying everywhere.'

'We'll come with ye, so we will. Where's Laura now?' Thelma's head went back as she looked reproachfully down the length of her nose at Rosaleen. 'Ye know, you should've kept the child in the country, so ye should.' Her voice was accusing and Rosaleen turned angrily on her.

'Do you think I don't know that? I'll never forgive myself if anything happens to her.' She blinked furiously to contain the tears before adding, 'Amy has her at the moment.'

Thelma had the grace to look ashamed. Rosaleen was bound to be feeling guilty without her piling on the agony.

Suddenly they both leapt to their feet and Thelma screamed,

'Jesus, Mary and Joseph ... what's that?' as a huge explosion rent the air and the house shook.

They bumped into each other in their effort to get out of the door to see what was wrong, and over and over again in Rosaleen's mind ran the plea: Laura ... Laura ... Oh, please let Laura be all right. Please ... please!

Once out on the street Rosaleen saw from the direction of the thick smoke that the explosion was round behind Iris Drive, further up Springfield Avenue. She was also relieved to see Amy turn the opposite corner, an excited Laura by the hand.

'Thank God you're all right.' Rosaleen hugged Laura tight, and eyeing Amy over her head asked, 'What happened?'

Amy mutely shook her head. It was a passerby who answered Rosaleen.

'A delayed bomb went off at the corner where Springfield Avenue meets Cavendish Street. It has demolished some houses, but thank God nobody's hurt.'

'Thank God indeed,' Rosaleen agreed with him, and her mind was full of the thought that it could just as easily have been her home.

As they worked side by side with Protestant women, making up camp beds and sorting out groceries, Rosaleen was close to tears. There were three hundred refugees here in St Paul's school and her father said as many again were in St Gall's and some further up the Falls Road in St Mary's Training School. And that was just this end of town; there must be thousands homeless. It was heartbreaking watching people wandering about in a daze. Some of them didn't even know whether or not the rest of their families were still alive, and each policeman, each air-raid warden that appeared was besieged with questions.

To add to their problems, as a result of fractured pipes, water was not reaching the houses and everybody had to queue up at water stands in the street to fill their kettles and buckets, and some houses were also without electricity.

Their duty done for the day, after a rushed scanty meal, Thelma offered to look after Laura, when Rosaleen and Annie voiced their desire to take a walk and see what damage had been done the night before. The radio had requested that sightseers stay away from the bombed areas, as they were hampering rescue work, but Rosaleen and Annie did not intend going too near. They just wanted to see for themselves what the town was like.

The sights that met their eyes as they walked down Divis Street, past Percy Street, where a bomb had taken sixty lives, were awful. They could see that complete rows of houses were demolished and piles of rubble were all that was left of what used to be prominent buildings. In some streets, pathetic heaps of furniture which had been salvaged from houses stood on the corner, as though rejected, furniture that had probably been someone's pride and joy.

Most of the bombs had fallen on civilian targets and soldiers still toiled digging bodies from the ruins, laying them side by side until such time as they were delivered to the morgue.

To their surprise the town centre appeared to be all right, although as they walked along Royal Avenue they could see that the Public Library was pitted all over and every window in the big Co-op Stores in York Street was broken. Even as they watched, looting was going on, furtive figures darting from buildings with stolen goods in their arms. They also observed that the nurses' home in Frederick Street was completely demolished, and wondered how many lives had been lost there.

It was soon obvious to them that it was the poor districts that had suffered most, and as they made their way home they pondered how lucky they on the Falls and Springfield Roads had been.

'I can't stand it,' Annie cried. 'We were very lucky last night, but that could be our street tomorrow. I know one thing – never again will I feel guilty about making bits of planes and bullets.' She thrust her face towards Rosaleen. 'I did, ye know. I felt awful when I thought that maybe the bullets I was helping to make would kill someone. But not any more … Oh no, not any more. I just hope the Germans are suffering like we are.'

They arrived home in Iris Drive to find their father on the doorstep. He was dropping with fatigue and didn't need any coaxing to stretch out on the settee.

'I came to warn you t'get away up the Falls Road early t'night. Don't wait for the siren t'go off. As soon as ye get your tea, start out.'

'Yes, Da, we're not stupid … that's what we intend to do,' Annie informed him. 'Are you coming home with me now for your tea?'

'Aye, I am Annie. And I hope to get a couple of hours sleep.'

'You'd need to. You're out on your feet, Da. Come on, the sooner we go, the longer you'll be able to sleep.'

Still he lay prone, too tired to move, his mind full of the horror of the night and the long day.

'It's been awful. They couldn't find anywhere big enough to store all the bodies. The City Morgue's stacked high with coffins, and there's a hundred and fifty more in St James's Market. So they came to the Falls Road. The Falls Baths are piled high with coffins, they're everywhere. They arrived in hearses, lorries, coalcarts … even the bin lorries brought some. And when they ran out… do ye know what we had to do?'

When Rosaleen and Annie could only shake their heads mutely, he continued, 'They let the water out of the pools and we wrapped the bodies in blankets and laid them on the tiled floors. There was just limbs … legs, arms … awful, I even saw a head lyin' on its own … it was awful.'

His voice trailed off and they sat some moments in silence, minds alive with horrible pictures of the scene he described, waiting for him to continue his narrative, until eventually it dawned on them that nature had taken its course and he had fallen asleep.

When Annie would have wakened him, Rosaleen stopped her.

'Don't. Let him be. I'll waken him at about seven and give him a bite to eat. That should be early enough, shouldn't it?'

'Yes, about seven … or even eight. That'll give him four hours sleep. Thank God I'm on the dayshift. It'll be awful on the night shift in Mackie's after last night … it was bad enough before. Me mam and I'll bring Laura down for you to get ready, at about half-eight and we'll go up to the Falls Park. All right?'

Rosaleen nodded, 'Yes, I'll have all Laura's things ready and we can call for Amy on our way out.'

The nightly journeys up the Falls Road to the park and countryside became a monotonous, boring habit and if it hadn't been for Laura, Rosaleen would have taken her chances and stayed at home, in spite of being so close to Mackie's Foundry. Thousands made the journey every night, and some didn't bother coming down again, staking claim to old barns and shacks. They had no homes to go to and the Corporation was finding it hard to find accommodation for everyone in need.

The Corporation had ordered buses to be kept ready at the depot at the bottom of the Glen Road, to take those who preferred to be further afield out into the countryside when the siren sounded. The first to arrive every night settled in the buses and a party atmosphere reigned as stories were told and songs sung, and the dreaded siren was awaited.

Days passed without any further raids and it was decided that the bodies that weren't identified would have to be buried. There was a notice in the newspapers, and for those who were homeless and unable to buy them, posters were pasted up all over town advising those with relatives still missing that they had two days left to try to find them.

The stench of the decomposing flesh and the risk of infection was too great to risk keeping them any longer, and arrangements were made for a communal burial. As she listened to her father, who had volunteered to help out in the Baths, recount tales of men and women hunting for their lost partners or members of their family, and then having to be sprayed with disinfectant as they left to lessen the chance of infection, Rosaleen's mind baulked at the horror of it all. Imagine not knowing whether or not one of those horribly mutilated bodies that were rotting away was a husband or a wife or one of the family. The stench would stay in your nose forever. No wonder so many people were wandering about in a daze, not caring what happened to them.

The funeral of the unclaimed dead was held on Monday, April 21st. There had been so many private funerals that people were used to seeing hearses go up the Falls Road and would bow their heads, say a prayer and then go on about their business, but for the communal funeral it was different. Thousands lined the road, and both men and women cried openly. The authorities had ordered the bodies to be examined, and any with crucifixes or rosary beads or prayer leaflets were deemed Catholics and the others taken to be Protestants. After separate religious services, by a Catholic priest and a Protestant minister, the bodies were taken in military vehicles to the City Cemetery where the Protestants were to be buried and then continued on up the Falls Road to Milltown Cemetery for the burial of the Catholics. Those with relatives and friends still missing formed a procession behind the vehicles and followed them up the road, stunned and despairing. It was a scene that would stay with those who observed it until the day they died.

Due to the demolition of the shipyard and aircraft factory, thousands of people were out of work and others had neither the energy nor the inclination to spend the night in the fields and parks and then go into work. So, according to the newspapers, production was down a quarter of what it was before the awful blitz on April 15th, and the government urged all hands to help get production going again in case of another raid. Mackie's, having received only a few minor hits, all taken care of quickly, was working all out, taking over some orders that Shorts' aircraft factory was unable to fulfil and employing more staff as a result.

One good thing emerged from all this desolation and trouble. A new affinity was created between Catholic and Protestant. As they gathered together night after night and listened to each others' tales of woe and sometimes even joy, like when a child was born or a beloved relative thought dead was discovered alive, they realised that they were all the same under the skin. They had the same aspirations for their children – better homes and jobs, a better start in life than they themselves had known – and many firm friendships were made that were to stand the test of time.

Rosaleen discovered that the people of the Shankill were just the same as the people of the Falls, encumbered with the same lesser paid jobs and slum areas that were a breeding ground for the dreaded disease TB, which was becoming very common among the working classes. How come she had thought that the Shankill

Road people were better off? Just because they were Protestants? She thought it was only the Catholics that were the underdog. Now it looked like she was wrong.

Disenchantment with the government and fear of Hitler brought to Catholics and Protestants a closeness they had never achieved before. They were also united in their resentment of the Corporation. Never was the prestige of the Belfast Corporation so low, and bitterness against it was rife as the homeless queued up for food.

'Other big cities were prepared. So why wasn't Belfast?' they asked angrily.

Other problems also gave cause for grave concern. The people on the Antrim Road and surrounding district were worried about what would happen if the zoo at Bellevue was bombed. Wild animals would be free to roam the countryside, so it was decided that all the dangerous animals must be put down. These included the beautiful lions, tigers, and wolves Rosaleen had been admiring at Easter, as well as a giant rat she hadn't liked the look of. The thought of their fate brought tears to her eyes, and she was not surprised when it was reported in the newspapers that the head gamekeeper had cried when his lovely animals had been slaughtered.

After many false alarms, Sunday, May 4th dawned bright and frosty, and as the day wore on Rosaleen was filled with hope. There was been no bombing since April 15th; perhaps Hitler was finished with Belfast! The afternoon was hot and sunny and it was the first day of the new scheme thought up by the government to save fuel by lengthening the hours of daylight. That morning the clocks had been put forward an hour, meaning dusk would be one hour late. Encouraged by the hot weather and the extra hour of daylight, Rosaleen decided to wash some bedclothes. For boiling bed linen and whites, she had a small boiler which was kept in a shed in the yard. Now she pulled this out into the warm sunlight and, filling it with water, stripped the beds and gathered together towels and whites. May as well make hay while the sun shines, she thought happily as she set the water to boil, and later, when Amy popped in on a visit, they sat out in the yard, lapping up the sunshine and watching the washing sway in the light breeze.

But the hope that lifted Rosaleen's spirits was soon dashed. The Germans chose that night to launch their second major bomb attack on Belfast and it was another night of horror.

This time the moonlight was so bright in a sky free from clouds that the planes didn't need flares to see their targets and their aim was accurate as they devastated the shipyards, destroying three corvettes that were nearing completion. They also managed to inflict more damage to Shorts' aircraft factory and hit the Harbour Power Station. York Street Railway Station was reduced to rubble.

It was on this night that St Paul's Parish suffered its worst damage. At dawn, as Rosaleen and company trailed wearily home from their night in the Falls Park, they saw as they neared Beechmount Avenue that a bomb must have fallen nearby. Smoke hung in a dense cloud over Our Lady's Hospital on the Falls Road just above Beechmount Avenue and wafted down on to the road, catching their breaths. Horrified, they deduced that one of the streets that ran off Beechmount Avenue must have been hit. Crowds were milling to and fro and Annie grabbed a man by the arm.

'Where did the bomb hit, mister?'

'The top of Beechmount Street, and it's demolished about eight houses,' he informed her.

Dazed, Annie stood as if turned to stone, and Rosaleen clutched her. They were thinking of Sean's family who lived at the top of Beechmount Street.

It was Thelma who took control. 'Rosaleen, you go with Annie and see about Sean's family. I'll see Amy home and then bring Laura to my house until you come back. We'll go down the Falls Road way, it's too smoky for Laura over there.' She nodded in the direction of Beechmount Avenue. 'Take your time. Stay as long as you have to, but don't leave until you know how Sean's family are. OK?'

'Yes, Mam. OK.' With a kiss on the brow for the sleeping child and a nod of farewell to Amy, Rosaleen slipped her arm through Annie's and led her down Beechmount Avenue. 'Come on, Annie, let's go and see what we can find out.'

At the bottom of Beechmount Street, air-raid wardens tried to turn them back but when Annie explained that her in-laws lived at the top of the street, they were allowed through. It was with apprehension that they climbed the street, to stand aghast at the sight that met their eyes. The houses at the top were completely demolished and covering their mouths and noses with handkerchiefs against the thick dust and grime, they watched fearfully as bodies were carried from the ruins. It was with relief that Annie hailed one of the stretcher bearers.

'Mr Devlin ... Mr Devlin!'

When the grime-covered figure turned at her call, she threw herself into his arms and sobbed against his breast.

'I'm so glad you're all right ... is the rest of the family all right?'

Jim Devlin nodded his head. 'Yes, love ... yes, we're all right. But that complete family has been wiped out.' He nodded to where bodies lay, but Annie kept her head down and refused to look.

'Why were they in the house?' she cried. 'I would've thought that anybody with sense would make for the open country.'

'I know, Annie ... I know. And normally they would've been away in the fields, but ye see, the man of the house was in a wheelchair and he was poorly, so his wife and son stayed to keep him company.'

'Oh, dear God ... how awful ... awful!'

'Ah.' He sighed and shrugged his shoulders. 'Who knows? Perhaps they would have preferred it that way. All to go together. They were a very close family. But look here, Annie ...' he glanced down at her kindly '... you must be tired. You can do nothing here, so away home. But thanks for coming to see how we've fared.'

With a gentle push, he sent her in the direction of Rosaleen. 'Take her home, love.'

Before he could turn away, Rosaleen caught his eye. 'Is your house all right?' she asked, and was relieved when he nodded. Then taking Annie by the arm, she pulled her away and down the street.

'Oh, thank God Sean's family is safe. Those poor, poor people.'

Rosaleen let Annie ramble on, knowing it would help relieve the tension, but when they passed Iris Drive, on their way to pick up Laura, and she saw Bobby Mackay leave her doorway and, seeing them at the corner, come towards them, she felt a shiver run down her spine. Bobby and her father were both wardens and had been partnered off. Somehow she was aware that he was the bearer of bad news. How, she didn't know, but she felt fear squeeze her heart.

Bobby stopped in front of them, bringing Annie's lamentations to an end, and they both gazed speechlessly at him.

Rosaleen had met him just once before, on the night she had returned from Dungannon, and he had reminded her of a great St Bernard dog with his long sad face and heavily lidded eyes. It was obvious from Annie's blank expression that he was a stranger to her.

The great hangdog face topped by a mop of untidy thick brown hair swung slowly from side to side, the slack jowls quivering with emotion.

'What's wrong, Bobby?'

Rosaleen didn't recognise her own voice and she was aware that neither did Annie because she turned on her with a look of amazement.

'He wouldn't listen to me, so he wouldn't. I warned him ... tried to keep him down on the main road, but he wouldn't listen. Insisted on going to check on those people.'

'Who on earth's he talking ...' Annie's voice trailed off when Rosaleen gripped her arm and shook it.

'Is he badly hurt, Bobby?' she asked fearfully.

The heavy lids lifted and big brown eyes full of sorrow looked from one to the other of them, begging their forgiveness. Why couldn't it have been him, a widower without child or chick? he lamented inwardly.

'I'm sorry, girls ... I couldn't face your mother, just couldn't ... they were so close.'

Rosaleen's mind was saying over and over again. Me da's dead. Me da's dead. Oh, sweet Jesus ... let me be wrong. Please let me be wrong.

But no, she was right, Bobby was continuing, 'He knew that there was a family in one of the top houses in Beechmount Street ... and he had just started off in the direction of the house to check that they were all right, when the bomb fell. I was at the bottom of the street and was lifted off me feet. He was thrown a great distance and when I saw him lying still ... well, I thought that he was just stunned. I never dreamed ... Ah, Rosaleen, it was an awful shock to find he was dead.'

Turning on her heel she quickly started to retrace her steps. One of the bodies at the top of Beechmount Street must be her father's. She had to go to him. Annie was whimpering and caught at Rosaleen's arm.

'Does he mean me da's dead?'

Rosaleen could only nod mutely and Bobby cried, 'Rosaleen ... he's not over there.' He nodded back towards Beechmount Avenue. 'He wasn't buried ... just caught by the blast ... they've taken him away. Look, you come with me and we'll find out where they've taken him. And you, love ...' he turned his gaze on Annie '... will you tell your mother?'

'Oh, Rosaleen ... Rosaleen!' The horror of it made Annie sway and she clutched her sister by the arm.

'Hush, Annie love. Look, you go and keep me mam company and I'll go with Bobby.' Seeing the tremor in Annie's face, Rosaleen asked gently, 'Will you be all right?'

'Yes ... yes ... you go find me da.' And Annie staggered away, her mind full of dread. How was she going to break this awful news to her mother?

In a daze, Rosaleen allowed herself to be led towards Cavendish Street. Her legs felt like lead weights and she was so weary, she was afraid she would pass out. With a great effort of will, she moved when Bobby moved, paused when he paused, and soon they were outside the Royal Victoria Hospital.

'We'll try here first, Rosaleen, and if he's not here we'll have to go down to the City Morgue.'

Once inside the hospital, Bobby left her standing and went to the crowd milling around the reception desk to ask directions. Weariness was like a great weight sitting on her shoulders and a bench in the corner seemed to beckon her over. With dragging steps she made her way to it, and with a sigh of relief gratefully sat down. However, she had barely touched the seat when Bobby was in front of her again, urging her up, leading her down long corridors and down flights of stairs, until at last they were in the morgue.

It was very cold and she shivered as she looked around. It was like a giant locker room, with great drawers lining the walls on either side. Once more Bobby left her, and followed an attendant along one wall, shaking his head as he examined each corpse. This time there was no friendly bench nearby and Rosaleen drooped as she watched the men, hoping they would not have to go downtown to the City Morgue, yet dreading seeing Bobby nod his head to confirm that her father was there. Even as she watched, more coffins were brought and stacked along the corridor, and Bobby had to inspect these.

When she thought that her legs would no longer bear her weight and she would collapse, Bobby shook his head for the last time and approached her.

'He's not here Rosaleen. We'll have to go to the City Morgue.'

Becoming aware of her fatigue, he exclaimed, 'Ah, Rosaleen, what on earth am I thinking of? Sure, you're out on your feet!' Putting a supporting arm around her, he led her forward. 'Come on, love. Let's get you a cup of tea.'

This was easier said than done. Each nurse he approached looked at him as if he was an idiot, asking for tea at a time like this, shaking their heads abruptly and then hurrying on about their business. At last, in despair, he led Rosaleen into a small office that was at the entrance to a ward. They found tea-making facilities and he put the kettle on to boil. Helping himself to some sugar and milk he prepared a cup.

'Just what on earth do you think you're doing?'

'I … oh … look, I'm sorry, but this young woman's in a state of shock. Her father was killed tonight and we're looking for his body.'

The harassed young doctor framed in the doorway looked at Bobby blankly for some seconds. Then, as if the words had just registered, he turned his tired gaze on Rosaleen.

'I'm just making her a wee cup of tea before we go down to the City Morgue. She's out on her feet, so she is, an' I want to waken her up a bit,' Bobby explained, his voice pleading. He knew he was in the wrong; had no right to be in the office, no matter making tea.

A long drawn-out sigh left the doctor's lips and he rummaged in his pockets. Producing a phial, he shook two small tablets into the palm of his hand. 'Here ... give her these ... They'll waken her up. You'd better hurry up, and not let Sister catch you in here.' And dismissing Bobby's thanks with a wave of his hand, he left the office.

'Here, take these with your tea ... the doctor says they'll waken you up,' Bobby said kindly, and waited until Rosaleen put the tablets in her mouth before pressing the cup of tea into her unsteady hands.

Rosaleen didn't think anything could waken her up; she just ached with tiredness, longed to close her eyes and sleep. Guilt added to her fatigue. What must people think of her, searching for her father's body and unable to keep her eyes open? She felt so ashamed. They must think her uncaring. But to her surprise the tablets did waken her up and by the time Bobby was ready to move on, she was wide awake and clear-headed.

They had just come through the gates of the hospital and were making their way down the Grosvenor Road when a car pulled up on the other side of the road and an arm waved them over.

'You wait here, Rosaleen,' Bobby said, before warily crossing the road, but after conversing with the occupants of the car, he beckoned her over. 'We're getting a lift down to the City Morgue,' he informed her. 'These young doctors have been sent to help out down there.'

And Rosaleen recognised the driver of the car as the doctor who had given Bobby the tablets.

The journey to the morgue, although a short distance by car, seemed endless. As they approached the city centre, they could see fires blazing. With a smothered oath, the doctor reversed the car and approached the morgue via Sandy Row and then across the back streets to the Donegall Road. On their journey, they could see streets demolished and smoking desolation.

Once at their destination, the procedure was the same as before. Corridors, stairs, more corridors, and then the morgue itself. There were coffins everywhere, the lids removed and resting against them for each viewing, and there was a long queue waiting to examine the bodies. They joined the queue and Rosaleen felt dazed and shocked as she viewed horrible corpses, all twisted out of shape, staring eyes, faces and hair thickly matted with dust. Young people, old people, some with the clothes blown off their bodies, one woman still clutching a child to her breast. And to add to the horror of it all, the smell of excrement permeated the air, causing the bile to rise in her throat. It took a great effort of will to choke it down again. Unknown to herself, she was whimpering. Taking her gently by the arm, Bobby led her outside and to a bench where other people were waiting.

'You wait here, Rosaleen. As you have seen, some of these bodies are not a pretty sight. If your father's here, I'll call you.'

She sat, full of dread. What if her father was disfigured? How would her mother react? She remembered the night of April 15th. Remembered her father talk about laying bodies on the floors of the swimming pools in the Falls Road Baths, and her heart sank. Is that what was happening tonight? Would she have to climb down into the swimming pool to identify her father? Dread made her mouth dry up and a great lump gathered in her throat, causing her to gulp as she tried to swallow it. If only Joe was here ... or Sean. They would know what to do. There would have to be a funeral. What did she and Annie know about funerals?

At last Bobby came and beckoned her forward.

'He's here, Rosaleen,' he said softly, and put a comforting arm across her shoulders. 'Come on love. He's in the morgue itself... it's not so gruesome.'

With dread she entered the room and, eyes downcast, approached the big drawer that the assistant held open. There was a big ball of fear where her heart should be. What if he was badly disfigured and she fainted?

As if realising the trend of her thoughts, Bobby whispered in her ear, 'It's all right, Rosaleen. It's all right. He isn't marked. And remember ... I was with him. I closed his eyes, straightened his limbs. You'd think he was just sleeping.'

He was right; except for a discolouration at the right side of his brow, her father looked as if he was just taking a nap. Unconsciously, she reached out her hand and gently touched his face. It was cold, firm and waxy. Tears blinded her as she turned away. He was dead all right.

'It's him,' she said, for the benefit of the attendant who was watching her gravely, and who now nodded and pushed the great drawer shut. 'I'll need you to sign a form and then I'll get the doctor to give you the death certificate,' he said softly, as he led the way out of the room, glad that another body had been identified.

The minute Rosaleen entered her mother's kitchen she knew Annie had not told her the bad news and her heart filled with bitterness. Why did she have to do everything? Annie should bear her part of the burden.

'Make Rosaleen a cup of tea, Annie. She looks foundered.'

At her mother's words, with a pleading, apologetic look, Annie disappeared into the scullery. Rising to her feet, Thelma greeted her daughter brightly. 'My, but you were a long time. Laura's asleep. I've put her up in my bed.'

'Mam ... Mam, please sit down, I've something to tell you.'

Thelma made no effort to obey Rosaleen. Instead she moved away from her outstretched hand and over to the fireplace. Here she stood warming her hands at the blaze and continued in the same bright voice, as if Rosaleen had not spoken: 'You can leave Laura here. When she wakens, I'll bring her down.'

With a sinking heart, Rosaleen realised that her mother guessed the truth and was afraid to face it.

Going to her, she put an arm gently across her mother's shoulders and tried to lead her to the settee, but with an angry thrust, Thelma pushed her away.

'He's dead, isn't he?' she cried, and great tears welled up and ran down her stark, white face. 'Do you think I don't know?' Her hand clutched at the regions of her heart. 'Part of me died with him. I knew something was wrong ... I just knew it. I couldn't understand why I felt so bereft. Couldn't understand ... It was as if I had lost something, but didn't know what. Just a feelin' that I'd lost something.' She fell silent for some moments and allowed the awful feeling to swamp her. 'Then, when Annie said that you were away somewhere with Bobby Mackay, I knew ... I knew ...' a sob gathered in her throat, almost choking her, and she gulped before she could finish '... just how much I'd lost.'

Full of compassion, Rosaleen tried to urge her mother towards the settee. 'Come on, love, sit down. Can I get you anything?'

Resisting her efforts to make her sit down, Thelma cried, 'Yes! Yes, ye can! Ye can get me your da.' She clutched at Rosaleen's arm, and eyes full of dread, asked, 'Where is he? Is he in the swimming pool?'

When Rosaleen shook her head, Thelma bowed hers.

'Thank God for that. He would have hated that. He thought it degrading.' Her eyes swung to the picture of the Sacred Heart that hung on the wall. 'Why are you doing this to me?' she cried. 'Eh? Eh? I didn't do anything wrong.' Then, bowing her head, she pleaded. 'Oh, sweet Jesus help me ... help me to bear this.'

Wiping the tears from her own cheeks with the back of her hand, Rosaleen once more tried to comfort her mother.

'He was a good man, Mam, he'll have been prepared.'

Another thrust sent her staggering and she plunged down on the arm of the settee and grabbed the back of it to save herself from toppling over.

'Prepared? Oh, he'll have been prepared, all right. I'm not worried about him. He'll have made his peace with God long ago, but what about me? What am I gonna do?' She wrung her hands in despair. 'Oh ... you don't understand, you don't understand.' She turned away, then swung back again, crying in anguish. 'Why couldn't he have stayed at home with his wife like other men? Eh? No ... no ... he had to be out saving strangers. It didn't matter about me.' She thumped her breast with her fist and bawled, 'If he had stayed at home, he might have died in his own bed and I'd have had some warnin'. Do you hear me? I'd have had some warnin', so I would.'

Stung on behalf of her father, Rosaleen cried, 'Mam, that's not fair! He was doing what had to be done.'

'Oh, I know, I know. Don't pay any attention to me. Ye see ... well ... Oh, you don't understand!'

Frustrated, Rosaleen felt like shouting, 'Well then, tell me. Explain.' But her mother was actually pulling at her hair … yanking at it … pulling it down with both hands, her eyes wild, her mouth trembling, and Rosaleen was afraid to question her. Then suddenly, just like air leaving a balloon, her mother's body sagged, her legs buckled, and with a great howl she collapsed. On her knees, at the settee, she buried her head in her arms and wept, great sobs tearing at her slight frame.

In the face of such grief, Rosaleen was at a loss what to do. Who would have dreamt that her mother had cared so deeply for her father? Was she being a hypocrite? If not, she had certainly hidden her true feelings all these years. Because of her offhand attitude towards her father, Rosaleen had in her own mind concluded that her mother had married him as a last resort. Of course she had cared for him, but not enough to warrant this breakdown, surely?

During her mother's tirade, Annie had come to the door of the scullery and was standing, her clenched fist pressed against her mouth, panic in her eyes. Now, catching her eye, Rosaleen mouthed the words: 'Get Doctor Hughes.'

Without a word, Annie lifted her coat and fled from the house, glad to escape from the sight of her mother's mindless grief. Stumbling down the Springfield Road, she felt ashamed. She was aware that she should have broken the news to her mother. Rosaleen had every right to be angry with her. When her mother had descended the stairs after settling Laura in bed, she had tried to tell her, but Thelma would not listen to her. She had rambled on and on, not letting her get a word in edgeways and, to her shame, she had been so tired she had drifted off into a doze as she listened to her mother's voice droning on and on.

As she entered the hall of the doctor's surgery, she whispered a quiet prayer that Doctor Hughes would be present. What would they do if he wasn't in?

He was not there. His housekeeper informed her that he was down at the Royal Hospital, lending a helping hand.

As she turned away, despair in her heart, the housekeeper said, tentatively, 'His father's here … I'll see how he is this morning.'

Annie knew that she was referring to old Doctor Hughes, who

must be about seventy and who had retired some years ago, and who sometimes, if he felt well enough, came out in an emergency.

To her relief he shuffled into the waiting room, and agreed to come and see her mother. Soon they were out on the Springfield Road, she slowing her step to suit his and he plying her with questions about her mother's condition.

When they entered the kitchen, they found Rosaleen sitting on the settee, her face buried in her hands. Of their mother there was no sign.

Going to Rosaleen, Doctor Hughes gently took her hands away from her face and asked, 'Where is your mother?'

'She's up cleaning the rooms.'

Her voice was bitter, scornful. After a quarter hour of mindless grief and belittling Rosaleen's attempts to comfort her, Thelma had calmly dried her face and risen to her feet. Watched by a bewildered Rosaleen, she had fetched her brush and dust pan, duster and polish.

'You'll have to excuse me now – I must clean the rooms for them bringing him home.' And without another glance in Rosaleen's direction, she had mounted the stairs, her back straight, her step firm. Imagine! Her husband was dead and she was worried about what the neighbours would think if the rooms were dusty.

Taking Rosaleen's wrist between his fingers, Doctor Hughes examined her face intently as he took her pulse. He felt heartsore for these two girls whom he had brought into the world.

'Rosaleen, you must not judge your mother by her actions. She's coping in the only way she can. You need to rest,' he said, with a gentle tap of reprimand on the back of her hand. 'I'll go up to your mother.'

Sitting down beside her on the settee, Annie tried to explain. 'I tried to tell her, Rosaleen. Honestly, I did, but she wouldn't listen to me.'

'I know, Annie. I know. She was the same with me. Listen …' the look she turned on Annie was full of dread '… what are we going to do? I wish Joe was here. How I wish he was here.'

'And Sean,' Annie fervently agreed. 'They'll get compassionate leave, won't they?'

'Huh! It depends on where they are and what they're doing,' Rosaleen cried in despair. 'Don't count on them getting home. We'll probably have to manage on our own.'

They fell silent when they heard Doctor Hughes on the stairs.

'I've given your mother a sedative. She'll sleep for about six hours and I'll leave some tablets ...' He opened his bag and took a small bottle from it. 'Make sure she takes two of these every six hours. They'll keep her calm.'

He placed the bottle on the mantelpiece and eyed the girls.

'Now ... what are we going to do about you two? You look dead beat.' His teeth gnawed away at his bottom lip as he stood deep in thought. 'Have you an uncle or male cousin? Someone to see to the funeral arrangements?'

'We'll send for Sean and Joe ... our husbands,' Annie informed him.

'That will take too long. Is there no one else?'

Before they could reply the door was thrust open and Amy entered the room, followed by Bobby Mackay.

'Oh, you poor, poor girls.'

Kneeling in front of them, Amy put an arm around each of them as she explained, 'Mr Mackay came for me. Wasn't that good of him?'

Clutching her, Rosaleen wailed, 'Oh, Amy, what are we gonna do? Do you know anything about funerals?'

'You leave all that to me, Rosaleen,' Bobby interrupted her. 'I'll make all the arrangements.'

Relieved that someone was in charge, Doctor Hughes produced more tablets from his bag, and pouring some into the palm of his hand he proffered them to Amy.

'Here, see they take two each ... it will make them sleep.'

As she listened to his words, Rosaleen felt hysterical laughter well up inside her and pressed her lips tightly together to contain it. Tablets to waken her up ... tablets to make her sleep. She'd feel like a pill bottle before this was all over.

'Thank you, Doctor. I'll see that they take them,' Amy assured him, and duty performed, Doctor Hughes bade them good day and left the house.

'Rosaleen?' Bobby hovered in front of her awkwardly. 'Before you take the tablets, can I have the death certificate? I'll need it to make the funeral arrangements.'

Rosaleen, who was still sitting with her outdoor coat on, searched the pockets. When she failed to find the sheet of paper, she panicked and began feverishly to search them again.

Gently, Bobby stilled her frantic hands. 'Rosaleen, I think you put it in your cardigan pocket for safety. Remember? Eh, love?'

With a relieved sigh, she unbuttoned her coat, extracted the certificate from her cardigan pocket and gave it to him.

'Will you need me here, Mrs Smith?' he asked Amy, and when she shook her head, said, 'Then I'll away down and set things in motion.'

When the door closed on him, Amy turned to the girls.

'Where's Laura?'

'Upstairs.'

'Well ... here's what I suggest, Rosaleen, you and I will take Laura and go to my house. That way I can look after her for the next few days and leave you free to support your mother.' With an apologetic look she turned to Annie. 'Will you be all right here, near your mother, in case she awakens?'

'Oh, yes ... yes. Don't worry about me. I'll look after Mam. But, what about Sean and Joe? Shouldn't we let someone know, so that they can be sent for?'

'Mr Mackay is seeing to all that, so he is. My, but he's a good man.'

'Do you know Bobby, Amy?' Annie questioned her.

'No ... no, Annie. I didn't know him from Adam when I opened the door to him an hour ago. He stood on the doorstep, big and sorrowful-looking, and informed me that he was Bobby Mackay, your father's warden partner. He said that your father had been killed and he thought I might be needed.'

'Oh, thank God for that,' Rosaleen exclaimed. 'That was kind of him. We were worried about the funeral arrangements. It's a relief to know Bobby's helping us.'

'Amy, do you think Sean and Joe will get home?' Annie was eyeing her beseechingly, and Amy was sorry to have to disillusion her.

She shook her head. 'I'm afraid not. I can't see them getting home in time for the funeral.' But when both their faces dropped, she hastily added, 'But ye never know … ye never can tell.'

Joe did get home; he arrived the day before the funeral and when Rosaleen opened the door and saw him, she fell into his arms and wept. She wept for joy at seeing him, and she wept because she was horrified at how thin and gaunt he was. Just like a bag of bones in her arms. She thought her heart would break as she hugged him close.

Her mother had refused to allow her father to be taken to spend his last night in the church. She said she wanted to keep him at home with her as long as she could; and near eleven, when everybody had departed at the sound of the sirens, she settled down in the chair she had occupied constantly since they had brought him home, near the trestles on which the coffin rested.

When the sirens had started their mournful wail, they had ignored them. Just as they had the previous night when a few planes had passed over the city and dropped bombs. Somehow, nothing seemed to matter any more. There was no way they were going to leave Tommy on his own, no way. They had been outraged when a neighbour had the effrontery to remark that they were daft and should get themselves away up into the fields, saying, 'Sure, ye can't kill a dead man. What about the child?'

Annie had rounded angrily on him. 'She's safe. She'll already be up in the fields, but we're staying with me da.' And she had bestowed such a look of wrath on him, he had said no more.

When Rosaleen retired to the scullery to make a cup of tea, Joe followed her in. This was the first time they had been alone since he had arrived that morning, and coming up behind her he put his arms around her waist and sank his face into her hair.

'How I've missed you, love … you'll never know how much I've missed you.'

She sank back against him, and closing her eyes pulled his hands over her breasts and revelled in the comfort of his arms. As she felt his passion rise, her heart soared. Surely this time it would work? It was different, she could feel the difference as he gripped her tighter still against his body.

Swiftly she turned in his arms and lifted her face for his kisses. Gripping her arms tight around him, she moved her body sensuously against his, her long months of frustration making her act like a wanton woman. Aware of her mother in the kitchen and Annie upstairs, she urged him so that his back was against the scullery door and no one could take them unawares.

Such was her great need to be held and loved, it was a minute or so before she realised that Joe was not responding to her frantic actions. He was actually squirming in her arms, and hot with shame she pushed her body away from his and turned away from him.

Her knuckles showed white as she gripped the edge of the stove, and wrapped in misery, fought for self-control. She was a fool! Why should it be any different? He was still the same man.

Sean's face surfaced in her mind but she pushed it away. She had no right to think how differently he would have responded to her actions. No right at all!

'I'm sorry ... I'm sorry, Rosaleen. I'm ... I'm very tired.'

Joe's voice, soft and apologetic, invaded her misery, and thinking grimly that it may as well be a headache, she avoided his outstretched hand and busied herself at the stove.

'It's all right. Never worry.'

Keeping her attention fixed firmly on what she was doing, she set a tray and when she had poured the tea, motioned for him to carry it into the kitchen. She was amazed at her own stupidity. Had she really believed that Joe would get carried away enough to make love to her, and her mother sitting in the kitchen? No, she had been daft ... but he could have held her and kissed her and suggested that they wait until they were alone. He could have softened the blow. After all, he was her husband. He didn't have to reject her like that. Make her feel cheap and dirty. Still, she should have known better. Joe would be appalled at the idea of her wanting to make love in the scullery and her father dead in the next room; she would have dropped another notch in his estimation.

When her mother had finished her tea, the sleeping tablets Rosaleen had insisted she take soon worked and she fell asleep.

'Joe, will you carry her over to the settee? She'll rest better there.'

After she had placed a pillow at her mother's head and gently tucked blankets around her prone figure, she turned to face him.

He looked so worn out that she wanted to go to him and hold him close, tell him everything was all right, but the rejection in the scullery still rankled and she found she could not make herself move towards him. She knew he needed to be held and comforted, and it was her duty to attend to him, but she had needs too ... and he always left her wanting.

'Joe, you can sleep in me mam's bed, I'll sleep with Annie, all right? That is ... unless you want to go home to Iris Drive? I must stay here in case I'm needed.'

'I'll stay here too. That is, if you don't mind?'

His look was pleading for understanding but she refused to meet his eye. Keeping her gaze on his shirt front, she shook her head and moved over to the coffin to say goodnight to her father.

'Ah, Da, if you can see us, if you know what's going on ... please help us through tomorrow,' she whispered, before heading towards the stairs. 'Gome on, Joe. I'll show you where you can sleep.'

He followed her up the stairs and on the landing she motioned him into her mother's bedroom. There was such a wealth of sorrow in his eyes that she felt compassion block out all the other mixed-up, hurt feelings. It was like seeing a child in pain. And wasn't that what he was to her ... a child? And who could reject a child?

With a sigh she followed him into the room and closed the door. He watched her, a hopeful expectancy about him. Pushing him gently down on to the bed, she started to unbutton his shirt.

The happiness that radiated from him was her reward, and cupping her face in his hands, he whispered, 'Thanks, Rosaleen ... thanks, love. You're too good for me.'

'It's all right, love,' she assured him, while her mind lamented. If only it was all right. If only it was.

When she undressed and crept into bed beside him, he gathered her close and she thought, ah, what the hell? We can at least cry together.

The next morning, Rosaleen awakened early and asked Joe to nip down to Iris Drive and light the fire so that later the water would be hot enough for her to bathe.

Early though it was, she discovered when she descended the stairs that Annie and her mother had beaten her to it.

They were both washed and dressed and although they were sipping tea, untouched breakfasts were pushed to one side.

'Did you sleep well?'

Annie's voice held an insinuation and Rosaleen realised that she was envying her Joe's return.

'Yes.'

Entering the scullery she reached for the pan and then hesitated. Would it look heartless to make Joe a fry? He must be hungry, he deserved a fry and one thing was sure … her da would be the last to begrudge him a proper meal.

She sat sipping a cup of tea and watched Joe wolf down the bacon and eggs, potato and soda farls. He must have lost stones in weight. Once she got him home she would soon fatten him up.

He'd be home for a week, she'd shovel food and vitamins into him while he was here. It would help to sustain him when he returned to war.

After breakfast, Joe departed for Iris Drive to carry out Rosaleen's wishes and as she washed his breakfast dishes, Annie joined her in the scullery.

'I dread the day,' she said mournfully. 'I just know it'll be awful.'

'So do I,' Rosaleen agreed with her. 'I wish it was over and done with. Although … mind you … me mam's coping better than I imagined she would.'

'Ah, but wait 'til they take me da away. Oh, the very thought of it fills me with dread. If I need you … if she's bad, will you stay the night?' Annie's voice was apologetic as she added, 'I know you'll want to be alone with Joe … but if I need you, won't you stay?'

'Of course I will. Joe'll understand,' Rosaleen assured her.

'Thanks, Rosaleen.'

However, things rarely go as expected and in the event it was Rosaleen who was worst affected.

Father Logan and the hearse were expected at eleven, and at twenty minutes to the hour the mourners gathered in the house to say the rosary. Someone suggested that Rosaleen, being the older daughter, should lead the prayers and bravely she tried, but halfway through the first decade her voice broke. At once Joe took over; with a comforting arm around her shoulders he recited the prayers in a strong voice.

Rosaleen let the Our Fathers and Hail Marys go over her head. She was standing beside the coffin and as she looked down on her father's features, she was suddenly swamped with guilt.

This dear, kind man had been so good to her. He had lavished love and affection on her all her life and she had accepted it all without so much as a thank you. When she was young, she hadn't known any better, but what about when she was an adult? She had just taken everything he did for her, as her due. As if it was his duty to attend to her. Not once had she asked if he was happy; if there was anything that she could do to make his life easier. No, she had been too wrapped up in her own problems. And the worst thing of all... she could never remember telling him how much she loved him. Probably when she was young she had told him, but never once had she said so when she was an adult. It didn't seem possible that she could have been so remiss, but it was true.

She heard the words of Hail, Holy Queen resound around the room and moved closer still to the coffin, sensing rather than seeing Joe's look of surprise as she left the shelter of his arm. The rosary was almost over, but she still had time to tell her father how much she loved him, before they put the lid on the coffin.

He was heavy, she couldn't get her arms under him to hug him, but she gripped the front of the shroud and kissed him feverishly. 'I love you, Da. Honestly! Honest to God! I just forgot to tell you.'

She felt hands try to move her away, was aware of the awful hush, but still, defying their efforts, she clung on.

'Da ... Da? Can you hear me, Da?'

It was her mother who at last managed to get through the wall of guilt that surrounded her. Gently, she put an arm around Rosaleen's shoulders.

'Come on, love. Come on now. He knows you loved him ... he

knows.'

'Really, Mam? You're sure?'

'Yes, love. Really ... really. I'm sure. Now we must let him go, in peace.'

With these words, Thelma led Rosaleen into the scullery, and whispering 'I'll be back in a minute,' left her with Amy and went to make her own farewell to her husband.

The next thing Rosaleen was aware of was wakening in her own bed in Iris Drive. Joe was sitting at the bedside holding her hand and when she opened her eyes he smiled at her.

'How are you feeling, love?'

A frown puckered her brow as she looked around the room. 'What happened?'

'You passed out.'

She struggled to sit up but he pressed her back.

'You need to rest.'

'You don't understand ... I promised Annie that I'd stay and help her with Mam.'

'It's all right ... Sean's home. His ship was in port loading cargo, and he got three days' leave. He arrived just as the funeral was moving off. He'll look after your mam and Annie. Now you go back to sleep. I'll see to everything else.'

She stretched herself. 'I ache all over.'

'That's shock. The doctor says you received a shock to your nervous system and it only hit you yesterday, when you realised that you would never see your father again.'

'Yesterday? You mean I've been sleeping since yesterday?'

'Yes. The doctor gave you a sedative.'

'How's me mam?'

'She coped very well ... surprised us all. Even came to the cemetery in one of the cars. Sean came down this morning to see how you are and he said she seems to have accepted Tommy's death ... ye know what I mean.'

Rosaleen gazed at him blankly. She couldn't understand her mother, but then, she had always thought her strange.

'Where's Laura?'

'Round at me mam's. Shall I fetch her? Do you feel well enough?'

'Yes, I feel much better now. Bring Laura home. There isn't much of your leave left. Let's not waste any more of it.'

With a grin on his face, Joe rose to his feet.

'I won't be long, love.'

When he left the room, Rosaleen swung her feet to the floor and rose shakily from the bed, surprised at how weak she felt.

Imagine her carrying on like that. What must everyone have thought? Now if it had been her mam, everybody would have understood. She couldn't understand herself what had possessed her. She knew her father couldn't hear her, couldn't feel her kisses, but she had felt compelled to try to reach him. If only she had been a better daughter. Well, she would make sure that she would have no such regrets when her mother died. From now on, she would make a point of showing her how much she meant to her. That would please her da. Yes, it would. Help to make up for her neglect of him.

Now she must see to it that Joe enjoyed the next few days. He was far too thin; needed to be fed and loved. Loved … why did the word love make her feel desolate? There were all kinds of love. Joe was probably right. Sex was just one facet of marriage, and a minor one at that. It was up to her to work at her marriage, and when the war was over, Joe would go and see about himself, wouldn't he? She could only hope so. But for now? Life must go on.

Chapter 6

It was with horror that Rosaleen learnt of the damage that was inflicted on Belfast on the night that her father was killed. Devastated by his death and preoccupied with arrangements for his funeral, she had only half listened when neighbours spoke of the raid, and her mother forbade the radio to be played whilst her father's body was in the house; said it would be disrespectful. So it was after the funeral before she became aware that the shipyard had been devastated, with three-quarters of its buildings destroyed, three corvettes burnt to a cinder and a transport ship sunk at her moorings. Three other vessels were also destroyed and many others were damaged. Like the shipyard, Short and Harland aircraft factory received direct hits, and planes, some already on the assembly line, were destroyed.

But then, things like this were expected, had to be tolerated. After all, this was what war was all about. This was why the soldiers went to Germany, to destroy their ships and planes. It was the news regarding the number of dead and the destruction of the centre of town that dismayed Rosaleen. She could not take it in that the town was almost flattened. Shaftesbury Square, she knew, had been hit, remembering how the young hospital doctor had made a detour away from that part of the city when going to the morgue. He had taken the back streets over Sandy Row, to the Donegall Road and by-passed that part of town, but they had seen in the distance the fires that raged; had been aware of the severity of the fires from the dense smoke.

Now she was being told that Donegall Place, Chichester Street, Castle Lane, North Street and Bridge Street were all wiped out, and the left-hand side of High Street was completely gutted. All those beautiful shops like Arnotts, Thorntons and the Athletic Stores, to mention but a few, were no more. Fires were the main cause of the damage. The whistling fire bombs had shot balls of fire far and wide, and lack of water to put out the flames had helped to destroy the town. All this, in spite of help once more sent post haste from the south.

St Paul's Parish escaped with only minor damage, a bomb at Beechmount and a few delayed bombs going off during the course of the next few days, but all, with the exception of her poor father (why did it have to be him?) and the family at Beechmount, without loss of life. It was hard to believe that the town was demolished, hundreds of people dead, thousands wounded and thousands more homeless. Indeed, she would have to go downtown and see for herself the devastation before she would be able to take it all in.

She also learnt that the City Hall had been hit, half of it demolished – the half that housed the beautiful banquet hall – and close by, the Water Commissioner's Office had received a direct hit.

Because of burst pipes, in some districts there was sewerage in the streets and water carts were touring the areas, delivering clean water. This meant that after spending nights in the fields, tired, depressed people had to queue, sometimes for hours, to have their buckets and pots filled, adding to the sense of hopelessness and despair. There was also an acute shortage of essential food, and many grocery shops were closed, with their owners lamenting that they were ruined. With nothing to sell and, because of another rush of refugees from town, unable to track down people who owed them money, they were in despair. How could they survive? Personally, Rosaleen thought that they should be grateful to be alive, and their shops still standing.

All this had been going on during the days of Joe's leave and she completely unaware of it. It was Amy who queued up at Hughes Bakery for bread and at the butcher's shop for meat, supplying them with their needs, and they were grateful to her for giving them these few short days to themselves. Even at night when the sirens wailed their warning, they had remained in the house, seeking refuge in the cubbyhole under the stairs, clasped in each other's arms; Laura asleep on the floor. They were content, if they must, to die together. However, after another slight raid on the 6th, no more bombs had been dropped, so far.

Joe needed a respite before returning to war and Rosaleen was determined to see that he got it, lifting and laying him, listening to his tales of hardship and, when he suffered nightmares, holding him in her arms and hushing him as she would a child, murmuring endearments, until the terror passed and he slept again. When he left to rejoin his regiment, she was glad to note that he was more relaxed, although she could detect the reluctance with which he departed.

'Surely it won't be long now?' she questioned him. 'Can the war last much longer?'

He hugged her close. 'I hope not. All I want is to be back here with you and Laura.'

Human nature being what it is, the retort hovered on her lips: 'Well, you didn't have to go! You didn't have to enlist!' But, hearing the misery in his voice, she bit back the words and defying the tears to fall, smiled brightly.

'If the Americans enter the war, it won't last much longer. We must pray that they join the fight against Hitler, and then you'll be home in no time,' she consoled him.

He nodded, but it was a mournful sight. He put her firmly away from him as the taxi drew up to the door. Lifting a weeping, bewildered Laura up in his arms he kissed her fiercely, then thrusting her at Rosaleen, hurried from the house. Rosaleen rushed to the window. Lifting the net curtain, she watched him enter the taxi. Then, with a final wave, he was gone.

Later that day, Annie and May arrived together. Rosaleen greeted them warmly, but with a surprised, questioning look in her eyes.

Seeing the look, Annie explained, 'We met at the corner, so we did.'

'Rosaleen ... imagine me not being at your da's funeral!' May exclaimed. 'But I didn't know. I only heard last night that he was dead. Ye see, we don't get the *Irish News*.'

'It's all right, May,' Rosaleen assured her kindly. 'I guessed that's what happened.'

She turned to Annie. 'How's me mam?'

Annie rolled her eyes towards heaven. 'Oh, Rosaleen, you don't know the half of it. Sean and I spent his entire leave roaming the streets looking for her. And he only got three days' leave, so he did. He wouldn't have got home at all only his ship was. in port for repairs.'

Concerned, Rosaleen pressed her: 'What do you mean? Roamed the streets? Why did you roam the streets?'

'Every time we left me mam alone for a minute, she took off. The first time was the day after the funeral. When Sean was down here telling Joe how well she was, she took off ... just a coat over her nightdress, and slippers on her feet. It was three hours later that she was found, wandering on the Shankill Road, and we had to go to the Shankill Road police station to collect her.'

Rosaleen groped behind her for a chair and sat down. 'Oh, my God! Why on earth didn't you come for me and Joe?'

'You weren't very well.' Annie examined her face intently. 'How are you now?'

'I'm fine.' Rosaleen felt colour rush to her cheeks as she recalled her behaviour on the day of her father's funeral, and overcome with embarrassment, she muttered, 'I feel such a fool. I don't know what came over me. Imagine me getting on like that.'

'Well, you were always closer to me da than I was. You were his favourite,' Annie said sadly, and Rosaleen was dismayed. Had her father favoured her?

But her sister was continuing: 'Mam was great at the funeral... and afterwards. When people came back to the house she sat and chatted, praised me da to the heavens, but the next day ... oh boy! She went berserk. The thing that surprised us most was that every time she took off, it was always the Shankill Road she headed for.

Imagine! Her that hated the Shankill. Wouldn't set foot on it when she was normal.'

Rosaleen's breath caught in her throat at these words, and she whispered fearfully. 'What on earth do you mean ... normal?'

Annie grimaced. 'She's in a bad way, Rosaleen. Sean told Joe that she was coping, but she wasn't. We thought that she would improve, but she hasn't. I haven't been able to get to work. I'm afraid to leave her alone.'

'Huh! You should've come for me. She's my mother too. I'd a right to know.'

'I waited 'til Joe's leave was over because ... well, God knows when you'll see him again.' She watched Rosaleen covertly as she added, 'Doctor Hughes wants us to put her into Grahame's Home.'

At Rosaleen's start of dismay, and seeing her mouth open to protest, Annie hurried on, 'Just for a short while, Rosaleen. He says she'd be well cared for, so he did.'

'And what did you say to that? Did you agree?' Rosaleen's voice was indignant, her look threatening.

Annie shook her head. 'No ... I said I'd have to talk it over with you first.'

'I'm glad to hear that. 'Cause no way is she going into that madhouse.'

Annie's head reared back defiantly. 'Hey, hold on now! It's all right you talking like that, Rosaleen, but I've to go to work.' The face she thrust at her sister was flushed with anger. 'Will you be able to look after her during the day, eh? Will you?'

'You don't have to go to work,' Rosaleen retorted, her face matching Annie's for bright colour. 'I'm sure Sean sends you plenty of money, and me mam has some insurance left, and ... she'll probably be back to work in no time. Anyhow ...' her lips tightened and her eyes flashed '... we'll work something out between us. No way is she going into Grahame's Home. No way! Do you hear me? Good God, do you want to send her around the bend? It's only natural that she's upset at the moment. Give her time to get over the loss of me da.'

'Doctor Hughes says it's not an asylum ... just a hospital for nervous disorders and people unable to cope. People like me mam who've had a bereavement. He says it would give her a chance to recover.'

May squirmed uneasily in her chair; she didn't want to sit listening to this private business. At the first lull in the conversation, she rushed in.

'Look, Rosaleen, I'll go down and see me mam and come back later, OK?'

Rosaleen came back to reality with a start, and turned to her friend.

'No! No, May. That won't be necessary. You'll have to excuse us, getting all het up in front of you. I'll go up and see me mam tonight. That's what I intended doing anyhow.' She glanced across and nodded at Annie. 'We'll talk then. Meantime, I'll make us all a cup of tea.'

Annie rose quickly to her feet. 'Not for me, thank you. I'll leave you and May to have a chat. I don't want to be away too long. Me mam's in Mrs Murphy's.' She turned to May with a wry smile. 'Wish we were meeting under happier circumstances, but that's life. Hope your mother recovers.'

May jerked her head in a hopeless gesture. 'We can only keep our fingers crossed, Annie. See you soon.'

When the door closed on her, Rosaleen turned to May.

'What did she mean about your mother?'

'Me mam's had a stroke, so she has. She's bad, Rosaleen, paralysed from the neck down.'

'Ah, May, I'm sorry to hear that.'

May blinked furiously to hold back the tears. 'I wish it'd been me da,' she ground out through clenched teeth.

'Oh, don't say that. Whatever you do, don't say that,' Rosaleen begged her. 'Never wish ill on anyone. It always rebounds on you.'

May grunted. 'Huh! You sound like Father Docherty. When I said that to him, he nearly ate me.'

Picturing the big, stern parish priest of St Peter's, to which May belonged, Rosaleen gasped, 'You said that to Father Docherty?'

'Why not? It's what I was thinking.'

'What did he say?'

'Huh … he said me mam was ready to meet God and me da

wasn't. He said I should pray for me da. Pray for him? I pray all right. I pray he'll roast in hell!'

'Oh, May, don't ... don't,' Rosaleen whispered, and a shiver ran down her spine. She wasn't really superstitious, but still... 'Will your mam recover?'

May's head swung slowly from side to side and the tears could be contained no longer. 'A couple of weeks ... maybe a couple of months. She knows nobody, can do nothing for herself, and the worst of it is ...' great sobs choked her and tears ran unheeded down her cheeks, to fall on her tightly clenched hands '...me da won't let me stay to look after her.'

'Is he back in the house then?'

'Oh, yes. He arrived the minute he heard about it, playing the concerned, doting husband. But he fools nobody. Everybody knows that he tortured me mam. And, Rosaleen ... I just know he won't look after her properly.' Once more sobs caused her to pause. 'The lads will do their best, but they're on shifts and a woman's touch is needed. Our wee Jenny's too young.'

'Ah, May.' Rosaleen's arms stretched out and clasped her close.

After a few moments, May wiped her eyes and pushing Rosaleen back, grimaced at her.

'It's me who should be comforting you. At least my mam's still alive. Your da's dead. I cried when Billy came home last night and told me. Your da was such a good, caring man. No wonder your mam's had a breakdown.'

Rosaleen shook her head sadly and went to the bureau in the corner. She didn't want to talk about her da. It was too soon; the pain too close to the surface, ready to fill her with guilt and remorse. Forcing it into the back of her mind, she opened the bureau and produced a bottle of gin.

'I think we need something stronger than tea, May, a wee drink, eh? Widow's ruin.' She held the bottle, which was half full, up for May's inspection. 'It's all I have. Do you fancy a drop?'

May was looking at her, a comic expression on her face, and Rosaleen, in spite of the misery that engulfed her, laughed aloud when her friend exclaimed, 'I never thought I'd see the day that you'd drink gin! But I'll be glad to join you.'

'Oh, I'm a changed girl, May. You'd never believe half the things I get up to.'

'No, I wouldn't!' May bestowed a wry smile on her. 'Your conscience wouldn't let you go far wrong.'

Rosaleen smiled grimly and changed the subject. If only May knew! Why, she'd be horrified.

'Where's the child, May?'

'Mrs Mercer has him. She's awful good, so she is. Says I'm to stay as long as me mam needs me, but that aul bugger won't let me. He got a great kick out of showing me the door, but I'll go back tonight when Colin's there. He won't take any nonsense from him.'

'Stay here, May. I'd be glad of your company and you'll be able to nip down to Spinner Street any time you feel like it.'

'You mean ... bring Ian here?'

Rosaleen nodded her head excitedly. 'Of course! Why not? Billy can come and stay as often as he likes, and I'll be glad of your company.'

'Billy's only working half time, ye know. You might be fed up looking at him.'

'Not working? I thought the Falls Flax had plenty of orders.' Rosaleen's eyes were wide with wonder. What on earth was wrong?

'They have! Loads!' May assured her. 'But the raw material's not getting through, what with the docks and the railways being bombed, so they're working a three-day week, until further notice.' The look May gave Rosaleen was puzzled. 'All the engineering works are either closed down or on short time. There's hardly anybody working. There's thousands on the outdoor relief. Only the like of Mackie's is working full time. They've taken over orders that Short and Harland can't do and they're working around the clock. I can understand Annie wanting to go back to work. If she doesn't, she'll lose her job. They'll give her a wee breathing space on account of your da dying in the blitz, but the work has to be got out. If she delays too long, someone else will be only too glad to fill her shoes.'

Rosaleen sighed. 'May, I'm not with it. With Joe being home, I haven't been out of the house. While he was here Amy kept us supplied with food and I didn't realise it was so bad.'

'We'll take a walk downtown this afternoon and let you see just how bad it is. Or ...' May grimaced, '... on second thoughts maybe we shouldn't, it's enough to depress a saint. You wouldn't know where one street ends and another starts. Honest to God, Rosaleen, you can stand in Castle Street and right down to the Albert Clock at the bottom of High Street is flattened.' Her gaze was vacant as if seeing the ruins in her mind's eye. 'The right-hand side of High Street is still standing, but Bridge Street's rubble ... so is Lower North Street and Donegall Street. All those big beautiful shops destroyed. And the clock itself is tilting to one side. Maybe it'll have to come down and all.'

Rosaleen took a gulp of the gin, grimaced with distaste, and proffered the bottle to May.

'No, thank you, I've enough here, I'll have to stay sober. Did you mean what you said just now? About me staying here?'

She watched Rosaleen closely, ready to back down if her friend looked dismayed. In case she had made the suggestion on the spur of the moment, and now regretted it.

She need not have worried, Rosaleen replied quickly, 'Of course I mean it. I tell ye, I'll be glad of your company.'

And they touched glasses and drank to that.

However, they had not reckoned with Billy. When May put the idea to him, he hit the roof.

'Are you mad? Do you think I'd let you take Ian over to live beside Mackie's? Wise up, woman.' He saw her lips tighten and softened his tone. 'Look, I know you want to be near your mother, but Ian must come first. Eh, love?'

May's face crumpled, and she wailed, 'I have to go ... can't you see? I ran off and left me mam in the lurch once before when she needed me. I can't leave her lying there, helpless, and that aul bugger ...' She turned aside and fought for control. At last she wiped her eyes and faced him again. 'I'm sorry, Billy, but I just can't stay. I'll leave Ian with your mam, and you can take him to the fields at night. All right?'

She watched him draw himself to his full height, his face a tight, angry mask, and gasped in dismay when he growled, 'No, it's not all right. I forbid you to go. You're my wife and your place is here with me and Ian.' Surprise was etched on her face as she gaped at him. Never before had he denied her anything, and that he should start now when she most needed his understanding, hurt her.

'Ah, Billy, you don't mean that.'

He nodded. 'Oh, but I do. I'd be a fool to let you stay over beside Mackie's. My God, May, they've hit everywhere else. If they come back, it's Mackie's they'll be looking for.'

'Billy ... I have to go.' Her voice was soft, pleading.

His lips tightened and he played his trump card. She might leave him, and the indications lately were that she would like to, but she would never leave Ian.

'If you go, Ian stays. And I don't want you coming every other day upsetting him.'

He watched her head rear back; her chin jut out.

'Don't blackmail me, Billy,' she warned, her voice tight with emotion.

He ignored the warning. 'That's the situation, May. If you love Ian, you stay and look after him.'

He was ashamed of himself, bargaining with his son, but he had nothing else to bargain with. Lately May had withdrawn into herself. She who had been so loving and warm was building a wall between them and he couldn't penetrate it. He was at a loss as to what to do, and the uncertainty was killing him. Had she met someone else?

They stared at each other, a hard, bitter look, then with a sad nod of the head, May moved towards the stairs.

'I'll pack me bags.'

Billy watched her climb the stairs, hurt and humiliation a tight ball in his chest, Well, he'd no intentions of backing down. Let her go! He wasn't going to beg. He'd gotten over the loss of one wife, he could do it again.

But you didn't love Diane, an inner voice taunted him, and in spite of his resolutions he followed her up the stairs.

Standing at the door of the bedroom he watched her remove

clothes from drawers and wardrobe and pack them into a suitcase. He avoided looking at the bed where she had given him so much joy. This plain, homely girl who held his heart in the palm of her hand. What had gone wrong? They had been so happy. He had let her have her way in everything. As long as she was content, so was he. Perhaps he had been too easy going. Perhaps he should have shown her who was boss long ago. Now it was too late.

May avoided looking at him. She longed to feel his arms around her, to beg for his understanding, but she was aware that sooner or later this had to happen. They could not go on as they had lately, and she would be the first to admit that it was her fault. She was the one who had changed, and the worst of it was, she couldn't tell him why. No. She had given him her solemn promise and she could not break it. When she had made the promise, everything in the garden was rosy; love had overcome all obstacles. However, the blitz had changed all that and she couldn't help how she felt now.

When the case was full, she pressed it shut. Raising her head she met his eyes.

'May, don't do this to me, please. I beg you.'

'I'm sorry, Billy, but I have to go.'

As she waited for him to move aside, he reached out and his arms gripped her close.

'Well, if you must … you must, but I didn't really mean what I said. You know, about upsetting Ian. You can come back anytime and see him.' He drew back and his eyes begged her forgiveness. 'Every day if you like. And when your mam recovers, or the worst comes to the worst and she … You'll come home, won't you?'

She nodded mutely, to show that she understood. The need for him was rising and knowing that it would serve no real purpose should she submit, she exerted pressure on his chest, indicating that she wanted to be free from his arms.

Silently, he released her and moved to one side.

Entering the back bedroom, May stood and gazed down at her son, tears blinding her. Billy was right. Ian should be looked after here. He would take him to the fields at the first sign of danger whereas she would probably want to stay with her mam. But she would have seen that the child was safe. Yes, she would have made sure that Ian was safe. She would have made Kevin take him and Jenny up to the Falls Park at the first sign of danger. No, he had been wrong to blackmail her like that. That hurt.

When she left the room, Billy sank down on the bed. Ears strained, he listened to her descending the stairs. Hoping against hope that she would change her mind and come back. When he heard the outer door close on her, he buried his head in his hands.

Where had he gone wrong? What had changed May?

Rosaleen's visit to see her mother started in fear and apprehension. Thelma had cut herself off from reality and when Rosaleen entered the room she ignored her and stayed huddled over the fire. Annie nodded in her direction and mouthed the words: 'I told you so. Maybe now you'll believe me.'

Then, touching her mother gently on the shoulder, she said softly. 'Mam ... here's Rosaleen to see you.'

Thelma made no sign that she had heard her and once more Annie bestowed on Rosaleen a knowing look.

Pulling a small stool close to her mother's chair, Rosaleen sat down. Taking her mother's hand between her own two, she exerted pressure on the cold, limp fingers until Thelma slowly moved her head and focused her eyes on her.

'How are you, Mam?'

After a short silence, Annie whispered with a shake of the head. 'She won't answer you. She hardly ever speaks.'

'I'm all right, Rosaleen.'

Thelma's words caused Annie to gape in amazement and Rosaleen had to smile when her mother added, 'Make Rosaleen a cup of tea, Annie. I'm sure she'd like one. It's cold outside.'

Grinning widely, in a happy, relieved, agreeable voice, Annie teased her. 'And how would you know that, eh, Mam? You haven't been out of the house for days.'

A confused frown gathered on Thelma's brow. 'I thought...' She turned and bestowed a worried gaze on Annie. 'Surely I was over in Mrs Murphy's today?' she queried.

Annie clasped her hand to her head.

'Of course you were, Mam. It's me that's confused … not you.'
She grimaced at Rosaleen's broad smile and headed for the scullery.
'I'll make the tea.'

And that was the turning point. Although Thelma was quiet and
withdrawn, and her days were spent sitting gazing into the fire,
she agreed to go to Rosaleen's house when Annie was working,
and Grahame's Home for the mentally disturbed was mentioned
no more. Rosaleen sometimes wondered if her mother had heard
the doctor speak about Grahame's Home and perhaps this had
hastened her recovery. Not that she had fully recovered, far from
it, but whatever the reason, the wandering up the Shankill Road
stopped.

It was some days before Rosaleen realised that all was not well
with May. When she arrived alone to stay Rosaleen had thought
it reasonable that Billy did not want his son staying over in the
shadow of Mackie's Foundry. And it was only natural that May
should be depressed. Wasn't her mother at death's door? Still, there
was something else. Something was drastically wrong, she could
sense it. Why hadn't Billy brought Ian to see his mother? Why did
May change the subject when she inquired after Billy? Rosaleen
was at her wit's end when at last things came to a head.

Kate Brady lasted just over two weeks and it was after her funeral
that Rosaleen learned May and Billy were separated.

Billy was at the funeral and returned from the graveyard to
Spinner Street to the wake.

It was late in the evening when the last mourner departed and
Rosaleen, who had stayed back to help with the washing up, made
her excuses and prepared to go home.

At once May was on her feet. Bidding her brothers goodnight,
she made it obvious that she was accompanying Rosaleen. A tight-
lipped Billy, in a voice that would not be denied, declared that he
would walk them home.

The short journey through the dark, deserted streets was a
nightmare to Rosaleen as she and Billy made inane conversation
and a silent May walked some steps ahead of them.

At the door, in a dilemma, Rosaleen said tentatively, 'Look, I'll
nip round and see how Laura and Amy are. It'll give you two a

173

chance to talk.'

Amy had offered to look after Laura, and Rosaleen was aware that, like the rest of the Falls Road, she stayed awake even when the sirens didn't wail their warning, just in case of a raid. Although fewer people trekked up to the Falls Park and countryside every night now, they didn't retire until about two in the morning, when it was assumed that the danger of a raid was past, so Rosaleen was confident that she would find Amy still awake.

'No!' May's voice rang out sharply in the still night air. 'Billy won't be coming in. He's a busy man. He won't have time to talk to me.'

'May!' His voice was, if possible, sharper. 'Stop this nonsense. Of course we must talk. We've arrangements to make.'

'We can do that through the solicitors, Billy. Now that Mam's dead, I can start to put my affairs in order.'

With these words, she brushed past them and entered the house.

Standing on the pavement, Rosaleen gaped at Billy in dismay. 'I'm sorry, but I can't ask you in.'

'It's all right, Rosaleen. It's all right ... don't upset yourself. Goodnight.'

Sensing the deep unhappiness in him, she gripped his arm as he closed the gate of the small forecourt.

'Billy, I don't mean to be nosey ... but what on earth's wrong?'

'Hah! I wish I knew, Rosaleen. I wish I knew. I've wracked me brains and I'll be damned if I can see what I did wrong. I gave her everything and this is the result.' He paused a moment, hating himself for asking the next question. 'Rosaleen ... is there anybody else? Another man?'

'Good Lord, Billy, of course there isn't. The past few weeks have been devoted to looking after her mother. I thought that's why you didn't come. I thought you were giving her a breather while she nursed her mam. All this has come as a shock to me.'

'You mean she hasn't talked about us?'

'Not one word, Billy. Not one wee word.'

'Oh.' He looked perplexed, then, 'Here, I almost forgot.' He plunged his hand into his inside jacket pocket, and produced a bulky envelope, which he thrust into her hand. 'I intended to give this to her, but I didn't get a chance … couldn't get her alone. And, Rosaleen … if she's ever in need, you'll let me know, won't you?'

'I can't make any promises, Billy. May is very proud and independent, you know that. If she doesn't want you to know how she is, well … she's my best friend and her wishes come first. I hope I don't get into trouble for taking this.' She wagged the envelope in his direction, sorry that she had been so ready to accept it. May would probably be angry with her.

'I understand, Rosaleen, but make her take that. After all, she is still my wife. Goodnight.'

With these words, he turned on his heel and strode down the street, a picture of misery.

When Rosaleen entered the house, May had already retired to the back bedroom and although Rosaleen tapped on the door, there was no reply. The next morning she was gone from the house before Rosaleen descended the stairs and it was lunch time when she returned.

'When on earth have you been?' Rosaleen greeted her reproachfully. I've been worried stiff about you.'

'Afraid I might commit suicide?'

A wry smile crossed Rosaleen's face. 'No, never that. You're too strong a person to give into despair.'

'You're right. Mine isn't the first marriage to flounder, and it won't be the last.' She squared her shoulders and proudly declared, 'I've been out getting meself a job. Our Colin told me that Mackie's were looking for two learners and I start work there on Monday.'

This news didn't come as a surprise to Rosaleen. May was not one to let the grass grow under her feet.

'Good for you,' she praised her, and going to the bureau, retrieved the envelope Billy had given her the night before. Tentatively she proffered it to her friend. 'Now, May, don't be angry with me … he made me take it.'

May opened the envelope and peered inside. Rosaleen could see that all the notes were big and white. Fivers! And quite a lot of them.

May's face twisted in a grimace as she fingered the notes. 'These'll help pay for the divorce, so they will. It means he can get rid of me sooner.'

'May, don't say that. Billy's terribly upset. I doubt if he wants to be rid of you.'

'Well then, explain this to me, Rosaleen. Explain this to me.' Her voice choked with emotion. 'Why did he not bring my son down to see me? Eh? I've been out of the house three whole weeks and he never once brought the child to see me. He knew I was stuck in the house, looking after me mam, and still he never came. I'll never forgive him for that. Never!'

Unable to think of a suitable reply to this accusation, Rosaleen groped about in her bewildered brain and at last said haltingly, 'Perhaps Ian was poorly.'

'All the more reason why he should've been in touch with me,' May interrupted her angrily. 'No, it's all over between me and Billy.' A harsh laugh left her lips. 'The neighbours in Spinner Street will be glad. They'll be able to say: "We told her so! She should have listened to us." '

She turned away for a moment. 'He didn't even mention Ian to me yesterday ... not one word. He was there for hours and hours and he never mentioned Ian once. Never told me how the child is.'

'Ah, May now ... be fair! You didn't give him a chance. You avoided him all day. Remember, I was there. I saw the way you kept him at arm's length. And he was probably waiting for you to inquire about Ian. How come you didn't ask about him, eh? Your only child, and you haven't seen him for three weeks, and you didn't ask about him.' The look she bestowed on May was scornful. 'It seems to me you were both at fault.'

May reacted angrily to her criticism. 'Don't you preach to me! You don't know the circumstances.'

Ignoring her anger, Rosaleen moved closer and beseeched her, 'No, May, I don't know the circumstances, but it seems to me that you should give Billy a chance to put things right.'

Tentatively, she placed a hand on her arm. 'May ... what went wrong? You and Billy were so close. I used to envy you, you were that close. What on earth happened?'

Even in her misery, May gaped at Rosaleen in astonishment. 'You envied me? You, who had everything, envied me?' A hand covered her chest. 'Me ... living in sin on the Shankill Road. Ah! Don't mock me, Rosaleen. You always thought that this would happen. Come on now, admit it. Right from the start you thought that Billy and I would break up.' She thrust a red, angry face close to Rosaleen's. 'Didn't you?'

Aware that, at the start, she had expected the marriage to flounder, Rosaleen answered honestly.

'You're right, May. At first I had deep misgivings about your marriage but, against all the odds, you and Billy made a go of it. You were so happy, so close. It was your closeness that I envied. With different backgrounds, and different beliefs, you were still so happy. It was a joy to watch the two of you together. But it was your closeness that I envied most. Not many couples are as much in harmony. You're a fool if you don't fight for your happiness.'

Seeing May's eyes go round with wonder, and guessing that she was wondering just why she and Joe weren't close, Rosaleen hurried on. 'You really should talk it over with Billy. I'm sure things can be sorted out.'

May's mouth opened to speak but shut without uttering a sound. How could she tell Rosaleen about her change of heart. Why, she would laugh at her. Tell Rosaleen that she, who had never been gospel greedy, was afraid of losing her soul?

'If you don't mind, Rosaleen, I don't want to talk about it.' And to change the subject, she confided. 'I'm moving back home to Spinner Street, so I am.'

'Will your da allow you back?'

'No way! But he's not staying there. It seems some fool of a woman has been looking after him while he's been out of the house.'

'Really? You know, May, I felt sorry for him yesterday. He seemed so lost ... so unhappy.'

'Huh! So he fooled you too? My da's crafty. There'll always be some idiot there to care for him. He must have some kind of charm, but I never saw it displayed in our house. No bloody fear. All I ever saw was scorn and dislike.' A puzzled frown knitted her brows. 'Do you know something, Rosaleen? I sometimes thought my da hated me. Even when the boys were young, he never hit them as hard as he hit me. Is it any wonder I hate him?' She paused and thought for a few moments. 'He used to shout at me: "If it wasn't for you, I wouldn't have married yer ma." It was a long time before I understood what he meant. Imagine blaming me on that, Rosaleen. Imagine me mam going through life, getting that thrown at her every time he was drunk.'

'Ah, May … you've had an awful hard life. You've been through the mill, so you have.'

The tears clung to May's lashes and the smile she gave was more a grimace, but there was no doubting her sincerity when she proudly declared: 'I've had over two wonderful years with Billy Mercer. Some people don't even get that, so I consider myself lucky.'

And as she turned away towards the bathroom, Rosaleen knew the tears were falling. But what could she do if her friend wouldn't confide in her?

With so many mills and engineering places shut down, there was a rush of young men to join the army, and it came as no surprise when, two weeks later, Billy arrived at Rosaleen's house to announce that he had joined up. He had Ian with him and as May hungrily reached for her son, Rosaleen lifted her coat and slipped quietly from the house, sending a prayer heavenward that things between Billy and May would be sorted out.

However, when she returned some hours later there was no sign of Billy and Ian and she found May huddled on the settee, crying as if her heart would break.

Taking May in her arms, Rosaleen sat and rocked her in silent sympathy. At last May drew back and, blowing her nose, confided, 'He's joined the army because of me, Rosaleen. He thinks I don't love him and he's joined up.'

'I wish I knew what to say. I wish I could help you.'

'Nobody can help me now, Rosaleen. I've made a mess of everything, and if it was only me that was suffering, I wouldn't care.' She started to sob. 'But Billy's unhappy, too, and Ian's fretting.'

Rosaleen gripped her by the shoulders and shook her roughly.

'Oh, May! You make me want to scream! If you love Billy ... GO SEE HIM! Tell him you love him.'

But May just shook her head in a hopeless gesture and Rosaleen slumped back on the settee in despair. How could she help if May wouldn't listen to her?

'Rosaleen?'

May's head was buried in her hands and her voice was so low Rosaleen had to lean closer to hear it.

'Yes?'

'If I tell you what's wrong ... promise you won't laugh?'

'May, I never felt less like laughing in my life.'

Voice stronger now, she continued. 'Well, do you remember the night your da died?'

Rosaleen nodded. Would she ever forget?

'Well, there had been so many false alarms, we didn't bother trekking up to the fields. We stayed in the house ... in the coalhole.' May's head lifted and she turned to Rosaleen. 'It was awful, remember? Those whistling fire bombs.' Her eyes were vacant and her lips trembled as she relived the experience. Then, with an abrupt shake of the head, she continued, 'Well, the row of houses behind ours was hit. I'll never forget it ... it was awful. The screeching whistle ... the thud ... and then our house shook. I thought it was going to fall in on top of us. I was sure that we were all going to die ...' Her voice trailed off and Rosaleen sat silent, not wanting to interrupt the flow of May's words. She could picture the scene. The whistling bombs had been terrifying, even from afar, but it must have been awful to have been enclosed and one fall nearby.

May gave a grimace and continued, 'I kept thinking of how I was living in sin, and the fact that Ian wasn't baptised ... that tortured me, so it did.' Her head rose and she fixed Rosaleen with a shamefaced look. 'You must think me a right hypocrite.'

When Rosaleen shook her head and smiled sadly, denying May's accusation, she continued: 'Well ... I was so worried, I promised God that I would put things right. And I really meant to ... but, you see, when Billy and I discovered that we shared a lot of interests and he began to get serious about me ... he asked me to make him a promise that I'd never badger him about bringing any children we had up in the Catholic faith.'

A harsh laugh left her lips as she thought of how naive she had been. Born in the shadow of Clonard Monastery, practically reared by the Redemptorist fathers, how could she have convinced herself that the Church didn't matter to her?

'Anyhow, I promised. I vowed I would never mention the Catholic faith to Billy. And to tell you the truth, at that time I wasn't worried. I was actually amused and surprised when you said that you were worried about my soul. Everything in the garden was rosy, and I was glad to get away from me da.'

'May, why didn't you confide in me?' Rosaleen was reproachful. 'We're best friends.'

'Now, honestly, Rosaleen, tell the truth – do you tell me everything, hmmm?'

Sean's face rose before Rosaleen's mind and she was glad that dusk was falling and May could not see her blush, as she admitted, 'Well… not everything.'

'I thought so. Mind you, I don't blame you. When you're married … well, your husband comes first and you just don't talk as freely. The worst of it was we'd just heard that Billy's ex-wife was one of the people killed in Percy Street … remember the sixty victims? Well, she was one of those. He would have thought that I was suddenly remorseful about the Church because he was now free to marry me in it.' She shook her head. 'I couldn't break my promise, but at the same time I was uneasy. What if there was another raid? What if I died in a state of mortal sin?' She threw another wry smile at Rosaleen. 'Imagine! Me of all people worried about my soul. I didn't realise that at heart I was a staunch Catholic. I began to avoid Billy … you know what I mean.' A smile flitted across her face. 'I never had so many headaches in my life before. I think he thought I'd gone off him. That I fancied somebody else.'

At Rosaleen's start of surprise, May fixed her with an intent look and she found herself offering the information that Billy had indeed thought so. May's sigh was heartfelt. 'Poor Billy. Poor, poor Billy. He can't figure out what's wrong … but at least I put something right. Do you know what I did, Rosaleen?' She leant forward and held Rosaleen's eye. 'On the morning after the fire raid, I baptised Ian.'

'You baptised him?'

May laughed, and admitted, 'I can smile at the idea now, but at the time I was deadly serious. I was shaking like a leaf ... afraid of not doing it properly. I nearly drowned the child ... he screamed blue murder, so he did. If anyone had come in, they would have had me up for cruelty.'

'May!' Rosaleen found herself laughing softly at the idea. 'Ah, May.'

'Aye, I know. You may well laugh, but I kept thinking that if we were all to die in a raid, at least Ian would go to heaven with Billy, and I deserved to join aul Nick down below.' The look she gave Rosaleen was questioning. 'Rosaleen, truthfully now, have you ever wished that you'd been born a Protestant? I mean, if they do something wrong ... but they don't realise it's wrong ... well then, it's not a sin. But if we do something wrong, we're damned, if you see what I mean.'

Rosaleen nodded her head. 'I see what you mean, but no ... I've never wanted to be a Protestant. But listen, May, you'll have to tell Billy the truth. You can't let him go to war thinking you don't care ... thinking you fancy someone else. You just can't do it. When does he leave?'

'In two weeks' time, but I can't back down on my word, Rosaleen. I just can't.' May was adamant, and Rosaleen had to admit defeat.

Not that she had any intention of giving up. She hadn't made any promises, and just in case May got the idea of extracting one from her, she changed the subject.

'What about Ian? What's happening to him while Billy's away?'

'Billy's parents are moving to Newry. His aunt has a house there and they're taking Ian with them, until the war's over. I'm glad, Rosaleen. It's all for the best. I can't have him with me, what with me working. He's safer away from Belfast, and sure thousands of children are evacuated away from their parents. And this way ... at least he's with his grandparents.'

A glance at the clock brought her to her feet. 'Look at the time. I've wasted your evening, but I'm glad I was up here when Billy called and not down in Spinner Street. I'd have hated him to go there. And it was good of you to leave us alone. Thanks, Rosaleen. Thanks for everything.'

Although it was a warm evening, Billy came through the gates of the Falls Flax, his step slow, shoulders hunched up around his ears as if from the cold. Rosaleen's heart went out to him, and when she hailed him and saw alarm fill his face, she felt like weeping. He hurried across the road and stopped in front of her, his eyes questioning.

'It's all right, Billy. Don't look so worried ... May's all right,' she hastened to assure him. 'Look, can we talk?'

'I'll walk you home.'

He fell into step beside her, his look still intent and questioning. All day she had been rehearsing what she would say to him, but now her mind was blank. She did not know where to start.

Suddenly, he smiled down at her. 'Well now, Rosaleen, I'm sure you didn't meet me just for the pleasure of my company. Is May well?'

'As well as can be expected.'

At once he stopped in his tracks and gripped his arm. 'What do you mean ... as well as can be expected. Is she ill?'

'She's suffering from a broken heart, Billy.'

'Hah!' His head went back and he looked down the length of his nose at her. 'And just who's breaking her heart? Eh, Rosaleen?'

'Come off it, Billy. You know there's no one else.'

'Well then, what the hell's goin' on, Rosaleen?' he cried in exasperation.

Haltingly, she tried to explain May's change of heart towards her religion, how the blitz had brought home to her that she could die in mortal sin. To her surprise, Billy heard her out in silence and then shrugged his shoulders.

'So that's what was wrong. A big change of heart, eh? It wouldn't have had anything to do with the fact that my ex-wife was killed, I suppose?'

'No. That's why she didn't tell you. She said you'd think that.'

He shrugged these words aside. 'What about Ian, eh? She spent weeks away from him. Showed no interest whatsoever in his welfare. Our son ... and she didn't give a shit whether he was alive or dead. Can she explain that away? Eh, Rosaleen? What has she to say about that?'

Deep dismay filled her. She had expected Billy to fall over himself to go to May, had pictured a happy reunion before he left for the army, but here he was deriding May.

'Billy, May dotes on that child! She's letting him stay with you because she knows that you can look after him better at present than she can. It will be different when the war's over. She'll want him back, and believe you me, she'll fight you tooth and nail for him. And another thing – May doesn't know that I'm here. I did this off my own bat. I thought I was doing the right thing. I thought you loved her ...'

He interrupted her sadly. 'I do love her, Rosaleen, indeed I do, but, personally I believe Ian will be better off if I rear him alone. He'll have less hangups away from the Catholic faith. And as for getting married in the Catholic Church ... no way. There's no way that I can do that. I made that clear to May before I married her and I haven't changed me mind. Ye see, Rosaleen, my da's in the Orange Order and it would break his heart if I married in the Catholic Church ... he'd have to leave the order. I couldn't do that to him. I'm all they have and I've loved my parents longer than I've loved May. So, as far as I'm concerned, unless May comes back on my terms, which, after all, are what she agreed to in the first place, she needn't come back at all.'

In the face of such determination, Rosaleen was dismayed. She could only hope that May never heard about her attempt to win Billy back.

They had reached the corner of Springfield Avenue and she stopped and offered him her hand. She had allowed him to walk with her in this direction, picturing May maybe being on the dayshift and coming along, and she and Billy having a wonderful, happy reunion while she looked benignly on. Now she was afraid of May coming along and Billy sighting her. Why, May would never forgive her for interfering.

'I'm sorry, Billy. Seems I should have minded my own business. Sure you won't mention it to May, if you happen to be talking to her?'

He put his hands on her shoulders and kissed her on the cheek.

'Thanks, Rosaleen. Thanks for caring. But as you can see it's a hopeless case. Ye know, it's right what they say. You should stick with your own kind.'

Mackie's workers were starting to trickle down the Springfield Road and Rosaleen drew away from him.

'I'd better go now, Billy.' She nodded towards the workers. 'Just in case May comes along. God, but she'd never forgive me for interfering! So long, and safe home from the war.'

She hurried down Springfield Avenue and Billy watched her out of sight. Then, aware that he might see May if he waited, he walked down the road and sheltered in the doorway of Hughes Bakery.

At last he saw her approaching and drew back out of sight. She looked awful – thin and haggard, and she obviously wasn't bothering about keeping her hair blonde, the roots showed black for about four inches.

He examined her critically. She looked common. Common as muck. Was this what he was breaking his heart over? His lips tightened angrily. He must need his head examined. Even so, as she passed by, it took all his willpower to stop him from hailing her. After all, who was he to think anyone looked common? With a mug like his, he was in a position to criticise no one.

He waited until she had passed by, deep in conversation with Colin, and then he headed back up the Springfield Road, his thoughts in a whirl.

Rosaleen was right; he knew in his heart that May doted on Ian. She would put his welfare first, before her own feelings. It was unselfish of her to let him have the child. It would be only right to let her see him before he went to Newry. Yes, he would have to arrange that. Even his mother thought his attitude towards May was hard. But then, she didn't understand. The next two weeks could not pass quickly enough for him. After that he wouldn't have time to brood. And if it wasn't for Ian, he wouldn't care whether or not he returned.

On Saturday morning Rosaleen was making her way down to the Post Office when May hailed her from the tram stop at the Falls Road junction.

'You're out early,' Rosaleen greeted her, and her eyes took in her friend's appearance. From the neat brown court shoes to the top of the pale, ash-blonde hair, she was pleased with what she saw. May had been letting herself go, but today she was back in form. Dressed in a dark blue suit and white blouse, with a beret tilted to one side on her head, she looked smart.

May waited until Rosaleen had finished her inspection and then jested: 'Well, do I meet with your approval?'

'You certainly do. You look smashing. Have you a date?'

May's eyes danced with laughter and she nodded her head.

Rosaleen was dismayed, she had been jesting, and May's smile broadened when she saw her friend's face drop.

'I've a date with a young lad called Ian,' she explained. 'Billy sent word in to work that if I liked – Imagine! If I liked – I could meet him in town to say goodbye to Ian. He's moving to Newry tomorrow.'

A smile of delight appeared on Rosaleen's face. 'I'm glad, May. Really pleased for you. I'm sure you're all excited.'

May grimaced, and confessed, 'I'm a bundle of nerves, so I am. I'm more worked up now than I was on my first date with Billy.'

Her eyes grew anxious. 'Do I look all right?'

'You look lovely. Billy's sure to be impressed,' Rosaleen assured her.

'Oh, here's the tram. I'd better run.' She gripped Rosaleen's arm. 'Say a wee prayer for me, won't you?'

'I will. And you let me know how you get on.'

'Oh, I will … I will. I'll come up the night and tell you about it.' She swung on to the platform of the tram and shouted over her shoulder, 'Bye for now.'

And she did come that night, subdued but happy. Billy had asked her to write to him while he was away and he had also arranged for his mother to keep in touch with her to let her know how Ian was progressing.

When she heard this news Rosaleen sent a thankful prayer heavenwards. There was hope for them yet.

Chapter 7

It was discovered that the damage to Harland and Wolff was not as bad as at first appeared. Although a vast number of the buildings and sheds at the shipyard were demolished, a number of important structures had survived the bombings. These included the power station, the building slips, and the pumping station, so although work was halted completely while unexploded bombs were hunted for and dealt with, urged on and supported by the ministry, work commenced building more ships much more quickly than expected. This was a blessing, taking hundreds off the outdoor relief, and as buildings were erected to house the homeless and accommodate the soldiers stationed in Belfast, more work still was available and unemployment fell dramatically.

Short and Harland also got off lighter than first thought, and determined not to be caught with all their eggs in one basket again, spread their processes across Belfast and outlying districts.

The King's Hall at Barmoral was taken over for the making of fuselages and components, and aircraft wings were produced at Long Kesh. At Lambeg, a linen mill was converted and tail planes and flaps were made there. Sheetmetal pressings were made on the Newtownards Road, and all over the north other factories and buildings were converted and used as stores for supplies.

As work got underway in these places, unemployment, although not wiped out, was lower than it had been for many a year, and even Joe's small business flourished, obtaining plenty of orders for repairing houses that had been bombed but were sound enough for repairs.

Proud and happy, Owen Black approached Rosaleen to ask her opinion about taking on a man to help him and someone to look after the yard and take orders while he was busy. He emphasised the fact that his wife would take on the job of looking after the yard if she didn't have the kids to worry about, and Rosaleen realised that, in a roundabout way, he was suggesting she look after it. She turned the idea over in her mind.

Why not? She wasn't stupid; she could answer the phone, write down orders ... she could even, with a bit of tutoring, do the books. And Amy was always willing to look after her beloved granddaughter.

Owen gave a nod of approval when she offered to look after the yard four mornings a week, and soon Rosaleen was caught up in the running of the business while the months slipped away unnoticed. The sirens were going off less frequently as Hitler's assaults on the west coast of England had decreased. The reason given for this was his decision to break his pact with Russia and launch an attack on them. However, to their surprise, the Germans were encountering far more opposition than they had bargained on from the Russians, and the planes that had formerly blitzed the west coast of England and the east coast of Northern Ireland were now turned on Russia.

The Russians, once regarded as those terrible communists, those awful Reds, were suddenly regarded by all as gallant allies, calling forth praise from all sides, as they put up a fierce battle against Hitler.

And then, the day everyone was praying for – the day America entered the war. It was the Japanese bombing of Pearl Harbor on December 7th 1941 that caused America to join the fight against the Germans, and everyone was convinced that with their help, the fighting would not last much longer.

With hope of an early end to the war and the long lull, free from air-raids, the refugees started drifting back from the countryside. With plenty of jobs going, the people of Belfast were better off than they had been for many years, and this in spite of shortages and rationing. In the midst of war and ruin, the ordinary, poor people of Belfast never had it so good; never before had wages been so high.

The IRA, although still fighting fiercely against De Valera's government in the south, had been dormant for some time in the north, and in spite of constant fear of air-raids, peace reigned in Belfast itself.

This was not to last. To the surprise of all, America chose Northern Ireland as their base from which to launch an attack on Hitler's Europe. On January 16th 1942, welcomed by the Governor, the Duke of Abercorn, and the Prime Minister, the Americans landed on Irish soil. They disembarked on Dufferin Quay to the strains of 'The Star Spangled Banner' and the cheers of the crowds who had gathered, although their arrival was supposed to be a well-kept secret.

The Yanks brought with them Hershey bars and comics for the children, silk stockings and charm that would have put the Blarney Stone to shame for the young women.

The girls of Belfast lapped it all up, surging in their hundreds down to the Plaza Ballroom every night. The Catholics, not wanting to miss anything, ignored warnings from the pulpit that they were in danger of losing their immortal souls and joined the throngs.

The arrival of the Americans also galvanised the IRA into action again, as they strove to show the Yanks how powerful they were.

In St Paul's Parish heartbreak was to result because of this.

On Easter Sunday, a few short months after the arrival of the Americans, Constable Murphy of the RUC force was shot dead. Rosaleen was on her way home from visiting her mother, coming down the Springfield Road with Laura by the hand, when it happened and all hell broke loose. First there was a great surge of people and Rosaleen thought, My, but the road's busy, so it is! And everybody's in a terrible hurry. Then premonition filled her with terror, turning her legs to stone as police cars screeched past and turned down Oranmore Street. She stood rooted to the spot, unable to move, Laura's head pressed protectively against her body as the crack of gunshots pierced her ears.

Then some man, a stranger to her, gathered Laura up in his arms and urged Rosaleen down Springfield Avenue. He knocked on a door and when it opened tentatively, pushed it roughly ajar and quickly thrust her inside, pushing Laura after her. She gripped her child close, he was gone, and the door was closed.

Rosaleen and the man of the house gazed at each other. His face was familiar to her, and she realised that she probably saw him at Mass on Sundays.

Now she apologised. 'I'm sorry, I have no right to be here ...'

'Never mind, missus ... never you mind. Sure, you're welcome to stay 'til the shootin' stops. Do you know what's goin' on?'

Mutely, she shook her head, then voiced her impression of where the shooting was. 'It's in one of those streets off Oranmore Street ... maybe ... Cawnpore Street.'

'Come in and sit down, missus. I think you'll be here for a while.'

With these words the man led the way into the living room and they joined his wife and young daughter at the fireside.

'Maura!' Laura greeted the girl with delight, and Rosaleen recognised the child as one who sometimes played with her daughter when they visited the Dunville Park. She also recognised the woman of the house and nodded in her direction, and everybody relaxed as Laura was led away to see Maura's toys. Now that the man realised that they were practically neighbours, he introduced himself as Bill Hanna and his wife as Rose. After all, one had to be careful. One never knew to whom one was talking. Now their conversation centred around the shooting.

'After all these months of peace,' Rosaleen lamented. Then, realising how absurd this sounded considering that they were at war with Germany, she added with a wry grimace, 'You know what I mean.'

With a laugh, Bill agreed with her. 'You're right! I know what you mean.' And Rose smiled and nodded to show that she too understood.

'As if we hadn't enough to worry about,' Bill continued. 'Sure they're just showing off. Putting on a show for the Americans, that's what they're doing. The bloody fools!'

The shooting was long over before Bill judged it safe to allow Rosaleen to venture out, and she hurried down Springfield Avenue and arrived in Iris Drive to find a distraught Amy waiting at the door for her.

'Oh, thank God you're safe! I was worried stiff about you, so I was. I knew you'd be returning home about the time the shooting started.'

Rosaleen recounted her experiences, bringing gasps of concern and dismay from Amy, and asked, 'Have you heard anything about it?'

'Just a rumour on the grapevine that someone's been killed. A policeman!'

'Oh, sweet Jesus.' Rosaleen bowed her head in reverence when she took the holy name in vain. 'You know what that means. More retaliations ... more innocent people suffering for things that they have no control over. You'd think the IRA would catch itself on, now that there's plenty of work for everybody,' she said, and gaped in surprise when Amy retorted: 'It's all right you saying that, Rosaleen. But you were too young to realise how bad it was during the 1920s. It was awful then ... you ask your mam. She'll tell you how bad it was. Then the IRA was all we had between us and the Black and Tans, and those bloody B-Specials picked up a thing or two from the B&Ts, and if anything they're worse now.'

It was the first time Rosaleen had heard Amy volunteer an opinion on something as touchy as the IRA, and she found herself apologising.

'I'm sorry. It's just that things have been going so well, in spite of the war ... or should I say because of the war?' And she smiled tentatively at Amy who, appeased, shared the smile. The IRA were not mentioned again.

On Easter Monday morning it was May who called and brought Rosaleen the news that a policeman had been shot dead, and that six young IRA volunteers had been arrested and charged with his murder. It was alleged that they had fired on a police car, and when chased had sought refuge in Cawnpore Street. In the gun battle that followed, the young constable lost his life.

'Do you know any of them?' she asked May apprehensively.

'No ... our Kevin went to school with two of them. Their families must be in an awful state, so they must. It's awful. They're only kids.'

When she heard their names Rosaleen realised that she knew some of their families and her heart bled for them. It was awful to think that your child could bring such sorrow to your door. She agreed with May; they really were just youngsters, five boys and a girl, all gullible fools, and they all but one belonged to St Paul's Parish.

There wasn't a dry eye in church the following Sunday when the priest prayed for the widow and children of the young constable, who was also a member of the parish. He then prayed for the families of the six who now stood accused of his murder. He went on to say that it was an act of folly for the youngsters to fire on a police car, and that those who had given them the firearms and sent them out on such a mission had a lot to answer for.

'Remember, "Thou shalt not kill!" is one of the commandments of God and must be obeyed!' he thundered from the pulpit.

Once more Belfast was put under curfew, and the streets were patrolled by armoured cars and 'cage' lorries. While on foot, patrols of the B-Specials strutted about, displaying their guns, egging the IRA on.

To everyone's horror, the six young offenders were condemned to die and the IRA retaliated with assaults on British army barracks and police stations, bringing misery and unrest once more to the streets of Belfast. The attacks only led to more and more arrests and the worst activists were either sentenced or interned in Crumlin Road Jail. Meanwhile, petitions were got up begging for mercy for the six young offenders. The Eire government took the matter to heart, and in Dublin a petition was launched and over 200,000 signatures collected. The American, Canadian and British Ambassadors in Eire added their voice in support of the plea for clemency.

The British government wanted the six to hang as a deterrent to the IRA during the remainder of the war, but with so many crying out for mercy, the sentences were commuted except for one young man. (An eye for an eye?) Tom Williams, from Bombay Street, was hanged in Crumlin Road Jail on September 2nd. It was a day of terrible depression, and black flags were flown from many windows. All day long prayers were offered up for the repose of his soul, and people lamented, 'It's the ones who gave them the guns that should hang!'

However, the Falls Road was used to these atrocities and once more the burden was shouldered and life went on as normally as the curfew would allow.

The curfew from 10 p.m. to 6 a.m. was always a curse, but as far as Rosaleen was concerned, it spoilt her life. Saturday night was her night out with either May or Annie (whoever happened to be on the right shift) and they went to the pictures. With the curfew starting at ten, there was only one show nightly and this began at half-past six or seven. It also meant that it was crowded and they had to go early and queue up, no matter what the weather was like. Then the show was over at half-past eight or nine and with being home so early, it spoilt the night out. She felt as if she had not been out at all.

Mostly they frequented the Broadway Picture House, further up the Falls Road, which was quiet and respectable, but sometimes they were lured to the Clonard Picture House by reports of a good film. The crowds that went to the Clonard every night were rough and ready, and although they went to the stalls, Rosaleen never felt comfortable there. She was not amused when May and Annie teased her, calling her a snob; remarking that they all came from the same district. Sometimes they even suggested that they go to the Diamond Picture House, which was down the Falls Road on the corner of Cupar Street and was nicknamed the 'flea pit', falling about laughing at her outraged dignity when she refused.

The rest of 1942 dragged on, and she had no idea where Joe was. She received his letters via the ministry and it broke her heart to read them. May was in the same boat as her as far as Billy was concerned, but Rosaleen was pleased to note that when she did receive letters, May was all sentimental and happy. Hopefully things would work out for them. As promised, Mrs Mercer sent her news of Ian, and May had even made one flying visit to Newry to see him.

Sean fared better than Joe and Billy. Being in the Merchant Navy, he managed to get a forty-eight- or thirty-six-hour pass each time the ship was in a convenient port loading cargo so at least Annie was happy, and how Rosaleen and May envied her.

Although at the beginning of 1943 Hitler's bombers had still not returned to Ireland, the war still raged in Europe and Rosaleen wondered why everybody had been so keen for America to join the fight against Hitler. They had been fighting over a year now and still there was no sign that the war would end in the near future, and many a heart was broken as the girls who were foolish enough to take the Yanks seriously, learnt to their cost how silly they were.

Easter Saturday saw Rosaleen, Annie and May all together for a change, due to the Easter holidays, at the Broadway Picture House. They queued up outside for half an hour and then settled down to enjoy the film: a musical, starring Betty Grable. Each had used some of their precious sweet coupons on a quarter of a pound of their favourite confectionery and when the lights went out and the film whirred to life, they wriggled down in comfort and sighed contentedly.

They were sitting in the back stalls and as the film progressed gradually became aware that there was a disturbance in the front stalls, near the screen. Then the lights went up, and to their amazement they saw that two armed men had the staff gathered together and were holding them at gunpoint.

Someone behind Rosaleen whispered, 'Oh, dear God ... it's Hugh McAteer. Ye know ... him that escaped from the Crumlin Road Jail a couple of months ago. And that's Steele with him.'

Only then did she realise that it was two IRA men, and fear made her heart bang against her ribs. Four had escaped ... were the other two behind them? A swift glance over her shoulder reassured her that the space at the back was empty.

What did they want? Was there anybody important in the audience? Were they going to shoot someone? She was not left in doubt for long as the two men forced the audience to take part in an Easter commemoration for 'The dead who died for Ireland'.

In the silence that followed, Annie and May exchanged worried glances with Rosaleen. They were only too aware that if anyone tried to apprehend the fugitives, blood would be shed. The men appeared nervous and it was awful to think of shaky fingers on the triggers of guns. They prayed that no one was foolish enough to do anything provocative.

After the short silence, when the men thanked them for their co-operation and left the cinema, everyone breathed a sigh of relief and burst out into excited conversation. This was brought to a halt by an agitated manager announcing in a shaky voice that the film would continue immediately. Then the lights went out and the film recommenced.

Later, as they sat in the ice-cream parlour at Broadway, eating sundaes, they expressed worried thoughts that Easter Sunday might once again bring trouble. 1941 had brought the blitz, 1942 the shooting of the policeman, and now this display in the Broadway tonight. Was anything else planned to stir up the Troubles over the holiday?

To their relief, the rest of the Easter holiday, at least in St Paul's district, passed without incident, and later in the year they read in the *Irish News* about the recapture of McAteer and Steele.

By the end of 1943 it was estimated that there were 100,000 American troops in the province. Rosaleen's mind baulked at the thought of so many (where on earth did they all stay?) but the newspapers quoted that number, so it must be right.

On her outings to town with Annie, she could well understand the young girls being bowled over by the Yanks. Unlike the Irishmen, the Americans showed their appreciation of a pretty girl. Wolf whistles followed them everywhere, and she and Annie could have had dates galore if they had been that way inclined.

The Yanks were also a great source of money, being open-handed and ready to spend, and the shops and places of entertainment never had it so good. In 1944, when they were moved to England to prepare for D-Day, Belfast seemed empty and dull and many a girl shed tears.

It was apparent that the war was on the wane when it became common knowledge that the anti-aircraft guns around Belfast had been dismantled and the barrage balloons around Northern Ireland withdrawn. And when the British Air Ministry removed Northern Ireland's allocation of night-fighters, it seemed certain that the Germans would soon be defeated. Joe, Sean and Billy should be home soon.

It was amidst this feeling of well-being that the dreaded yellow telegram arrived at Rosaleen's door.

Amy was with her the day she received it; she had witnessed others receive one and had prayed that her turn would never come, but now it had. With hands that shook, she tore it open, but was dismayed to find that her eyes would not focus on the typescript.

As she stood gazing blindly at it, Amy gently took the slip of paper from her hands, and in a voice that shook, read aloud the printed message.

' "We are sorry to inform you that Private Joseph Smith has been wounded in action. Letter to follow with further details." '

'He's alive, Rosaleen. Thank God, he's alive.'

'Thanks be to God,' Rosaleen whispered, and then they were crying in each other's arms.

It was two long drawn-out weeks later that the promised letter at last arrived. In it she was informed that in one week's time, Joe would be in Belfast, but that he would be taken direct to the Royal Victoria Hospital as he required further treatment for his wounds.

Full of apprehension, Rosaleen and Amy reported to the hospital the day that Joe was due to arrive. At the reception desk they were directed to a ward and then a young nurse escorted them to Joe's bedside. Rosaleen warned herself to try to appear normal as shock registered at the sight of him. His face was grey and gaunt and he looked like a tired old man.

She heard Amy's intake of breath, and bent to kiss Joe to block out the dismay on his mother's face and give her a chance to get her features under control.

'How do you feel, love?'

As she spoke, her eyes ranged over the bed and relief flooded through her when she observed that he had all his limbs.

For the past three weeks she had been tortured by thoughts of Joe legless or armless, but although he was worn and ill-looking, he was at least whole.

'A lot better … now I'm home.' He lifted her hand to his face and held it against his cheek. 'I'm so glad to be home, Rosaleen. I could never, ever explain to you how glad I am.'

Holding his other skeletal hand out to his mother, he said, 'Don't look so worried, Mam. I'm going to be all right.'

Having regained her composure, Amy quickly agreed with him.

'Of course you are, son. We'll soon have you back on your feet. Won't we, Rosaleen?'

Mutely she nodded and smiled through her tears. She was glad when the nurse told her that the doctor wanted to speak to her; glad to escape from this skeleton with dark orbs sunk far back in his head. After the shock of his appearance, she needed a breathing space to get a grip on her emotions. When she entered the doctor's office, he rose to his feet, offered her his hand and introduced himself. She acknowledged his introduction with a nod of her head and then he motioned for her to take a seat.

'Your husband is a very sick man, Mrs Smith,' he said, and his voice and face were grave.

'I can see that!' Rosaleen answered sharply. Did they think that she was blind? 'Is he going to recover?'

'Well … let me explain. Joseph had a lot of shrapnel in his body. So far he has undergone surgery four times. All successful … but each operation takes a lot out of him. There are still two pieces to remove. One we'll remove when he has regained his strength from the last operation, but the other piece we can't touch. It's lodged close to his heart, too close for surgery.'

'Does that mean he's going to die?' Rosaleen asked fearfully, dismay in her heart. Her voice was shrill and she saw the doctor's eyes narrow.

'Are you feeling all right, Mrs Smith?' he asked solicitously.

Inwardly, Rosaleen fumed. Why didn't he just come out and tell her the truth? Not keep her on edge like this!

'I'm all right. Tell me! Is he going to die?' she insisted.

'No. At least, we don't think so. It's like this … we have experienced cases like this before, and most times the patient has lived to a ripe old age. However, some patients have died young. We shall keep an eye on Joseph, and if the shrapnel moves away from his heart, we will operate. Meanwhile, once we operate on his leg, he can go home and live as normal a life as possible.'

Rosaleen wanted to question him, ask what would happen if the shrapnel moved towards Joe's heart, but she held her tongue. After all, didn't she already know the answer to that?

It was a further three months before Joe was allowed home from hospital, and when all the well-wishers who had gathered to welcome him home had departed, he lay back on the settee, drained and tired, but happy.

'You know something, Rosaleen? I never thought that I would survive the war. It's great to be home ... and soon I'll be able to go back to work. I'm proud of the way you've been helping Owen to keep the business going.'

'It'll be a while yet, love, before you're able to work,' she said, as she tucked a blanket around him. 'A long time. But the work's still rolling in. We'll never be rich, Joe, but if things keep on the way they're going, we'll never want, either.'

'What's the new man like, Rosaleen? Tell me about him. Is he handsome?'

Rosaleen looked at him in amazement at these words. What difference did it make whether or not the new man was handsome?

'He's nice ... quiet, and a good worker. He has two children and another on the way.'

Joe sighed with relief. The new man was married. He could relax.

Thoughts of children made Rosaleen sad. Laura was now five, and she longed to give her a sister or brother.

Joe had been through so much, had spent such a long time in hospital, would he ever want to go see about his problem? She doubted it very much.

By the autumn of 1944, Joe was back at work, looking pale and frail, but except for the recurring nightmares, he seemed to be slowly making a full recovery. To be truthful, he wasn't able to do much work, just got in the way, but it pleased him to potter about, sort nails into different boxes, plane pieces of wood, and Rosaleen didn't mind – he was company for her when Owen and Andy, the new man, were out on jobs.

He attended the hospital once a month, but so far the shrapnel near his heart remained lodged in the same spot and the doctors were inclined to think that it was there for good, and once more assured Rosaleen that her husband would probably live to a ripe old age.

By the end of 1944, he was more or less back to normal but still pitifully thin, and Rosaleen had become aware that the reason he attended the yard each day was to keep an eye on her. It wasn't that he felt able for work. No, it was jealousy that brought him down to the yard each day. His jealousy was becoming overbearing.

He was full of plans for after the war; plans to build a house on the Upper Falls Road, a house with a garden for Laura to play in. When he had first arrived home from hospital, Rosaleen had settled him in the back bedroom, using the excuse that he needed a bed to himself for a while.

She could see that he didn't agree with her, but in the months that followed, after a few unsuccessful attempts at love-making, he bothered her no more and they lived as brother and sister. Rosaleen refrained from pestering him to go and see a specialist, hoping that as his health improved he would suggest going himself, but she waited in vain.

Billy was invalided out of the army early in 1945, and Rosaleen was not surprised when May confided in her that they were going out to Canada. Billy had two uncles out there and if they liked it, they were going to settle.

'I'm happy for you, May, but I'll miss you,' she wailed, as she pictured the lonely life ahead of her. May was her only chance of a night away from Joe. He was so possessive and jealous, and only her nights out with her friend and her rare outings with Annie kept her sane.

'Listen, Rosaleen.' May was only too aware of Joe's jealousy. 'You keep on going out. Do you hear me? Get Amy to go to the Broadway with you every week.'

Rosaleen had to smile at this idea. Amy was being courted by Bobby Mackay and had very little time to spare.

May saw the smile and realised at once the cause of it. 'Oh, I forgot. Any word of a wedding yet?'

Sadly, Rosaleen shook her head. 'No. I think she's letting Joe influence her. He doesn't like Bobby.'

May's face grimaced in disbelief and she cried, 'Doesn't like Bobby? Sure, you couldn't dislike Bobby if you tried. He's a wonderful person, and so good. Joe needs his head examined,' she finished in disgust.

'I think Joe's jealous of him. You see, he has always been the only one in Amy's life and he doesn't like coming second. And there's no doubt about it... Bobby comes first with Amy now. She'd be mad at me for saying so, but she's like a teenager in love.'

'And why shouldn't she, eh? Why shouldn't she? She's been a widow a long time. Joe should be glad that she has met someone to keep her company in her old age. Not that she's all that old! She can't be fifty yet.'

'No, forty-seven! She must have married young. I'm surprised that she never remarried. She's a fine-looking woman ... must have been a beauty in her day.'

'Aye, indeed. Anyhow, Rosaleen, it'll be a while before I go, so let's not worry until we have to.'

As usual, May had underestimated Billy. Once he got an idea into his head he neither stopped nor stayed until all arrangements were made, and soon Rosaleen was wishing May a tearful farewell.

'You'll write, won't you, Rosaleen?'

'Of course I will.'

'And if we like Canada and decide to stay after the war ...' May's head swivelled to where Joe stood with Billy. 'Joe ... after the war ... you'll bring her to visit us, won't you?'

'That's a promise, May. I'll bring her out to visit you. I've always wanted to see Canada and America,' he assured her and, bathed in tears, May allowed Billy to propel her towards the customs, to enter the plane.

May's departure left a great gap in Rosaleen's life. With Annie being on shifts, she saw little of her, and her mother had got herself a part-time job in Mackie's Foundry. Four mornings a week she packed ammunition into cartons. Rosaleen was glad to see her filling out, see a bit of colour return to her cheeks, but they could not get her to go out and enjoy herself. Once home from work, she remained indoors and brooded.

To Rosaleen's surprise, Amy volunteered to accompany her to the pictures once a week.

'Ah, Amy … I don't want to come between you and Bobby.'

Hot colour rushed to her face and Rosaleen thought how lovely she looked. Why had she never remarried? Unthinkingly, she voiced the question.

'Amy … why did you never get married again? I'm sure you must have had plenty of chances.'

'Oh, yes … they were queuing up, so they were,' Amy jested. 'Look, Rosaleen, Bobby won't mind. In fact, he'd be only too pleased to accompany us. So how's about it, eh?'

'Thanks, Amy. It's kind of you to think of me. To tell you the truth, I need to get out on my own, now and again.'

'I know you do, love. I know you do. So come round to my house on Saturday night at six sharp and we'll go down to the Classic.'

'Oh, how lovely. I haven't been in the Classic for years.'

Amy smiled at her, glad to see the despair lift, if only momentarily.

If Joe wasn't careful, his jealousy would drive them apart. She knew just how obsessive his jealousy could be. Hadn't he ruled her life until Bobby came on the scene?

In his heart, Joe had been relieved to see May go to Canada. She was a bad influence on Rosaleen, expecting her to go to the pictures with her every Saturday night. Now Rosaleen would stay at home at the weekends, keep him company. So anger was in his heart as he watched her prepare for her night out with Amy and Bobby. What on earth did his mother see in that man? She was making a fool of herself and every opportunity he got, Joe told her so. Now he chastised his wife.

'You know, Rosaleen, you shouldn't encourage me mam to go out with Bobby Mackay.'

'Why not?'

Rosaleen's voice was reasonable, she had no intentions of agreeing with Joe about Bobby. He was a wonderful man and he adored Amy.

'Because she's too old for that kind of thing.'

'What kind of thing? Bobby treats her like a lady, and I think that if you would unbend a little ... we could soon be hearing wedding bells.'

'Good God! You don't think she'd really consider marrying him, do you?'

'Why not? They're both old enough to know their own minds! I think they make a lovely couple. Just what have you got against Bobby? Eh?'

Rosaleen frowned at Joe and his lips tightened as he glared back at her. 'Nothing ... so long as he keeps out of my way.'

Rosaleen shrugged and refused to be drawn into an argument. Putting the finishing touches to her make-up, she put on her coat. 'I'm off ... see you later.'

The film in the Classic Picture House in the centre of town was a comedy, and as they left the theatre after the show they were all relaxed and happy.

It was a lovely, warm night and Bobby suggested that they walk home and call into Victor's in Divis Street for some ice-cream. As she walked along, licking away at her ice-cream cone, Rosaleen remembered the night that Sean had walked her home from the Club Orchid. Thoughts of the events at the Dam returned to haunt her and sadness enveloped her. If only she had been wiser, how different her life might have been.

When they arrived at her corner, she invited them in for a cup of tea. At once Amy demurred, but Bobby gently overruled her.

'A cup of tea sounds lovely, Rosaleen.' He turned courteously to Amy. 'Do you not fancy a cup of tea?'

She gazed at him, and whatever she read in his eyes caused her to change her mind.

'Why not... why not indeed?'

The expression on Joe's face when Bobby entered the room made Rosaleen seethe with anger, and the look she threw him stopped the protest that hovered on his lips. He acknowledged Bobby with an abrupt nod.

'Your mam and Bobby have come in for a cup of tea, Joe. Would you like one?' she asked him, and even to her own ears her voice sounded false. She hated him for placing her in a position where she had to play-act. They eyed each other but Joe found that even to please her he could not make 'that man' welcome in his home, so rising to his feet he headed for the stairs.

'No, thank you. I was just about to retire. Goodnight.'

As the door closed on him Rosaleen turned to Bobby. 'I'm sorry … I'll make the tea.'

He reached out and caught her by the arm as she passed him on her way to the kitchen.

'Hey now, don't you be upset. He's a sick man, Rosaleen. I keep telling Amy that we'll have to wear him down. So just keep inviting me in and let me do the rest, OK?'

Rosaleen looked at the big, long face that still seemed sorrowful even when he was smiling. He had been so good to her since her dad's death that it hurt her deeply that Joe should slight him; now she nodded, she would do as he asked.

'I'll make a pot of tea and we'll enjoy it,' she vowed, 'even if it chokes us.' And they all laughed at the idea.

When they had departed, Rosaleen climbed the stairs two at a time and burst into Joe's room without knocking. He was sitting up in bed reading a book and the look he gave her was venomous.

'Don't you ever again treat a friend of mine like that. Do you hear me?' she hissed at him.

'You're forgetting that this is my house, and I'll treat people any way I like in it,' he hissed back at her.

'Oh, yes? Well, the next time you let me down, in my home … remember it's your house, but I have to live here … I'll leave you. And that's a promise!'

With these words she left the room and it was a long time before she got control of her temper.

The next day she made a point of calling in to see Amy when she knew that she would be alone.

'I came to apologise, Amy. What Joe did was unforgivable.'

'Bobby didn't take offence … he's not like that. He could find excuses for Aul' Nick himself. He's a wonderful person, Rosaleen.'

'I know that, Amy. That's why I can't understand Joe's attitude.'

Amy eyed her and gave a long drawn-out sigh. 'Sit down, Rosaleen. I think it's about time I explained something to you.'

Mystified, Rosaleen sat down on the settee beside Amy and eyed her questioningly.

A grimace crossed Amy's face and her voice shook.

'This isn't easy for me to talk about. I'm not proud of my actions ... my only excuse is that I was very young when it happened.'

Rosaleen sat silent, watching her gravely.

'You see, Rosaleen ... I've never been married.'

She felt her jaw drop, and gulped to close it. Amy had never been married? That meant that Joe was ...

As if she had followed her thoughts, step by step. Amy nodded sadly.

'Yes, that's right. Joe's illegitimate.'

Unable to think of anything to say, Rosaleen just repeated, 'Illegitimate?'

'Yes. That's why he's so bitter towards me. Why I let him rule my life for so long. But not any more. I told Bobby about my past and he advised me to tell you. Really I should have told you sooner, but I was embarrassed and ashamed.'

'No, Amy. There's no reason why you should have confided in me. Your past is your own business ... it has nothing to do with me,' Rosaleen assured her.

'It would have helped you to understand Joe better had you known, but you see ... he didn't want you to know.'

Rosaleen's face was a picture of confusion and Amy explained: 'To Joe it was a terrible stigma. And it is a stigma ... I know that, but Joe took it even more to heart than others. It was my fault. I should have told him when he was young, but I kept putting it off. You see, when I was expecting him, I moved here to be near our Belle. You know, Bill Murray's mam? It was near the end of the '14–'18 war and everybody thought that I was a war widow, so I didn't enlighten them. There were a lot of young pregnant war widows about, and I was only too glad to hide my shame. The man I was in love with got me this house to rent.' Her voice became bitter. 'Payment for favours received!'

She sat silent for some moments and Rosaleen's heart went out to her. She heard herself whisper, 'What about your parents?'

'They were both dead, and our Belle did not want to advertise that I was a fallen woman so she encouraged the widow idea.' She looked Rosaleen in the eye and laughed. 'It got to the stage where I nearly believed I was a grieving widow. I was grieving all right.'

Once more her voice trailed off and Rosaleen gripped her arm. 'Amy, don't torture yourself opening old wounds ... I don't need to know!'

'It's all right, Rosaleen, I want you to know.' And she continued, 'I led Joe to believe that his father had died when he was a baby, and when he started school I was glad that I had. You see, kids are cruel. There was one young lad who was illegitimate and the other youngsters tortured him about not having a father, so I kept up the pretence. It was such a shock to Joe when he found out.'

'How did he find out? Who told him?'

Rosaleen could imagine just how shocked Joe had been. He was so strait-laced; forgiveness would not have come easy to him. Poor Amy! She was even more dismayed when Amy continued her story.

'He found out when he tried to enter the ministry. You see, from when he was no age he wanted to become a priest.' Seeing Rosaleen's mouth gape open, she asked, 'He never told you that he once wanted to be a priest?' Her eyes rounded in disbelief.

'No ... never.'

'Ah, Rosaleen ... Well, I was over the moon. My son a priest? I couldn't believe it. I never dreamed it would matter that he had been born out of wedlock, but it did.' She paused to wipe away the tear that had trickled down her cheek and then wailed, 'It was awful. He was accepted and all, and so happy, and then they asked for his birth certificate.' She grimaced at Rosaleen before continuing, 'It shows you how thick I am. Even then, I didn't think it would make any difference. I was worried about what Joe would think, but I thought that he would be understanding. But the minute Joe saw it, he knew. He knew it would prevent him from entering the priesthood. He went berserk! Would not speak or eat. This went on for some time and I was in despair. And then, he started speaking to me, but it was as if the episode had never happened. The priesthood was never mentioned again, and when he met you and you agreed to marry him, he made me promise never to tell you. I thought that you must know. When you were married, you must have seen the birth certificate.'

At her look askance, Rosaleen shook her head. 'Joe attended to all that.'

So many conflicting emotions were fighting for control of Amy's features, Rosaleen clasped her arm tightly.

'Don't torture yourself. Please, Amy, don't.'

Her heart was breaking at the thought of how Joe had kept his mother at arm's length all these years. How could he? How could he have been so cruel?

'He made me promise that I'd tell no one ... but Bobby said he was wrong to extract a promise like that from me. He said that you had the right to know.'

'Is his father still alive?'

'Oh, no. He died when Joe was about ten. He left some money in his will ... that's how Joe was able to start his own business.' She turned and looked Rosaleen full in the face. 'This may seem strange to you, but Thomas was a good man. It was just that he had so many commitments, and when I became pregnant ... he couldn't leave his wife.' She smiled wryly at Rosaleen's start of surprise. 'That's right! He was a married man. A prominent figure in the Church. The scandal would have ruined so many lives. I was very bitter at the time but I agreed to move away from the district, and as a reward Thomas granted me a small allowance so that I need never want. I wasn't quite seventeen and I loved Thomas dearly ...' Her voice trailed off and Rosaleen moved closer and took her in her arms.

'I'm sorry, Amy. I'm so sorry for you.'

'That's life, Rosaleen. I've never wanted to marry. Joe was my life and I was so happy when he met you. I'm glad you're my daughter-in-law. However, I'm very fond of Bobby and I'll not let Joe spoil it for me.'

'I should think not! We'll do as Bobby says and wear him down.

Eh, Amy?'

She smiled and they nodded at each other, but neither was very hopeful of success.

The long anticipated victory in Europe caused a festive air as the people of Belfast waited for the government to specify which day the celebrations would be held. In due course May 8th was named as a day of festivities to celebrate the Allied victory in Europe, V. E. day! The crowds went wild in the streets, and for the first time in six years the sky was aglow with lights from the bonfires. Buntings were strung across the streets, drums were beaten, and effigies of Hitler were burnt or strung up on lampposts.

On the 8th no work was done, and Joe and Rosaleen took Laura with them and joined the throngs that were heading for the City Hall to hear Churchill's speech relayed over the air by loudspeakers.

At three o'clock, everyone stood silent as he gave details of the German capitulation. When he had finished, the city rang with cheers. Then the church bells rang out loud and clear, and the factory horns blared in accompaniment, while bin lids were rattled to add to the din. Hoarse but excited they returned home for dinner, but that night they were there again to witness the floodlighting of the City Hall for the first time in six years, and to join in the singing and dancing in the town centre.

It was late when they made their way to where Joe had parked the works van. Laura was asleep in his arms and he placed her on the floor of the van, rolled up his coat as a pillow for her head, and with Rosaleen in the cab beside him, drove slowly and carefully home so as not to jar the sleeping child.

The feeling of well-being persisted as Joe rekindled the fire and Rosaleen put Laura to bed. Afterwards, as she prepared a light supper, her thoughts turned to the future. The war was over and Joe was making good progress. Surely now she could broach the subject of more children without making him huffy or angry?

She could but try; she owed it to Laura to attempt to give her a sister or brother before she got much older.

With this thought in mind, she eyed Joe covertly as he ate the sandwiches she had made. He still looked frail, but contented and happy. When they had finished eating she retired to the kitchen to wash the cups and plates, all the while going over in her mind the things she would say; how she would broach the subject.

Returning to the living room, she sat on the floor beside Joe's chair and rested her head against his knee. He had an appointment at the hospital on Friday. Surely he was well enough to ask for advice about his problem? She was ashamed of the way she had settled him in the back room when he arrived home from hospital, using the same excuse he had offered her when she was pregnant with Laura: that he needed a bed to himself for a while. At the time she had felt justified in what she was doing, and when he needed her she was always out of bed and in with him, the minute he had one of his nightmares, to hold him close until it passed and he slept again. But she could not bear to lie beside him night after night, frustrated and unhappy. Now, with the war virtually over, she felt uneasiness about the future. She wanted a full married life, but Joe seemed content with things as they were. After the few unsuccessful attempts at love-making he had tried no more, and seemed content for them to live like brother and sister. However, she must make it plain to him that she wanted more out of life than a house up the Falls; that she didn't want the chains of jealousy to tie her to the home. She must make it plain to him that she wanted more children.

She pressed closer. Surprised, Joe placed his arm across her shoulders and drew her between his knees, his hand ruffling her hair.

It was a long time since she had shown any open affection towards him, and he was not fooled, he could guess what was on her mind.

'Joe ...' Her voice trailed off. How should she phrase it?

'It's all right, Rosaleen. I know what you're going to say.'

Her head twisted round and she looked at him with brows raised inquiringly. He answered her look. 'You want me to go and see about myself, don't you?'

She laughed softly. 'How did you know what I was thinking? Are you psychic?'

He sank his face down against the silky softness of her hair, breathing in the sweet perfume of it.

'I think it's the relief that the war's over at last. Tonight, I bet everybody's making plans for the future ... so why not you?'

'Yes, and ...'

He interrupted her. 'Let me finish. Yes, I do intend seeing about myself. I promised you I would, and I'll keep my promise.'

When she raised a happy, bright face for his kiss, he cupped it with his hands and whispered against her lips. 'Can I sleep with you tonight, Rosaleen?' And as if afraid of rejection, he rushed on, 'I just want to hold you ... be close to you.'

At the longing in his voice, shame engulfed her. This man was her husband; she should have been holding him every night, but it had been so frustrating. From now on things would be different, she vowed silently.

'Yes, love. I'll go on up and move Laura into the back room.' She rose to her feet and kissed his brow. 'Don't be long.'

A half hour passed and at last Rosaleen rose from the bed, pulled on her dressing gown and descended the stairs again.

He had fallen asleep ... probably the heat of the fire had made him drowsy. In sleep, he looked young and contented, his head back against the top of the armchair, his eyes closed. His hair had tumbled down over his forehead and she gently pushed it back. He needed to have it cut, she'd make him go to the barber's tomorrow. Then awareness came over her and her hand shook as she touched his shoulder.

'Joe? Joe ... wake up, love. Please Joe, don't tease. Joe, wake up!'

She realised that she was shaking him roughly and forced herself to stop, aware that he would never open his eyes again.

For some minutes she knelt beside him, explaining that she hadn't meant to be hard, that she had thought it best he slept alone. That in her own way she loved him dearly.

Well then, why hadn't she told him so? Why hadn't she held him each night?

It was as if Joe had said the words, and tears of regret blinded her as she rose to her feet. Realising that it was too late for excuses, she tightened the sash of her dressing gown around her waist and went to awaken her neighbour. They would need the doctor and the priest. The shrapnel had moved the wrong way.

Chapter 8

The journey back from the graveyard seemed endless and when the car turned down Cavendish Street, Rosaleen moved restlessly to the edge of her seat, preparing to get out when it arrived in Iris Drive. Everyone had tried to persuade her not to go to the graveside but she had felt compelled to; had imagined that Joe would want her to be there.

She found it hard to convince herself that it was Joe in the coffin she had seen lowered into the wet clay. She could not believe he was dead, that she would see him no more; even though she had helped wash him and dress him in the shroud, and had kissed him for the last time before they put the lid on the coffin. Somehow, it was as if she was a bystander and someone else was going through the motions. Had she been a good wife to him? Plagued by guilt, she had started to shake uncontrollably as she peered down at the coffin. Did her father know what was going on? Was he aware that Joe was joining him in that dark hole? Oh, how she hoped they would be company for each other. Afraid that she would break down, Annie had ushered her away from the grave and into the car, and it had left the graveyard immediately.

At last it slid to a halt, and glad to escape her tortured thoughts, leaving Annie to deal with the driver of the limousine, Rosaleen left it and hurried to the door, hoping the neighbours would give her a few minutes to herself before calling to pay their respects for the last time. Although her hand was shaking, the key slid into the keyhole at first try and she quickly entered the house, darkened and cold, just as it should be after death had claimed the master.

Tea ... she must make tea for the mourners coming back from the graveyard. The neighbours had been marvellous. Early that morning they had arrived at her door with freshly cut sandwiches and savoury dishes, and it was all laid out on a table in the kitchen. How they had managed it, in the face of all the food shortages, she did not know, but manage they had and she would be forever grateful to them. Now all she had to do was make tea. Soon, in a few short hours, she would be alone to face the doubts and regrets that kept tormenting her, but now ... now she must brew the tea.

Glad that they were the first to arrive, Annie raised the roller blinds, which had been down for the past three days as was the custom, letting the daylight into the cold room. Then, after removing the black bow from the door knocker, she pulled out the damper at the back of the grate to set the fire glowing and followed Rosaleen into the kitchen.

Taking her by the arm, she led her gently out again and pushed her down on to the settee.

'You sit down and rest ... talk to people when they come. People will want to talk to you and Amy. Mam will be here soon and she and I will attend to the tea.' She turned with a weary sigh at a knock on the door. 'And here's the first of them now.'

She was relieved to see that first to arrive were her mother and Amy, accompanied by Bobby Mackay. Bobby was kind, he would answer the door and let people in, and he would look after Rosaleen and Amy while she and her mam made the tea. Poor Amy. She was bearing up well under the strain, but then, Bobby had a lot to do with that. He was taking care of her.

When someone came to Rosaleen and clasped her hand, murmuring words of comfort and praising Joe's goodness, she must have made the right replies because they moved on to Amy and someone else took their place until, in due course, her duty was fulfilled and tea was served. There were so many mourners; men she had never seen before, assuring her that if she needed anything, just to let them know. Some Joe had lent money to, to start up in business. Others he had done work for; honest work. Everybody sang his praises, many shed tears.

To her surprise she noticed that some of the men were drinking beer, and her eyes sought Bobby's. He winked and nodded at her. How good he was. She had not even thought about beer. Funny how attached Bobby was to her family now. Even Joe had welcomed him towards the end. Hopefully, this would make Amy put him out of his misery and marry him. It was obvious that she loved him, but Joe had been the stumbling block. Poor Joe, so ashamed of his illegitimacy.

At last the mourners started to drift away and soon it was just family and close friends that were left. When Rosaleen slumped back in the corner of the settee like a wilted flower, Annie eyed her in dismay and then turned to her mother, a worried frown on her brow.

'Mam, will you be all right if I stay here with Rosaleen tonight?'

At once Thelma nodded her approval but Amy quickly interrupted with the suggestion that Thelma accompany her home. They had supported each other at the graveside when Joe had been laid to rest on top of Billy, and Amy had felt the tremors that had coursed through Thelma's body. In a way, looking after her had helped Amy. Helped her to keep at bay the pain that it was her only son who was being buried. Now, if Thelma accompanied her home, they would be a comfort to each other. However, Thelma demurred, shaking her head emphatically at this idea. Amy, catching Annie's eye, shook her head also.

Annie knew what she meant. Her mother had insisted on going to the graveyard, but it had upset her to see the grave opened, to be aware that her husband's body was down there. She had yet to come to terms with her loss and this could start her wandering again. No, she couldn't be left alone. Annie stood undecided and it was Rosaleen who solved the problem. Rising shakily to her feet, she said, 'I just want to be alone. Just Laura and me ... please? Will you fetch Laura for me?'

'Ah, Rosaleen, I don't like leaving you.'

If only Sean were here, Annie thought, he would take charge. Poor Sean, he would get an awful shock. Perhaps his ship was in the middle of the ocean and he would not get home. They could only hope. He had been sent for but had yet to arrive. Joe had gone so quickly, everyone was still in a state of shock. Why, Rosaleen had yet to shed a tear. She looked so tense, so drained, that Annie was afraid to leave her alone, to brood.

'Please, Annie? I'll be all right. All I want is to be alone. Just me and Laura ...' Rosaleen's voice trailed off forlornly, and this decided Annie.

'All right! If that's what you want,' she said resignedly. 'I'll fetch Laura.' And with these words she went next door to bring the little girl home. Before they left, Bobby built the fire up.

'That should last you 'til bedtime, Rosaleen. An' later on, see and make yourself something to eat, won't ye?'

'Yes, Rosaleen, promise me you'll make yourself a bite to eat,' Annie backed him up. She could not remember when she had last seen Rosaleen eat.

'I promise, Annie. I promise.'

She would promise them anything to be rid of them. If only they would get out and leave her alone. Her soul was crying out for solitude. She had not been alone since Joe died. Someone was always there keeping her company, preventing her from thinking. Did they not realise that she needed to grieve?

At last Amy and Bobby prepared to leave, and as she hugged Amy she envied her the tears that flowed. When at last she closed the door on her mother and Annie, she stood with her brow pressed to the smooth, cool wood. Now she could think; now she could grieve.

A small hand being pushed into hers brought her back to reality, and lifting Laura up in her arms, she hugged her close. Poor child, so bewildered and confused. Sitting on the armchair close to the fire, she took Laura on her knee.

Normally, Laura would have slid off, considering herself too big for cuddles, but now, as if as much in need of comfort as her mother, she pressed close.

'Would you like something to eat, love?'

'No. Mrs Gray gave me dinner. Mammy, is Daddy in heaven, or will he have to stay in purgatory for a while?' Laura asked, her eyes keen and searching, causing Rosaleen to pause and think before answering her.

'I don't know, love,' she answered truthfully. Had anyone ever came back to verify that there was a purgatory? 'I honestly don't know. I imagine he's in heaven. He was a good daddy, wasn't he?'

Laura nodded and big tears welled up and rolled down her cheeks. Glad to see them, Rosaleen encouraged her to cry, wishing she could join her, but she felt that there must be no moisture left in her body, otherwise surely she would have cried before now. When Laura sagged exhausted in her arms, Rosaleen gathered her up and climbed the stairs with her. And when she was snug in bed and asleep, she wearily descended the stairs again and sat huddled over the fire. If only she could get relief in tears it might help her, but she felt nothing. She was so cold. Perhaps if she took a hot bath she would be able to unwind. This thought brought her to her feet, and entering the bathroom she ran the bath full of hot water, but all to no avail. Even after a long soak, she still felt numb and tense. Wrapping herself in Joe's old dressing gown, she hugged her arms around her body and pressed her cheek against the shoulder of the dressing gown, desperately seeking warmth and comfort.

'Joe, I'm sorry – I'm so sorry. I failed you, didn't I?'

She had tried to love him. In a way she had loved him, dearly, just as she would have loved a brother. And he hadn't wanted anything else. Had he? Had she been fooling herself that he was happy the way things were? She must have been; he had sounded so sad the night he died, when he had asked to sleep with her. If she had tried, could she have made his last months happier?

Had she been a comfort to him? She had done her duty, comforting him when he had a nightmare, nursing him and caring for him after his operation, but had she successfully hidden her frustration and despair? Doctor Hughes had thought that she was the perfect wife, but what about Joe? How had he regarded her? Had he found her wanting in warmth and understanding? Had he guessed the way she secretly yearned for a normal life, for love and companionship free from jealousy?

When the knocker was lifted and dropped gently, breaking in on her misery, she ignored it. Let them go away. She could not bear to listen to any more platitudes. When it sounded again, she covered her ears and buried her head in the cushions to block it out, but when the knocking persisted and became urgent, with a sigh of regret she slowly rose and entered the hall.

Remembering Joe's warning never to open the door at night without first making sure it was someone known to her, she whispered. 'Who's there?'

'It's me, Rosaleen. Sean!'

The key was icy to her touch but at last it turned in the lock and her cold fingers struggled with the bar at the top of the door, then the one at the bottom. Then Sean was in the hall, and the door was closed, and she was clasped to his breast, the tears free to flow at last.

There was infinite tenderness in the way he lifted her in his arms, inwardly lamenting at how light she was, and carried her to the settee where he sat with her on his knee.

'There now, love ... that's right. Cry it all up.'

He held her close, rocking her gently, murmuring endearments, until the last shudder trembled through her body, and the last hiccup left her lips. Then, tilting her face up to his, he tenderly wiped the tears from her cheeks.

Taking the handkerchief from him, she blew her nose. 'I'm sorry ... imagine greeting you like that.'

He smoothed the hair back from her damp brow and assured her, 'My shoulders are wide enough to bear your grief.'

She gazed back at him, sad-faced. Her hair was lank and lifeless, her nose and eyes swollen and red, but to him she was beautiful.

Embarrassed at the look in his eyes, she turned aside.

'I must look awful.'

He wanted to tell her that she could never look awful to him, but there lay danger, so instead he asked, 'Have you eaten anything today?'

When he had arrived home an hour earlier, after a bite to eat, Annie had urged him straight out again, and pressed on him the need to make Rosaleen eat something.

A guilty look passed over her face and she shook her head. 'Sure, you won't tell Annie?' she pleaded. 'I promised her I would eat something, but when Laura said she had eaten next door, I couldn't be bothered to cook for meself. Besides, I'm not hungry.'

'Have you any eggs?'

At her indifferent nod of the head, he eased her gently on to the settee and rose to his feet. 'I'll make you an omelette.'

When the omelette was ready, he buttered crusty bread and poured a cup of strong tea. Pulling a small table over close to the fire, he made Rosaleen sit at it and watched until she had finished every last crumb of the meal and washed it down with the tea.

'Now, do you feel any better?'

With a faint smile she had to admit that she did. 'Thanks, Sean. You're very kind.'

KIND! The word struck into the depths of his being. If only he was free to show how he felt…

He poured her a small sherry and a whiskey for himself, and sat facing her. 'I'm sorry I was too late for the funeral. It must have been awful for you.'

She nodded and took a sip of sherry. Then to his dismay, with a hand that shook, she placed the glass on the table and buried her face in her hands.

'Ah, Rosaleen … Don't torture yourself, love.'

He fought the desire to go to her and hold her close again. He was only human and her need for comfort was putting a great strain on his self-control.

Her muffled voice barely reached him.

'I feel so selfish … Here I am, filling my face, and Joe's down a hole in the damp earth on his own.'

Suddenly her head jerked up and she gazed imploringly at him. 'Do you think me da and Joe will be company for each other?'

'Of course they will!'

He would tell her black was white if he thought it would ease her pain. His resolve to keep away from her crumbled. Moving to the settee, he ordered, 'Come here. You still look frozen.'

She also was aware of the danger but she needed to be held,

wanted to feel his arms around her, so she rose slowly from her seat and joined him on the settee.

His arms opened to hold her. When he tenderly pressed her close, she melted against him and felt all the tension flow from her body as his hands warmed and caressed her.

It was without surprise that she found herself naked in his arms on the rug in front of the fire. His face above hers was full of love and awe, bringing a lump to her throat at the wonder of it. Then Annie's face rose before her mind's eye and she tried to demur, to push him away as her conscience smote her, but he would not let her.

'Hush, Rosaleen … don't think, just feel.'

Mesmerised, she obeyed him, and all else was forgotten as for the second time in her life, she reached for heaven.

They lay for a long time at peace. If only they could stay like this forever. If only he was hers, to have and to hold, how wonderful life would be. If she had listened to him at the beginning, how different her life would have been. But then she had been so naive and innocent. Innocent? Ignorant was more like it!

At last he broke the silence. 'Rosaleen … we must tell Annie the truth.' He felt her body jerk in revulsion at the idea, and hastened to add, 'Not right away, but eventually. You know how it is between Annie and me. She doesn't care … all she thinks of is having a baby and I can't give her one. She'll be hurt for a while, but we must tell her.'

When she would have pushed him away, he tightened his grip on her. She had sent him away once before. This time he was determined to win her over.

'Listen, love. There's no point in everybody being miserable, now is there? That would be stupid, wouldn't it? We'll go down south or over to England … anywhere you like. I'll leave the navy and get a job, and together we'll make a home for Laura.' His eyes held hers fearfully as he asked the next question. Would she mind having only one child?

'You won't mind if you don't have any more children, sure you won't?'

Mind? Even if he really was sterile, if she was childless, she would not mind. Just to be with him was all she desired. His words washed over her. He made it seem so easy. Just grab their happiness and take off. If only they could. Oh, if only they could. Why, it would be heaven to know that he was hers to have and to hold, to depend on forever. But that kind of romance was just for novels. Life wasn't like that! There was Annie to consider. In spite of what he thought, Annie loved him. She was just letting her desire for a child get in the way. If she had to choose between him and a child, she would choose him. This Rosaleen knew; this she was sure of. Besides, there could be no divorce. Annie would be tied to him for life, and they would be living in sin. No, she did not believe that happiness could be found at other people's expense. They would come to hate each other. No matter where they went, they would not be able to hide the truth from Laura. To her he would always be Uncle Sean, and she would be bound to inquire where her beloved Aunt Annie was. And to tell her and Sean the truth? No! That must never happen. How could Laura ever cope with that? No, she must not be swayed. She must convince him that she did not care enough to go away with him.

Gently, she extricated herself from his arms and sat up, her arms around her knees, her back to him.

Propped up on his elbow, he watched her in silence, determined not to let her send him away as she had before. They were two halves of a whole. They were meant to be together. He should never have married Annie. Why had he been in such a rush? It was the war. Wanting to keep the family name going. Hah! That was a laugh. Well, many a hasty marriage had been entered into during the war. Three of his mates in the navy were getting divorced. But Catholics could not get divorced. That was the snag! He would have to persuade Rosaleen to live with him. He was very much aware that she would call it 'living in sin'.

He remained silent. Let her weigh the pros and cons. Let her measure life with him against life on her own. Surely she could not fail to see that they were meant to be together? With or without the Church's blessing.

Rosaleen gathered all her resources about her. She had to convince him that she did not love him, that she had used him. Only if she convinced him of that would he leave her alone. There was no way she could square her conscience and go off with him. Hurt Annie? Bring shame on her mother?

No! It could never be.

When she was sure she could control her voice, she spoke. 'Sean, you've got it all wrong. I'm grateful to you for being here when I needed you ...'

'Don't talk a lot of bullshit!' he interrupted her angrily. 'You love me! I know you do, and I won't be sent away again.'

'You listen to me, Sean Devlin,' she whispered fiercely, afraid of a bawling match. What if Laura awakened and came down? 'I admit that I needed you. Oh, yes, I needed you. And I know I shouldn't have used you, but I was missing Joe so badly ...' Her voice broke as she uttered these lies to the man she loved above all others. But to Sean it sounded as if it was because of her longing for Joe and he rose from the floor in a fury. Gripping her by the shoulders, he hauled her to her feet and shook her roughly.

'Look me in the eye and tell me you don't love me!' he ordered. 'Come on ... look me in the eye.'

He gripped her chin and pulled her face towards his. Unable to do as he asked, she pulled angrily away from him, but his arms tightened around her and he pressed her closer still against the hard muscles of his body, defying her to deny her need.

As always, when close to him, she went weak at the knees and passion welled through her, causing her to tremble in his arms.

He smiled grimly in triumph. 'Go on. Deny you want me,' he growled.

Fear filled her mind. She must not let him take her again or all would be lost. There would be no turning back.

'You're despicable!' she hissed. 'You're taking advantage of my vulnerability, my unhappiness. Go home to your wife. Annie trusted you to come here alone to help me ... and look how we repaid her trust.' She put her head high and looked him in the eye. 'I'm so ashamed of my actions ... but it will never happen again, Sean. Believe me, it will never happen again.'

'I don't believe you. After how you behaved just now?' He saw the hot colour spread across her face, down her neck, and laughed harshly. 'Ah no, Rosaleen … you'll have to do better than that.'

Her heart sank. She must convince him.

'Lust, Sean?' She hardly recognised her own voice, it was so cold. 'You don't recognise lust when you experience it?' She forced a light laugh from her lips. 'Mad animal lust? Hah! You surprise me. It's all I know.'

He winced, and slowly relaxed his hold on her. His eyes examined her face and she returned his look without blinking. She sounded so sincere. Was she speaking the truth? For her, was it lust that lifted them above all reason; above right and wrong? Was it because he loved her so much that he'd believed she felt the same? Had she just used him to assuage her longing for Joe?

Free of his grasp, she groped for the dressing gown and thrust her arms into it. As she tied the sash around her waist, she felt better, stronger. He had murmured over and over again how the sight of her bare body set him on fire. How he had pictured her often; longed to caress her milky skin. But now she must put out the fire. Try to deny her love for him.

Stunned and bewildered, he stood uncertainly, examining her face through narrowed, searching eyes. Head back she returned his look and just when she thought that she would break down, he reached for his clothes and started to get dressed. Unable to watch the hurt and pain on his face, she turned away, her heart aching. She had burnt her boats all right. He would never bother with her again.

When he was dressed, he stood silent, waiting, until she was forced to turn and face him. A ghastly smile twisted his lips and she cringed inside at the contempt in his eyes.

'Well… you know where to come when you need to be serviced. I enjoy it, Rosaleen, and I'll oblige anytime.'

With these cutting words, he turned on his heel and left the house.

In despair, she slowly sank to her knees and huddled in front of the fire. If only he hadn't married Annie! If only … She stayed on her knees for a long time but there was no relief in tears. The hurt went too deep.

The light was bright, and coming from the darkened house, Rosaleen shaded her eyes as she gazed up at the tall, young man in army uniform, standing on the pavement.

He returned the look, unblinking, noting the signs of grief and pain etched on her delicate features.

'Well, can I do anything for you?' Rosaleen's voice was sharp; it was the second time she had asked the question.

With a start of dismay, the man straightened to attention.

'I beg your pardon. Are you Rosaleen Smith?' he asked. He didn't need to ask the question. He knew who she was; had seen many photographs of her. None of which had done her justice.

She nodded and he delved into the pocket of his overcoat and extracted a letter, which he handed to her.

'Your father asked me to give this to you.'

'My da? You knew my da?' she asked in wonder. How could this soldier know her da?

'Yes, I knew him well ... very well indeed,' he replied gravely.

She gazed at him in bewilderment. 'He's dead, you know.'

Once more he surprised her. 'Yes, I know. I was informed. I would have come sooner but I've just returned from abroad.'

Her bewilderment grew and swelled. He had been informed?

She fingered the bulky envelope. From her da? Sure, he had hated writing. Would have done anything to avoid putting pen to paper. She examined the envelope; it was his scrawl all right.

Still looking bemused, she stood aside and with a jerk of her head motioned him into the house, closing the big outer door before following him into the living room. Since Joe's burial she kept the big door shut. The neighbours were very kind, but she couldn't think with them popping in and out at all hours and she needed to think, to face up to her shame. Besides, she was afraid of Sean coming back, she had to keep him at bay. She must never be alone with him again.

Once inside the living room, she tore open the envelope and counted the pages. Six! She found it hard to believe that her father would ever write six pages, but here they were in black and white.

Becoming aware of the bulk of the man standing watching her, she said abruptly, 'Here ... gimme your coat, and take a seat.'

He struggled out of the army overcoat and her arms sagged under its weight as she took it from him and hung it at the foot of the stairs.

'Sit down. Go on … sit by the fireside,' she ordered, and when he obeyed her, she sat on the armchair facing him and turned her attention once more to the letter.

Tears stung her eyes as she read. In her head she could hear her father's voice. It was as if he was talking to her, a voice from the grave.

My dear, lovely Rosaleen, when you read this letter, I'll be gone. Gone to meet my Maker and receive my sentence. It will also mean that I have died before your mother, so I want to put the record straight. You see, Rosaleen, it's my fault that your mother is the way she is. My fault! Mine alone, and I shoulder the blame gladly. I have seen you look at me in surprise from time to time when I apparently let your mother walk all over me, but you see, Rosaleen … I deserved it. Your mother will never defend herself, she's a very private person and she'll let you go on believing that she is cold and hard. This is far from the truth, because behind that rough front your mother shows the world, is a very shy, passionate, loving woman.

Sharing a bed as we had to, she could not always deny her need for me, because in spite of what I did, in spite of the pain I caused her, she still loves me. That surprises you, doesn't it? But she does love me, and although I'm sure she had her chances (a lovely woman like your mother?) and she may have been tempted to get revenge, I know she never betrayed me. Besides, her good Catholic upbringing would never have let her commit adultery, so sometimes she needed me, and it was when she needed me that she scorned me most. For me, those were the moments that made up for everything else.

When I first met her, your mother was like a breath of spring. Very like you in looks, and pure and good. She could have had her pick of any man in the neighbourhood and she chose me. I couldn't believe my luck when she agreed to walk out with me. Me! Tommy Magee, a mill worker, when she could have had an electrician or a joiner or a schoolteacher. They all fancied her, but right from our first meeting there was a bond between us. I hope you and Joe are experiencing this bond. I've watched you together and sometimes I've been uneasy for you, but I hope and pray that you are happy, Rosaleen.

She paused, startled at these words. Imagine her da sensing that all was not well between her and Joe. Perhaps if she had talked to him about their difficulties at the start of their marriage, things might have worked out differently. Ah, but sure you couldn't talk to your da about a thing like that. Besides, although she had not been aware of it, she was already pregnant. When she had found out, would she have gone to her da and told him that? That she was expecting another man's child? No way! There was no way she could have admitted that to her da. Sad for chances lost, she continued reading.

But to get back to me. The day your mother married me, I was the happiest man in the world and I swore that she would never regret it. That I'd spend the rest of my life making her happy. And I meant it, Rosaleen. I wanted no other. All I wanted was to care for her and when you came along, my happiness was complete. But I was weak and the promises so easily made, were even more easily broken. I didn't mean to betray your mother's trust … ah no, I didn't set out to do it, but betray it I did.

Let me explain. We were invited to a party. A mate of mine got the key to a house in Leeson Street and threw a house-warming party.

Your mother was expecting Annie at the time and the day before the party she was confined to bed for a couple of days. Her blood pressure was giving concern. Nothing serious, but she had to rest, and going to a party wasn't allowed. I didn't want to go without her but she insisted. Said I must give the happy couple the wee present she had bought for them. So I went alone – and, oh, how I lived to regret it.

It was like this … it was a long night and there was plenty to drink. I didn't realise I was drinking so much, and I wasn't used to it.

Anyhow, I got drunk and was foolish with a girl. We were thrown together because we were both on our own, and later, it seemed only good manners to walk her home. I don't remember much about that night and I don't want to put the blame on her. It takes two. But one thing I did know – I knew I'd done wrong and I prayed your mother would never find out. As time passed and I never set eyes on the girl again, I breathed a sigh of relief. It was going to be all right and I had learnt my lesson. I would never get drunk again. And in spite of what your mother often implied, I never did. Tipsy, now and again, but never blind drunk. Ah, no, it had cost me too dearly.

Alas, our sins have a way of catching up with us, Rosaleen, and mine did. Just when I thought that I could breathe easy, thought that I'd got away with my misdemeanour, there she was one night, waiting for me coming out of work. Pale and tense-looking, she told me that she was pregnant and that I was the father, and I remember grabbing hold of the gate of the mill to steady myself, I was so shocked. I stood in a daze and wished that the ground would open up and swallow me. The one thought in my mind was ... how on earth was I going to tell Thelma of my betrayal?

Rosaleen paused once more and gazed blankly at the page for some seconds. She couldn't take it all in. She glanced at the stranger; he sat leaning forward, elbows on knees, gazing into the heart of the fire. What had he to do with it? As if aware of his scrutiny, he slowly turned his head and met her gaze; his eyes sharp, probing orbs. Flustered, she looked away and gave her attention once more to the letter.

The girl was in an awful state. She wasn't young, about thirty, and plain. She was actually grateful to me for giving her a child, said it would make her life worthwhile. I didn't know where to turn, Rosaleen. So when she explained that she was an only child, born late in life to elderly parents and she would not have approached me at all but for the need of help during the pregnancy, I could have wept with relief. She did not intend to cause a scandal and, living on the Shankill Road as she did, with a bit of luck, if I was careful, your mother need never know. The relief, Rosaleen ... never in this world could I explain the relief I felt.

To get more money, I gladly gave up smoking. My lungs were starting to bother me even then, so your mother was delighted when I stopped. Funny ... she never inquired what I did with the extra money, but then it wasn't much, I wasn't a heavy smoker, and Annie was only a couple of weeks old and she was preoccupied with the two of you. So every now and again, I met Ruby and gave her as much as I could afford towards the birth.

Then tragedy struck. Ruby died giving birth to my son. You can imagine how I felt ... I felt as if I had killed her. Her parents were wonderful, said that they would rear the boy, said it would give them something to live for now that Ruby was dead, but I decided that the time had come to confess to your mother and to ask her to adopt the baby boy.

It was awful! I had diarrhoea for two days with the worry of it, and there was your mother worrying and fussing over me, while I was trying to find the courage to admit my guilt. I'll never forget the look on her face when I told her. The look of horror, dismay, and ... rejection. It was like a physical blow. Of course she didn't believe that it had only happened once. She thought that I had been playing around with Ruby when she was carrying Annie and I could not convince her otherwise. I know it's hard to believe, Rosaleen, but it was only the once.

She closed her eyes and swallowed deeply. She believed him all right. Oh, yes, she believed him!

It was as if an invisible wall was between us and I never really got close to her again. Physically, yes, but spiritually, no. It was the end of happiness for me.

She refused to adopt the boy. Would not even see him. I was hurt, but in my heart I didn't blame her. I was the one at fault. Your mother had done no wrong. No wrong at all.

Once more Rosaleen looked towards the man and this time he was waiting.

'You're … you're my half brother?'

He nodded. 'Yes.'

Her eyes scanned his face. Yes, now she knew the truth, she could see the resemblance. The planes of his face, the dark chestnut hair. He was her father's son all right.

Not knowing how to react, she gave him a weak smile and returned to the letter.

However, one thing I couldn't do, not even to please your mother, and that was to sever all connections with my son. Every Thursday night I visited George. I watched him grow up and I contributed all I could to his upkeep …

Rosaleen recalled how she couldn't understand her mother's attitude when her father went to visit his old friend every Thursday night. Her bitterness and anger. How could she have been so blind? How did she not realise that something was wrong? Very wrong.

Rosaleen, be kind to him, please. He's a good lad and his grandparents are now dead. He has no one to call his own. Befriend him. For my sake, love, please befriend him. I know that during your mother's lifetime you will not be able to call him brother, but let him visit you and get to know you … and Joe and Laura. I leave it up to you whether or not to confide in Annie. She's different from you and might not take kindly to keeping a secret from her mother, so use your own judgement. I hope you never have to read this, but if you do, pray for me.

Goodbye, love.

Your loving dad

Rosaleen folded the letter and sat fiddling with the pages. How on earth had her father managed to keep this secret all these years? He must have been very, very careful, or the neighbours would have found out.

Covertly, she examined the man. His face in repose was sad and weary. Compassion filled her; here he was home from the war and no one to greet him. But he was from the Shankill Road. They would have nothing at all in common. Nothing! Still, for her father's sake she would have to try to befriend him.

Unknowingly, she sighed, a long deep sigh, and the man's heart sank as he watched her. He grew more apprehensive, afraid that she did not want to know him.

At last she spoke. 'I'm afraid you're too late to meet my husband. He was buried a week ago.'

On his feet instantly, he was full of apologies.

'I'm sorry. Oh, I am sorry. I didn't know or I would never have come. I'll leave now. Not intrude any longer on your grief.'

He hesitated before asking haltingly, 'Perhaps you will allow me to come back at a later date?'

As he reached for his coat, her voice stayed him.

'No! Don't go. I'm glad of your company. Sit down.' She smiled kindly at him. 'I'll make us a cup of tea and we'll have a chat.'

In the sanctuary of the kitchen as she waited for the kettle to boil, she smiled wryly to herself. At least now she knew who she took after. Like father, like daughter. However, unlike her father, she could not blame drink. Each time she had been with Sean her senses had been her own. Very much her own.

Her poor mother ... no wonder she nearly went out of her mind when Da was killed. Now it was clear to her why Thelma had been in such a state. To have withheld her forgiveness until it was too late. It must have been awful for her. All those wasted years when they could have been so happy. What had held her back? Pride? Probably ... pride, and fear of what people would think was an awful thing. That was what her mother would have dreaded most, the neighbours finding out.

To her surprise, once the first awkward moments were over, she and George got on like a house on fire. They discovered that they had a lot in common, and she learnt of a side to her father that she had never known. She enjoyed watching the different expressions flit across George's face, bringing her father close, and she noted that he had the same dry humour, being funny without realising it.

They had been talking for about an hour when a glance at the clock brought her to her feet. It was almost time to go and fetch Laura from school. When she voiced her thoughts, he looked so disappointed that she found herself asking him to accompany her and he eagerly agreed.

'But first I must change.' Embarrassed colour tinged her cheeks when she glanced down at the old soiled skirt and jumper she wore. She had been so careless of her appearance of late. 'What must you think of me? I look awful.'

Gallantly, he assured her that she looked lovely, and fetching clean clothes, she retired to the bathroom.

For the first time since before Joe's death she took trouble with her appearance, and she was pleased at the admiration in his eyes when she returned to the kitchen. Somehow, he made her feel at ease and she was grateful to him.

As they passed down the street, she greeted neighbours and was puzzled when her greetings were returned with abrupt nods.

Dismayed, she realised what they must be thinking. They would be saying, 'Now we know why she keeps the big door closed!' And they would also be thinking that she must have been carrying on before Joe died. How cruel people were, to condemn without knowing the whys and wherefores.

In the following weeks, George visited her regularly and they became close friends. Rosaleen grew to rely on him. She had decided not to tell Annie about George. Her sister was kind, very kind, but a bit of a blabbermouth, and it would be her mother who would suffer if Annie failed to hold her tongue. Not knowing the truth, she joined the neighbours in their condemnation, and a hurt Rosaleen refused to offer any excuse for her friendship with George. While her mother lived, they would have to think what they liked; she would not risk having Thelma hurt again.

How she would have survived without George, when morning sickness sent her retching to the bathroom every day, she did not know.

TWICE! Twice in her life she had been with a man and each time had resulted in a child. How could life be so cruel? Annie longed for a child and was unable to conceive, while Rosaleen certainly did not want this one! How would she manage to rear two children on her own? Especially with the business to run.

George comforted her; told her he would do all he could to help. He assumed that the child was Joe's and she realised that in ordinary circumstances it could be his. But try telling the neighbours that!

And Sean ... what would he think when he heard?

George had just left the house late one night when a knock on the door brought her back to it, a smile on her face. He must have forgotten something.

When the door was knocked out of her hand she reared back in alarm, and then Sean closed the big door and bundled her into the living room.

'How dare you! What do you think you're doing?' she cried as she twisted out of his grasp. She could smell the drink on him and was afraid.

'Who is he? WHO IS HE?' he ground out through his teeth, and his words were slurred. It tore at his guts to think that she could have someone so soon after Joe's death. What kind of a woman was she?

'Shush! It's none of your business. I'm not accountable to you for my actions, Sean Devlin, so get out of here. Go on!' She flapped her hand at him. 'Go on ... get out!'

What if he made a scene and the neighbours heard him? Oh, no, she couldn't bear that. They had enough to talk about already.

He swayed on his feet, shook his head and then sank down on to the settee.

'I'll not go 'til you tell me who he is.'

'It's none of your business!' she hissed. Then, softening her tone, she coaxed, 'Go home, Sean. It's very late.'

'Hah!' He scowled at her. 'That's a gag. I've been waiting out there.' He jerked his head towards the street. 'For him to leave. And you tell me it's late. Why didn't you tell him that, eh? Why didn't you tell him that?'

He looked so unhappy her heart was torn with pity, and as she gazed at him, temptation reared its ugly head. The urge to go to him in his misery and comfort him, as he had so often comforted her, was strong. To put her arms around him, hold him close and ease away the pain. To get lost in that wonderful well of passion that he inspired. As her emotions rose, the longing for him grew and swelled, blocking out all rational thought. As every nerve edge came alive, she argued with herself. Would it be so wrong? Annie need never know, and wouldn't he be easier to live with if he was contented? They could be careful … she would just see him now and again. That way the neighbours need never suspect. Her hand reached out tentatively to him and then commonsense prevailed.

Who did she think she was kidding? WOULD IT BE SO WRONG? It would be a mortal sin! And she was not the type to keep running back to confession with the same sin. She would be cut off from God's grace! How could she live like that? And no matter what he might say now, he would never be content with an affair. He wanted to own her, body and soul, and if he was free, he could own her body and soul. But that was the snag … he was not free! He watched the different emotions flicker across her face and when her hand dropped limply to her side, felt that he had been judged and found wanting.

Glaring up at her, he taunted, 'Were you enjoying his company too much to notice the time? Come on, talk to me, Rosaleen! Talk to me!'

'You're drunk, Sean. Come on.' She leant down to assist him to his feet, and when her face was close to his he caught and held her gaze appealingly.

'Why, Rosaleen? Just tell me why?' His hands stretched wide in despair. 'If you must be serviced, why him? Why not me? Eh? Why not me?'

Anger straightened her back and the full weight of her body was behind her hand when she slapped his face.

Taken unawares, without thought he was on his feet, retaliating. His slap sent her spinning and to her amazement, she found herself on the floor, gaping up at him.

At once he was on his knees beside her, cradling her in his arms, begging her forgiveness. 'I'm sorry, love. Oh, please forgive me … I'm so sorry.'

Great tears welled up and slid silently down her cheeks, and frantically he kept mopping at them.

'Ah, Rosaleen … don't cry, love. Please … please … I'm sorry. I didn't think. Ah, Rosaleen, sure … I wouldn't hurt you for the world.'

At last the well dried up. Relieved, he mopped her face for the last time, and rising clumsily from his cramped position, assisted her to the settee.

She sat curled up, for a long time her face in her hands, and he watched her anxiously. Rosaleen drew a deep breath and straightened as she came to a decision. She had examined her predicament from all angles and could see no way out. There was no alternative. If she didn't want him to think badly of her, she would have to tell him the truth about George. It didn't matter what anyone else thought of her, she could not bear for him to think that she was a whore.

With another long sigh, she rose resolutely to her feet. 'I have something to tell you. But, first, I'll make us a cup of coffee.'

He pushed her gently down on to the settee again and put a cushion at her head, a stool at her feet.

'I'll make the coffee.' He held out his hands for her inspection. 'Look, steady as a rock. I won't break anything. I've sobered up.'

And he had. The shock of lifting his hand to Rosaleen had sobered him. When he handed her the cup of coffee, his fingers touched hers and they were icy. Placing the cup on the table, he took her hands in his and chaffed them until they felt warm, and then handed her the coffee.

They drank in silence. She trying to form words to tell him about George and that she was pregnant, without rousing his suspicions, and he putting off the moment when he heard from her own lips that she loved this other man.

At last, unable to bear the silence, he took the empty cup from her, placed it on the table, and said gently, 'You were going to tell me something?'

She nodded and rose once more from the settee. Going to the desk in the corner, she removed her father's letter from the drawer and thrust it at him.

'Read that.'

Mystified, he withdrew the sheets of notepaper and started to read, glancing up at her now and again in growing concern.

231

When he had finished reading, he folded the letter and returned it to the envelope before speaking.

'Then this man's your half-brother?'

She nodded.

'Why on earth didn't you tell us?' he cried in surprise. 'Why, Annie thinks you've a ...' His voice trailed off in embarrassment and she smiled grimly.

'I know what my sister and my mother and the neighbours think. They think I've a fancyman, and I bet they think I've been carrying on before Joe died.' Her voice rose accusingly. 'Even you thought ... thought ...'

'I know. I'm sorry, but you should have told us. Ah, Rosaleen ...' his voice broke on the words '... you don't know what I've been through.'

'You read the letter! Me da left it up to me whether or not to tell Annie, and I decided not to. She's a blabbermouth. You know she is and I won't have Mother hurt any more. She must have been too proud to forgive me da all those years ago. We can't let her know that we know her dark secret. It would send her over the edge. Annie said that she's been in a state since the grave was opened again.'

'I know, I know. But why didn't you tell me?' His look was full of reproach. 'You nearly sent me over the edge.'

'I haven't seen you since George came on the scene, remember?'

He nodded sadly. This was true. He had been avoiding her, until listening to her mother and Annie discussing the 'other man', his jealousy could be contained no longer. His leave had been extended by the celebrations of D-Day but now he had but one week's holiday left and, fortified by a couple of drinks, here he was.

For some time he sat deep in thought and she watched him in silence. Drinking in the look of him. Longing for his touch. Loving the way his hair tumbled boyishly over his forehead. Admiring the strong jaw, the straight nose, the sensitive lips. Those wonderful lips ... wonderful! His voice brought her back to reality and she gulped to regain control of her emotions.

He spoke haltingly. 'Rosaleen, do you not think ... that ... perhaps you should tell your mother about this man?'

She reared back and her brows climbed her forehead in amazement. 'And send her round the bend? Remember how bad she was when me da died?'

She was shocked; could not understand his reasoning.

'Ah.' His finger wagged. 'Listen, now. Listen to me, Rosaleen. Where did we always find your mother when she wandered off? Eh?' He nodded his head. 'Just you think about it.'

Comprehension dawned and she gazed at him open-mouthed.

'You mean ... you think Mam was up the Shankill looking for George?'

'Maybe not knowingly, but yes, I think guilt drove her up on to the Shankill Road.'

She continued to gape at him and he smiled faintly at her expression.

'Tell you what ... why not bring him up to meet her? Just introduce him as a friend and see what happens.'

'He might not come. She rejected him, remember.'

'What kind of a person is he?'

She thought of George – big, easygoing, kind – and smiled.

'He's a wonderful person. Me da all over again.'

Sean returned her smile. 'Well, if he's like your father, he won't hold spite. When will you see him again?'

'He's calling tomorrow night.' Now was her chance to let him know. 'You see, he's been trying to cheer me up. I've discovered that I'm pregnant.'

He tensed and she saw his fists clench as he gazed at her in amazement. She held her breath. Would he twig or would she be able to convince him that Joe was the father?

Stunned, he sat silent, then his head bowed and he examined her closely from under drawn brows. 'You mean Joe ...?'

'Of course! Who else? But the neighbours will never believe that he's the father. You can see the pickle I'm in. They'll swear George is the father, unless me mam claims him as her stepson, which I can't really see happening, but I can bear it if I have to. I don't want me mam hurt any more. She's suffered enough already.'

She watched him, her heart in her mouth. Would he believe her? She knew it was only Annie's strong belief that he was sterile that made him so naive. Would he twig on?

Sean gulped deep in his throat as pain seared through him. To think that a wreck of a man like Joe was able to give Rosaleen another child and all these years a big fellow like him had been unable to make Annie conceive. Feverishly, he pushed all self-pity from his mind. Time enough for that later, now he must think of Rosaleen.

'Well then, she'll have to be told,' he said determinedly. 'Does this George fellow look like your father?'

'Yes … well … he's not the spit of him or anything like that, but once you know who he is, you can see the resemblance.'

'Try and get him to come up with you tomorrow night. Just introduce him as a friend, and we'll play it by ear. Your mother knew your father better than anyone else, so she should recognise him.'

'Will you be there?'

'I'll be there,' he promised. He continued to linger, and rising to her feet, she said, 'You'd better go now. Annie will wonder where you are … and the neighbours will wonder what we're doing.'

On his feet, he faced her. His eyes examined her face, the eyes heavy from weeping, a bruise already discolouring her jaw, and shame smote him.

'Rosaleen, I'm sorry. Can you ever forgive me?'

He made to draw her into his arms but with a deft movement she eluded him.

'Sean, I'm tired. I want to go to bed.'

The old teasing look came into his eyes. 'Now is that an invitation … or is that an invitation?' he whispered softly, and love flowed between them. He was relieved to see a slight smile drift across her face and she waved her hand at him.

'Away you go. Go on.'

'Good night.'

Still he lingered, and with a slight push she sent him in the direction of the door.

'Good night, Sean.'

As she climbed the stairs to bed, she was weary in mind and body. Was she doomed to spend the rest of her life alone? Even if she was lucky enough to meet another man who attracted her, who would want to take on a woman and two children?

The rain was cool on his cheeks as he walked home and he was glad it hid the tears. Imagine a skeleton of a man like Joe being able to give Rosaleen another child, while a big fellow like him could not make his wife conceive. He felt so helpless. So inadequate. Other couples were childless, but the women didn't go on like Annie. Wait until she heard this latest bit of news ... her tongue was as sharp as a razor when she scorned him, but wait until she heard about this! He supposed she was right. He should listen to her and go see a doctor. Annie had done all she could, and the doctors could find no fault with her. So the defect must lie within him. If only she had been patient just a little longer. He had been talking himself into going to have the tests done, but she had to jump the gun. He would never forgive her for setting everything up and then expecting him to perform. What did she take him for ... some animal?

He wiped his cheeks with the back of his hand. Why was it considered unmanly for a man to cry? He felt better for it. He would have to decide what to do with his life. Perhaps this George fellow would be a blessing in disguise. If Thelma was to recover enough to live on her own, Annie might at last agree to buy a house somewhere far away from Rosaleen. Not that Annie would know that he was running away from Rosaleen, but if they could just get away on their own, perhaps then he would go and see the doctor. And if hardy came to hardy, he would even consider adoption ... but first things first. For all their sakes, Thelma must recognise and accept George. He could not live his life hoping for crumbs from Rosaleen's table. No! He owed it to Annie to try and make her happy.

As Rosaleen walked by George's side up the Springfield Road the next evening, she was in a dither.

Watching her covertly, George smiled. Reaching for her hand, he pulled it through his arm and pressed it close to his side. 'Relax, everything will be all right.'

Easing her arm free, she gave him a grateful smile. He didn't know what was at stake. It would never dawn on him that the neighbours would think him the father of her child, and it would never do to arrive arm in arm with a strange man at her mother's. Annie would have a fit. Besides, the neighbours had enough to gossip about without that.

The hall door was open, and tapping on the kitchen door she entered the room. From the scullery, Annie looked at her in surprise and her jaw dropped with amazement when she saw Rosaleen motion George into the kitchen.

Where was Sean? He had promised to be here. Even as she thought of him, he was on the stairs, his voice welcoming as he greeted George.

Annie gaped at him. He had been as much against Rosaleen's fancyman as the rest of them, yet here he was fawning all over him. And how come he knew him?

'George, this is my wife Annie, and her mother Thelma.'

Good manners forced Annie to greet George civilly but she would have something to say to Rosaleen when she got her alone. Imagine bringing her fancyman into their home and parading him in front of their mother. Who would have thought that their Rosaleen would become such a shameless hussy? Thelma was in her usual position at the side of the fire and paid little attention to them, but at the sound of her name she glanced in their direction.

After a brief nod of acknowledgement at George, she returned her gaze to the fire. Rosaleen looked beseechingly at Sean. What were they going to do? Her mother didn't recognise the visitor.

'Sit down, George. Here, sit here by the fire.'

Sean deliberately motioned him to the chair facing Thelma's. Tommy Magee's chair. 'The throne' it had been called when Tommy was alive, and well dare anyone sit in it when Tommy was in the house.

'How's about a cup of tea, eh, Annie?'

It was with bad grace that she entered the scullery. Sitting beside Rosaleen on the settee, Sean gave her arm a reassuring squeeze and spoke across to George.

'You live on the Shankill Road, don't you?' he asked, and was relieved to see that Thelma was watching George covertly. Would she see the resemblance? He could see Tommy so plain in this young man, but he knew the truth. Would Thelma guess who he was?

'Have you always lived on the Shankill, George?'

'All my life.'

'And your parents ... did they always live on the Shankill Road?'

'My mother was born and reared on the Shankill. She died when I was born, but my father was a Falls Road man. He died during the blitz.'

Thelma tensed, and Sean pressed on. 'You're something the age of my wife, aren't you?'

Before replying, George examined the woman his father had loved. She must be about forty-nine but she looked sixty. Snow white hair was pulled back severely from a skeleton face, and the green eyes had a wild look about them. They were examining his face, and he saw a flicker of disbelief pass over the pale face.

It was obvious that she was far from well. Why, he had seen men look like this when shell-shocked. There was nothing that he would like better than to help this woman, but supposing they were wrong and it went the other way? Could they afford to take the chance? Shouldn't a doctor be present? However, Sean was nodding encouragingly at him so he replied, 'I think there's about six months between your wife and me.'

Annie heard his words as she entered the kitchen carrying a tray, and gasped aloud. How did this man know what age she was? Had Rosaleen told him?

Sean took the tray from her and placed it on the table, then lifting a cup of tea, he approached Thelma.

'Here, Thelma ... here's a nice cup of tea for you.'

He placed a comforting hand on her shoulder as she gazed beseechingly at him. Would she believe what her mind was telling her, or would she choose to close her mind and retreat even further from the world? It was in God's hands. They could do no more.

Rosaleen sat on the edge of the settee, clasping her cup of tea, and prayed. It would make so much difference to her if her mother accepted George, but she was afraid to hope.

Conversation flagged, and an uneasy silence reigned.

George felt Thelma's eyes on him and he moved slightly, bringing his face round so that the light from the window fell on it. However, he kept his gaze averted. The brightness of the woman's eyes worried him. He sensed that she was treading a narrow line between sanity and madness. Rosaleen had explained how the opening of their father's grave to receive Joe's body had knocked her back into despair. His father had stressed that he was sure that she loved him. Would she want to come face to face with the result of his sin?

At last the silence was broken by a great shuddering sob and at once George was on his feet, hovering anxiously over this poor, tormented woman.

To his relief, he saw that the madness had left her eyes and she was weeping quietly.

'Tommy sent you … didn't he? He's forgiven me … hasn't he?'

On his knees by her side, he gathered her hands in his.

'Yes, he sent me. He's forgiven you.'

As Thelma tentatively reached out a hand to touch George's face, Rosaleen released her long-held breath. And when a bewildered Annie would have broken the hush, Sean, with a finger to his lips, ushered her and Rosaleen out of the house, having the presence of mind to pick up their coats on the way out.

Once outside, Annie rounded on them. 'What's going on? Who's that man? I thought he was your …' Her voice trailed off and Sean and Rosaleen shared a happy smile. Annie could be told the truth.

It was Sean who spoke first. 'Rosaleen has something to tell you, Annie.'

Her eyes swung from him to Rosaleen.

'You're in for a bit of a shock. George is me da's son.'

'Me da's? You mean …?'

Rosaleen laughed at her shocked expression. 'Yes, that's right! Me da had an illegitimate child.'

'I don't believe you!' Annie cried indignantly. 'Me da loved me mam too much to have a fancy-woman.'

'You're right… he didn't have a fancy-woman. But he did have a

238

one-night stand and George is the result.'

Still Annie looked scandalised. 'I don't believe you! Me da was too good-living to do anything like that.'

'I'm not saying me da wasn't a good man. He was wonderful. The very best. But even the best can fall, so they can.'

Rosaleen was unprepared for the picture of her actions with Sean that chose at that moment to rise in her mind, and turned away, confused. For the first time she was actually aware of the enormity of what she was doing to her sister. When she was with Sean it all seemed so natural, but no matter how right it felt, it was adultery. What if Annie ever found out? She had turned her anger on Sean. 'And you knew all about this, and you never said a word to me?'

'No! No, I didn't know until last night,' he defended himself, only to find that he'd jumped out of the frying pan into the fire.

'You were at our Rosaleen's house last night?' Annie's eyes darted from one to the other of them suspiciously. 'I thought you were at the pub with Jim Gourley.'

'I was at the pub ... but I was a bit drunk, and you know how you hate to see me drunk, so I called into Rosaleen's for a cup of coffee to sober me up,' he blustered.

'Oh, indeed?' Annie's voice dripped with scorn. 'So you don't mind if our Rosaleen sees you making a spectacle of yourself?'

Sean's voice was bitter when he answered her, 'Rosaleen's kind! She's not like you! You take after your mother.'

They had reached the corner of the street and Sean turned and strode up the Springfield Road, a hurt, vulnerable set to his head and shoulders. Rosaleen longed to go after him and assuage the pain, but she had not the right.

'Go after him, Annie!' she urged. 'He's hurt!'

Tight-lipped, her sister stubbornly shook her head. 'No! It wouldn't do any good. We're always at each other's throats. It's got to the stage where we can't look at each other without snarling.'

Seeing the misery on her face, Rosaleen slipped her arm through Annie's and led her gently down the Springfield Road.

'I know what we need ... a drink. Come on, I've a bottle of sherry. Let's go drink it.'

'You don't ...' Startled out of her misery, Annie drew back and

239

gazed in open-mouthed amazement at her. 'Surely you don't … do you?' she gasped. Rosaleen smiled grimly when she realised what Annie was thinking.

'Tut! Of course I'm not a secret drinker. I haven't reached that point … yet. It's a bottle left over from the wake.'

Still uneasy, Annie said, 'What about me mam?'

'We can safely leave her in George's capable hands. You'll like George once you get to know him, he's me da all over again.'

'I can't take it in. Me da doing that …'

Rosaleen laughed softly. 'I know how you feel. I couldn't believe it either. No wonder me mam nearly went out of her mind when he died.'

'Me poor mam,' Annie said softly. 'To have lived with that knowledge all her life. How could me da have been so cruel?'

'He didn't set out to hurt me mam,' Rosaleen defended him.

'He must have known what he was doing!' Annie interrupted her. 'He was far from stupid. He must have guessed that there could be consequences, and that me mam would be heartbroken.'

'It was only a one-night stand, Annie. He explained in a letter to me. He was drunk.'

'Still … I can't believe that me da would do a thing like that.'

They had arrived at Rosaleen's house, and opening the door she ushered her sister inside.

'Let's have a drink and forget all about it,' she said as she filled two glasses and joined Annie on the settee. 'Here! Cheers!'

After a couple of glasses of sherry, Annie was mellowed enough for Rosaleen to risk questioning her.

'Annie … do you not think that you're making too big an issue out of not having children? I mean, lots of couples don't have children, but they don't get on like you do.'

To her astonishment, Annie rounded on her angrily. 'Would you not be mad if your husband refused to go see about himself? That's all I ask of him. And then … if we can't have a family … fair enough. But the big fellow won't even go to the doctor, and then he's mad when I make all the arrangements …' Her voice trailed off and Rosaleen was surprised to see a blush stain her cheeks.

'All what arrangements?'

Annie shrugged, and sighed. 'Oh, I suppose I can tell you. I made arrangements to go see a specialist ... all Sean had to do was perform before I went. That's all he had to do, and I'd have done the rest. But no ... he hit the roof! Stormed from the house.'

A puzzled frown furrowed Rosaleen's brows. 'I don't understand.'

'It's simple! He performs ... I go straight to the hospital ... and they can take a sperm count without even seeing him. But he went mad, said I should have discussed it with him first. Said he was no performing animal. Well, as far as I'm concerned he'll never perform again.'

'You mean, you set all this up and never told him?' Rosaleen cried, aghast. 'No wonder he was mad. You'll be driving him into another woman's arms, so you will.'

'Huh ... you don't know what it's like being married to him. He's away so often and I thought I was doing him a good turn, setting it all up. I honestly never meant to offend him, but now it's as if a brick wall is between us.' There was an edge of tears in her voice. 'I've tried,' she admitted, 'but he doesn't want to be friends again.'

'Annie, will you take a bit of advice from me?'

Her reply was sulky. 'Maybe.'

'Put on your sexiest nightie and make it up with him before he goes back to sea. Swallow your pride or you'll lose him. He's a very handsome man, and very passionate.' Horror made her pause at this blunder. 'At least, I imagine he would be passionate. Many a girl would be glad to accommodate him.'

She breathed a sigh of relief when Annie answered her. Obviously, she had not noticed the slip of the tongue. Funny how you trusted your own. Would not dream that they would betray you.

'I suppose you're right. Not that I'm worried about other girls. As you say, he is very handsome and girls are inclined to throw themselves at him, but never once have I seen him show a flicker of interest in return. And, strange though it may seem, I trust him.' She lapsed into silence. Then: 'I think maybe he cared deeply for someone before he met me, but she must have died or maybe she was already married. He never confided in me. I respect his privacy. Anything that happened before we married is water under the bridge as far as I'm concerned. I had my moments too.'

Observing Rosaleen's start of surprise, she laughed. 'Oh, nothing serious. Just some mad passionate embraces. But the monastery fathers soon put me back on the straight and narrow when I went to confession. And I'm glad, mind you. Sean married a virgin, so he did! No matter how fast me mam thought I was.'

'Forget about a baby, Annie. Just love him wholeheartedly and maybe you'll conceive.'

'Fat chance! There's nothing wrong with me.' She glared at Rosaleen. 'I've seen a specialist and he could find nothing wrong.'

'But sometimes the doctors are wrong. Maybe you're trying too hard.'

'Hah! Listen to you. I suppose you think you know better than the doctors?' Annie sneered.

'No, but give it a try, Annie. Show him you love him. Tell him it doesn't really matter whether or not you have children. Or, mark my words, you'll lose him.'

'Do you know something that I don't know?' Annie's voice was shrill and her eyes suspicious again. 'Has he been talking to you about me?'

'No, he hasn't. Oh … I give up. I'm away to the loo and then we'll go up and see how things are with Mam. And I forgot to tell you … I'm pregnant!'

In the bathroom Rosaleen faced herself in the mirror. She would stay here until Annie got over the shock of her being pregnant. How she wished that she could change places with her. Everything would be okey-dokey if it was Annie who was pregnant.

Why was she trying to get Annie and Sean to hit it off? Because if they should part, she did not want to be the cause. If they parted with no help from her, then and only then … She pulled her mind back to reality. Now she was treading dangerous ground. Maybe when the baby was born she would have no choice in the matter and everybody would know the truth. It might be a boy, the picture of Sean. She was hardly likely to produce another green-eyed daughter. Then, if Annie chose not to forgive them, then and only then would she feel free to go away with Sean. Live in sin. Damn her soul. All she could do was wait and see. She might never get the chance.

Annie was still sitting on the settee when she returned to the living room. She turned an anguished look upon Rosaleen.

'Is it Joe's baby?'

'Of course!' Fear gripped Rosaleen's heart. Would Annie guess? But then, she thought Sean was sterile. Would this make her doubt her belief? 'You can understand why I'm so grateful that Mam has accepted George, otherwise everyone would think that he was the father.'

Annie smiled wryly at her. 'I'm ashamed of the way I acted towards you, you know ... about George. I should have known that you wouldn't do anything underhand. Am I forgiven?'

Embarrassed, feeling a traitor, Rosaleen avoided looking at her and headed for the door. 'Come on. Let's go and see how me mam and George are getting on.' And when Annie joined her and squeezed her arm, Rosaleen gave her what she hoped looked like a forgiving smile, inwardly hating herself.

Sean had already returned to the house, and when they entered the kitchen, glanced quickly at them and away again.

Amazed at the change in her mother, Rosaleen perched on the arm of her chair and hugged her.

'It's wonderful to see you looking so relaxed and contented, Mam.'

'I've you to thank for that, Rosaleen.' She smiled across at George. 'You brought him to me. How I've longed to see him, but I didn't know where to start lookin'. And ... I was too ashamed to ask for help.'

'Ashamed? Why ashamed? You didn't do anything wrong, Mam,' Rosaleen assured her.

'Oh, but I did! I committed the worst two sins of all. My pride got in the way of my love for your da, and I wouldn't forgive him. That's the worst sin of all – to hold spite. I made his life a misery.'

Seeing that she was getting all het up again, Rosaleen said earnestly, 'Mam, me da loved you dearly. He was happy just to be with you, but he will be pleased ... wherever he is ... to know that you have accepted George.'

Thelma gripped Rosaleen's hand. 'You think he'll know?'

'I think he'll know,' Rosaleen muttered, and squeezed her tight. In her heart she really did think her father knew. 'But now I'll have to go down and collect my Laura. Amy'll think I'm lost.'

She eyed George and he stood up. At once Thelma was on her feet, eyeing him beseechingly.

'You'll come back, won't you?'

He smiled kindly at her. 'Just let anyone try to keep me away. You'll be fed up looking at me, so you will.'

'Never! Never, son, and I mean that.'

During this conversation, Rosaleen had been covertly watching Annie as she sat beside Sean on the settee. She saw her take his hand and whisper in his ear, and saw Sean nod and return the pressure of Annie's hand, and she breathed a sigh of relief. Perhaps everything would work out all right. Only time would tell!

Chapter 9

It was with apprehension that Annie stepped from the trolleybus and eyed her surroundings. It was one thing coming out the Antrim Road to Bellevue Zoo or the Cave Hill for a day's entertainment, but another matter entirely to consider living out here, so far away from her mother and Rosaleen. It was all right for Sean, he was away for months at a time, but she would be here day in, day out. As her eyes took in the lush, vivid green of the grass, and the yellow of the gorse, and her ears picked up the sounds of the countryside, she had to admit that it was lovely, and so quiet and peaceful. It was hard to believe that on their journey down they had passed through districts with streets missing and work still going on razing condemned buildings to the ground. A reminder of the past few years. It would be a long time before Belfast was back to normal.

The Cave Hill reared up behind them. So close, she felt that if she reached out her hand she could touch the legendary Napoleon's nose, etched sharp against the skyline. It struck her as strange that she had stood on that nose not so long ago and looked down over these fields and houses, out over the lough, and now Sean wanted to buy a house out here. Wonders would never cease!

In front of them, the fields and hedges tumbled down steeply to the small village of Greencastle. Beyond that, in the far distance, Belfast Lough could be seen, shimmering and sparkling in all its glory, and away to the right of it, the cranes of the shipyard were prominent. Even the sky seemed brighter out here, with clouds scurrying across a curtain of deep blue, and the spring sun was a pale, yellow, hazy blur. But then, there wasn't much of the sky to be seen on the Springfield Road. Out here, there was no built-up area to obstruct your view. No mills and foundries casting dark shadows, so you were more aware of the sky and its beauty.

Sean watched her intently. It meant so much to him that she should like it here, and agree to live on the Serpentine Road. He knew he was asking a lot of her. She was used to living in the heart of the city; shops, churches, schools all close at hand. Out here, there was no tram at the corner and the nearest shop was in Greencastle, some distance away. The houses were spaced out and secluded, although the one he wanted to buy was semi-detached so perhaps the next-door neighbour would be nice, and good company for Annie. He realised that the cards were stacked against him, but they needed to be alone, to try and make a go of their marriage. He would just have to persuade her to give it a try. Now that Thelma was so much better and George was a constant visitor to see her, they could leave her to live alone without feeling guilty. And he needed to get away from Rosaleen.

He wanted a settled life, a home of his own, the chance to make Annie happy. And, God willing, maybe some day they would have a child. Slipping his arm through hers, he hugged it close to his side and led her across the Antrim Road, over to where the Serpentine Road started its meandering down to Greencastle.

'Wait 'til you see the house. It seems huge compared to your mother's,' he explained excitedly. 'It's semi-detached and there's a wide driveway. Maybe one day … who knows, we'll be able to afford a car, and we'll have room to build a garage. Now the war's over, anything's possible.'

A happy laugh left his lips and rang out on the still air and Annie laughed in return, pleased to see him so relaxed. It was a long time since he had laughed spontaneously; during his past couple of leaves he had been morose, if not actually unhappy. But then, that was her fault, not his. He had tried to please her. Any other woman would have been beside herself with joy at the flowers and gifts bestowed upon her, but she could see no further than the fact that after years of marriage, she was still childless. Ignoring Rosaleen's warning, she had nagged him often.

She could not help herself. All she wanted was for him to go and see about himself. Was that asking the earth, when so much was at stake?

Now she rubbed her cheek affectionately against his sleeve, and was rewarded with a quick kiss.

The Serpentine Road sloped gently down, winding in and out, just like the river it was named after. They dandered along, pausing now and then to admire the houses set back off the road. Some were detached, some were sprawling cottages, but all had one thing in common – they were well maintained, with rockeries and lawns a delight to the eye. And always, around each bend, to their right in the distance was the lough, calling for admiration.

At last Sean drew her to a halt. 'There it is.' He pointed upwards to two houses, set on an incline, looking very imposing. 'It looks all right, doesn't it?' he asked, nodding towards the right-hand house.

She smiled and nodded in return and followed him slowly up the drive, her eyes examining everything around her.

The garden was overgrown, but that could soon be put right. The house was not very old. It had belonged to an aunt of one of the sailors on Sean's ship, built by an uncle who had died at war, and when his aunt died suddenly, to his surprise Sean's shipmate had inherited it. It was quite by accident that Sean had heard it was going on the market, and going at a bargain price for a quick sale.

Sean's letters had been full of it, and once home on leave he had gone straight to view the house. Having fallen in love with it, he was now praying that Annie would like it; would consent to live out here. Covertly he watched her reaction to the house. He just had to persuade her to live here. It was a beautiful house. They would never get a bargain like it again. Normally it would be beyond their pocket, and once it went on the market it would be snapped up.

They left the drive and climbed four steep steps, passing the big bay window. Annie noted as they did so that the top panes of glass of the window were lead-lighted and the fanlight above the door likewise. From here they paused and turned to survey the scene before them.

The house was well up off the road, and opposite it green pastures soaked up the peaceful, warm sunshine. In the distance, the lough could be seen, shimmering and gleaming. And to the left, the road meandered on, sloping in and out between secluded houses.

'Isn't it lovely?' Annie whispered, as if to raise her voice would shatter the stillness. 'It's like being in a different world.'

With a nod and a grin, Sean happily agreed with her, before turning and mounting another step up to the entrance of the house.

The big door was of hard wood and varnished, and the upper half of it framed a beautiful leadlight window.

He was surprised to note that his hand shook when he put the key in the lock, and smiling wryly, he admitted to Annie, I'm as excited as a child visiting Santa Claus.'

Pushing the heavy door open, he turned and smiled down mischievously at her.

'Hows about me carrying you over the threshold?'

With a quick glance at the next-door house, Annie grinned and declined his offer with a shake of her head. Stepping around him, she entered the house.

They stood close together and surveyed the hall. Annie was aware just what he had meant when he said that the house seemed huge compared to her mother's. Why, you could set her mother's hall in the corner of this one. It was wide, more than twice the width of the hall in Colinward Street, and ran almost the full length of the house. To their right two doors opened off the hall, and facing them at the far end was another door. A wide staircase rose to the floor above. Sean opened the first door and ushered her in. It was a wide, spacious room, with a high ceiling, a deep frieze and a big bay window. The floor boards had been sanded down and varnished and gave off a dull glow. In the wall facing them a slate mantelpiece commanded attention, the light from the window reflecting on its muted shades of blue and grey and making the marble hearth glisten just like washing soda. That was what came to Annie's mind, the rough washing soda, white, shot with colours.

'Well, what do you think?'

'Lovely … very nice indeed,' she replied cautiously, amused at his impatience.

The next room off the hall also had a bay window which looked out on the drive at the side of the house. Smaller than the first room, it was nevertheless larger than her mother's kitchen or Rosaleen's living room. Here there was a smaller grate with a wooden mantelpiece and a tiled hearth. Sean pointed to the back of the grate.

'That's the back boiler, for heating the water. Just imagine, Annie, hot-water at the turn of a tap. No waiting for kettles to boil, to have a wash.'

'Now that would be nice,' she replied, and saw by his smile that he was pleased at her answer.

There was also bright oilcloth covering the floor and a small armchair at each side of the hearth. At her querying look, Sean nodded.

'Yes, they go with the house. They're not bad. They'd do until we decided what kind of furniture we want.'

The last door led to the kitchen. It was the width of the house but not very deep. An old, well-scrubbed wooden table took up a lot of the floor space. The window was to their right, above a deep sink with cupboards built around it. Annie was surprised to note that what she would call the 'back' door was actually at the side of the house, leading out on to the drive, and was relieved to see that the enamel stove was gas. A step down from the kitchen led to a small back hall and here, on the left side, facing the 'back' door, was a small room lined with shelves. This, Annie decided, must be the larder. It was much bigger than Rosaleen's, you could walk right into it.

Sean opened the door and stepped outside to survey the back garden, rolling his eyes heavenward when he saw the jungle that it had become.

'Dear God, Annie. You could lose half of Colinward Street in here,' he jested, as his eyes, bright with happiness, travelled the length and breadth of it.

'I'll soon get that mess cleared up,' he promised.

Silently, she wondered when he would find the time to clear it, he was away so often. Really, a house this size was too big for a couple on their own, and it was so cut off, so out of the way. What if the neighbours hated them? Besides, time enough to buy a big house if they ever had a family.

Aware of her silent contemplation, Sean escorted her back through the house and up the wide staircase, all the while pointing out the advantages and beauty of the hall. At the top of the stairs was the bathroom. Here, the ceiling and walls had been fitted with light oak tongue and groove panelling and the bathroom suite gleamed, obviously well cared for. There were four doors off the landing; three of these opened on to bedrooms and the fourth was an airing-cupboard and contained the hot-water tank. One of the rooms overlooked the back garden, and from the window there was a breathtaking view of the Cave Hill. Annie stood entranced and Sean relaxed. It was obvious that she liked the house. However, he would not have been so happy if he had been aware of her thoughts. She was warning herself not to fall in love with the house. It was too big, too isolated. She would be out herie on her own for weeks on end, depending on Rosaleen, her mother or George taking pity on her and paying a visit.

The other two bedrooms overlooked the front of the house and from these the view of the lough was breathtaking. The smaller of the rooms immediately sprang to Annie's mind as a nursery. She could picture murals on the walls, a big cot in the corner, and tears came to her eyes. Would she ever have a child?

She pushed these thoughts from her, knowing Sean would not want to hear her lament about a child, and as they descended the stairs, she smilingly agreed with him that the house was indeed a bargain.

'Well … what do you think?' His voice was apprehensive. She was too quiet, too unenthusiastic, and he feared the worst – that she did not want to live here. 'It's going for a fraction of its real price, Annie. We'll never get a chance like it again,' he pleaded.

Their tour of the house completed, they sat side by side on the bottom step of the stairs, admiring the spring sunlight coming through the leaded light in the door and casting coloured rays over them. He waited anxiously for her reply, and after some moments of thought, she answered him.

Tentatively, not wanting to just dash his hopes, she countered, 'It's lovely ... very nice ... but do you not think it's a bit big for two people?'

Abruptly he rose to his feet, his face flooding with hot, angry colour, and glared down at her, causing her to draw back in dismay.

'Could you not let one leave go by without harping on that?' he cried bitterly. 'Eh? Are children the beginning and end of all for you?'

'No, but ...'

'Oh, but YES. I'm sick of listening to you harp on about being childless. I'm sick watching you drool over other people's kids.' As suddenly as his temper had flared, all the fire left him. His shoulders slumped and his hands stretched out in a wide, hopeless gesture. 'I've been giving our marriage some thought, Annie, and I've come to the conclusion that perhaps we should try for an annulment.'

She was aghast. This was a bolt from the blue. 'What on earth do you mean?' she asked, and it was her turn to be apprehensive.

'I mean ... since we can't get divorced, and since we're so incompatible, perhaps the Church will grant an annulment. Set us free of each other. We can at least ask.'

'The Church would never do that!' Annie cried, amazed that he could think such a thing. 'We married for better or worse, so we did. The Church doesn't grant annulments just because you can't have children. That's God's will! You have to learn to live with it. You can only get a marriage annulled if it's not consummated.'

His finger pointed accusingly at her, and his eyes scornfully raked her face. 'But you can't live with it... sure you can't, Annie,' he taunted. And turning on his heel, he strode down the hall, through the kitchen and out of the door, to stand gazing blindly in front of him. The back garden, about seventy feet of it, stretched before him and the Cave Hill loomed high above it. He eyed it bleakly. Annie was right. This was a house to rear kids in. That big garden was made for swings and slides, the tree made for tomboys to climb. He'd been a fool to think that a house like this could ever belong to him.

Alone on the stairs, Annie sat stunned. She wanted children, yes, but Sean was her world ... from the first moment she had set eyes on him, she had loved him, and no other man had ever received a second thought from her. Why, without him she would die. Slowly, she rose to her feet and followed him, pausing at the door.

'Sean?'

He remained outside, his head averted. His cheeks were wet with tears that he did not want her to see. He felt ashamed. Imagine crying over a house.

Going to him, she put her arms around him and pressed her cheek against his sleeve, delighting in the smell of him, the feel of the rough tweed of his sports jacket under her cheek.

'Sean, I'm sorry,' she said softly. 'I realize that I've been a selfish fool. If you want this house, buy it, and we'll give it a try.'

Astounded, tears forgotten, he turned to face her. 'You mean that? Honestly now, you're willing to give it a try?'

The sight of his tears dismayed her, tore at her heart.

'Ah, Sean ... Sean. Forgive me. I've been blind.' Her fingers smoothed his cheeks, wiping the tears away. 'I've been a blind fool, so I have.'

'Listen, Annie, I've been selfish too. I should've gone and seen about myself long ago, but I was afraid.' A tense silence yawned as he gripped her tighter still. Then the fear that was constantly with him poured out. 'What if I can never father children?'

Regret gnawed at her mind. She had been so wrong. She had been blaming him, thinking that he didn't care enough about children, and all the while ... he had been afraid of the result of the tests.

'It won't matter, Sean. Honestly, love. Just so long as we have both tried.' Her voice was earnest, compelling. She must make him understand that he came first. 'Much as I want children, I can live without them as long as I have you. But, love, don't you think it's worth a try? A visit to the doctor? That's all I ask. That we both try.'

Feeling humble, he vowed. 'On my next leave, once you know

just when I'm coming home, you can set up an appointment for me with the doctor, and I promise I'll go.'

And as his lips claimed hers, hope was deep in their hearts.

Both Rosaleen and Annie gazed adoringly at the baby lying on the rug in front of the fire. He was a beautiful child, his chubby limbs flailing the air, gurgles being emitted from his widely yawning mouth.

On her knees beside him, Annie tickled him under the chin. She was rewarded with a lovely, gaping, toothless grin and a gurgle of pure happiness.

'He's lovely, Rosaleen … beautiful. Such a good baby. I wish he was mine.' She gave a long, heartfelt sigh. 'You don't know how lucky you are to have two lovely children.'

Rosaleen leant forward in her chair, the better to enjoy the beauty of her son. She agreed wholeheartedly with Annie. Her son was beautiful. The pregnancy had been hard, the child spending most of his time lying on a nerve and causing her unending pain and misery, but the result was worth waiting for. Her eyes examined him intently. The chestnut hair, just like her father's, the big blue eyes … Would Sean see the resemblance? No one else had noticed. If he did notice, what would he do? Could she bluff him? Did she want to?

Annie continued gently to tickle the child, and as he gurgled and kicked, she examined him.

'Do you know something, Rosaleen? My desire for a child must be affecting my mind.' With a wry grimace she raised her gaze to Rosaleen's. 'I can actually see Sean in young Liam.'

Leaning forward as she was, their faces just inches apart, and taken completely unawares, there was no way Rosaleen could have controlled her expression, her change of colour.

Open mouthed, Annie gaped at her in dawning horror. She saw the colour flood her sister's face and creep down her neck, the guilt and dismay register in her eyes. Aghast, her eyes returned to the child and feverishly examined each feature. He had her colouring … just like his grandfather. He even resembled his grandfather in features, which meant that he favoured her. Why, this was how a child of hers and Sean's could look, chestnut-haired, blue-eyed. But then, thousands of children had blue eyes, she assured herself.

Not this shade of blue! her mind shouted back.

Such an unusual shade. She had noticed the eyes before but had assumed that they were inherited from Joe's father. Perhaps they were, she warned herself. She must be cautious, not accuse Rosaleen. Perhaps she was wrong. Once more her eyes returned to her sister but Rosaleen now had her emotions under control, her features schooled, and gazed innocently back at her.

Annie blinked in bewilderment. Had she imagined that look? No! No ... she had not imagined it. But she must have. Surely she must have? There was no way that Sean could be the father. Wasn't he sterile? Besides, he wouldn't ... not with Rosaleen, not with her sister! Would he? Would he do that to her?

Afraid to speak in case she said the wrong thing and made matters worse, Rosaleen watched Annie grapple with her doubts.

Confused, she shook her head as if to clear it and stumbled to her feet. Towering over Rosaleen, she wailed piteously, 'Tell me it's not true. Oh, Rosaleen, tell me I'm wrong. Please tell me I'm wrong,' she begged. 'Don't let this happen to me.'

'What? What's not true? I don't know what you're talking about.' Rosaleen replied, looking bewildered.

And all Annie's doubts fled. She knew! She was sure. How she didn't know, but she was sure that Rosaleen lied. Her voice was too easy ... her manner too innocent.

Blinded by tears, she groped for her shoes and pushed her feet into them, all the while her mind insisting that it could not be true. It just could not be true! How would she be able to bear it if it was true? With shaking hand, she reached for her coat and shrugged it on.

Rosaleen watched her in silence, afraid to speak, flailing about in her mind for words that would make everything right, but none were forthcoming. At the door Annie turned and gazed wildly around the room.

The peaceful scene of mother and child by the fire enraged her.

Her world was falling apart and nothing had changed. Everything still looked the same.

With a cry of pain, she lifted a vase that sat in pride of place near the door, and crashed it against the wall. As it shattered, Rosaleen was on her feet.

'Now wait a minute … just what do you think you're doing?'

'Don't you come near me, you mealy-mouthed, sanctimonious bitch, or I won't be responsible for my actions,' Annie hissed, her fist lifted threateningly in the air. 'You slut! You dirty, rotten wee slut!'

'I don't know what you're talking about,' Rosaleen blustered. 'But that was an expensive vase, and I'll see that you replace it. You're right. You are crazy. You need your head examined.' Then, her voice softening, she implored, 'Look … sit down. Let's talk this out.'

'Sit down? Are you nuts? I'll never sit in this house again. Never again.'

Pain was etched sharply on Annie's face and her voice broke on a sob that tore at Rosaleen's heart when she asked, 'Does he know?'

'Does he know what? I don't know what you're talking about, so I don't.'

'Oh, you know! You know all right! You lying cat!'

As the door settled back on its hinges and the sound of Annie's footsteps storming up the street receded, Rosaleen sank slowly down on to the settee, shame and regret tearing her apart. It was awful to hear Annie call her a slut, but wasn't it the truth? And didn't she still covet her sister's husband? What would Annie do? Would she confront Sean? If so, how would he react? Swamped with unhappiness, she argued with herself. Was it so wrong of her to want Sean? Perhaps Annie was meant to notice. Perhaps it was fate and at last she was going to get a chance at happiness. Was she not entitled to some happiness? All those wasted years married to Joe, frustrated and unhappy. And most of the time Annie and Sean were at loggerheads. Annie longed for a child and obviously she was barren. Sean was miserable married to her. He was right! She should have listened to him. Why should everyone be unhappy?

Still, was she brazen enough to cause a big scandal? Run off with him and live in sin?

Annie's feet hardly touched the ground in her mad race up the Springfield Road. She kept her gaze straight head, ignoring people who spoke to her, not in a fit state to converse with anyone, very much aware that some stopped to look after her in amazement. And why wouldn't they? She must look demented. At the corner of Colinward Street her feet faltered, then continued on up the Springfield Road. George would be with her mother and she just didn't feel able to see him, make conversation.

George was so good and kind, her mother doted on him, treated him as the son she never had. It had surprised everyone the way she proudly introduced him as her stepson. Deep inside it must have hurt her to announce to one and all that her husband had sinned against her, but she seemed intent on punishing herself. She probably looked on it as penance, and her brave act brought her nothing but admiration.

Young Maureen Murphy also doted on George, but he kept her at arm's length, and Annie was aware that this was because his religious beliefs differed from hers.

Annie knew that she was just thinking of George to keep her mind off… Sean. There, she had let his face surface. How could he have done this to her? Him and Rosaleen. Her mind baulked as she tried to picture them together. Where had they met? Sean had been home so rarely during the war, and for such short periods … how had they managed to have an affair? Was he leaving Rosaleen and coming directly to their bed? But then, hadn't she been rejecting him? It had been wrong of her to withhold sex, to try to compel him to see a doctor. Was this why he had turned to Rosaleen? Hadn't she, hypocrite that she was, warned Annie that she would lose him? That some other girl would be glad to accommodate him. And all the while she was accommodating him, was already pregnant by him. She remembered how surprised she had been when Rosaleen had told her that she was expecting another child. The idea that a physical wreck like Joe could father a child, and a big healthy man like Sean could not, had stuck in her guts; made her, in her mind, scorn her husband. And all the time it was Sean's child that Rosaleen was carrying, and gullible fool that she was, she had believed Rosaleen that it was Joe's.

Pain seared through her, bringing sobs to catch at her throat. Angrily she choked them down. This was no time for tears. What she needed to do was think. She must have been blind! But then, wasn't the wife always the last to know? It's a wonder that the neighbours hadn't dropped hints. They delighted in doing that, and they must all have known. They must have been nudging each other and laughing at the idea of it. Well, what the neighbours thought had never bothered her before, so she would not let it matter to her now. No, she would not let it hurt her!

It was her own fault! She had been obsessed with the idea of having a baby. She had nagged and repulsed Sean and driven him into Rosaleen's arms. No, it was Rosaleen's fault. Good-living Rosaleen!

She, who cringed with distaste when a smutty joke was told. She, who would never take the Holy Name in vain. She had been letting Sean get his leg over. Oh, now, wouldn't Rosaleen be shocked at that expression? Wouldn't she just be shocked at anything so crude? How had she squared her conscience with committing adultery? Pure, holy Rosaleen! And what about Sean? It took two! But didn't the priests say that if there were no bad girls, there would be no bad boys? Didn't the women always get blamed. Weren't men weak, and wasn't it up to the women to keep them at arm's length? As for Rosaleen … how Annie had admired and looked up to her. All her life, because Rosaleen was such a good, pious person, she had thought it right that her mother and father should favour her, hold her up as an example. She had always been second best; only with Rosaleen and Sean had she felt that she came first. Rosaleen had been her friend as well as her sister, and look how she had betrayed her. How was Annie ever going to face her again? Her mouth trembled at the thought of her loss. Hurt and pain once more brought tears to her eyes, but she brushed them angrily away. She had no intention of wallowing in misery; she wasn't going to give in to self-pity. If Rosaleen thought that she was just going to walk off with Sean, she had another thought coming. He was her husband, and she would fight tooth and nail for him, child or no.

At the Dam she paused, then slowly made her way down the grassy bank, off the road. She could sit here for a while, gain control of her emotions before facing her mother. It was a lonely place, and as she gazed down on the water she shivered. Many nasty rumours circulated about the Dam, but the way she felt, it wouldn't matter if someone finished her off and pushed her in. Indeed, they would be doing her a favour.

As her anger abated, the house on the Serpentine Road came to mind, like a sanctuary in a storm. Sean had set things in motion the day after she had consented to live there and now it belonged to them, lock, stock, and barrel. So why not go there? But sure she couldn't. Except for the table and two armchairs, it was empty.

They intended moving in during Sean's next leave, but why wait? George would help her. He had a car; she could depend on him. First thing tomorrow morning she would go down and order a bed. It being a Saturday, the first day she could expect it to be delivered was Monday, but meanwhile she could sleep on the floor. It wouldn't kill her to live rough for a few days. Not after the nights spent in the Falls Park during the war. What about the chimneys? They needed to be swept. Sean had been warned not to light a fire until the chimneys had been swept. Well, it was just at night that it got chilly. The weather was changeable for June, but not really cold. She would survive. They had been told that a man in the village swept chimneys. Tomorrow she would find out where he lived and go and ask him to sweep them as soon as possible.

Now that a course of action was open to her, she turned and quickly retraced her steps up on to the road. She must catch George before he left to go home, make arrangements for him to help her move cooking utensils, bed linen and her wedding presents.

Once she had moved into the house on the Serpentine Road, she would be able to think, to decide what to do.

George and her mother had finished their inspection of the house and were now enjoying a cup of tea in the kitchen. Sitting at the old wooden table on two dining chairs borrowed from her mother, surrounded by pots and pans and boxes.

'It's lovely, Annie. You must be real proud to own a house like this.'

'Your mam's right ... it's a beautiful house,' George agreed with Thelma. 'Well-built and sturdy. But will you be all right here on your own?'

There was a worried frown on his brow, and from her perch on the edge of the draining board, Annie smiled reassuringly at him.

'Yes. Once I get the gas and electricity turned on, I'll be fine. Meanwhile I have your Primus stove and oil lamp. I'll be all right.'

'You should have asked Rosaleen to come and stop with you for a couple of nights, just 'til ye get settled in. I'd have minded the kids, so I would. Surely you knew that?' Thelma admonished her. 'I don't know what the big rush was for. Ye said you'd move during Sean's next leave ... what changed your mind?'

'Oh ... I thought I may as well be doing some decorating ... have some of the rooms ready for Sean coming home,' Annie replied airily. 'Anyhow, Rosaleen's too busy looking after her wee business, and to be truthful, I prefer to be alone.'

'Rosaleen'll be surprised when she hears about your movin'. She'll probably come down t'morrow t'see the house.'

'No. Tell her that I don't want her to come down. She'll understand, so she will.'

George watched her from under drawn brows. There was something wrong here. He sensed a deep unhappiness in Annie. Had she and Rosaleen quarrelled? Surely not. They were such close friends.

When they were ready to leave, and Thelma was in the car out of earshot, he whispered to Annie, 'I'll come down tomorrow afternoon and help you start cleaning out the rooms. I'll bring some food, so don't worry about cooking on the Primus stove. But do make yourself plenty of hot drinks.'

'Thanks, George. Thanks a lot,' she whispered back, 'I'll look forward to seeing you.'

Cold and unhappy, she was unable to sleep. Early next morning, an orange glow radiating from the front of the house brought her from the back bedroom to investigate – to stand at the window in awe and gaze entranced at the sun rising on the lough. Everything was orange and gold. The sky dazzling her eyes with its glow, and the lough shimmering and glowing like a thick gold chain brought a sigh of pure rapture to her lips. The sun was free of the lough and lightening the sky, and some sort of normality was apparent before she turned away from the beauty of it all. Imagine waking to that every morning. Wait until Sean saw the beauty of it, he would be enchanted. Thoughts of Sean dampened the joy that engulfed her. Would she ever be able to think of him without pain? Only time would tell, time and Sean's introduction to his son.

She had bought some ceiling white, and making up a thin paste with this, whitened the window panes. The house was high up and back off the road, and so far she had witnessed little traffic, but she still felt exposed by the curtainless windows, and the whitened panes made her feel easier, more private. With earning good money in Mackie's, she had some savings of her own. Tomorrow she would measure up for curtains and go into town to see if she could get any bargains. Something cheap to tide her over until the house was decorated and she knew just what kind of curtains she needed. They had decided that they would furnish the house slowly. Buy things as they could afford them. Only the best would do.

She had sent in word to her supervisor that she was ill. That gave her a week's breathing space, but could she travel to Mackie's every day? It would mean taking two trams … she would wait and see how she felt at the end of the week before making any decisions.

She had just finished her breakfast when there was a knock on the door. To her surprise it was the chimney sweep. Small, wiry, grinning from ear to ear.

'I couldn't let you spend another night without a fire, missus, so if it's all right with you, I'll clean yer chimneys now. Will ye allow me t'work on a Sunday?'

His infectious grin brought an answering smile to her face as she answered him.

'Of course, of course! I'm grateful to you for thinking of me.'

As she led the way into the sitting room, she said over her

shoulder, 'I'll be glad to get the chimneys swept.' She gave a slight laugh. 'But as for lighting the fires, I haven't any coal, so I'll have to wait until tomorrow to light them.'

'You've no coal, missus?' he cried, aghast.

When Annie smiled wryly and shook her head, the small man cried, 'Well now, we can't have that. Sure we can't. It gets chilly at night, so it does. There's a shop in the village that sells everything, an' it opens on a Sunday. When I've done the chimneys, I'll fetch you a small bag of coal and some kindlin' t'tide ye over. But I've t'go t'Mass, so it'll be about lunch time before I get back.'

Annie smiled at him; she loved his strong brogue. Much broader than the Belfast tongue. Even stronger than the older folk like her mother.

'Oh, thanks very much. That's kind of you. Is the Catholic church far away?'

'It's just down in the village. Have ye not bin down?'

Once more Annie shook her head. This man would think her a fool. 'I just arrived here yesterday ...' she began apologetically.

He interrupted her. 'Never you worry. I'll take ye down t'Mass, that's if ye don't mind travellin' in the van, an' then, sure, ye can buy yer coal and sticks yerself an' I'll run ye home again. I'll be finished in time for ten a'clock Mass, so I will.'

He waved her thanks away and started to connect his brushes, preparing to sweep the chimney. Not wanting to stand over him, she left him to it and went to get ready for church.

Annie turned the bend in the road that brought her house into view and shock brought her to a standstill. Monday had dawned brisk but sunny, just right for walking, so when her bed had been delivered earlier that morning, she had decided to walk down to the shops for some fresh milk and bread and meat. She had enjoyed her tour of the village and was in an easier frame of mind as she dandered up the Serpentine Road. Now she stood undecided, unrest once more agitating her. A figure sat on the step outside her door, a child in her arms and another youngster playing on the lawn. Rosaleen was gazing out over the lough, and Laura had her back to Annie. Should she turn back before they became aware of her? Should she stay away until they tired of waiting and departed for home?

Anger bubbled inside her. How dare she? How dare she come here, to Annie's home, to contaminate it. How dare she! With steps that dragged, she continued on up the road and was at the gate before Rosaleen, lost in a world of her own, became aware of her. As she closed the gate behind her, Annie tried to form words to tell Rosaleen that she did not want her in this house, would prefer her not to come visiting, but her mind was blank, and when an excited Laura threw herself into her arms, she hugged her close.

'Auntie Annie … Auntie Annie … we've come to see your new house, so we have.'

'Have you, pet? That's kind of you.'

Rosaleen had risen to her feet. Clutching the baby to her breast, she watched Annie fearfully. She had every right to refuse to let her in. Would she? As Annie drew close to Rosaleen, the baby, with a happy gurgle, held out his arms to her and she instinctively reached for him and hugged him close, her cheek softly caressing the silky hair of his head. Her actions surprised her. She had thought that she would never be able to look at this child again, yet here she was, hugging him.

Over the child's head their eyes met. Annie was pleased to see by Rosaleen's ravaged face that she too had suffered. Rosaleen looked how she herself felt: miserable beyond description.

'Annie, it was only the once.'

These words brought a howl of protest from Annie's lips.

'Don't you add insult to injury!' she cried. 'On Friday night you didn't know what I was talking about, and now you dare to insult my intelligence … me mam didn't believe me da, and I certainly don't believe you. Do you think I'm soft in the head?'

She stopped her tirade to glance down at Laura who was pulling at her skirt for attention. 'All right, all right, Laura,' she said testily. 'Let's go around the back. I've the back door key.' And with these words, she was committed to entertaining Rosaleen in her home, having to laugh when Laura exclaimed: 'This isn't a back door … have you no back door, Auntie Annie?'

'No, love. I'm rich, so I am … I've a side door.'

Begrudgingly, she showed Rosaleen over the house, receiving tight-lipped her obviously sincere words of praise.

When they retired to the kitchen, Rosaleen produced an apple tart from her shopping bag and proffered it to Annie. 'I'm hoping you'll offer me a cup of tea. And, Annie … we've got to talk.'

However Laura, who had kept the conversation going while they viewed the house, disappeared out into the back garden and the tea was drunk in silence. Both of them sat deep in thought, and the apple tart lay untouched. Once finished, Annie suggested that they sit out in the sun. That morning she had rescued two old deckchairs from the shed and they retired to these.

Rosaleen was having difficulty forming words to explain to Annie how she came to be pregnant. She had decided not to mention that Sean and she had been friends before he met Annie. If she once heard that, there was no way Annie would believe that it was only the one time and she must never learn about the first time, never! No one must ever learn about the night up at the Dam. Annie must be convinced that it had been a one-off event. It was the only way that her marriage could be saved. The vague ideas and longings Rosaleen had harboured, that maybe Liam would bring Sean and she together, had slowly died in the face of her sister's awful desolation. Annie loved Sean … And he?

Well, she must not put him to the test. Sean must never learn that Liam was his son. Only she, Sean and May knew that they had dated, and only Sean and she knew about the night up at the Dam. May was in Canada. Somehow she must get word to Sean, and he must warn Betty never to mention to Annie that he had once been interested in her sister.

Now she began, choosing her words carefully. 'Annie … honestly … it was only the once.'

The hope in the look that Annie turned on her made her want to weep, but it was quickly replaced by scorn.

'I don't believe you.'

'Well, I can't help that!' Rosaleen cried in exasperation. 'I've come here to explain … I don't want you picturing Sean creeping down to my house every now and again.' Her head jerked from side to side in denial. 'It just wasn't like that. It wasn't like that at all! It was just the one time. Sean's not like that. You must know that he would have come out in the open about it … if … we'd been having an affair.' Her eyes begged Annie to believe her. 'It happened just after Joe died. I was unhappy and vulnerable. Sean comforted me … and one thing led to another.'

Annie desperately wanted to believe her. Accidents did happen and she remembered how devastated Rosaleen had been when Joe died. And hadn't she herself pushed Sean out of the house? Insisted that he go to see Rosaleen, and him just home after months at sea. Long, lonely months without a woman. Nevertheless they shouldn't have, they had no right … he was Annie's husband. But if they did, and if it was only the once, was there an excuse for them? Angrily, she pulled her mind back to reality. Rosaleen was trying to fool her. Once? And there was a child? No, it was hardly likely.

'I don't believe you.'

But seeing that Annie was weakening despite herself, Rosaleen asked, 'Well, if you don't believe me … what do you intend doing about it?'

'What do you mean?'

'I mean, I want to know where I stand. Are you going to acquaint Sean with the knowledge that he's a father, or shall I?'

'He doesn't know?'

'Tut, Annie! Do you think he would just look the other way if he knew?'

Annie felt this was true. Sean had no inkling before he left that the child Rosaleen had just given birth to was his. She had already convinced herself of this. There was no way he would have asked her to make an appointment with the doctor if he had known that there was nothing wrong with him. Rosaleen had fooled him as well.

Now Rosaleen had her attention. 'Do you intend telling him?' Annie asked fearfully.

'Not unless you are going to act stupid. Sean is a wonderful person … as you well know. Are you going to let him go?'

'No, I am not!' Annie's voice was shrill. Imagine Rosaleen thinking she could walk off with Sean! 'I'll fight you tooth and nail for him.'

'You don't have to fight me,' Rosaleen interrupted her. 'Sean need never know about Liam, if you keep your mouth shut.'

Annie turned the words over in her mind, then her head swayed from side to side in despair.

'He'll know. The minute he sets eyes on Liam, he'll know.'

'Why?' At Annie's surprised look, Rosaleen repeated, 'Why? No one else has noticed.'

'I did!'

'Only you noticed. Look at him.' She pointed to where Liam lay sleeping on a rug. 'He's not the picture of Sean, is he?'

In sleep, Liam looked like the Magees. To Rosaleen's relief, Annie shook her head. Not a very definite shake, but a shake nevertheless, and she pressed on: 'He could have inherited his blue eyes from Joe's side of the family, couldn't he?'

A nod this time from Annie, and Rosaleen knew she had won – or lost? – her case.

'You have the right to maintenance, so you have,' Annie said mournfully.

Rosaleen tossed her head in disgust. 'Huh! I don't want maintenance. I'm far from rich but the business keeps me in comfort. I promise ... I swear ... that Sean will never hear from my lips that he's Liam's father.' She spread her hands wide. 'I can do no more.'

Annie looked at her intently. At the heavy, pale gold hair, the classic high cheek bones, the wide-spaced green eyes, so like her own, and without thinking, she asked, 'Are you in love with him?'

The colour rushed to Rosaleen's face and then receded, leaving her deathly pale.

'Of course I'm not!' And Annie was sorry that she had asked, because it was obvious to her that her beautiful sister was indeed in love with Sean.

The following day, Annie met her next-door neighbour. She was in the back garden gathering rubbish up and putting it in a pile at the bottom of the garden to burn, when a light voice hailed her from the other side of the hedge. The hedge wasn't very high and at first Annie thought her imagination was playing tricks on her, then the branches were parted slightly and she saw a small pale face with twinkling blue eyes.

'Hello, I'm Minnie Carson.'

'Hello. My name's Annie Devlin and I'm very pleased to meet you. Can you come in for a cup of tea?'

'I'd love to. I won't be a minnit.'

A few minutes later Minnie arrived around the side of the house, her arms full of flowers. The bunch was so big it almost dwarfed her. She was five foot tall, if that, about sixty years old, and bright and cheerful-looking.

'Thank you very much.' Annie sank her nose into the flowers and cried: 'Oh, they're lovely! Let's go inside and I'll put them in water.'

As they sat at the kitchen table, Minnie told Annie all about herself. She was a widow, with two married sons who lived on the opposite side of town. 'I was away at the weekend and I was going to call on you yesterday but you had company,' she explained.

'That was my sister and her children,' Annie replied, and Minnie nodded her head.

'I thought so ... you are very alike.'

'You think so?'

Annie had always thought that she and Rosaleen were as different as chalk and cheese, but Minnie disagreed with her.

'The planes of your face are the same ... and your eyes, it's just your colouring that's different.'

Annie grew silent. This tiny woman had noticed a lot, considering Rosaleen and she had been completely unaware of her. Had she overheard their conversation?

Minnie realised that she had given away more than she had intended, and sought to put matters right. From what she had overheard yesterday, fate had handed this young girl a bitter blow. She needed to be admired and her courage bolstered up.

'I saw you from the back bedroom,' she lied, with a nod up at the back of her house. 'I've a sewing machine up there ... I was making curtains.'

'Oh, I see.'

'Do you sew?'

'I was a stitcher before the war, but I haven't a sewing machine,' Annie said regretfully.

'You can borrow mine. I'm away every weekend. You can have it any time you like. I visit the boys alternate weekends.'

'Oh, that's kind of you. Curtains are so expensive. I would love to make my own. You must get on well with your daughters-in-law to visit them so often.'

'I do. But to tell you the truth, I'd prefer to stay in my own home. But since my husband died last year, the boys worry about me, and they insist I visit them.' Her face lit up. 'Perhaps, now that this house is occupied, I won't have to trek across town every weekend. And before I forget, I'll tell you another thing. I can get you material very reasonably. I've a friend in the business.' She drained her cup and rose to her feet. 'I'd better go now, but tomorrow you come and visit me.'

They beamed at each other, and Annie said softly, 'I'm glad to have you for a neighbour.'

'And I'm glad you're my new neighbour. I was dreading strangers coming, but I can tell that you and I are going to become friends. See you tomorrow ... about eleven.'

Coming out of the docks, Sean flagged down a taxi, too excited to wait for a tram or trolleybus. He sat in the front of the taxi, beside the driver, and directed him to approach the Serpentine Road via the Shore Road. He wanted to see what Greencastle looked like. As they approached it, his eyes took it all in. It was bigger than he expected: a row of small shops and a pub, the Railway Bar, on the right-hand side of the road, and another row of shops and whitewashed cottages on the left-hand side. This was all he had time to note as the car turned off near the start of the village and travelled up the Whitewell Road. Here, on the left-hand side, there was a housing estate and he observed that Greencastle had not escaped the blitz scot-free. No, some streets were partially demolished, but he also noted that as they left the Whitewell Road and climbed the Serpentine Road, it was barely touched.

When his house came into view, he breathed a sigh of utter contentment, his eyes darting all over it in admiration as they approached. He had been surprised when Annie had written to tell him that she had decided to move into the house. Surprised, but pleased.

She had been living there for over three months now. Had left Mackie's a month ago to devote herself to decorating. Was she happy? Her letters were different. Not so demonstrative. All about the house … he had been perplexed, but soon would be able to judge for himself whether or not Annie regretted buying the house. He hoped not. He could picture them growing old together happily in this house.

When he had paid the taxi driver and turned to enter the driveway, he was puzzled that Annie had not come out to meet him. Perhaps she was busy?

He walked along the side of the house and stopped in amazement when he saw the changes made in the back garden. Annie was there, awaiting his reaction.

'You've been a busy wee woman!' he exclaimed, as he walked along the lawn, admiring the shrubs that had been trimmed, the borders bright with flowers. Even the big tree had been pruned. 'It's lovely, Annie. Very nice.'

She, too, looked lovely … beautiful, even … standing there. The late September sun highlighted the chestnut hue of her thick hair, showed up the spattering of freckles that spanned the bridge of her small, straight nose, and turned her eyes to hazel. The short, yellow cotton dress she wore showed off her long slim legs and honey-coloured skin, and he found himself examining her intently. Gone was the cocky young teenager that he had married, and in her place was a beautiful, composed woman. All this hadn't happened overnight. How come he hadn't seen the changes taking place? His conscience would not let him escape from the truth. It wasn't because he was away so often. No, he had been too busy thinking of Rosaleen. Too preoccupied to see the beauty that his wife had become.

'You look lovely,' he told her sincerely, his eyes still on her face.

She had made no effort to greet him. No face proffered for his kiss.

'Thank you.' She smiled wryly, and flapping her hand at the garden, confessed, 'Not all my work. I had a handyman in, an afternoon each week. I thought we'd better not let it go another winter.'

As he approached her, she turned and led the way inside, saying over her shoulder, 'The kitchen's pretty much the same as it was ... just a lot cleaner.' She smiled at him, but he was aware that it didn't reach her eyes. 'Come see the sitting room.'

Slowly he followed her through the kitchen, along the hall, to pause on the threshold of the sitting room. As before she kept her distance from him, and awaited his praise.

And she deserved it; obviously long hours of work had been put into the room and the result was lovely. The high ceiling was snow white, as was the frieze, and the picture rail and deep skirting board and framework of the wide bay window a warm cream. The walls were papered with a flowered paper, a mixture of blues and greys, and a dark blue border, about three inches deep, ran along under the picture rail. At the window hung heavy damask curtains, a mixture of darker hues of blue and grey. All highlighting the beautiful colours in the slate mantelboard and contrasting with the pale grey of the marble hearth.

'I thought perhaps you would like to help choose the suite and carpet and a picture or two?' Her head tilted and her brows rose. 'Am I right?'

He nodded, and with a sweep of the arm embraced the room. 'All your own work?'

'Well, now. I have to confess that George helped me with the ceiling, but I did all the papering and painting,' she confessed proudly.

'It's lovely, Annie, you must have worked hard,' he praised her, but he was preoccupied. He was vaguely aware that something was wrong.

Any other time when he came home, if they had the house to themselves, they were straight up the stairs. Yet today, in this big empty house, she seemed to be avoiding him. Of course, she was anxious to show him the result of her labours. Still, she could just as easily have done so from the shelter of his arm. Not keep a wide berth between them.

'How's about showing me the bedroom, Annie,' he teased, and was surprised to note her dismay.

'Oh, I haven't decorated the bedroom yet!' she exclaimed, and he saw her squirm uneasily.

'I would still like to see it,' he insisted, and putting his arm around her waist, drew her out of the sitting room.

Annie allowed herself to be led up the stairs. His hand was gently moving along her ribcage, setting her aquiver, and when his other hand cupped her breast she thought she would faint with the longing and need that he was arousing in her. How could she let him? She should be ashamed of herself for wanting him so. After the way he had betrayed her. And with her sister. God, how it hurt, even after months of mulling it over.

Would she be able to pretend that she didn't know? She'd have to if she wanted to save her marriage, she would have to hold her tongue. Something that she was not noted for. Blabbermouth was her nickname, but once he knew he had a son ... oh, it didn't bear thinking about. She was the one who was barren. There was nothing wrong with him. And she had gone on and on at him, making him miserable and afraid.

As he slowly undressed her, Sean kept his eyes on her face. She flinched each time his fingers touched her bare skin, and he thought he detected tears on her long dark lashes. What on earth was wrong with her? He felt as if he was seducing her. He let his hands grow still, and she stood there unmoving, gazing down at them.

'Annie? What's wrong?'

Her head swung in a wide arc, causing the tears to slip over and slide silently down her cheeks.

'Annie ... look at me,' he commanded.

Slowly the dark, wet lashes rose and he gave a start of dismay. Never before in his life had he seen such despair. Did she hate living out here so much?

'Annie, is it because we bought the house?' he asked anxiously, his hands cupping her face, thumbs wiping away the tears. But as fast as he wiped them, more fell. 'Do you hate living out here so much?'

She gasped in alarm. 'No! Oh no ... I love this house. It's the loveliest house in the world.'

How would she have survived without this haven?

He was bewildered and showed it. 'Then why on earth are you so miserable?'

Pulling free, she wiped the tears from her cheeks with the back of her hands, and grimaced.

'I'm just tired. I couldn't sleep last night, and I've a headache.'

The music hall excuse. Would he believe her?

He did not. 'That's strange, coming from you.' He reached for her again, drawing her near, but not allowing their bodies to touch. 'But anyhow ... it's not your head I'm interested in.'

Putting his finger under her chin, he tilted her face up and gazed deep into her tear-filled eyes.

She was trembling, and aware that she wanted him, he asked gently, 'Do you really want me to stop? I will, if that's what you want.'

She shook her head, her eyes clinging to his, and for the time being the cause of her misery was forgotten as he clasped her to him, and they responded to the urgent need created by months apart.

Once their reunion was over, Annie was more at ease. She blossomed under his teasing as together, the next day, they stripped the paper from the walls in the bedroom.

However, Sean was aware that things were far from well, so he questioned her.

'Did anything happen while I was away?' he asked, watching her intently.

'No ... nothing important.'

Her eyes fell away from his. What a lie. Her world had fallen apart and the worry of what would happen when he saw Liam was with her night and day ... and she was telling him nothing important had happened.

It was obvious to him that she lied, but he let it pass; she was still in a tearful mood and he did not want to upset her.

'Have you made an appointment for me to see the doctor?'

'Yes … yes, I have. I have to go next Wednesday.'

'You have to go?' His voice was sharp.

Her lip trembled and her voice shook when she replied, 'Please, Sean, do it my way … please? You're a Catholic. You know masturbation is a sin. I want to go to a specialist who is a Catholic, and that's the way he works things.'

It was a source of wonder to him just how good-living Annie was. When he had first met her, her forwardness, her cocky sureness, had convinced him that she was easy. Not cheap, oh no, never cheap, but he had thought that she would be easily won over. He could not have been more wrong. Even with the engagement ring on her finger and war in the background, she had kept him at bay. Kisses and hugs, yes, she did not object to close embracing or long kissing, which were forbidden by the Church, but anything else … no way. He had to wait until they were married, and he had been surprised at how proud he had been of her for sticking to her principles. And now, she preferred to go through the hassle and embarrassment of being examined herself rather than let him go.

'All right, all right… don't be upset.' He pulled her into his arms, and lightly rubbed his nose against hers. 'We'll do it your way,' he consoled her, and was rewarded by a wobbly smile.

On Wednesday morning, he walked to the top of the Serpentine Road with her. She had refused point blank to let him accompany her to the hospital, and as he assisted her on to the tram, he said, 'I'll keep my fingers crossed.'

She smiled and nodded at him, feeling a traitor. She knew that there was nothing wrong with him and she was letting him worry needlessly, but what else could she do? She had no choice. At least once the results came through he would know that there was nothing wrong with his sperm count. If Rosaleen was telling the truth, it would be high. Very high.

Thoughts that were never far from her mind returned to haunt her as she waited to see the specialist. Would Sean see the resemblance Liam bore him? He was owed a lot of holidays now the war was over, and he would be home for four months this time.

He had seen Liam on his last leave, but the baby had just been a few weeks old and had slept the whole time. There was no chance that he would not see the child this time, even though they lived so far away. Already he was planning on having her family down to spend Christmas Day with them. How would she survive it? The worry of it was having an awful effect on her; she was a bundle of nerves. She could see herself ending up in Grahame's Home, unless she got control of her emotions.

When the result of the tests eventually arrived, Sean greeted them with a great sigh of relief.

'Phew!' He took her in his arms and held her eye gravely. 'Now, Annie, there's nothing wrong with either of us. So let's just take things a day at a time and see what happens. Eh, love? Remember what you said? If it's God's will, we'll have a family. If not ... well, we'll just have to live without them.'

And as she raised her face for his kiss, Annie was only too happy to agree with him.

Chapter 10

Pressing her forehead against the window, Rosaleen peered out into the gathering dusk to where, in the far distance, passengers were descending from the plane.

George watched her; he was worried about her. Since Annie's mad gallop down to live on the Serpentine Road, Rosaleen was a changed person. Withdrawn and touchy, she had even Thelma, usually unaware of undercurrents, muttering about her moods and easily aroused temper. On the journey down to Aldergrove Airport to meet her friends who were coming home from Canada to attend a funeral, he had tried to pump her. Tried to find out what had destroyed the close friendship shared by the two sisters, but she had evaded his leading questions, assuring him that nothing was wrong between Annie and herself. He was equally fond of both these girls who had welcomed him into their homes and hearts, and it dismayed him to sense the deep unhappiness within them. What on earth could have happened to cause such a rift?

Many times, he had gone over in his mind the week preceding the change in the girls but could think of nothing to account for their behaviour. He remembered that Annie had been distraught the night she had asked him to help her move things into her new home, but he had thought that whatever was wrong would soon blow over. But no … Annie had made it clear, at least to him, that she did not want Rosaleen visiting her. He had thought that when Rosaleen had gone down to Greencastle in spite of Annie's obvious rancour, all would be well, but alas, no. Rosaleen had obviously not been invited back, and Annie never came near her mother's, content to see her during working hours at Mackie's.

Suddenly Rosaleen turned to him, her face wreathed in smiles. He grinned happily back at her, glad to see the strain gone from her face. It was a long time since he had seen her smile spontaneously. Perhaps this friend they were meeting would take her out of herself; maybe even help to breach the great divide between Annie and her.

'I can see her! I'd know her from any distance!' Gripping his arm she pulled him close to the window. 'See the big tall guy, halfway up the steps? That's Billy! And there's May behind him … in the blue coat.'

They watched until all the passengers had disappeared into the tunnel leading to the Custom Offices, and then made their way down to the waiting room.

Her eyes fast on the door through which May would come, Rosaleen confided in him, 'You'll like her, so you will! Billy too.'

'I feel as if I already know her!' he exclaimed. 'I've heard so much about her. You two must have been very close.'

'We're like sisters.'

Pain shadowed her face at these words and he guessed that she was thinking of Annie, but it passed and then she was rushing across the room to embrace a small, obviously pregnant, young woman.

'May … ah, May! Here, let me look at you.'

Pushing May away from her, Rosaleen examined her critically. 'You look marvellous!'

And she did. Her hair was pale silvery blonde, obviously cared for by an expensive hairdresser, and even after the long journey, the bloom of pregnancy gave a glow to her skin. Lucky May! No morning sickness for her; she just sailed through her pregnancies.

'I wish I could say the same for you!' May eyed her in dismay.

'You must be about six stone. Does she not eat?' she demanded, turning to George.

'Not very much, from what I hear.'

'Oh, never mind about me, I'm all right. Billy ...' Rosaleen's voice trailed off in confusion when she realised that he had a companion with him.

'Rosaleen, this is my cousin Andrew. And ...?' He glanced in George's direction, his brow raised.

'Oh, excuse my manners.' Taking George by the arm, she pulled him forward. 'This is my brother, George,' she announced with a wide smile, and her pride in him was apparent to all.

'I feel as if I know you, George.' May gave him an impish grin. 'My ... everybody must have got an awful shock when you turned up!'

'MAY!' Billy gave her a reproving look, dismayed at her audacity.

George just laughed. He had just been warned that May didn't pull her punches. 'Likewise. I've just been saying to Rosaleen I feel as if I already know you.' And after shaking each hand in greeting, he grabbed one of the cases and led the way out to the car park.

As they crossed over to George's car, aware of the other man examining her, Rosaleen thrust out her hand towards him.

'I'm sorry ... I neglected to greet you. You must think me awful, but I wasn't expecting anyone else.'

'He made up his mind at the last minnit, Rosaleen.' May threw him an exasperated glance. 'I hadn't time to warn you.' But the smile she bestowed on him showed how fond of him she was.

Rosaleen felt suddenly shy as Andrew held her hand longer than was necessary, and when he leant towards her and said, 'I'm very glad, now, that I decided to come.' She felt the colour rush to her face and was glad that the artificial lighting would conceal it. Imagine behaving like a schoolgirl!

In the car, she suddenly remembered the reason for this visit home and turned in dismay to Billy.

'I'm sorry about your father. You must think me awful but I was so pleased to see you, I forgot the reason you were here.'

'Don't worry your head, Rosaleen. The state me da's heart was in, it came as no surprise. He's been on borrowed time for years. I'm just sorry he didn't last long enough to see Canada. He'd have loved it out there.'

On the journey home, each time Rosaleen turned to speak to May or Billy in the back of the car, she met Andrew's eyes, dark and intense, examining her face, smiling faintly at her discomfort.

When they arrived at Iris Drive, Rosaleen dished up the supper she had prepared beforehand and once it was consumed George suggested that the two men would be better getting a move on. He was driving them over to the Shankill Road to Billy's mother's and did not want to arrive in the early hours of the morning. Strange cars were suspect at all times on the Shankill Road, but in the early hours of the morning – well, then you were really taking a chance.

May was staying with Rosaleen, and as the men donned their coats and bade them goodnight, a grave-faced Andrew assured Rosaleen that he would be back to see her, bringing bright rosy colour once again to her cheeks.

Annoyed at herself, she just gave him a curt nod. Who did he think he was? And just why was she blushing?

He was not someone that she would normally have given a second glance! Just an inch or so taller than herself, he was ordinary … ugly, even. The nicest thing about him was his eyes, the colour of dark chocolate and warm as velvet.

When they were curled up in armchairs each side of the fireplace, a gin and tonic in their hands, prepared for a long natter, May winked across at Rosaleen.

'Andrew is smitten.'

'Huh! Don't be silly!'

'He is … he is! A blind man could see it.'

'He's quite old, so he is. Is he not married?'

'He hasn't had time to bother with women. Not that they don't chase him, mind. Believe you me, they do! He's quite a catch … has his own small publishing business. And he's not all that old … he's only forty. You could do worse, so you could.'

'May, you haven't changed a bit! You always thought you knew what was best for me.'

'Well, I was right about Joe, wasn't I?'

Her eyes leaving May's searching gaze, Rosaleen gave a brief nod before retorting: 'Well, I'm not interested in any men at the moment.'

And to change the subject, she asked, 'How's Ian?'

'Great. Andrew's sister has him. She has two of her own so he won't be lonely.' Her hand fell to her bulging stomach. 'I hope this is a girl. Billy would love a daughter.' She grinned across at May. 'I can't wait to see your wee son … and Laura. I bet she has grown inches. I've a wee present for her.'

'She has grown … and cheeky with it!' But Rosaleen smiled as she said the words; she was very proud of her daughter. 'I don't know what I'd do without Amy. She's always willing to look after the kids, even at a moment's notice.' Suddenly apprehensive, she wondered what May would think of Liam. Would she see the resemblance he bore Sean? She hadn't thought of that. Best to try and keep them apart, but it would not be easy.

Now she said, 'You'll have to wait until after the funeral. Do you still want me to accompany you tomorrow?'

'Please … I'm not looking forward to it. Billy's worried about his mam. Thinks she'll want him to stay in Belfast, although, thank God, she has agreed to move in with one of her sisters, 'cause there's no way he'd leave her on her own.'

'How would you feel about that … staying home?'

'To be truthful, I want to stay in Canada. It's a better way of life over there. You'd love Canada, so you would.'

'There's not much chance of me visiting you, now that Joe's gone and I've two kids to rear.'

'It was awful sad him dying so young. I wish I could have been with you.'

'It was terrible, but your letters were a comfort to me, and Bobby Mackay was a tower of strength. I honestly don't know what I'd have done without him.'

'You must have had an awful shock, Rosaleen, when you discovered you were pregnant after Joe's death … especially after such a long break.'

'That's life. I wanted a brother or sister for Laura, but not the way it happened.' Her lips twisted wryly as she repeated inwardly: NO! Definitely not the way it happened.

'What are you smiling about?'

'What?' Rosaleen blinked and came back to reality. She had been smiling at how amazed May would be if she knew the truth of Liam's birth. Now she blustered, 'I'm not smiling.'

'It looked very much like a smile to me. Did I say something funny?'

'No ... no. Tell me, what do you think of George?'

May gave her a reproving, 'You're not fooling me' look, but condescended to change the subject.

'Oh, he's lovely. You can see your da in him, all right. There's no mistaking that he's your da's son.'

Her eyes grew round with wonder. Imagine ... your da of all people! I nearly died when you wrote and told me. How on earth did he keep it a secret?'

'I don't know! I have often wondered that meself. In spite of visiting George every week, he managed to cover his tracks. Perhaps if George's mother had lived, he'd have been caught on.'

'He wouldn't have been able to keep it a secret in Spinner Street, I can tell you that. Old Ma Rafferty knows everybody's business.'

'There's one in every street, so there is. In Colinward Street it was Mrs Mullen, God rest her soul. But me da still managed to keep his secret.'

'All the same ... it must have been awful for your mam. I don't know what I'd do if Billy suddenly confessed that another woman was expecting his child.' May lapsed into silence for a few moments. 'I think I'd murder him,' she confessed. 'Yes, it must have been awful for your mam, living with the knowledge that your da had a son.'

'That's life. We all get our crosses to bear.'

'Oh, listen to you! Like you've had crosses to bear?' She grimaced in dismay. 'Sorry ... I know you were widowed young. But other than that, you were born lucky. And I'm sure Joe left you comfortable, eh?'

Rosaleen laughed outright. May didn't believe in beating about the bush.

'Yes, he left me comfortable,' she said, deliberately not telling May what she wanted to know. 'Now, how about you?'

'You'll never believe it... but Billy has consented to make an honest woman of me. Before this child is born,' she patted her bump, 'he's going to marry me in the Catholic Church.'

'Ah, May, I'm glad to hear that.'

'He's not turning, mind, but he has agreed the kids can be brought up Catholics. Ye see, it's different out there! Nobody cares what religion you are, so he doesn't have to worry about the effect it will have on his relatives, 'cause they'll be none the wiser. It's only here that Catholics and Protestants distrust each other, Rosaleen.'

Noticing the fatigue around May's eyes, the tired droop to her mouth, Rosaleen rose to her feet and relieved her of her empty glass. 'Do you want another one ... or do you want to go to bed?'

'I think I'll retire, Rosaleen. I can hardly keep my eyes open.'

'It's great to have you home, May. Two whole weeks! Think of the fun we'll have.' Her voice trailed off. 'You know what I mean,' she finished lamely, thinking of the funeral.

'I know what you mean. It's sad ... but once the funeral's over, we'll be free to enjoy ourselves. Seeing that Andrew enjoys himself will help Billy cope with his grief. He'll want Andrew to see all over the north. He was only seven when his parents emigrated. You'll not mind Andrew tagging along, sure you won't?'

'No ... just as long as you don't try any matchmaking. Promise?'

'I can promise that with a clear conscience,' May assured her. 'Andrew doesn't need any help.' She grinned impishly. 'In spite of his ugly mug, he's a charmer. So, you have been warned. Come on. Let's go to bed, or I'll never make it to the funeral tomorrow.'

Once the funeral was over, Billy, with Andrew in tow, spent another two days attending to his mother's insurance policies and settling all accounts attached to the funeral. Then his mother went to stay with her sister, shooing Billy off to show Andrew around Northern Ireland.

Meanwhile May and Rosaleen shopped in town, May, having obtained some precious coupons from Billy's relatives, determined to buy some Irish linen gifts to bring back to Canada.

Then Billy, burying his pain deep within, determined that

Andrew would enjoy the first break he'd had in years, and set about arranging a good time for him.

Although he and Rosaleen were thrown together a lot, Andrew never again expressed any romantic interest in her. In spite of all May's warnings, he never put a foot wrong; never said a word out of place. This pleased Rosaleen; it meant that she was able to relax and enjoy herself, and they became friends.

Billy hired a car and the four of them toured all over the north, showing Andrew around the Glens of Antrim, the stark splendour of the Giant's Causeway, the beauty of Cushendun and Cushendal, and wonderful Ballycastle where the Auld Lammas Fair was in progress.

Then, in Belfast itself, they took the tram out to the Zoo at Bellevue and then climbed the Cave Hill and stood on Napoleon's Nose, admiring the scenery for miles around, Rosaleen pointing out a winding road far to the left and explaining that it was the Serpentine Road and that Annie now lived there. The Botanic Gardens and Ulster Museum also received a visit, and the pride of Belfast, the Castle itself, was toured and exclaimed over by an admiring Andrew.

Then in the evenings they visited the Opera House and St Mary's Hall, and the Empire Theatre, where Andrew was delighted at the variety concerts. The two weeks went past in a flash and to Rosaleen's amusement, on the night before they were about to fly back to Canada, May and Billy had some very important business to attend to, leaving Andrew and she alone. Rosaleen realised that Billy would want to spend the day with his mother, but not his last night in Belfast. And May had apparently decided to spend the night with Billy at her mother-in-law's house. Rosaleen could see that she and Andrew were being set up.

She was a bit embarrassed, it was so blatant! Surely May could see that she and Andrew were not attracted to each other? At least not in that way. She found him a wonderful companion, felt contented in his company, but there was no physical attraction. During the past fortnight he had been kind and courteous, treating her like a lady, and it was true she would miss him. Life would be dull when he returned to Canada.

After first checking with her that it would be all right, he booked a table for a meal in one of the posh hotels in town and arranged to pick her up at seven o'clock.

She spent the afternoon preparing for their date, grateful to Amy for looking after the kids yet again; she'd had them so often since May's arrival, leaving Rosaleen free to enjoy herself. First a long, leisurely bath, perfumed with bath oils brought over by May. Then she shampooed her hair and rolled it in curlers. While it was drying, she manicured her nails and varnished them her favourite pale pink.

As she stood in front of the mirror smoothing her best petticoat down over her slim hips, she had to admit that May was right – she was too thin, except for her bust which was firm and full and swelled seductively over the lace at the top of the petticoat. She could do with some new underwear! But now that she could afford the best, there was not enough clothing coupons to buy them. Although the war was over, its effects were still being felt, and she had used all her coupons on a new coat for herself and clothes for the children.

Not that it would make any difference. Andrew had no chance of seeing her underwear … no chance at all!

She wore the suit and blouse that she had worn for her first date with Sean. Pre-war but that didn't matter. Everybody was wearing dated clothes, and this was the first time she had worn the suit since that evening and she knew it became her.

Once ready, she viewed herself from all angles, pleased that her hair just failed to meet her shoulders and swung like a bell around her face, casting shadows on her cheeks and making her eyes dark and mysterious-looking. The jacket of the suit, being boxed, was all right but the skirt didn't hug her hips as snugly as before; nevertheless, it swung seductively around her calves and called attention to her slim ankles, so what more could she ask for?

Satisfied at what she saw, she gave a wry smile. Anyone would think that she was going out with a lover. But still … she wanted to do Andrew proud, wanted him to remember her looking her best.

When he arrived, he stood inside the doorway and his glance slowly swept over her from head to toe, full of delighted admiration.

She lapped it all up; it was a long time since she had seen such admiration in a man's eyes.

'You look beautiful,' he said sincerely, and she nodded in acknowledgement of the compliment. Lifting up her handbag, an exact match for her smart court shoes, she indicated that she was ready to go, aware that he had kept the taxi waiting to take them to town.

Once at the hotel, Andrew came into his own. Not used to dining in such opulence, Rosaleen asked him to choose for her, and this he did competently, conferring with her to be sure that she liked what he chose. In fact, Rosaleen noticed a touch of arrogance in his manner and guessed that he was used to being in charge, and often dined out. It was with surprise that she found herself wondering if he had a special woman friend. May was right; he was charming, and any woman would be proud to be seen with him.

When they were settled, waiting for the prawn cocktails he had ordered for starters, the wine waiter having poured the wine of Andrew's choice, he leant towards her.

'You know, I'm going to miss you,' he said softly.

'I'll miss you too,' she whispered back.

At this admission, he smiled and his hand reached across the table towards hers. His eyes were warm and caring and reminded her of her father's.

Without thought she said, 'You remind me of my da.'

It had been meant as a compliment but the minute the words left her lips she regretted them. She could see that he was hurt and offended. The smile slid from his face and his hand was slowly withdrawn.

However, he quickly recovered his composure and her muttered 'I'm sorry,' was waved aside as he raised his glass to toast her.

'I wish you all the best in the future, Rosaleen. May you meet somone you can be happy with.'

'Andrew ... I'm really sorry.'

'Don't be! We can't help how we feel. Look, let's just enjoy ourselves. I'll probably never see you again after tomorrow and I want to remember you smiling and happy.'

But her words had put a damper on their spirits and the delicious meal was eaten in comparative silence.

Andrew had arranged for the taxi to return for them at half-past nine and as they awaited its arrival, they sat in the foyer and sipped brandy. Once more Rosaleen tried to breach the gap that was yawning wider between them with every minute that passed.

He was sitting, head bowed, swirling the brandy round and round in the glass. Impulsively, she reached across and touched his knee.

At once he was full of apologies. 'I'm sorry. How ignorant of me.'

'Andrew,' she interrupted him. 'Please let me explain ... please!'

His hand covered and squeezed hers. 'There's no need. I was foolish to think you liked me.'

'I do! I do!'

'As a father figure?' He smiled slightly. 'That's not quite what I had in mind.'

'I was paying you a compliment. My father was a wonderful man ... just like you. Kind and understanding ... comfortable to be with.'

His grip on her hand tightened and he leant towards her. 'Rosaleen, are you telling me that you care for me?'

This brought her up short. She liked him, but obviously he wanted more. Just how did she feel towards him? She hadn't really given it any thought; had just enjoyed his company. Not wanting to lie, she groped about in her mind for words that would not give offence.

As the silence lengthened he relaxed his hold on her hand and with a sigh, drew back. Unable to think of anything to say, she was glad when he nodded towards a man hovering in the doorway.

'I think our taxi has arrived. I'll just check that it's ours.'

As she waited for him to return, she berated herself. She could have assured him that she was fond of him! What difference would it have made? Tomorrow he would be gone. She could have put on an act. But would it have been an act? She was all mixed up, hadn't thought of him in that way. Hadn't expected him to become serious.

The journey home was strained and when they arrived at Iris Drive, she turned to him.

'Don't send the taxi away. You must have packing and things to see to. Thank you for a lovely meal. I'll see you tomorrow.'

He threw her an angry glance and followed her from the cab. When he had paid the driver his fare, he faced Rosaleen. 'I think the least you can do is offer me a cup of coffee or a drink.'

At his tone of voice, her head reared in the air.

'Of course!'

Inside the house, she headed for the kitchen, leaving him to hang up his own coat, should he care to remove it. She was angry, very angry.

So she had compared him to her father! So he had taken offence! Well, she had done all the placating she intended to do. The sooner he drank his coffee and left, the better she would like it. On second thoughts ... it would be easier to pour him a drink. What had she to offer him? There was some Old Bush, left since God knows when. Would it be all right? Yes, of course! Whiskey matured with age, didn't it? But did it keep once the bottle was opened? She had no idea. Ah, t'hell! she'd risk it. It was all she had ... besides a little gin for herself.

He had removed his coat and loosened his tie and was sitting sprawled out on one of the armchairs, making the chair appear too small for his bulk. Avoiding his eyes, she handed him the glass of whiskey and then sat down on the settee.

'Rosaleen, we got off on the wrong foot tonight. Will you accept my apology? I was childish to take offence.'

For the first time since they had entered the house, she looked him in the eye. They were full of pleading and her anger, already on the wane, disappeared altogether.

'We were both at fault, but I was honestly paying you a compliment.'

'I realise that now ... and thank you. I didn't mean to throw it back in your face.'

'It's all right.'

Now that she was relaxed and the warmth of the fire warmed her limbs, the gin, following so swiftly on top of the wine and brandy and more than she usually consumed, took hold of her, sending her floating on a happy cloud. The room was slowly revolving around her and she closed her eyes to stop it, but that only made it go faster. She stared hard at the fire which helped.

In her dreamlike state, it came as a surprise to her when, prising the glass from her reluctant fingers and placing it to one side, he said, 'Come on ... it's bed for you.'

Gripping her hands, he pulled her to her feet. 'Come lock the door after me. I'll see you tomorrow.'

He reached for his coat, but without his support she swayed and he drew her gently into his arms to steady her. Her eyes, almost on a level with his, were inviting and her lips swayed tantalizingly near.

Aware that she was not in command of her actions, he started to put her from him, but then she licked her lips as if anticipating his touch and he was lost.

For the second time in her life Rosaleen found herself on the rug in front of the fire, naked in a man's arms. His kisses were long and soul searching, his touch thrilling. She wanted him. How she wanted him! But even through the blur of pleasure that was lifting her towards fulfilment, warning bells rang. Was she prepared to carry another child? No! Oh, no! She couldn't take the risk.

Feverishly, she pushed at his chest; he drew back and looked deep into her eyes. 'What's wrong? Do you ...?'

'I don't want another baby ... I can't have another child. You see, Joe isn't here to blame it on. Everybody will know I'm a whore.'

He gave her a slight shake. 'Rosaleen, listen to me ... I promise you that there'll be no baby. Do you hear me? There'll be no baby.'

Her eyes sought and found reassurance in his and she nodded, and as his mouth lowered once more towards hers, her arms closed around his waist and gripped him tight.

Sounds downstairs awoke Rosaleen the next morning and she opened her eyes fearfully. Was it a prowler? Or Amy? Her eyes sought the bedside clock. Six! Too early for Amy ... it must be a prowler.

Then, when she heard him mount the stairs, whistling happily, memory came rushing back.

Had he stayed the night? Had she really made love with him? It wasn't a dream then?

When he entered the room she was sitting up in bed, the bedclothes pulled up under her armpits, her eyes wide and wary.

'Good morning. I've brought you some tea and toast.'

He settled the tray across her legs and stood looking down at her, a wide grin on his face.

'My, but you'd be a sight to awaken beside every morning.' His grin became rueful. 'Pity I can't say the same about myself.'

Still she didn't speak. She wished she could remember all that had happened the night before; she couldn't even remember coming to bed.

'Eat your breakfast and then we'll talk.'

Obediently she lifted the cup of tea, but waved towards the tray to indicate that she did not want the toast.

He lifted it. 'Would you mind if I smoked? I don't usually smoke in the bedroom but I want to talk to you and at the moment I need a cigarette.'

She nodded her consent and he left the room.

When he returned he sat on the edge of the bed, drawing smoke into his lungs, deep in thought.

He was naked to the waist and as she sipped her tea she examined him covertly. Thick black hair covered his arms and chest. At last he lifted his eyes and met hers.

'How much do you remember about last night?'

'Not much,' she admitted, her eyes fearful.

'Rosaleen … I want you to believe something. I didn't take advantage of you. You were all for it.'

She gulped in her throat. So they had made love. Had she conceived?

As if reading her mind, he continued, 'But I can assure you, there will be no baby.'

The relief that flooded through her sent all the tension from her body and she relaxed, slumping back on the pillows with a sigh.

He was in a dilemma. She had made some statements the night before that he would like enlightenment on but obviously she had forgotten them. Should he pursue the matter or let it go?

A whore! She had called herself a whore. Well, he had met many whores, and having spent the last two weeks constantly in her company, knew she was not one of them. But there was something bothering her ... he decided to try and find out what it was.

'Rosaleen, you said some things last night that puzzled me.'

The fear was back in her eyes. What had she said? She shouldn't have drunk so much.

'What did I say?'

'You called yourself a whore.'

Her face blanched and at the stricken look in her eyes, he reached for her. She pushed him roughly away and turned her head from him.

'If you must know ... I spoke the truth.'

Cigarette crushed out, he sank to his knees beside the bed, and endeavoured to pull her round to face him.

'You did not! You're not even promiscuous!'

Slowly, she turned her head towards him. 'How would you know? Eh? We've just met.'

'I know women and you are no whore. You said Joe wasn't here to take the blame ... am I to assume one of your children wasn't fathered by him?'

'Neither of them are Joe's.'

She laughed bitterly at the stunned look in his eyes.

'Now do you believe me?'

Speechless, he gaped at her, his mind in a whirl.

Tears were swelling in her chest, and determined not to let him see her weep, she once more pushed at him.

'Would you mind leaving me now, please? I want to get dressed.'

Bewildered, he rose to his feet, trying to sort out his jumbled thoughts. Then he saw the tears spill over and slide silently down her cheeks and he sat down on the bed again. Ignoring her efforts to evade him, he gently gathered her into his arms, cradling her head against his chest.

'Cry it all up ... get it out of your system and then tell me about it. Because no matter what you are. I've fallen in love with you.'

The shock of these words stopped the tears falling and in the comfort and warmth of his arms, with the kindness in his voice soothing her, she found herself telling him things she had told no one but the priest in the confessional.

Everything came tumbling from her lips: her night with Sean; Joe's impotence; her relief when he accepted Laura as his own. Her anguish when Sean married Annie. How, after Joe's funeral, she had again conceived Sean's child.

He interrupted her one time only.

'Is this Sean fellow stupid? Did he not guess?'

'Annie had him convinced that he was sterile, it was easy deceiving him.' She wiped her eyes dry on the corner of the sheet and grimaced at him. 'Now you can see how evil I am.'

'No ... no.' Tenderly, he pushed the damp hair back from her brow. 'Ah, Rosaleen, no ... you are a victim of circumstance. What about other men? Is there anyone you see?'

'Just Pat McDade.'

'Who is he?'

'He lives around the corner in Oakman Street. It's not serious ... well, not on my part. He wants to marry me.'

'But you don't want to marry him?'

She shook her head. Handsome though Pat was, he had never inspired any deep emotion in her; they were just friends.

'Is it a relationship?'

Uncomprehending, she looked blankly at him, then the penny dropped.

'Oh, no ... no. I told you it wasn't serious!'

His look was full of sadness. So much of her life had been wasted. She was so sensual, so passionate. And she called herself a sinner!

He glanced at his watch. 'I'll have to be going soon. Look, Rosaleen ... will you write to me?'

'Of course! If you really want me to.'

'I really want you to. And ... I know that Sean is the great love of your life. I don't begrudge you that. But it's over! You must look to the future. I'll take anything you offer ... it's up to me to teach you to love me, because you obviously need someone to take care of you.'

Wide-eyed, she stared at him and then her jaw slowly dropped when he rose and started to remove his trousers.

'Move over … If you don't remember last night, then I'll have to refresh your memory. I want to be sure you think of me often.'

Smiling at the eager way she made room for him, he slid into bed beside her. And proceeded to love her, teaching her as he went along, opening new avenues of pleasure for her. Stopping only when she was completely sated.

'I wish you had a shower, Rosaleen. That bath is going to be a tight squeeze for us.'

'You mean … us … us … bathe together?' she squeaked.

His great throaty laugh filled the room. 'Yes … us … together!'

Then he gathered her up in his arms and descended the stairs, satisfied that he was leaving her plenty to remember him by. He was only glad that he had been in time to catch her. She was ripe for the picking and if that fool McDade hadn't been so slow, she would have been lost to Andrew forever.

The following weeks were lonely for Rosaleen, but with each letter she received from Andrew a warm glow enveloped her and she walked around in a contented haze. Memories of him were constantly with her. Often she recalled the day she and George had driven them to the airport. When all their goodbyes had apparently been said, Andrew led her away from the rest and kissed her long and ardently.

Then he had whispered, 'Remember you're mine and I'll be sending for you.'

And hugging these words close to her heart, she had returned to the company, rosy with happiness; to delighted grins from May and Billy and a pleased smile from George.

There was only one cloud on the horizon now. Annie! The awful sin she had committed against her sister festered like an open wound.

If only Annie had not guessed the truth, they could still be friends and Rosaleen would be able to discuss with her the great change Andrew had made in her life. And now Sean was home, would they come visiting? Would he see the resemblance?

May had! It had been with apprehension that she had watched her friend's first encounter with Liam. Stunned incredulity had showed on her face, but Rosaleen had been ready for her.

Smiling and at ease she had said, 'Isn't he lovely? I think he's like me da, but Amy say's he's the picture of Joe's father,' she lied, and must have sounded convincing because May relaxed, and if she doubted Rosaleen, managed to hold her tongue. But what about Sean? What would happen if he guessed the truth?

To think that a few short months ago she had been hoping that he would recognise his son and persuade her to run off with him to live in sin. Imagine her contemplating living in sin! As if that was the answer to anything. In time, the shame would have tarnished their great love for each other and they would have been unhappy cut off from family and Church.

Soon it would be Christmas. The family always gathered together then. What would Annie do?

For the first time in her life Rosaleen dreaded the festive season, and her gratitude to Andrew increased. His letters kept her from despairing. Though he never mentioned marriage. But then, he was up to his eyes in work. He wrote about his business ... about launching books ... but she didn't understand. It only made her aware that he had a hectic social life, and she felt jealous. It was obvious that he was a passionate man. Was he sharing his bed with someone? Oh, she hoped not! What if, in his case, it was out of sight out of mind? He had certainly made sure that she remembered him.

At night she hugged herself as she relived the feel of his arms around her, the rapture of his touch, and prayed that he would send for her. It would solve all her problems. Meanwhile, there was Christmas to get over, but that was out of her hands. It all depended on what Annie decided to do. She could only hope and pray everything worked out all right. Her sights were set on Canada; it was her only hope of a happy, fulfilling life. Please God, don't let anything spoil my chances, she prayed.

Chapter 11

For Sean, the following weeks flew past as, weather permitting, he toiled in the front garden each day building a rockery. He would disappear for a time and then arrive back, weighed down by a huge boulder; laughing at Annie when she chastised him, afraid of him wrecking his back. They were lucky to have Minnie living next door. She had connections, and even though wallpaper was like gold dust, managed to obtain some for them. None of the current paint and stippling for their rooms, and as Sean papered walls and painted woodwork he was contented and happy. He even built shelves in the alcove beside the hearth in the living room, displaying a talent for decorating to equal Annie's own. She assisted him in every way she could and each evening as they relaxed for an hour or two in the living room, before retiring for the night, there was a closeness and harmony between them such as they had never experienced before. Nevertheless, Sean was aware that Annie was not completely at one with him. There was a shadow in her eyes that all his teasing could not banish, and behind which he was not allowed to see.

He watched her sitting across the hearth from him, the light from the table lamp turning her hair to burnished copper, her face pale in its shadow; knitting needles clicking away as she knitted a pullover for him. The wool had been salvaged from a pullover of Tommy Magee's. She had ripped it out and wound it into hanks. These had been washed and dried and then rolled into balls, and now a new pullover was appearing on the needles. Annie was a wonderful homemaker; thrifty and wise, she flourished where others would have foundered, and most pleasing of all ... the house was coming alive under her influence. What pleased him most was the fact that she really must love the house, because not once had she suggested that they go out visiting, seeming content to remain at home with him. Knowing how close she was to her mother and Rosaleen, this surprised him. Different from him; a flying visit to his parents was sufficient for him, but then, daughters were closer to their parents than sons. However, was he not being selfish, shouldn't he offer to go visiting? Didn't she need to see her family? While he was feeling generous and willing to waste some of his precious leave visiting, he suggested: 'How's about you and me going out tomorrow night, Annie?'

Her head jerked up and she queried, 'Out? Out where? Where would we go?'

For a moment, the guard in her eyes slipped and he thought he saw fear there. But what would she be afraid of?

'Well, I thought perhaps we could go up and visit your mother and Rosaleen. Take them out for a quiet drink.'

Her gaze swerved away from his and he saw her knuckles grow white as her hands tightened on the knitting needles.

'Do you particularly want to go out?' she asked, the shadow back in her eyes as they gazed at him.

Bewildered at her attitude, he replied, 'Well, yes ... why not? You know what they say ... all work and no play makes ... even someone as fascinating as me a dull boy.' He grinned as he teased her, but her figure remained tense, her face serious. He continued, 'While we're up there, we can invite them down for Christmas Day. Let's invite George as well, shall we? And perhaps he has a girlfriend he could bring. The more the merrier.'

Fear was welling up inside her. Before it could swamp her and he became aware of it, she agreed with him.

'All right … let's go visiting,' she said resignedly, and to turn the knife in the aching wound that was her heart, added, 'Young Liam will be quite a big boy now, almost ten months. He's a lovely child.' Her voice trailed off as she gazed into his eyes and remembered that Liam's were identical. She bit on her lip before finishing: 'He's beautiful, so he is.' After all, Sean had to see the baby sometime or other and better tomorrow than to have an almighty row when they came on Christmas Day.

Hearing the misery in her voice, Sean regretted his impulsive suggestion. Obviously, that was why Annie was staying away from the Springfield Road – she could not bear to see Rosaleen's children. He wished that he had not opened his big mouth, but he had committed himself now. Should he back down? No … she should not retreat from reality! It wasn't right that she should avoid children.

It was brought home to him just how wrong he had been to suggest visiting the Springfield Road when, that night, for the first time since he had arrived home, Annie stayed rigidly on her own side of the bed. He had been stupid to think that she was happy here. She was still fretting for a child, and it looked like they were doomed to be childless. What was to become of her? She could not avoid children for the rest of her life. Perhaps he should broach the idea of adoption?

He had been thinking about adoption for some time now, but was reluctant to take the final step; to admit to himself that they were apparently doomed to be childless. Now he dithered. Not yet… not just yet… he would wait another while.

There was a sharp frost the next day and this increased as it wore on. The thought of the steep climb up on to the Antrim Road and then the hanging about in the cold waiting for a tram or trolleybus, followed by another wait in town for a tram up the Grosvenor Road to the Springfield Road, sent Sean out to the nearest phone box to order a taxi to take them to Colinward Street.

Sitting hunched up in a corner of the car, Annie felt physically sick as it drew up to her mother's front door. Would Rosaleen be there? Would she have Liam with her? To her relief, she was reprieved. Her mother and George were alone in the kitchen.

'Why … come on in, come on. It's nice to see ye, Sean. I was beginnin' t'think that I'd done something to annoy you.'

Sean answered her mother's greeting by lifting her up in his arms and giving her a bear's hug.

'We've just been awfully busy,' he informed her. 'We're getting the house ready, so that you can come down and spend Christmas Day with us.'

'Oh, but we're goin' down to Rosaleen's house for our Christmas dinner, so we are. Ye know how it is, Sean, we want to see the kids' faces when they see what Santa Claus has left them.'

'Oh, don't you worry about that. We're inviting Rosaleen down too. You can see the kids open their presents at home and then come to us. Santa will have visited our house with toys as well. We want to see the kids' faces and all.'

A sudden thought made his eyes seek Annie's face as he spoke. Had he done the wrong thing again? Did she want the kids down at Christmas? Not once had he asked her opinion. He had just assumed that she would love having them all down, had thought that he was pleasing her. However, Annie had her back towards him, she was busy hanging their coats at the foot of the stairs, and he did not know how she was reacting to his suggestions. He was stupid; he should have talked this over with her, not just rushed in where angels feared to tread. But the damage was done, his invitation received with a smiling nod.

The moment passed as George welcomed him and soon they were settled close to the fire and were brought up to date on all the news.

When Thelma rose to make a cup of tea, Sean stopped her.

'How's about something stronger? Do you fancy going down to the Clock Bar for a drink?' he asked. 'I thought we could call into Rosaleen's on our way down, and if Amy will babysit she can join us.'

George was on his feet instantly. 'That's a smashing idea, Sean. Let's not waste any more time. Come on, Thelma.' He lifted her coat, and before she had time to demur, assisted her into it.

'He looks after me well, so he does.' Thelma smiled fondly at George before adding, 'Did ye know that George lives here now?

He's being instructed in the faith, so he is.' At Annie's start of surprise, she grunted, 'Huh! Of course ye don't know! You haven't been here since ye left Mackie's. Did we do something to offend you?'

'No, Mam. I've just been very busy, so I have.'

Although she was happy for George, this news dismayed Annie. At the back of her mind was the idea that if Sean recognised young Liam as his son and wanted to leave her, she could return to her mother's home until such time as she made other arrangements. Now where would she go? There were only two bedrooms in her mother's house.

Seeing Annie's dismay, Sean covered up for her, although he could not fathom why she should be unhappy at the idea. Wasn't she very fond of George? Glad that he had come into their lives?

'That's the best news I've heard in a long time,' he said. 'Tommy will be pleased.'

At once Thelma's eyes swung to meet his. Was he jesting? 'You think he'll know?'

And when Sean nodded his head vigorously and said, 'I think he'll know', she sighed contentedly and her smile stretched from ear to ear.

The two men walked ahead as they made their way down the Springfield Road. Annie was left to walk with her mother.

'Our Rosaleen's not a bit well lately, so she's not,' Thelma confided in her. 'She's lost an awful lot of weight. Wait 'til ye see her. Her clothes are hangin' on her. I think she works far too hard at that wee business. It's not worth it! I keep tellin' her money's not everything, but she doesn't listen to me. Will you have a word with her, Annie? She'll listen to you, so she will.'

'I don't think she'll listen to me, Mam. I'm the stupid one of the family, remember.' And inwardly she added, Stupid and blind!

At this Thelma drew back and looked at Annie in surprise. 'Stupid, my foot … you were the brainier of the two of ye. You took after your da.' A deep sigh left her lips. 'Your da was wasted, ye know. With a bit of education, he could have gone places, made something of hisself. It broke his heart that we couldn't afford to keep you on at school. You were so bright.'

'I didn't even know I was good enough,' Annie said, her voice full of disbelief. Had they really thought that much of her? Well then … why hadn't they told her? Made her feel as beloved as Rosaleen!

'Oh, did ye not?' When Annie shook her head, Thelma continued, 'I thought ye knew … we probably made light of it because we couldn't afford to let you go to St Dominic's. How your da regretted that he hadn't a better job! But even with my wee cleanin'job, we just couldn't manage it.'

This was all news to Annie, but it was too late for regrets. However, her mother sounded so sorrowful, she hastened to reassure her.

'Well, I didn't do too badly, did I?'

These words made Thelma laugh. 'No, ye did not. You'd go far to get better than Sean, so ye would. And now ye have that posh house.'

They had arrived in Iris Drive, and to Annie's relief she was reprieved again: Rosaleen was not at home. It was Amy who answered their knock on the door and informed them that Rosaleen had gone out for a few hours. Where she did not know.

After an exchange of greetings and a bit of a chat, they bid Amy farewell and continued on down the Springfield Road and along the Falls Road to the Clock Bar. Situated at the corner of Lower Clonard Street, this was one of the popular pubs and the lounge was crowded. And who should be sitting in one of the corners but Rosaleen.

Both Annie and her mother gaped when they saw who Rosaleen was with – tall, handsome Pat McDade, well known for his womanising and gambling. What on earth was she doing with him?

Rosaleen did not see them, and glad that the lounge was packed Annie made her way to the only empty table, in the opposite corner from Rosaleen and her companion, glad that they did not have to sit beside them.

Once the women were seated, Sean and George went to the bar for drinks and Annie watched Rosaleen, her eyes taking in the new coat that she wore. It had obviously cost a bob or two, not to mention clothing coupons, but then, Rosaleen's business was doing well.

Annie sighed. She had felt quite attractive in her dark brown two-piece wool suit, even though it was pre-war. Now she felt dated, mousy. It was all right for Rosaleen, her house had been furnished before all the rationing started; she didn't have to use her coupon allowance for curtain material and soft furnishings.

She found herself envying Rosaleen her new coat. Emerald green in colour, it highlighted her fairness, darkened the green of her eyes. Completely unaware of them, she was deep in conversation with Pat, laughing into his eyes, obviously teasing him. She looked beautiful, her hair a soft, shining, silvery cloud, her eyes glinting like emeralds. Annie agreed with her mother, Rosaleen had lost a lot of weight, but this just emphasised the high cheek bones, the small pointed chin, and when she threw back her head in laughter, her teeth gleamed, even and white. Even as Annie watched, she saw her glance at the bar, and the amazement and joy with which she met Sean's eyes brought fear rushing to Annie's heart. Sean was gaping back at her in surprise and a lump gathered in Annie's throat, threatening to choke her.

Rising abruptly to her feet, she made her way to the Ladies' room and was relieved to find it empty.

In front of the wash-hand basin she gazed mournfully at her reflection. Her eyes, dark and haunted, stared sorrowfully back at her. How was she going to get through the evening? Before she had time to regain control of her emotions, Rosaleen arrived on her heels and their eyes, green on green, met in the mirror.

'This is a surprise,' Rosaleen greeted her, and Annie's throat was so tight with unshed tears, she found that she could only nod in reply.

It was obvious to her that her sister was very much in love with Sean, but how did he feel?

'Were you up at my house?' Rosaleen asked, and when Annie once again nodded, she sighed. 'I wish I'd known that you were coming ... I'd have stayed at home.'

Then she would not have been taken unawares and gaped at Sean like that. He would always have the power to lift her on high, but she knew that she would be better off with Andrew. He knew all her secrets and she would not have to watch her words or actions with him. Now she was worried that Annie had seen her greet Sean.

At last Annie found her voice and her look held disbelief. 'And missed your date with Pat McDade? Eh? What on earth are you doing with him?' she asked, and was glad to find that her voice sounded composed.

'What's wrong with Pat?' At Annie's incredulous look, Rosaleen added, 'He's good company, so he is, and I'm lonely. What with you sulking down in Greencastle and May in Canada ...'

'Sulking?' Annie interrupted her angrily. 'Sulking?'

'Well ... aren't you? Why can't you just let bygones be bygones?'

Annie was saved from answering her by the door opening to admit their mother. She had to make do with a withering look. Bygones, indeed! And Sean the father of her child?

'Are you all right, Annie?'

'Of course I'm all right, Mam. Why shouldn't I be?'

'Well, ye rushed away from the table so suddenly, without so much as an "Excuse me", that I thought ye must feel unwell.'

Aware that both women were eyeing her, Annie retorted, 'Sorry ... but nature called. It's this cold weather, I'm always running, so I am.'

And although Thelma examined her face intently and noted how pale she was, she accepted the excuse, and they all returned to the lounge together; a worried Rosaleen well aware that Annie had not visited the loo.

Had Annie seen her greet Sean? That was the second time she had been taken unawares. She would have to find some way to warn him. Obviously Annie had not confronted him, but after the way she had gaped at him ... who knew what Annie might do! If only Andrew would send for her, before all her guilty secrets were unmasked. That was if he intended to send for her. It was three weeks since he had written, and when questioned, May was noncommittal about him in her letters. She just dismissed him airily, writing that he was very busy and they saw little of him. She was urging Rosaleen to sell up and join her and Billy, and Rosaleen was sorely tempted. What did it matter if Andrew thought that she was chasing him? Even if he had changed his mind about her ... well, she needed to get away from Belfast. In Canada she could start afresh. Until then, she would have to be more careful when she met Sean, and to keep her attention away from him, she turned all her charm on Pat.

The next two hours were the most miserable Annie had ever spent. She tried not to watch Sean, tried to keep her attention general, but it's hard to smile and chat when your heart is aching, and her nerves were stretched to breaking point, as the time crawled by.

After her first greeting, Rosaleen ignored them, giving all her attention to Pat. He was obviously lapping it all up, although a trifle perplexed looking.

Annie was aware that Sean covertly watched Rosaleen, a frown puckering his brow now and again, and when he went over to buy her and her companion a drink, Annie found that she could not bear it and escaped once again to the toilets, unable to watch them together. She returned to the lounge to find that it was her turn to be covertly examined by Sean, and this worried her. Was he comparing her with Rosaleen? Dismay filled her heart. How could she do other than come out second best?

Relief flooded through her when, near closing time, Sean refused an offer to return to her mother's house for a bite of supper, saying it was too late and that they would get a taxi straight home from the pub. She had been dreading returning to her mother's or Rosaleen's, couldn't bear to prolong the agony, and for the first time in hours relaxed, glad that her ordeal would soon be over.

When she saw them preparing to leave, Rosaleen came over to say goodnight, kissing Annie on the cheek, shaking Sean's hand and accepting his invitation to spend Christmas Day with them.

The journey home was conducted in silence. Sean reached for Annie's hand and held it between his own, but it was obvious to her that his thoughts were miles away. Was he thinking of Rosaleen? Wishing that it was she who was returning home with him?

Sean was indeed thinking of Rosaleen. The small piece of paper that she had pressed into the palm of his hand when saying goodnight was now burning a hole in his pocket. What was Rosaleen writing to him about? Why all the mystery?

When they arrived at the house, while Sean paid the taxi driver, Annie used her own key and entered the sanctuary of her home.

Immediately, she felt calmer and with swift steps hastened to the kitchen and busied herself preparing a pot of tea. Sean always had a cup of tea before retiring, and while he drank it, she would plead a headache and escape to bed.

From the doorway of the kitchen, Sean watched her. He noticed the sad droop to her wide, sensuous mouth, the shadows under her eyes, and unable to bear it, he turned abruptly away. If only he could make her happy. But how could you please someone who kept a barrier between you?

'I'll be down in a minute ...just going to the loo.'

Once in the bathroom he bolted the door and sitting on the edge of the bath, took Rosaleen's note from his pocket and opened it out. There was no greeting, just four lines squeezed on to a small scrap of paper.

'Sean, Annie knows about us. She guessed ... I told her it was just the one time, after Joe died. She must never know that we were friends before you met her. Never!'

Stunned, Sean read and re-read the small scrap of paper. How, after all this time, had Annie guessed? He sat for some time trying to figure out how she could have learnt about him and Rosaleen. It was Annie's voice, hailing him from the hall, that brought him back to reality.

'Sean, your tea'll be cold! Come on down.'

'I'm coming now.'

He tore the paper into small strips and putting it down the toilet, flushed it away before descending the stairs. It wouldn't do for to leave that lying about!

Annie passed him in the hall on her way up to bed.

'Sean, I've an awful headache. I think it was all the cigarette smoke in the small lounge tonight. I left your tea in the living room, it's warmer in there.'

He gave her a small, tight smile and she blushed, knowing that he was not in the least fooled. He was aware that she was avoiding him, but she could not help herself. Tonight she could not bear for him to touch her. Not after seeing him and Rosaleen side by side. How could he prefer her? Rosaleen was beautiful!

The cup of tea on the mantelpiece was ignored as Sean stretched out on the armchair, his feet on the hearth, almost touching the grate where the fire was banked down. It would be silly to disturb the coal, start it blazing, when he would be retiring soon. Now, casting his mind back, he reflected on the evening's happenings.

First, the surprise of seeing Rosaleen with that big good-looking guy, and not feeling in the least bit jealous. The joy that had radiated from her, when he caught her eye in greeting, had embarrassed him and he had been glad that he was not sitting beside Annie when it occurred.

Then when she had pushed the note into his hand, he had felt dismay. Had she changed her mind about him? If she had ... well, it was too late! He had all he wanted in the house on the Serpentine Road. That was where he belonged, his niche in the world; he was happy with Annie.

He had been in a dither coming home in the taxi. Clinging to Annie's hand like a drowning man. Unable to make conversation. Then when he had read the note, he had wanted the floor to open up and swallow him. He remembered reading Tommy Magee's letter and knew just how he had felt. As if the bottom had fallen out of his world.

What puzzled him most was Annie's attitude. Now, he could understand her reluctance to let him make love to her when he first came home. It must have been awful for her, picturing him and Rosaleen together. He could imagine how he would have felt if he had heard that Annie had been with someone else. But... the big but ... why had she not challenged him? She was so forthright, he could not imagine why she had not. A fleeting smile touched his lips at the next thought. Why had she not hit him with something? It would not have been the first time. Her temper, once roused, was fierce, but once the air was cleared she never held spite; never referred to past quarrels. He would have expected her to rant and rave, shout and yell, clear the air as it were, but no, without a word, she had suffered him to make love to her. Not that she hadn't enjoyed it ... oh, yes, indeed she had, but against her will. Very much against her will. Was that how it had been between Thelma and Tommy? Now he knew why each time they made love, she was quiet, not her usual joyous self. Was he doomed to be like Tommy

Magee? Doomed to live in the shadow of his sin for the rest of his life? If only she would challenge him ... then he might be able to convince her that he wanted no other but she.

Meanwhile, Rosaleen was coming down on Christmas Day, just a week away, and he would have to pretend that he was unaware Annie knew the truth or she would know that Rosaleen had told him, and would torture herself with thoughts of him sloping off to meet her sister. She would be hurt, and he had hurt her enough already, so he would have to make sure that she didn't realise that he knew.

Dear God, why had he suggested that they go visiting? Now he was in a quandary. He would have been better living in ignorance.

He remained downstairs for a long time, wanting Annie to be asleep when he retired. However, she was still awake when at last he crept up the stairs and into the bedroom. He knew by the deep, even breaths that she was faking, that she was awake but wanted him to think her asleep, and as he lay beside her still figure, he agreed with Tommy Magee. Your sins did catch up with you. Aye, and when you least expected it.

Once she was sure that Sean slept, with a sigh of relief Annie rose from the bed and flexed her limbs, cramped by trying to lie motionless, and feign sleep. Shrugging into the silk kimono Sean had brought her from abroad, she quietly left the bedroom and entered the small room. From the window, she stared out over the frost-covered hedges and fields to the lough, sparkling like a diamond necklace as it reflected the lights on the opposite shore. Each season gave the view a new beauty. She had seen the summer, the autumn and now winter. Each view different, each beautiful in its own way. Now, not a mark sullied the virgin whiteness. Not a cloud marred the moonlit sky. Even the lough was still, like a bright diamond band lying in the frost. She was surprised at how easily she had adapted to life out here, cut off from all the things she had once thought necessary for happiness. Indeed, the two trams to and from work every day had taken up too much of her time. She had given up her job when Sean's leave drew near, anxious to decorate the sitting room, wanting to spend all her time in the house. She could not picture returning to live on the Springfield Road. This was where she wanted to rear her child. Here in the fresh air of the countryside, far away from the smog of the mills.

Protectively, her hands cradled her stomach. Was her child to be the one without a father? She was sure that she was pregnant. There had been no morning sickness and, when she missed her second period, she had not dared to hope, having been disappointed so often in the past.

Now, she was sure; she had missed her third period and her breasts were swollen and tender, her nipples darkened. Funny how once she had stopped striving to conceive, she had been caught right away. Tomorrow she would go to the village on some pretext or other and go on down to Whitehouse, the next village down the Shore Road, where Minnie had told her Doctor Canavan lived. She had recommended him and told her to mention her name, so she must know him personally. Then she would know for definite, one way or the other.

'Oh, Sean. You startled me.'

Sean's hands circling her waist, brought her back to reality.

'It's beautiful, isn't it, Annie?' he whispered as he gazed over her shoulder at the lough.

When she nodded, he continued, 'It never looks the same twice.'

His hands slid up and cupped her breasts, as he nuzzled the nape of her neck. Cradling their weight in his palms, he chided her, 'You're putting on weight, Mrs Devlin. I'll have to keep an eye on you, or you'll become a wee roly poly.'

Annie's breath caught in her throat. Would he guess? Before he could ponder, she replied, 'Ever hear tell of middle-aged spread? Mm?'

He laughed 'You're a bit young yet for that.' Then, in a more serious voice, he asked, 'Are you all right, Annie?'

'Yes. Just restless.'

She relaxed against him, glad that he had not guessed. First she must find out how he felt about Rosaleen. Only if she was sure that he didn't love her sister would she tell him about the baby.

Now his voice was husky, as, haltingly, he whispered, 'Annie … I've never tried to tell you how much you mean to me.'

Her heart gave a skip and she waited breathlessly. Was she about to hear the words she dreamed he would say to her?

Sean continued, 'I love this house. You'll never know how grateful I am that you consented to live out here. How much I appreciate the work you've put into…'

With a vicious twist and push she was out of his arms and facing him, her eyes flashing green with anger.

'Yes! Oh, yes, but indeed I do realise how much you love this house. You're making it your god!' she hissed at him, disappointed that he had not said what she wanted to hear. Building her up like that, for nothing. 'But never you fear, I'll continue to slave away making it into a home. Think of the money you're saving. Why, if divorce had been allowed by the Church you would have got rid of me long ago, wouldn't you, Sean? Eh? And then you'd be out a fortune in housekeeper's bills. Or … ' Dismayed, she bit on the words that hovered on her lips, and turned abruptly away. She had been about to say: 'Or our Rosaleen would be living here.'

The words were spat at him in fury and he could only stand and gape at the empty doorway when she had turned on her heel and left him.

He stood still, dismay seeping through him. Wasn't it true what she had just said? If divorce had been allowed by the Church, wouldn't he have asked her for a divorce after Joe died? Annie had every right to be angry at him, to keep him at a distance; he had never been a true husband to her. He had enjoyed her body, whilst longing for Rosaleen. What a fool he had been! Was it too late to win her over?

Rejected, he went down to the living room, and dawn was breaking when he at last judged it safe to return to bed.

On Christmas Eve as they returned from Midnight Mass it started to snow. Arm in arm they climbed the Serpentine Road, more at ease that they had been all week. It had been a miserable time, with Annie finding fault at the slightest provocation, and Sean biting on his tongue to keep the peace. Mass in the tiny Star of the Sea church, set on a hill on the outskirts of Greencastle, had been beautiful and peace had settled in Annie's heart, as she placed her happiness in God's hands. God's will be done. Why was she fretting and worrying? Had God ever let her down before? Whatever happened would be for the best. This she must believe.

Side by side, Sean and she had received Holy Communion and she knew him well enough to know that if he was doing wrong, he would not commit the sacrilege of receiving the Holy Host, so there was peace in her heart as they climbed the Serpentine, the snow flakes settling on and around them.

Once home, they discarded their wet outer garments and retired to the sitting room. Arms entwined, they stood at the big bay window and watched the snow fall, slowly at first, great, large flakes drifting gently down to lie and amass on frost-covered hedges and fields. Then thickening and swirling, until a blizzard beat against the window panes, obscuring their vision completely.

With a happy laugh, Sean squeezed her close and confided, 'It looks as if God has answered my prayers. Now that sledge I bought for Laura won't go to waste.'

Annie smiled happily up at him. Perhaps her prayers would also be answered.

Christmas Day dawned crisp and clear, with about eight inches of snow covering the land as far as the eye could see, and the lough a heaving silver necklace. Behind the house, the Cave Hill rose like a giant iced cake. Sean went out to clear the steps and driveway for their visitors, and Annie dusted and tidied the sitting room. This was the only room that was completely redecorated with new furniture and she was proud of it. Disliking the utility furniture made during the war, they had decided to wait and save until such time as changes were made before tackling the kitchen and bedrooms, making do with wardrobes and chests of drawers bought second-hand and painted white by Sean, and she had to admit that he had done a good job; their bedroom was quite presentable. Now, plumping up the cushions, she surveyed the sitting room with pride. They had decided not to cover the polished floor boards completely, and these glowed around a great square Persian carpet, brought home a long time ago by Sean, who had been unable to resist its beauty. Cream and blue, it lay in the centre of the floor and was soft and thick beneath her feet. After much discussion, and through one of Minnie's many contacts, they had chosen a dark blue velvet-covered suite. The settee they placed against the wall behind the door, facing the hearth, and the beauty of the mantelpiece was complimented by the two armchairs placed on either side of it. Annie had brightened the suite with pale cream satin cushions, and near the window the Christmas tree rose to the ceiling. Below the window a long, dark oak table reflected the lights of the tree, and under it, gaily wrapped parcels were piled. The fire, built high and burning brightly, threw a warm, cosy glow over everything. Pleased at the result of their labours, Annie uttered a satisfied sigh and retired to the kitchen to prepare the dinner.

Sean, once his task in the snow was finished, covered the old table (now in the living room) with a linen cloth and arranged the chairs, four of which they had borrowed from Minnie who had gone to spend Christmas with her youngest son. Then he set out their best cutlery, before joining Annie in the kitchen.

They worked side by side in harmony, Annie surprised at how calm she felt. She had dreaded this day, worried herself sick over it, but now that it had arrived, she was quite calm. It was probably because she now knew for sure that she was pregnant. Whatever happened today ... whatever she lost – she would have a child. Sean had said it was all she wanted out of life; he was wrong. Without him, she would be only half alive, but at least now she would not be alone.

Liam was sleeping in Rosaleen's arms when they arrived in George's car, and after Sean had admired him and exclaimed at how he had grown, Annie led the way upstairs, and Rosaleen laid the child on the bed. The sisters eyed each other, and then Rosaleen held out her hand.

'Please say you forgive me ... please, Annie.'

Slowly, she reached for Rosaleen's hand and clasped it, but her heart wasn't in it. Rosaleen had caused her too much heartache to forgive and forget, and what if Sean recognised Liam? She and Rosaleen were of the same flesh, the same blood ran in their veins, and how she wished things could have been different, but the damage was done; they could never be close again. Rosaleen had hurt her too much. Not only had she committed adultery with Sean and bore him a son, she had also done Annie out of the joy of sharing the knowledge of her pregnancy with Sean. Together, they should be able to confide in her mother and sister that at last they were about to become parents. Instead, she had to hide the fact and pray Sean would not realise that Liam was his son. If it was up to her, she would never see Rosaleen again ... would avoid having to watch Sean and her together.

'Annie, I want you to know that I've decided to sell the business. I made up my mind during the week and discussed it with Owen Black and he's going to buy me out. I'm putting the house up for sale and Bobby is going to look after that for me. So I'll be emigrating to Canada as soon as possible. May's been urging me to come out. Billy Mercer's uncle is willing to claim me and the kids.'

Annie's heart lurched in her breast; Rosaleen going to Canada could solve a lot of problems. Still, in spite of her relief, she found herself lamenting. 'Ah, Rosaleen, how I wish things could be different.' And suddenly she did. But it was too late for regrets.

Rosaleen gave a wry smile. 'Perhaps it's just as well,' she teased. 'If I don't go ... you might end up with Pat McDade for a brother-in-law, and I don't think you'd relish that.'

Annie knew she was jesting to relieve the tension, and smiled through her tears.

'Oh, well then, you'd better go. You're right! I could never bear that.'

The meal was a happy, leisurely occasion, everyone eating too much, and Annie's cheeks were warm with the praise lavished on her for her cooking. She knew that she deserved it. Everything had been cooked to perfection. The turkey succulent, the vegetables just right, not too soft yet not undercooked, the roast potatoes crisp, and the creamed potatoes fluffy. And her gravy, usually a bit lumpy, had been creamy and smooth. The plum pudding, which she had baked months ago to allow it time to mature, was rich and moist, and covered in brandy cream had finished the meal off to a 'T'. Yes, it had been worth the sacrifice of doing without while Sean was at sea and saving her meat and bread rations for the Christmas spread.

They retired to the sitting room to drink their coffee, and afterwards, Thelma, unable to keep her eyes open, asked permission to retire upstairs to join Liam in a nap. Then, as if on cue, he signalled by a loud wail that he was awake.

Sean rose to his feet at once. 'I'll fetch him. I've yet to see him awake.'

They could hear him talking to the child as he descended the stairs, and both Annie and Rosaleen eyed him fearfully when he entered the room, but Sean was unconcerned as he knelt on the carpet near the tree and started to open the presents they had bought for Liam. With a relieved glance at each other, they relaxed. George joined him on the floor, and as they laughingly vied with each other for Liam's attention, Rosaleen caught Annie's eye and smiled encouragingly at her.

'Uncle Sean ... Uncle Sean ... you promised me that after dinner we'd go sledging, so ye did. Mam, you take Liam. Please!'

'Now, Laura, don't be impatient. Wait until Liam sees his toys,' Rosaleen admonished her daughter, and when at last Liam clutched his woolly lamb and small car to his breast, she held out her arms for him.

As Sean was about to lift the child and carry him to her, she said, 'No, let him be. Let him walk.'

'You're joking!'

'No, he's toddling about.'

Carefully, Sean set Liam on his little chubby legs and they all laughed when he promptly sat down.

Once more Sean stood him upright and this time Rosaleen encouraged him. 'Come on, love. Come to Mammy.'

He swayed for some moments and Sean hovered anxiously over him, then Liam tottered across in a rush into Rosaleen's arms.

'Ah, imagine! Ten months old and he's walking. Oh, he's a wonderful child, Rosaleen,' Sean praised him, and added, 'He's the picture of your father, so he is.' Then seeing the hurt look on Laura's face at all the attention that Liam was receiving, he cried, 'But now I must take your wonderful daughter out and let her push me on the sledge.'

'No, Uncle Sean!' All smiles now, Laura giggled at the idea. 'You and Uncle George are going to push me!' she explained, and rushed to the hall to get her coat and mittens.

'Put on your hat, Laura,' Rosaleen warned, 'or you'll get an earache.'

Sean assured her as he followed Laura out into the hall, 'Don't worry, Rosaleen. I'll take care of her.'

And sadness settled on her at his words. If only he could take care of them all, but alas it could never be.

Once they were gone and Rosaleen and Annie were alone in the sitting room, with a raised eyebrow, Rosaleen said softly, 'Didn't I tell you he wouldn't notice?'

Annie nodded and sighed. 'I wish you weren't going to Canada,' she whispered. Then, in case Rosaleen was tempted to change her mind, hastily added, 'But it's all for the best, so it is.'

And Rosaleen nodded sadly, in agreement with her. Children changed, as they grew up, and perhaps one day Liam would look more like Sean than he did at present. Her decision to emigrate had also been influenced by the fact that Laura was beginning to act like Sean. She didn't resemble him in the slightest, no ... but a turn of the head, a raised eyebrow, brought him to mind. So, yes, it was all for the best that she should go to Canada. If only Andrew had kept his promise to send for her everything would have been fine. Now she would have to do everything herself.

'May will be glad to see you,' Annie consoled her and asked, 'How is she?'

'She's fine ... being married in the Church has made a big difference to her. The new baby is a girl. They're calling her Rosaleen.'

'Ah, that's lovely. I'm sure you're pleased.'

'Yes, as a matter of fact I am.'

'I'll miss you, Rosaleen.'

'Not once your baby's born.'

Annie gasped in dismay at these words. 'How did you guess?'

'It's obvious.'

'Sean doesn't know yet. And, mind, I want to tell him myself,'

Annie warned.

'I was about to say it's obvious to me … there's a bloom about you. No one else seems to have noticed, and I certainly won't tell Sean.'

'When do you leave?'

'Not for a while. These things take time, but the fact that someone is claiming me should hurry things up a bit.' Not wanting to start talking about Andrew, whom Annie had never met, Rosaleen changed the subject. 'When's the baby due?'

'June.'

'I think I'll be away before then.'

Sadness settled on them, and to try to dispel it, Annie asked, 'Why didn't George ask Maureen Murphy to come down with him?'

'He's not ready for a relationship yet, and somehow or other I don't think it'll be Maureen he'll pick. I think he fancies Mary Mitchel. I think that's why he's being instructed in the faith.'

At these words Annie gasped, 'Mary Mitchel? Her that lives in the big house up on the front of the Springfield Road? The builder's daughter?' Her eyes flashed derision. 'She'd never look twice at him. Why, she can pick and choose! No, I know her. She's got big ideas … he'll never get his boots under her bed.'

'I think you're wrong, but time will tell.' Rosaleen smiled at Annie's amazement and confided, 'He's been out with her a couple of times.'

'Well, I never! Good luck to him. She's not short a bob or two.'

'Ah now, Annie, you know that doesn't count where George is concerned,' Rosaleen chastised her.

'No … no, of course you're right. Still, it'll be a feather in his cap if he marries her.' She nodded her head and repeated, 'Aye, a big feather!'

There was relief in Annie's heart as she watched them all bundle into George's car that night, to travel home. The day had been enjoyable and Sean had treated Rosaleen as he would a sister. What more could she ask for? Still, she was glad to see them go.

The relief that Sean felt as he waved them off was heartfelt. It had been a strain, being careful how he looked at Rosaleen. Not that he wanted to ogle her. No, he was relieved to find that those days were gone. But he was worried in case she … He brought his thoughts to a halt. Did he really think that Rosaleen might ogle him? She was the one who had turned him down. But remembering her joyous look in the Clock Bar, he had been a bit worried, and was glad to see them go, glad to be alone with his lovely wife, in his beautiful house.

It was after tea on Boxing Day when Sean was washing his hands at the sink that Annie blurted out the news about Rosaleen going to Canada. She had been bracing herself all day to tell him, wondering how he would react. Now she saw his body go still as he paused in his task, and she berated herself.

Coward! Weak, stupid coward.

Why hadn't she told him face to face? Because she was afraid of what she might see in his eyes?

Annoyed at herself, she asked, 'Well, what do you think of that?'

Sean let the relief that this news created seep through him and when she spoke again, he commenced washing his hands.

His voice when he answered her was mild. 'I think that's a good idea. A very good idea. May and Billy are out there. They'll take care of her. And with her looks, she'll soon meet another man. What do you think?' he queried, as he lifted the towel and turned to face her.

Annie's eyes searched his face; it was calm, he was relaxed. There was no sign that he cared where Rosaleen went. But… would he have been the same if she had told him face to face? If she had taken him unawares? Well, fool that she was, she had missed her chance. Now she would never know.

To her surprise, unable to let the matter drop, she heard herself reply, 'It's not what I think that counts. It's what you think.'

He let his hands drop slowly to his sides, the towel trailing the floor unheeded, and eyed her through narrowed lids.

'Now just what's what supposed to mean?'

Was he going to get a chance to clear the air? Plead his case? His innocent demeanour made Annie throw caution to the winds. Rising to her feet, she bawled across the table at him: 'Stop looking so bloody innocent! I know about you and Rosaleen ... do you hear me? I know that you and Rosaleen had an affair.'

He breathed a sigh of relief. Annie in a temper he could handle. It was the cold, silent treatment he could not penetrate.

'And just who says that Rosaleen and I had an affair?' he asked, his voice still mild.

This infuriated Annie more. 'I got it straight from the horse's mouth, so I did. So there!'

Annie was warning herself to be careful, she must get a grip of her temper; she must not mention Liam. Not if she wanted to keep Sean. But did she want to hang on to him? Hang on to someone who had never even pretended to love her. Who, not once in their years together, had said he loved her. It had cut her to the very core when, mulling over the past, she had realised this. Oh, he made love to her as if he cherished her (was it better with Roslaeen?), and he called her 'love' and 'sweetheart' and 'darling', but these were endearments that he lavished on everyone. Not once had he said, 'I love you, Annie.' And she, fool that she was, had thought that because he had married her, he loved her. Whereas he had probably just wanted someone to call his own when he was away fighting during the war.

'Rosaleen told you?' Sean felt shock register in his brain. Had she confessed? No. In her note she had said that they had been together once. He must be careful. Not say something that might betray how he had once loved Rosaleen.

This thought startled him. Once loved? Leave that for now, he chastised himself. Pay attention to what Annie's saying.

'Yes, Rosaleen told me.'

'If she told you that we had an affair, she lied, and I can't see why she should.'

'Well, she did tell me ... she admitted that you and she ...' Her voice broke and clamping her lips tightly together, she blinked furiously to contain the tears and headed for the door. He was there before her, barring her escape.

Gripping her tightly by the arm, he said in a controlled voice, 'Now listen here ... don't think that you can throw accusations like that at me and run away, and then tomorrow act as if nothing's different. You've been doing that a lot lately … starting to say things then ignoring me for a while, and I won't have it, Annie. Do you hear me? I won't have it. So … just what did Rosaleen say?'

Annie's head reared back and she fixed a hard gaze on him. 'You tell me! You were there!'

'It was only once.'

He made himself hold her eye, feeling ashamed. He became aware that he would prefer to tell her the truth, right from the beginning. Clear the air, once and for all. But Rosaleen had set the stage for this conversation and he could only play it by ear.

'When?'

Dismayed by her persistence, he released his grip on her and his eyes held contempt.

'After Joe died … do you want graphic details?'

In spite of herself, the tears that filled her eyes spilled over, but as they streamed down her cheeks, her head rose proudly in the air. 'No, Sean, that won't be necessary. I've pictured it often,' she replied proudly, and there was dignity in her walk as she left the room and climbed the stairs. After all, as she reminded herself, she had done no wrong.

Pain closed like a fist around Sean's heart. Pain for the hurt Annie was now feeling, hurt he had inflicted on her. He started to follow her, but changed his mind. What good would it do? He had thought that if it was once out in the open, he could explain, put things right, but he found that he could not tell more lies.

In the back hall he pulled on his Wellingtons and waterproof coat, and tugging his cap down low on his brow, left the house.

From the bedroom window, Annie watched him plough through the snow and leaving the drive, turn up the Serpentine Road. He would be frozen, she fretted, catch his death of cold, but then … she was frozen, and she was in a warm room.

As he battled against the elements, Sean tried to sort out his emotions. How come Rosaleen, whom he had loved dearly for years, now failed to raise a flicker of passion? For a moment he felt bereft at the loss of his first love; it had been a part of him for so long. When had he stopped dreaming about her? When had Annie eroded her way into his heart? He didn't know! All he knew was that he had made a terrible mess of his life. Was he to lose Annie too?

He was very much aware that without Annie he would feel lost. Somewhere along the way, she had become the pivot of his life, the heart of his home. What would he do if she left him? Turn to Rosaleen? He was so confused. Less than two years ago he would have jumped at the chance of starting afresh in Canada with Rosaleen. Would have, at a nod from Rosaleen, taken off. Now it looked like Annie held his happiness in her hands and he could not reach her. He didn't deserve her; all these years while she had longed for a family, he had ignored her need. He should have paid attention to her, gone to the doctor, found out about adoption. Would Annie consider adoption? Would she give him another chance to try to make her happy? Despair engulfed him. Why should she? When she had needed him most, he had been pining for Rosaleen. God forgive him!

When he returned to the house, he was not surprised to find blankets and pillows piled on the settee. He smiled wryly as he gathered them up, remembering how Annie had vowed that no one would ever sleep on her beautiful settee. Was this her answer? Was there no hope of a future together for them?

He tossed and turned most of the night, and as a result slept late. Annie had already breakfasted when he entered the kitchen. She rose from her seat at once to prepare his breakfast.

'I'm not hungry. Just a bit of toast… that's all I want.'

While he was eating, Annie poured herself a cup of tea and sat facing him. Her face was pale but calm, and he noted that there was no sign of tears. She, obviously, had had a better night than he.

Annie sat pondering for a few moments before speaking. After much soul searching, she had decided that Sean must be free to make up his mind just what he wanted out of life. If he would be happier with Rosaleen, well… had she the right to keep him tied to her? She was aware that they would still be tied to each other as far as the Church was concerned, but she felt sure that she would not want to marry again, and it was Sean and Rosaleen's own business whether or not they wished to live in sin.

Now she started to speak, tentatively. Although she wanted him to be free to choose, she did not want him to feel that she wished to be rid of him.

'Sean … I've been thinking about us.'

He paused, toast halfway to his mouth, and eyed her from under raised brows. 'Mm?'

'Well, I'm all mixed up. I can't offer you a divorce … I haven't the right. And divorced or not I'd still feel married to you, but I'll understand if you want to feel free.' Her voice trailed off and she waited expectantly. When he remained silent, disconcerted she continued, 'I would like to remain in this house for awhile, until I can make other arrangements. Will that be all right with you?' Again she paused. Why didn't he speak? 'I'll try to be gone before your next leave.'

The toast reached his mouth and his voice was muffled when he at last answered her. 'Yes … stay as long as you like.'

He tried to keep his voice airy, unconcerned. After all, she had already made up her mind. Obviously she had ceased to love him and he had no one to blame but himself, but there was no need to let her know how much he hurt.

With an abrupt movement, Annie rose from the table. She was in despair. He did not care. Did not even question her reasons. Was probably glad of the chance to be rid of her.

'Thank you . '. . thank you very much. I'll make sure that I'm out before you return.' And with these words she quickly left the room, fearing her composure would crack.

Breakfast finished, Sean toiled out the back clearing snow, his heart and mind as heavy as the mist that obscured the top of the Cave Hill. Annie's rejection of him cut deep. This was the third time that he had been rejected, but it didn't get any easier. Especially when knowing that he was his own worst enemy, had brought all his troubles on himself, made it harder to bear. He would have to sell the house. It would be an empty shell without Annie's warm presence. How could he have been so stupid? To have won Annie's love and lost it by his indifference. He was a fool.

It was a long time later that he climbed the stairs in search of her. He had wrestled with his desire to hide his pain from her, and the chance to try one more time to make her change her mind. What if she rejected him again? She had every reason to. Would he be able to bear it? Rejection or no, he had to try one more time.

As usual, she was in the small room, leaning on the windowsill, gazing out over the snow-covered beauty of the fields to the lough. The amount of time she spent in this room surprised him. From their bedroom she could look out on the same view, and sit in comfort while doing so, but she preferred to stand in this small, empty room. She was unaware of him until he spoke her name.

'Annie?'

Slowly she straightened up from her bent position but did not turn to face him. He knew from the way her head tilted up that her chin was thrust out, ready for battle.

'Yes?'

A great, deep sigh left his lips. He was going to throw himself on her mercy and he had no idea, no idea at all, how she would respond.

'I don't know how to begin. Look ... I know I haven't been the world's greatest husband, but you have had some good times with me, haven't you?'

The chestnut hair bobbed forward in a nod, and he continued, 'I was wondering, Annie, would you not give me another chance? I've been thinking ... you want a child. Well, what about adoption? Would you consider adoption? Would that please you?'

Slowly, she turned to face him, her eyes wide and questioning. 'You'd consider adoption?'

He nodded eagerly, 'Yes, I would.'

'Does ...' She paused, now knowing how to phrase the next question. Why couldn't he be more explicit? 'Does this house mean so much to you?'

His brows gathered in a frown. 'The house?' Then comprehension dawned, and he bawled, 'Have a titter of wit, Annie! Do you really think that I'd consider adoption to remain in this house?'

It was her turn to frown. 'Well, why?'

'Look, Annie, I love this house, I admit that, but without you it'd be an empty shell. If you want to move back to the Springfield Road or even the Upper Falls, I'll move gladly. If only you'll give me another chance.'

She was in a dilemma; she wanted nothing more in the world than to believe him, but Aul' Nick was whispering in her ear. Did he want to move to be near Rosaleen? Was he holding on to her while he sought to win Rosaleen over? His betrayal of her had made her wary.

'Annie.' He moved closer and reached for her hands, clasping them against his breast. 'Please give me a chance to prove how much I love you. How much I need you.'

For some moments she stood motionless, her eyes tightly closed, and let his words wash over her, balm to her tortured heart.

He loved her ... HE LOVED HER! A great bubble of joy welled up and burst inside of her and his voice trailed off in amazement when she pressed close to him, eyes ablaze with happiness.

As his lips claimed hers, her kiss was full of joy, like it used to be. He gripped her closer still, unable to believe his luck, and when at last she freed him, he sank his face in her hair.

'Ah, Annie, Annie ... I thought I'd lost you. I was in despair. Please don't ever shut me out again. You're my world ... the heart of my home.'

Eyes brimming with happiness, she drew back and looked at him. 'Ah, Sean, you've just made me the happiest woman in the world. Listen ...' A wave of her hand embraced the room. 'I've pictured this room often as a nursery. I'll paint the walls white and get some prints of nursery rhymes and flowers ... and Minnie has a lovely cot that she is willing to lend me.' Her voice was excited and happy. 'It'll be lovely in this room, I can just picture it. It's huge ... it will do a child until it's three years old. It would cost the earth to buy. Isn't Minnie kind?'

Still afraid to believe his luck, he clung to her, but fear penetrated his heart. He wished now that he'd mentioned adoption before, but she must be made to realise that it took time. She was going too fast.'

'Annie, please love, don't set your hopes too high. I've been asking around about adoption and it can take years ... and sometimes you can be turned down for no apparent reason.'

'Sean, we don't have to adopt.' Her eyes teased him. 'You were right. I am too young for a middle-aged spread.'

Her hand drifted down and patted her stomach.

He stared at her uncomprehending, and she repeated slowly, her eyes holding his, her head swaying from side to side, 'The weight I'm putting on isn't a middle-aged spread.'

His brows drew together. 'You mean ...'

She nodded, and watched his jaw drop with amazement.

'You're pregnant?'

'I only found out for sure last week.'

'And you never told me?'

Her eyes held his steadily. 'I didn't know what you wanted out of life, Sean. You might have wanted to join Rosaleen in Canada, and I didn't want you to feel tied. You see, I was convinced that you didn't love me.'

'But you must have known that I do.'

'No ... you never said.'

Her voice was sad and he squirmed inwardly when he realised that what she said was true. How could he have said it? He had thought he still loved Rosaleen.

'Ah, Annie. Annie, my love.' The back of his hand caressed the curve of her cheek, her jaw, her throat; sending shiver after shiver of anticipation coursing through her. 'Annie ... you'll be fed up listening to my declarations of love from now on.'

'Never ... never! That's something I'll never tire of, and don't you ever stop.'

His hands cupped her face. 'I love you, Annie Devlin. I love you so very much.'

The shadow had gone from her eyes and he felt humble as he gazed into her very soul, at the love shining there. Overcome with the wonder of it, wanting to hold back the tears that threatened to overwhelm him, he asked gruffly, 'When's the baby due?'

'June.'

'It'll be born before I come home again,' he lamented. 'Will you be all right, out here on your own?'

'Minnie will look after me.' Her eyes danced with happiness. 'She's adopted me. Says I'm the daughter she always longed for. And remember, she has a phone. I'll be all right, so I will.'

'Annie, there's something else I've been thinking about but I couldn't mention it while you were so distant.'

'Yes?'

Her eyes clouded over. Was there a snag?

'Well ... do you think you could bear to have me under your feet all the time? I want to leave the navy, get a job ashore. What do you think?'

'Oh! I think that's wonderful ... wonderful.' To think that he loved her that much, to want to leave his beloved sea and stay at home with her. A warm happiness enveloped her and her look became mischievous. 'I think I could just about bear to have you at home.'

With a happy laugh, he bent towards her and as his lips closed on hers, she felt a flutter as the child in her womb moved noticeably, for the first time, and sent a prayer heavenward that Rosaleen would find happiness in Canada and never, ever, return to Ireland.

Sean gently led Annie from the 'nursery' and into their bedroom. Now he knew why she spent so much time there. Soon they would have a child, and perhaps in a few years they would have another one. This house would need at least three children.

He voiced his thoughts to her. 'Annie, once this child is born, we'll space our family ... say two years apart.' His voice trailed off as Annie's hand covered his mouth.

'There'll be no birth control, Sean. We'll live up to our religion. God will take care of us.' Her words dwindled away and her eyes grew fearful. 'Do you agree with me?'

'Anything you say, Annie. For my part, I would like at least six,' he assured her.

She smiled happily and nodded, relaxing contentedly against him.

'Ah, Sean ... Sean.'

He held her close and settled her against his body. There now ... that was where she belonged. Slowly, he began to undo the buttons down the front of her dress.

'Let's have an early night, eh, Annie my love?'

She giggled softly. 'Sean ... it's nearly lunch time.'

He smiled at her amusement. 'Well then, let's have a mid-morning nap. Eh, love?'

Her arms crept up around his neck and her eyes danced with laughter. 'We might miss lunch, mind.'

'I think I could bear that,' he whispered, and at the look in his eyes, her heart turned over and no more words were needed as he gently lowered her on to the bed.

Wrapping Liam in a blanket, Rosaleen rubbed her nose gently against the sleeping child's before laying him on the settee. She sighed as she looked out of the window. Unlike the Serpentine Road, there was no large expanse of virgin snow here. Grey slush littered the footpaths and snowladen skies seemed actually to sit on the rooftops, darkening the rooms as if it was evening instead of early morning.

She had promised to take the children to spend Boxing Day with Amy and Bobby but she felt so depressed all she wanted to do was stay at home and weep. God forgive her! She should be counting her blessings instead of giving in to misery. And she had so many blessings: a lovely daughter, already on her way to visit her granny and Bobby. A beautiful healthy son. No money worries. Just why was she so depressed?

It must be the aftermath of spending Christmas Day at Annie's. The strain of being in Sean's company now that Annie knew the truth. The knowledge that Sean was uneasy and afraid in her company had filled her with a great aching pain. To think that Sean could fear her; be afraid of her spoiling things between Annie and him. As if she would! That's why she was unhappy.

Then on top of all that, the fact that Andrew had let her down deepened her unhappiness. She had been so sure he cared for her, but it appeared she had been wrong. Three weeks ago a doll had arrived for Laura, and a huge soft cuddly bear for Liam, but since then, nothing! Not one letter in answer to hers. And she had written twice! She squirmed when she thought of the drift of her letters. She had not actually asked him his intentions ... but she may as well have. And he had not been man enough to answer her. Tell her he had changed his mind. And tonight she had to face Pat and tell him that she had decided to emigrate to Canada.

Her actions in the Clock Bar a week ago had given him the wrong idea and she knew he thought that his long, careful courtship was paying off. At the beginning of their friendship she had warned him that she wanted nothing more from him, but she had seen his hopes rise when she had fawned all over him in the pub and guessed that he was just biding his time. Now she had to dash his hopes, and dreaded how he would react to her news.

As she tidied the kitchen, determined to leave everything spotless before joining Laura at Amy's, dismay filled her when she heard the living-room door open and close. It must be Pat. She would have preferred to confront him at night. Not so early in the day, when she felt weepy. But so be it. She may as well get it over with.

'Is that you, Pat? Take a seat... I won't be a minnit.'

As the silence stretched, she turned slowly towards the living room, a frown on her brow. There was no way Pat McDade could stay so quiet.

The figure standing near the door was very still; large snowflakes melted on his dark hair and on the shoulders of his black Crombie overcoat, and Rosaleen felt the colour leave her face and her knees go weak at the sight of him.

'You are expecting ... Pat?'

She longed to throw herself into his arms, feel the comfort of them around her, weep all over him, but the look in his eyes kept her motionless at the kitchen door. As usual when she was ill at ease, she resorted to sarcasm.

'What's it to you? Has another death brought you over?'

His face was stern, his eyes no longer warm and caring but dark and probing, but before he could answer her there was a light knock on the door and Bobby Mackay entered the room.

Startled and confused, he shuffled his feet in embarrassment and looked from Rosaleen to Andrew and back again.

'I'm sorry if I'm interrupting something, but the footpaths are in an awful state, Rosaleen. That snow coming down on top of the hard slush is treacherous so I came round to carry Liam for you.'

'That's kind of you, Bobby. He's ready to go.'

She nodded towards the sleeping child. To reach him she would have to pass close to Andrew and her feet would not obey her and move in his direction. It was Andrew who lifted the child and placed him gently in Bobby's arms.

'Bobby, I don't think you met Andrew when he was last here. He's Billy Mercer's cousin. Remember he came home for his uncle's funeral?'

'Of course ... of course. No, I never did have the pleasure. Pleased to meet you.'

The two men shook hands but Andrew never spoke, just nodded in acknowledgement of Rosaleen's introduction, and Bobby quickly turned to leave the house. As he said to Amy later, the tension was so thick it was like waiting for the thunder to roll, heralding a storm.

'I'll go on round, Rosaleen. You take your time ... there's no hurry. We'll expect you when we see you.' And with another nod at Andrew, he hurried out.

When the door closed on him, Andrew moved slowly towards Rosaleen but when he reached for her she hissed at him: 'Don't you touch me!'

She had endured weeks of torment because of this man, and he thought he could just walk in and take up where he left off.

Unable to stop herself, she let her tongue run away with her. 'You're too early! I've not had any drink yet,' she taunted him.

He drew back as if she had slapped his face. Was that the only way she could stomach him? Had all the plans and preparations he had made been in vain?

Had Pat McDade won Rosaleen over? Well, May had warned him not to delay too long. Hadn't she sung the praises of tall, handsome Pat? Everything that he was not. She had cautioned him not to keep Rosaleen in the dark about his plans. He should have listened to her, but he had wanted to surprise Rosaleen. But it had backfired ... he was the one who was being surprised.

He dragged his eyes from the cold, haughty beauty of her and glanced at the clock. 'What time are you expecting him?'

'I'm not really expecting him ... when I heard the door open, I just thought it might be him. I certainly didn't expect to see you.'

'Oh.' He frowned. Why had she not expected to see him? Had she sent him a letter telling him not to come and it had gone astray?

At a loss to understand, he sighed. 'Well, I'm very tired, Rosaleen. Do you think you could give me a cup of coffee before you show me the door?'

'Of course. I'm sorry … look, take off your coat and sit down. Are you hungry? Will I make you a fry?'

'No … no, I'm not hungry. Just a cup of coffee.' It wasn't food he was hungry for. He had hungered for her for long months, but it seemed he had delayed too long.

As she prepared sandwiches while the kettle was boiling, she chastised herself. He had travelled halfway across the world and look how she had greeted him. Not one kind word! As usual, she had let her hurt pride rule her tongue. She should have thrown herself into his arms and let nature take its course. God knows she had wanted to, but the look in his eyes had stopped her. There had been contempt in their depths … how could he look at her like that. Surely he didn't think that she was playing about with Pat? Would she be able to put matters right?

Drawing deep breaths into her lungs, she sought to compose herself. However, in spite of her efforts, her hands still shook as she placed a plate of sandwiches and a pot of coffee on a tray to carry into the living room, only to find him stretched out in the armchair, completely relaxed, his eyes closed, apparently asleep.

'Andrew …' she whispered, but he was out to the world, and returning the tray to the kitchen, she fetched a blanket and gently covered his prone figure.

He looked exhausted and shame once again smote her as she recalled the way she had greeted him. Well, when he awoke he would make amends, but first she must see Amy and ask her to mind the children, yet again. Then she would call in and see Pat McDade and inform him of her intentions to emigrate; she did not want him calling around and upsetting the plans she was going to set in motion. With these thoughts in mind, she quietly left the house.

It was two hours before Andrew showed signs of awakening.

Stretching, he craned his head this way and that, and it must have hurt because he grimaced as he opened his eyes. Awareness came slowly to him, as his eyes took in the room and at last came to rest on her.

Rosaleen watched him from where she sat curled up on the settee and smiled as she observed the surprise in his eyes as they roamed over her figure. The oyster-coloured silk pyjamas that she wore were very fine and hid nothing. Amy had supplied the coupons for them and Rosaleen had saved them for when Andrew should send for her, but now she felt the need to woo him. She had brushed her hair and it framed her head like a bright halo while her skin gleamed luminous in the dim firelight. Desire raged through him as he watched her rise from the settee.

Never having set out deliberately to charm a man before, she felt shy as she approached him.

Leaning over him, the pyjama coat open and revealing, she said softly, 'I'll make that coffee, now you're awake.'

He gripped her hand and motioned her to her knees beside his chair. They both started to speak at once.

'We must…' He stopped.

'It seems we …' She also paused and he nodded for her to continue.

'It seems to me we got off on the wrong foot again,' she whispered, and her eyes begged his forgiveness.

He smiled wryly. 'I must admit I've had better receptions.'

'I'm sorry … but I was so surprised to see you.'

His grip on her hand tightened. 'That's what I can't understand. Didn't you receive my letter?'

'No. It's almost four weeks since I received a letter from you.'

'It must be because of the Christmas mail. I wrote and told you that I would be arriving on Christmas Eve … but then the plane was delayed.' He pulled her closer against his thigh. 'I've spent forty-eight hours sitting at the airport dreaming about you. I thought I'd never get here! So you can understand how I felt when you seemed to be expecting Pat.'

Her gaze was compelling. 'I thought you had changed your mind. Even May's letters were so strange. She wrote that she rarely saw you. Then she urged me to sell up and go out to her and Billy. Is it any wonder that I thought she was warning me off? I was sure you had a woman out there and that May was trying to break the news gently to me.'

'That's my fault, Rosaleen. May was under threat of what I'd do to her if she told you what I was arranging. As for urging you to sell up and … well, I imagine she was trying to help me, by getting you ready to move.'

'Oh.'

'You see, I was buying a house. May assures me that you'll love it. I hope she's right. But I realise now that I should have asked you how you felt about it.'

She reached up and touched his cheek. 'You're sweet, Andrew … but yes, you should have warned me.'

He leant closer. 'Have you missed me?'

She nodded shyly. 'Awfully! I've thought of you often. Longed for you to send for me … when you didn't, I thought you had abandoned me.'

'Ah, Rosaleen, how could you think that?'

'It was very easy to doubt you. Thousands of miles away and no word of sending for me …. no offer of marriage …' Her voice trailed off in embarrassment. 'At least… well… are you offering me marriage?'

'Of course!'

He released his hold on her and, twisting in the chair, felt in the pocket of the jacket draped over the back.

'May also assured me that you would love this. I chose it because it reminded me of your eyes.'

She opened the small jeweller's box and gasped in delight at the ring nestling within. A large emerald surrounded by diamonds.

'It's beautiful,' she whispered. 'May's right, I love it.'

'If it doesn't fit, it can be altered.' His hands cupped her face and there was reverence in his voice. 'Will you marry me, and make me the happiest man in the world?'

At her shy nod, he removed the ring from the box, but when he lifted her hand to place the ring on her finger, he hesitated, eyeing the wedding band that Joe had placed there almost nine years ago.

Slowly, Rosaleen slid it from her finger. 'I shall keep the rings Joe gave me, until Laura grows up,' she said, and stretching up she placed the wedding band on the mantelpiece.

Then she held out her bare hand to Andrew. The ring fitted perfectly and she raised her face for his kiss.

'Have you been drinking?' he asked, dryly.

Hot colour blazed in her cheeks.

'I'm sorry ... that was an awful thing to say. Can you forgive me?'

She was tugging at his arm, indicating that he join her on the rug. Instead he rose to his feet. Gripping her hands, he pulled her up to face him.

'Rosaleen, much as I enjoyed my romp on the rug with you, I prefer the comfort of the bed.'

Her lips twitched in amusement, and laughing, he bent and kissed them hungrily. 'Does that make me sound old?'

She shook her head. Gazing down into her passion-filled eyes, he said softly, 'Ah, Rosaleen ... you are so beautiful. I can't believe my luck.'

His hands pushed the pyjama jacket off her shoulders and down her arms. For some seconds he gazed on the loveliness of her then, with a smothered exclamation, swept her up in his arms and headed for the stairs.